PARADISE TALES

Geoff Ryman

Small Beer Press
Easthampton, MA

Small Beer Press
150 Pleasant Street #306
Easthampton, MA 01027
www.smallbeerpress.com
www.weightlessbooks.com
info@smallbeerpress.com

Distributed to the trade by Consortium.

Library of Congress Cataloging-in-Publication Data

Ryman, Geoff.
Paradise tales / Geoff Ryman. -- 1st ed.
     p. cm.
ISBN 978-1-931520-64-5 (alk. paper)
I. Title.
PR6068.Y74P37 2011
823'.914--DC22

                              2010048947

ISBN 978-1-931520-64-5 (alk. paper)

First edition 1 2 3 4 5 6 7 8 9

Set in Centaur MT.
Cover photo by Giovis Dimitrios.

This book was printed on recycled paper in the USA.

Contents

The Film-makers of Mars

The films just started showing up, everywhere, old forgotten silent movies turning to jelly in warehouses all over SoCal: Anaheim, Burbank, Tarzana.

I got a call from Al at Hannibal Restoration. "They're mindblowing!" The old hippie.

Eight reels of a film about Santa Claus from 1909. Filmed in Lapland. And *forty* reels of a film it says was produced by Edgar Rice Burroughs. In 1911?

Cinefex sponsored a program at the LA Film Festival. They invited me, of course; Hannibal invited me as well. I gave the second invitation to my friend Amy.

I don't know what I was expecting. L. Frank Baum went bust producing Oz movies. They're terrible and have very silly special effects, but you couldn't film them now, or even fake them. They just look like they're from their era, or even maybe from Oz itself, if Oz were poverty-stricken.

We all sat down. Al's partner Tony came on and mumbled something through his beard about provenance and how grateful he was to the sponsors, then Hannibal screened the first film about Santa Claus. For all his work, Al only had one reel to show.

Hannibal had done a beautiful job. The team had remade each frame of film digitally, filling in scratches, covering up dirt, enhancing contrast—sharp, clear, monochrome images. It was like going back in time to see the premiere.

They had Santa Claus bronco-busting reindeer. Santa was pretty damn robust, a tall rangy guy in a fur-trimmed suit. The reindeer were not studio dummies but huge, rangy, antlered beasts. Santa wrestled them

GEOFF RYMAN

to the ground, pulled reins over their heads and then broke them in bare-back like it was a rodeo.

Think Santa Claus western—snow drifts between evergreen trees. Santa chewed tobacco and spat, and hitched up his new team behind a sleigh pulled by even more reindeer.

The next shot, he's pulling the team up in front of Santa's palace, and the only thing it could possibly be is a real multistorey building made entirely from blocks of ice.

So far, I was saying to myself, OK, they went to Lapland and filmed it almost like a documentary.

Then he goes inside, and it's not a painted set, the ice blocks glow like candle wax. Santa finds that the elves have been eating the toys.

Remember the first time you saw *Nosferatu,* and the vampire looked like a crossbreed between a human and a rat? Well Santa's Elves looked like little Nosferatus, only they were three feet high and deranged. One of them was licking a child's doll between her legs. You could hear the whole audience go *Ew!*

Rat teeth stuck out; fingernails curled in lumps like fungus. One of them snarled at Santa, and the old guy cuffed it pretty smartly about its pointed ears, then knocked it to the ground and gave it two smart kicks to the groin.

Then the reel ended.

Amy looked at me, her face seesawing between wonder and disgust. "That was a children's film?"

The festival director bounced up to a lectern, trying to look spry. He joked about the movie. "It was called *The Secret Life of Santa Claus,* and I think that must be the first X-rated Santa feature."

He introduced a representative of the Burroughs family, and a fresh-faced college student hopped up onto the stage. He was, the director said, Edgar Rice Burroughs's great-grandnephew. He couldn't have been older than twenty—sun-streaked hair and baggy trousers that sagged just suf-ficiently below his underwear line to be cool. He had that Californian polish of sun, wealth, opportunity, and honed parenting.

Appropriate. I knew that everything this guy did would be appro-priate. His name was the perfectly appropriate John Doe Burroughs, and

2

he made a perfect and predictable speech about how much he admired his famous forebear and how the film had been found inside a family safe.

"It really had been shut for about ninety years. It was recorded in the ERB estate inventory with a request not to try to open it, so we didn't. Then strangely, the safe appeared to open itself."

Oh yeah, sure.

"And inside were about forty reels of film, in other words about three hours' worth."

In 1911? That would make it an epic on the scale of *Intolerance*, only *Intolerance* was made in 1916.

Then my friend Al came up on stage. Soft-spoken, sincere, a fan of old radio shows, a native Angeleno who remembers the Brown Derby restaurant, Al had been my mentor. For a while. Where do nice guys finish?

He talked for thirty minutes about the restoration. I know, restoring old films is an art, but an art that's best when it shuts its mouth. It's like all those DVD extras about costume design.

Al gave us film history. The producer was Burroughs himself, and the director was called Nemo Artrides... unknown and probably a pseudonym. The actor, however, was known. He was Herman Blix, who stared in one Tarzan film in 1927 and then married Edgar Rice Burroughs's daughter.

So what was he doing in 1911? "More questions than answers, but the biggest mystery is the technical achievement of the film itself." Al, sweet Al, smiled with pleasure.

From the three hours of film, so far he had twenty minutes to show us.

The lights went down. Up came the first frame. A black-and-white panel, hand-painted with about ten pieces of information in one screen... title, Edison company logo, all in that art nouveau lettering.

Directed by Nemo Artrides from the histories by Edgar Rice Burroughs
Filmed by permission of the incomparable Jahde Isthor.
No cast list.

The first scene looks like what you'd see through a spyglass. There's a cotton gin, plants and black slaves. The spyglass opens out and we see on opposite sides of a cotton field rows of troops, one side in gray, one in the dark uniform of the Union army.

"So," I whispered to Amy. "It *is* D. W. Griffith."

She chuckled. "Shh."

Herman Blix in Confederate uniform rides into shot. He manages to swagger while on horseback. Like old photographs of General Beaufort, he looks crazed, with huge whiskers and a mad stare, and thick, dirty, plastered-down hair. From amid the rows of cotton, a slave stares up at him.

That's when I first sat up. There was something in that face. You couldn't paint it on with makeup; you couldn't buy it from Hollywood.

The slave looked as old as the Bible, starved and gnarled. His neck was thin in strands, his chin had no flesh on it; and the skin around his eyes, his cheeks, and even on his nose was crisscrossed with lines of repeated stress cut as deeply as whiplashes. His eyes swam with misery, outrage, a lifetime of abuse.

In the book, Burroughs bangs on about race. His history of Mars is a history of racial triumph and decline; race explains culture. His hero is a warrior for slavery and an Indian fighter; the opening of the book swiftly combines all of America's racial catastrophes.

Our supposed hero raises his sword and strikes the old black man down.

I sat back in shock. What the hell was that supposed to be? A racist assault? An apology for it?

There's a gap, a break I guess, where the film was unsalvageable. Somehow we jump to Mars.

We see a huge thing with six legs and swivel-eyes hauling Blix by a chain around his neck.

The brain processes at high speed. Mine said, *No.* This is never 1911, this is CGI, now. The glassy frog-eyes turn on stalks; the thing has six perfectly functioning limbs with hands for feet. A Thark, in the books. As I watch, it drops down onto its middle set of legs and starts walking on those as well. The motion is perfect, the design totally disorientating. The thing's scrawny and bloated at the same time; it moves as tensely as an erect cobra.

The ground all the way to a near horizon is carpeted with spongy fungus. Herman Blix doesn't walk across it; he bounces blearily, like he's on a trampoline.

He's stark, bollock naked. Unswervingly naked. You can see he's circumcised, and even weirder for 1911 Hollywood, his pubes are shaved smooth.

The audience rustled.

The title panel said:

No water on a Mars that suffers from climate change.

Climate change?

In the low Martian gravity, he does not know his own strength.

Blix stumbles, fights to regain his balance and springs up into the air, out to the end of his chain, like a guy in weightless simulation. The Thark jerks him back, and he slams down into the moss. He lands badly, rolls, and nurses his knee.

Distance shot. A caravan lumbers and sways and ripples with a myriad of limbs. It looks like one living thing, a giant centipede. I'd say a hundred extras at least.

Back to close-up. A Thark rides something that at first is difficult even to see, shapeless and wrinkled. An eyeless, featureless wormlike head splits open, its mouth lipless, like a cut. It seethes forward on what look like thousands of grappling hooks.

One of the Dead Cities of Mars, says a title.

The city looks like a chain of deliberately dynamited municipal parking lots, only with statues in the corners and mosques attached.

"No, no. No, no," I said aloud.

This wasn't a matte painting held in front of an unmoving camera. This wasn't a miniature. The actors did not troop past some dim rear projection of models. No silvered, masked, stuffed lizards stood in for monsters like in *The Thief of Baghdad*. No well-designed full-size dragons moved stiff puppet jaws like in *Siegfried*.

An accidentally good set of swivel-eyes I could take. Maybe, like Babylon in *Intolerance*, they just built the Martian city for real. Maybe they found the young Willis O'Brien to animate the Tharks.

But not all of it, all at once.

"This is a fake," I said deliberately loudly. "No way is this 1911!"

People chuckled.

But the thing was, the film didn't look like Now, either.

First off, the star really was Herman Blix.

Herman Blix was twenty-seven in 1927, so he could only have been eleven in 1911. OK, so they got the date of the film wrong. More like 1928 maybe, when he'd already married the boss's daughter. But Blix didn't look twenty-eight either. His hair was brushed back, which made him look craggier and older. Older and somehow mummified. Maybe it was all the dry desert air. But in close-ups, there were thousands of tiny wrinkles all over his face. The eyes looked fierce, almost evil, the mouth a thin, downward-turning line. And the eyes. The old film made his eyes, probably blue, look like ice. You could imagine them glowing slightly as if sunlight shone into them.

And the audience couldn't stop giggling at his willy. It was a very nice willy, even retracted. But it made the film feel like a silent, slow-motion *Flesh Gorden*.

"Pre-Hays Code," Amy murmured, amused.

Another blip.

Blix is now wearing a helmet, the hollowed-out head of a Thark. There's bits hanging down, and speckles of gore on his shoulders, but Blix looks bemused. He starts forward in surprise.

The silver screen fills with the image of a woman. Her head is lowered. Then suddenly she looks up, jerks in quick time as if the film were speeded up. The audience giggled. But not like they do at Princess Beloved in *Intolerance*. This was a nervous blurting chuckle. Because one stony stare from that woman and something around your heart stopped.

The Incomparable Jahde Isthor, said the titles.

Think Garbo, or Hepburn, but with no makeup. No 1920s bee-stung lips, no ornate metal twirls to cover the nipples. The cheekbones are too high, too large, and the eyes look like a plastic surgeon has pulled them too far back, all the way to the ears.

THE PRINCESS OF MARS!

Her tongue flickers like she's tasting the air. She wears what looks like a cap of snow white feathers.

The camera pulls back and she's naked, too, but her pudenda have a fan of white feathers clamped over them.

Amy giggled. "She looks like a stripper."

The Princess sees Herman, and all the feathers on top of her head stand up, like the crest of a cockatoo.

Jahde Isthor was no kind of actress. She bounced forward, a kind of bunny-hop, and you could see her glance down at the floor.

She was looking for her mark.

The hero moves closer to her and bows, but she isn't looking at him. She's peering right into the camera, as if wondering what it is.

Right, first find your deformed Greta Garbo and make sure she can hop. Acting might be well down your list of priorities.

That's what I'm thinking when, gathering herself up, Jahde suddenly jumps two-footed like a giant robin onto the top of a table. She reaches up for a hanging lamp and under her arms is a web of skin, like she has residual wings. They're tufted with flightless feathers. Jahde Isthor holds up the lamp and points it at the human.

The camera looks at his illuminated legs, his genitalia held in an unflinching gaze.

Our hero's face moves to speak and a title panel intervenes.

I am a man but not of this world.

"This is unbelievable," said Amy.

I am Herman, Lord of the Tharks.

At that point, the audience just loses it. They howl.

The camera eyes up the Princess's legs. Her knees double back in the wrong direction and she has the thick thigh muscles of a swan. Her shins are as long and thin as a walking stick, covered with scales. She has the feet of a whooping crane.

"It's different from the books," I said. "She laid eggs, but she didn't have feathers. She had ordinary legs."

"She laid eggs? Yuck!"

"Her name is different, too. All the names are different."

Jahde Isthor looks at the camera with the expression of an ostrich, and snaps forward. She's pecked at the lens.

The film ended suddenly, bang.

There were forty reels of that? It would have cost millions even at 1911 prices. In 1911, Edgar Rice Burroughs was still selling pencil sharpeners in Chicago and the story was only just being serialized in magazines for the first time.

In 1911 there was no film grammar for something that long. *The Birth of a Nation* had not yet been made. Naw, naw, naw, that was 1927 at the earliest.

The applause was light, scattered. People were in shock. It had been too good. It had been too weird.

I knew I had my story. "That's a fake, and I'm going to prove it."

After the next screening, a particularly nauseating silent version of Jack the Ripper, I talked to Mr. Appropriate. God, was he ever. Fresh-faced, I would say, like Andy Hardy on smart drugs.

He was indeed a distant relative of Burroughs, and he claimed with UCLA-freshman directness to have gone to do the inventory himself. So I said how convenient it was for everybody that the safe opened itself.

I couldn't dent his wide-eyed innocence. "That's the weirdest thing! It had a time-lock, and it could only be only opened from the inside."

He made me feel old and mean, and down and cynical, but I thought, "Gotcha, kid!"

I looked him up in the UCLA directories and found him, guilelessly open to public inspection. It said he was studying dentistry. Come on, I thought, you're a film major.

Like I'd been. So now I'm a journalist. Who only writes about film.

I know how it goes. Nobody gives you a break, so you fake something to get some publicity, maybe get your toe in the door. What's your story? You got a famous relative? Your, what, great-great-uncle twice removed? Cash in!

The family papers had indeed been kept in a SHOguard storage facility in Burbank. The guard at the entrance was huge, Samoan, and well, guarded. He said hardly anything, except that yes, the safe had been stored with his company and other chattels from the ERB estate. I showed him my press pass; said I was doing a story on the film. How long had it been stored there? He said he didn't know, but gave me names to write to. I did, and got a simple letter back. The Burroughs family inventory had moved there when the previous company upped sticks from Hollywood in 1965. I got the name of that company and the old address. The building was now an office block. The story, as far as I could push it, checked out.

My best-selling book—I mean, the book that sold the most copies though it remained well below the Borders threshold of perception—was called *A History of Special Effects*.

If the film was a fake, I knew all the people who could have done the work. There are only about forty companies in the entire world who could have animated the Tharks. I wrote to all of them, and visited the five or six people who were personal friends. I told them what I'd seen.

There had been at least two serious attempts to make an ERB Mars movie in the '80s. Had anybody done a particularly fine test reel?

Twice I thought I'd found it. Old Yolanda out at Pixar, a real pioneer now doing backgrounds, she told me that she'd been on board a *John Carter of Mars* project. She still had some of the production design sketches. We had a nice dinner at her place. I saw the sketches. The princesses all wore clothes. The clothes showed off their lovely and entirely human legs.

I visited Yong, a Thai animator who now worked for Lucas. I told him what I'd seen.

"I know, I heard," said Yong. He'd done some work on a Burroughs project in the '90s. "Look, you know that only us and a couple of other companies are that good. And if it wasn't that good, somebody like you, you'd spot it straight away." He nodded and chuckled. "It's gotta be a publicity stunt for a new movie."

"Well whoever did it, they're hot. This stuff was the finest FX I've ever seen. But the weird thing was the whole style, you know, of the titles? That was all perfect for a silent movie."

Yong chuckled. "I gotta see this. It sounds good. Really, really good."

I went home and took out some of my old scripts. Those would have made perfect little films. Only they didn't.

One was about a mother whose son and his boyfriend both had AIDS. She gets over it by counseling the boyfriend's mother, an evangelical. Would have been a great two-hander for Streep and MacLaine. Way ahead of its time. I had the delight of seeing it starring Sallie Anne Field, made for TV. Somebody at the agency just ripped it off.

Another was a crisscross Altman thing about race in LA. Sound familiar? The script is just dust on a shelf now.

One of my best isn't even dust. It was a new take on the Old South. Now it's just iron molecules on a scrambled hard drive. Always do your backups. That script now is as far away as Burroughs's Mars.

At twelve I was an ERB fan. I still had some of my old books, and got one down from the shelf. It was the Ace edition with the Frank Frazetta cover.

I'd forgotten that Burroughs himself is a character in the book. He says he knew John Carter, a kind of uncle. His uncle disappeared just after the Civil War and returned. He stood outside in the dark, arms outstretched toward the stars. And insisted that he be buried in a crypt that could be opened only from the inside.

Something else. John Carter never got older. He could not remember being a child, but he could remember serving kings and emperors. And that was why, somehow, he could waft in spirit to Somewhere Else, Barsoom, which even if it was some kind of Mars, did not have to be our Mars.

I got a call from John Doe Appropriate. "There's been some more film show up," he said. He sounded like someone had kicked him in the stomach. "In the mail. It's . . . it's in color."

Even he knew they had no color in 1911.

"Can I say that I'm not surprised?" He didn't reply. "I'm coming over," I said.

When he opened the door, he looked even worse than he sounded. He had a line of gray down the middle of his cheeks, and the flesh under his eyes was dark. When he spoke, it sounded like slowed-down film. "There's somebody here," he said, and left the door wide open behind him.

Someone was sitting with his back to us, watching a video. On the screen, a cushioned landscape extended to a surprisingly close horizon. The ground was orange and the sky was a deep bronze, and a silver zeppelin billowed across it, sails pumping like wings.

The man looked back over his shoulder, and it was Herman Blix.

Herman, as he looked in 1928 or 1911 or 1863, except that he had to lean on a cane. He heaved himself out of the chair and lumbered forward as if he had the bulk of a wounded elephant.

Did I say that he was stark naked?

"Not used to clothes," he said, gasping like he wasn't used to breathing.

Blink.

Your world turns over.

I saw as he spoke that he had tiny fangs, and that his eyes did glow. Looking into them made me feel dizzy, and I had to sit down. The strangest thing was that I knew at once what he was, and accepted it. Like meeting those little Nosferatu elves. No wonder he could waft through space: he wouldn't need a life-support system.

"Can you make films?" he asked me.

His eyes made it impossible to lie, and I heard myself say yes, because it was true, I could. The kid bled next to me, expendable.

"You're coming with me." Blix bore down on me, hauled me off the sofa, hugged me, and everything gasped cold and dark.

Mars was only the beginning.

The Last Ten Years
in the Life of Hero Kai

Kai was already an old man when he mastered the art of being hero. He was a student of war and a student of God. He was a particular follower of the text *The Ten Rules of Heroism*.

The Text is one hundred palm leaves long, but these are the Ten Rules.

1. Heroism consists of action
2. Do not act until necessary
3. You will know that the action is right if everything happens swiftly
4. Do whatever is necessary
5. Heroism is revealed not by victory but by defeat
6. You will have to lie to others, but never lie to yourself
7. Organized retreat is a form of advance
8. Become evil to do good
9. Then do good to earn merit and undo harm
10. Heroism is completed by inaction

The last ten years of Hero Kai's life are considered a perfect act of Heroism. One rule is exampled by each of his last ten years.

Heroism consists of action

It is Hero Kai's fiftieth year. He is lean and limber, his gray hair pulled back fiercely. People say his eyes are gray with age. Others say his eyes were always as gray as the eyes of a statue, except for the dark holes of his pupils.

His sword is so finely balanced that it can slice through sandstone walls. Kai himself can run up a vertical surface, or suspend his breathing for hours.

Kai starts each day with his exercises. He stands on tiptoe on the furthest leaf of the highest branch of the tallest mango tree in the region. He holds two swords and engages himself in fast and furious swordplay. He walks on his hands for a whole day.

Yet he takes no action.

He goes to funerals to chant for the dead. Rich men hope to earn merit by paying him to recite the traditional verses called the Chbap or Conduct. This is a Chbap.

The happy man is one who knows his limitations
And smiles formally even to a dog
If a neighbor owes him money
He applies an even gentle pressure like water falling over rocks . . .

. . . etc., etc. The Chbap are all about being tame and making things easy for superior people.

Kai's kingdom is very badly ruled. The roads have fallen apart; the rivers are choked with weeds; and the King spends his day performing gentle magic for which he has no talent.

The Chbap are the only thing that holds together the Kingdom of Kambu's Sons. The Chbap keep people toiling cheerfully in the rice fields. The verses remind them to give alms to the poor, thus staving off starvation and revolt. They insist that people care for their families, so that everyone can look forward to an honored old age. The Chbap prepare poor people to accept placidly an early and often excruciating death.

Kai believes in the Chbap to the extent that they are useful. He knows them in their thousands and recites one or two of them each evening as he is massaged by the boy he bought. The boy's name is Arun, and he gets up early each morning to sweep the monastery floors—and goes to bed late after scattering dust over those same floors to teach him acceptance.

On the day of his fiftieth birthday, Kai's acolytes present him with a handsome gift.

It is something new and dangerously different. In Kai's language, the words for "different" and "wrong" are nearly identical.

The gift is a tiny round bronze ball; and if you fill its tank with water and light a fire under it, it starts to spin.

Alone before going to sleep, Kai thinks about this different miracle long and hard. He decides that there is no magic in it. It is as hard and as fair as drought or pestilence.

The Westerners are building whole engines that work like steamballs. And the Neighbors are buying them.

The state of Kambu is so weak that the King has to pay to keep the neighboring states from invading. Kambu's King is so powerless that his own army is run by advisers from these states, and so helpless that he enforces their corvées of Kambu labor.

Kambu troops are being used to corral or even kidnap the Chbap-reciting farmers, herding them away to work on a new kind of road in the Commonwealth of the Neighbors.

Hero Kai sits on the beautifully swept floor. His little steamball spins itself to a stop. Candlelight fans its way through the gaps in the floorboards and walls. Everything buzzes and creaks with insects. In the flickering light, Kai thinks.

If only the King were strong. If only the Sons of Kambu stood up as one against the Neighbors. If only there were ten of me. Our army is controlled by our enemies. Our wealth pours out to them and when they want more, they just take it. The King's magic makes girls pretty, fields abundant, and rainfall regular. It holds back disease and the ravages of age.

The Neighbors make the magic of war.

Kai finds he cannot sit still. He stands on one leg and hops so lightly that the floorboards do not shake. He makes many swift passes with his sword, defeating imaginary opponents.

He loses heart and his sword sinks down toward the floor.

The unquiet spirit spends his strength in cutting air . . .

Kai takes out an incising pen and cuts a letter to the King in a palm leaf. He fills the grooves with ink-power and burns it so the ink hardens in the grooves but can be brushed away from the surface.

Then he wakes Arun and gives him the letter. Kai tells him to walk to the lake and take a boat to the distant, tiny, capital.

What can a mouse do when caught by the cat?

Do not act until necessary

A year later Kai stands with the farmers in revolt.

His monk robes are gathered up over his shoulders to free his arms and legs. The cloth is the color of fire. His body is hard and lean, as if cut from marble, with just the slightest creases of age across the belly and splotches around his ankles.

His sword is as long and lean as himself.

The Commonwealth of Neighbors is hot and smells of salt and drains. The sea hammers a coast that used to belong to the Sons of Kambu. The rich plains get all the rain that the mountains block from Kambu. Everything steams and rots.

Kidnapped fathers sweat in ranks, armed with hoes and pickaxes. Some of them simply carry rocks.

They have been starved and beaten until they are beyond caring. Families, fields, home are all hundreds of miles away.

They have nothing to lose.

The Road of Fire grins like an unending smile. The lips are burnished tracks of metal that gleam in mathematically parallel lines. The teeth are the wooden beams that hold the tracks in place. The Road of Fire looks like evil.

The Army of Neighbors looks beautiful.

They are naked except for white folded loincloths. Their bodies are hard but round from food and fighting, and their eyes are gray. Their earlobes are long and stretched, bearing heavy earrings.

Every one of them is a holy man.

The Army of Neighbors is famously small and famously bears no arms. For a moment or two the armies look almost evenly matched.

Then the Neighbors start to chant.

They chant and the sound seems to turn unhappily in place. The air starts to whimper. Kai has time to sniff magic. Magic smells of spit.

The eyes in the head of the man standing next to Kai explode. The man howls and drops the rock he had meant to throw.

There is a ripping sound. Kai turns in time to see the skin being pulled from a young man's body. The air lifts him up and plays with him as he is disrobed of his hide.

A farmer with a lucky mole on his chin is having his intestines pulled rapidly out of his body.

Kai's sword heats up. It becomes as hot as coals. Everywhere about him men scream and drop their hoes or their shovels.

Kai stands his ground. The sword belonged to his master, and his master before that. Kai holds on to it as it scorches his flesh. He focuses his mind on resisting the heat. His skin sears and heals, sears and heals in repeated waves of agony.

The rebels turn and flee.

The Dogs of Magic hound them. There is a slathering in the air as magic tastes, selects, destroys.

Magic licks Kai.

All of Kai's skin starts to boil. He can see the fat within bubble. He holds his focus, turns and calmly, somewhat stiffly, walks away. He survives through willpower.

He stumbles down rubble toward cool reeds before having to sit. He steams his way down into damp mud.

In the morning he wakes up after dreams of canoeing on the lake. In a circle all around him plants have burned or shrivelled. The dew steams. Kai hears the clink of hammers on rocks and smells a butcher's shop.

He stands. Sons of Kambu work in lines, their heads hanging low. They recite.

The happy man is one who knows his limitations
And smiles formally even to a dog

Tears pour down Kai's face, stinging the singed flesh with salt. He stands still, building a wall in his mind against despair.

Oh, familiar kindly Chbap, why do you have no answer to this? Do you have no song to bring victory and not defeat?

And somehow one comes to mind. Why this one? It's called the Problem Chbap, the one nobody understands.

> *Magic is the way of men of power*
> *They do not love kindness and nor does magic.*
> *Magic perfumes the air and sends men to hell.*
> *Push the particles of reality far and fast*
> *And magic will die, succumb to what is likely*
> *In the land where what you put in tea perfumes*
> *And magic is what is ground in the pestle.*

Kai stands transfixed. Suddenly it makes sense.

A guard struts forward, howling orders. He is a humble Neighbor without magic. Still contemplating the Problem Chbap, Kai spins on his heel and sends the Neighbor's head still shouting through the air.

Then Kai spins in the opposite direction and starts to march.

What do you put in your tea? Cardamom.

The Cardamom Mountains.

You will know that the action is right if everything happens swiftly

Kai arrives at his old monastery, still smoldering from heat.

The acolytes and the lay preachers and the old masters touch his skin, and their fingers hiss. His eyebrows flame and sputter, go out and flame again. The acolytes give him water and it boils in his mouth, but he has to drink it. Tears stream out his eyes and evaporate as steam.

An old master says, "You have become a fulcrum for the universe. I've cast the yarrow, and you came up all strong lines, changing to weak ones."

Kai tells them what happened in the lands of the Commonwealth, and of the Problem Chbap.

An acolyte says, "There are many like that. Remember the Dubious Chbap?"

Even trees mislead,
The worn path bends the wrong way
Undo cries the air, undo says the wise men,
And the trees open up.

Kai realizes. These problem Chbap did not make sense to us because we were not listening. These Chbap bring another kind of wisdom. They provide the balance to others.

These Chbap tell us how to fight.

"And how about this one. The masters love to set this as a test."

The mind observes and makes happen what it wants to see.
This is magic.
The motes of reality coast to what is most likely
And that is called the real.

Steaming, shuddering, fighting the spell, Kai's mind becomes his sword. For once.

His mind now cuts through a different kind of sandstone wall. This is a wall of beautiful, repetitive images: celestial maidens, virtuous monks, and skilled warriors . . . all that hardened rooster shit.

Kai says, "There is a machine that destroys magic in the Cardamom Mountains. We have to go and find it and use it on the Neighbors."

Immediately, ten young strong warrior monks volunteer. "We pack our bags now."

"No, no, Kai needs to rest," says one old monk, a rival of Kai.

"He should ask the King's permission," says another.

"That old fart!" says one of the warrior monks. "Let him sit at home and make earrings!"

Kai's voice rumbles from the fire within. "We go now. We go slowly, because if I am distracted I will burst into flame."

The young men exclaim: we take nothing! Just clothes, swords, stout shoes. A blanket against the cold in the mountains. We will hunt our food and cut it down from trees.

"More like you'll steal it from the poor peasants," growls Kai's rival.

"You mean like the King does?" The thrill of rebellion has made the acolytes forget respect.

They bustle their packs together.

The boy who Kai bought creeps forward. "Can I come as well?" Arun asks. His name means Morning Sun.

Losing focus, beginning to crackle from heat, Kai can only shake his head.

"Please." Arun begs. "I am so bored here. I learn nothing. I just sweep."

Eyes closed from concentration, Kai nods yes.

So the acolytes, proud sons of significant people, are joined by the slave. "Boy," they say, "Carry this."

Kai growls. "He works for me. Not you."

The acolytes bow and withdraw. They generally do, when faced with power.

They leave that night in the rain. The raindrops sputter and dance on Kai as if on a skillet.

"Swiftly" in a country without roads or waterways can mean many things.

It means you are welcomed in a village, and feted, and asked to wait so that you can chant at the wedding of the headman's daughter. You abide some weeks in preparation.

Arun says, "Teach me how to focus against the heat, Master. That way I can still massage your shoulders."

To Kai's surprise, he does.

One of the young men falls in love with one of the bride's sisters. It takes another week to persuade him to leave.

"Swiftly" means waiting out the rainy season as the plains of Kambu are milled into dough. It means the toes of the young men rot as they squelch through mud.

It means they wait all afternoon under a covered bridge as raindrops pound on the roof.

"Swiftly" means being lured into a welcoming village and then held as bandits, accused of theft and berated for rape.

The trial lasts weeks as all the ills of the village are visited on your head. The wretched people really think they can revenge all the wrongs done to them by killing you.

Kai practices forbearance, calmly pointing out that they were not in the village when the wrongs were done. He looks at the headman playing with Kai's own sword. He waits until the headman tires of admiring it and lays it to one side.

Then Kai stands up and says, "I am so sorry. I am afraid there's nothing we can do now except become another great wrong done to your people."

Kai can sing a note that makes his sword throb in harmony. The sword wobbles, weaves, and bounces itself into his hand.

"Many apologies," he says, and slices a pathway through the villagers, leading his acolytes out the door.

The dry season comes and the rivers shrivel. Kai's men march far out to the muddy borders of the lake, looking for a boat. They are told it will return from the city of Three Rivers within the week.

You swiftly wait sitting in mud, slipping in mud, catching frogs for supper. Each day, the lake is farther way, and you must walk again further out.

Arun says, "Let me oil and clean your sword, Master, so that it does not rust."

The hissing sword does not burn Arun's fingers. Kai thinks: this Arun has talent.

The noble acolytes look at the fish and frogs they have caught. Must they eat the frogs raw?

"No," says Kai, and cradles the frogs in his hands, passing them back crisp and brown.

Finally the boat comes and sets out through winding channels between reeds. It gets mired behind the abandoned hulk of a bigger boat, and starts to settle sideways in ooze.

Kai walks to the abandoned hull, and blesses it chanting, and where he touches it, the wood catches alight. The wreck burns bright as a torch, down to the waterline. The monks wade in the next day, and clear it.

Their boat proceeds to Three Rivers, the graceful capital.

Their voyage is made even swifter by messengers from Kai's rivals. They rode all night and day to warn the King.

The King's men await them along the marbled waterfront. They greet Kai with distanced politeness and invite him and his men to the Palace. The King himself spares five minutes to greet them. In a silky voice, he insists they must stay and rest.

The acolytes escape the Palace in darkness by running up and over its high walls.

Kai stays behind to rescue Arun, who cannot run up vertical surfaces. He loads the boy over his shoulder and walks toward the main gate.

A Neighbor wearing only a loincloth awaits him.

"You dress like that at this time of night?" says Kai. "You must be chilly. Or are you just trolling for trade?"

The Neighbor whispers with disgust, and there is a smell of spit.

But once you have been magicked, it is very difficult to magic you again.

Kai says, "Let me warm you."

He embraces the Holy Warrior. He holds the man until his arms have burnt to the bone. A burning fist over his face stifles his screams and will scar his mouth permanently closed. Kai and Arun walk flickering with unfocused flame into the night.

Then Arun throws up.

Most swift of all, are the Cardamom Mountains.

There was once a great trade route east through Cardamom, to the Tax Haven of the Others. But the Neighbors magnanimously protect the Sons of Kambu from the Others (and most particularly from any haven from taxation). They closed the trade route.

Where once there were broad clear pathways through the forest, Kai and his acolytes have to hack their way through vines, undergrowth, and stinging thorns.

After two months of hacking, mosquitoes, bad water, and ill wind, it becomes evident to even the meanest intelligence that something out of the ordinary is going on.

Steep paths snake their way up a hill, only to end up back at the bottom of the valley.

Kai's followers turn a corner and find that the last man in their caravan is now walking ahead of them all.

Kai cuts his name in the bark of a tree with one long flowing swordstroke.

They pass that sign again two days later. Kai throws down his sword.

"We stop walking," he says. He sits in meditation thinking about what has happened.

Even trees mislead,
The worn path bends the wrong way
Undo cries the air, undo says the wise men,
And the trees open up.

Kai stands up and shouts, "Undo!"

Up and down the valleys, the air echoes, "Undo!"

Trees crackle as they unwind, and stand straight. Paths grind as they heave their way back into shape, finally going somewhere.

The air yawns open from relief, being allowed to stretch at last.

Suddenly the path leads to a building, a simple building of red varnished wood. It stands out over the hillside on stilts. Beyond it, on the other side of the valley, rice terraces rise up thousands of feet.

A dog barks. The young nobles advance.

Kai groans. He sinks to the ground and starts to weep. Arun goes to him, takes him by the shoulders, and his hands leap back. Arun says, "He's not hot! The spell is broken."

There is a whole village built on stilts over the hillside. There are shaky wooden walkways and windmills. The rice fields go up this side of the valley as well, forming a natural amphitheatre. Sounds boom and roll or seem very close to your ear.

The air smells of mud and sweat and smoke.

Kai shudders, then chuckles, and stands up. "There's no magic here."

From out of the houses creep people with terrible broken teeth, spots, and age marks. The younger and more able-bodied of them stand with swords that look like pig iron, cast once and never smelted. Some of the men bear flint scythes that will shatter at the first blow.

"Hello," they say, glumly. "What do you want? We've not got much to take, we can tell you that for free."

Kai smiles with inner peace. "We want to see your machine."

They grin. They need dental magic urgently.

They lead Kai to a stone wall that shores up the cliff face. The whole village is in imminent danger of collapse.

Far below is a circular valley, where perhaps once a whirlpool wore away the rock. In that cavity, as red as tiles, a huge coiled tube stretches at least two hundred arm's lengths across.

"You're welcome to *try* to loot that," the locals say.

"Please," adds one of them, and they all laugh.

"Turning the thing off would be a start," one of them mutters.

The machine is smooth and huge, like a serpent that has swallowed its tail so that both ends merge. There is a series of bolts closing what look like long sideways windows. From this great height, Kai can see that along the top, one window has been left open and unbolted. What look like stars dance over the opening.

"It's never been properly turned on," says one old man.

"Don't give him any ideas," grunts a younger. He uses the tip of his little finger to pump out gross amounts of pus from his ear.

The air and the distance all whisper like defeat.

Kai slumps to the ground. "We can't move it," he says. "We can't take it to fight the Neighbors."

It is a year to the day since he set out on his quest.

Do whatever is necessary

At the gates of the royal palace, Kai hugs another Neighbor. He burns the man right through the middle.

This time Arun maintains his countenance. "Almost surgical," he says.

Kai's noble followers dance through the gates more silently than settling dust.

Two court officials approach in deep discussion, wearing purple cloth with gold-embroidered flowers.

With a whisper, swords slip through them. The cuts are so thin that blood seeps slowly. The bodies are arranged on cushions to look as though they are still in conversation.

Kai and his men whisper into the Sycophancy Salon. The Staircase of Effective Entrances sweeps up to the Royal Chambers.

Two strong Sons of Kambu guard the top of the steps.

Kai somersaults up the staircase, gathering speed like an avalanching boulder. He rolls to his feet and elbows their swords out of their hands. He holds his own sword close to their throats. He has lost focus, and the sword, even its handle, glows cherry red.

"You are Kambu," says Kai. "We don't want to hurt you. We are here to defeat the Neighbors. To do that we must get the King out of their clutches. Are you with us?"

They say yes. All Sons of Kambu, they say, want the King safe from influence and out of Neighborly attention.

The noble warriors surf up the balustrade of the staircase.

Among them is Arun. "I'll take that," he says and relieves one of the Kambu of his fine imperial sword.

A sword must be either inherited from a master or taken in battle. Arun grins and licks the sword's black laminate.

"Now, Master," he says. "I look to you for training."

In the royal apartments, the rooms are stuffed with foreigners—Neighborly advisers who run things, observers who write interesting reports, or guest troops who kill the enemy, i.e., the Sons of Kambu.

Kai and his ten are like a bladed whirlwind. They spin through the rooms, harvesting heads.

When they are done, five of the Ten stand guard outside the main doors.

Five plus Arun and his master go into the royal chamber.

The King is hunched over a tiny spinning steamball. "Remarkable this, don't you think?" he says, and only then turns around to look at the swordsmen. "But what use is it, I wonder?"

He is a beautiful man, tall, willowy, and graceful, with long thin fingers that look as though they could pluck heartfelt melodies out of the air. His eyes are full of sympathy for their plight. "Have you come to kill me? You will be reborn as toads."

"We've come," says Kai, "to take you home."

The King flutes some kind of mellifluous reply. It is muffled in Kai's ears. He cannot quite hear what the King says, rather as though his majesty was talking with his mouth full.

Then Kai remembers that he is immune to magic. This includes the magic of charm, of sweetness, of sympathy—the magic of kindly deception.

Whuh, whuh, whuh, the King seems to say. It is not entirely meaningful to say that Kai squints with his ears, but that is more or less what he does. He can just make out the King saying, "You surely don't want to hurt your King. It's a very humble thing to be a King. Your body mirrors the health of the nation. Hurt me and you hurt yourself."

The young men are drawn. "No of course not, Father. Not hurt you. Help you. Get you away from these Neighbors."

"Ah, but these Neighbors are our friends...." Kai lets the words unfocus back into *blah, blah, blah.*

Everyone is entranced. Kai keeps his eyes on them all as he steps carefully backward. There is a cabinet with crystal doors full of items under purple silk. Kai looks, then strikes. His sword cuts through the bolts.

"Oh dear," says the King. "I've been meaning to change those locks."

Kai gathers up the things. The King's voice is entirely unintelligible to him now. It drones like a call to prayers.

His own men turn around and face him, swords drawn.

Kai has a voice as well. "Nobody will hurt you, Father. Isn't that so, boys? We don't want to hurt the King. But he will have to follow these."

The King's eyes go wide and tearful.

Kai hugs to himself the Sacred Sword, the palm-leaf Royal Chronicles, the cymbals, the earrings, and the cup.

"All of this paraphernalia means you are king. Without it you can't give titles and buy the support of nobles. Without it you can't work your magic. Where these go, you have to follow. Or you are not king."

The King falters, looks sad and lonely, an old man, too frail for travel. What Kai has said is true.

Kai strides out of the room with all the symbols of his power, and the King trots after him. Kai can make out his tones of sad complaint. Kai's own men stand their ground. Their swords are still drawn.

"Earplugs," sighs Kai. He snatches up four candles, tosses them into the air, and slices them into eight with his sword. He catches them between his toes, and they light themselves from his heat.

Then Kai spins himself into the air, hugging the royal paraphernalia to his chest. Before even his trained acolytes can ward him off, Kai has filled their ears with melted wax.

"Now you can sing as sweetly as you like, King." He smiles.

His acolytes shake their heads, blink in confusion and then shrug.

Kai says, "King, if you call for help, I'll spit down your throat. Your vocal cords will be scalded and you'll never speak again."

Then he and his men jog through rooms soaked in blood and out into the courtyard. All of them run up the walls of the Palace, including Arun, although he carries a king.

Heroism is revealed not by victory but by defeat

The Neighbors fall for it.

They need the docile Kambu King. He is oversubtle where he should be bold, precise where he should be roughshod but quick.

The horrors of the Palace have shown them that they face a formidable adversary. They abide.

Finally, they hear where the King's new forced capital can be found. Cardamom.

And so, drawn, they march their magic army into the trap.

Kai stands on the new battlements of what he has renamed the City of Likelihood. Air moves, eagles fly overhead, and far down below at the mouth of the valley, the Army of Neighbors marches.

They number only three thousand. All of them are already through the narrow pass, which looks particularly ragged at the top. The hillside is crowned with heaps of rubble, with logs among them.

Kai smiles.

The Sons of Kambu face the Neighbors in ranks across the valley floor.

This is no rag-tag revolt of corvéed labor. These Kambu troops wear armor and carry weapons. The smithies of Likelihood have been busy. The corvéed labor hobbled hundreds of miles to find the new capital, but they have had time to rest and time to train.

Many sons of nobles have come as well, because there is no way for them to get a title but to receive it from the King.

And in flaming orange is a battalion of Kambu warrior monks. They have crossed into Likelihood as well, crying, "Undo!"

The King stands beside Kai now. Without his magic, the King looks stooped, wizened, and frail. "Are you sure this is a good idea?"

Kai smiles.

Someone must have given the Neighbors the word Undo. That someone hopes to be rescued.

The best argument is action not words. Kai does not answer him.

Down from the battlements to the valley floor are fine threads of silk, invisible to the Neighbors because they are too real.

Kai utters one piercing shriek, like an eagle's call.

On the distant hillsides, over the pass, teams of oxen drag the great logs. The tree trunks turn sideways, which is all that is needed.

The trees will open.

Oxen hauled those stones up the hillside, but love spurred on their masters.

You could say therefore, thinks Kai, that love moves mountains.

The rocks pour down.

Slowly like a lady's hand putting down her fan, the rubble falls the great distance. The Neighbors have time to turn, elbow each other, and clutch their sides. Their thin laughter wafts across the distance.

How stupid, the Neighbors seem to say. These Kambu wanted to rain down rocks on our heads and waited until we were all through!

The beauty of the Machine, thinks Kai, is that it is not a presence. It is an absence. There is nothing for the Neighbors or any of their mages to sense.

Then a cry goes up from the Neighbors.

They have cast their first spell, and it hasn't worked.

The stones settle with a crash and a raising of dust, closing the pass. The Neighbors cannot get out.

There is no magic here, only swords. The Neighbors are unarmed.

The ten acolytes of Hero Kai leap from the battlement walls onto the single silken threads, and they slide down. They balance holding out two singing swords in each hand, outstretched like wings. They somersault onto the ground.

Then they whirligig their way across the plain, spinning into the soft and real flesh of the Neighbors.

The monks, the farmers, and the sons without titles advance.

To be sure of victory, the Neighbors sent three thousand of their finest warrior sorcerers.

Within five minutes, all of them are dead.

Again, Kai cries like an eagle and flings his swords over his head. Blood whips from the blades in midair as if the weapons themselves are bleeding.

The Sons of Kambu cheer. They run to Kai and pat his back. They dip and hold up their hands in prayer toward him. Some of them prostrate themselves on the ground to him, but laughing, he shakes his head and helps them stand.

"We have all won!" he cries, and all the valley tolls like a giant bell of stone, ringing with many voices.

Kai laughs and turns, and he runs up the silken thread. True he slows somewhat near the summit, but he gains the top of the battlements and all the citizens roar all the louder.

He hops down from the wall in front of the King. The King looks like a skeleton.

Kai knows from the man's face. He had thought his only duty was to stay in office. This King liked the Neighbors because they kept him in his palace.

"You are a king for real now," says Kai. "Better start ruling and stop consuming."

The King gives a sad, sick smile. Kai seizes his hand, pulls him to the top of the battlements, and holds the King's hand aloft. All Likelihood cheers its King and all his sacred paraphernalia.

The fiction is maintained.

You will have to lie to others, but never lie to yourself

It has been a year without wonders.

The mountain rice paddies require unending maintenance. Gates have to be opened to let them drain. The gates must be closed promptly or the terraces dry out. Heavy stones must be rolled back into place. Spills of precious topsoil must be scooped back into the fold. The replanting of nursery rice keeps people bent over for a week. The ligaments in the smalls of their backs tear.

The monsoons are late and small. Water has to be pumped up from the valley floor.

Too many people crowd in, and there are disputes. The original villagers had no system of land registration. The newcomers steal their terraces only to have them stolen in turn.

So the King assigns fields. What happens when those assigned fields dry out and there are no more fields to register?

The King is pleased. He looks less of a man than ever, like someone recovering from malaria, but he smiles. "Of course, in the old days, I could have called up rain like that." He snaps his fingers.

Kai's reply is placid. "Now you have the opportunity to be responsible in a new way. You will have to join us in thought."

The King chuckles. "Responsible? The King is not supposed to be responsible. The King just is the King. Unless he is prevented from embodying the health of the country."

"You never did. You embodied the disease."

Kai goes for a walk.

He walks through the court that has gathered around the King. It is thriving, full of superior people in blue cloth with gold flowers. They gather murmuring in distinguished groups, and turn and mutter as Kai passes them.

He is relieved to be free of them. He clambers down the wooden ladder that is the entrance to the royal palace. The palace is one of the original, graceful, dilapidated village buildings. He likes it. What better way to say that here everyone shares the wealth and the labor? He himself plants rice.

Kai loves this new Kingdom. Everywhere he sees the work of God, God who hates miracles because they are so unfair.

He smiles at a beautiful Daughter of Kambu. She grins a strange closelipped smile that looks neither serene nor spontaneous. She is smiling so that she does not show her rotten teeth.

Kai walks through the market. The Neighbors harass caravans bound for Likelihood. The old trade route is kept open only through continuing force of arms. The noble sons who guard the passes come home wrapped in silk for cremation.

The high mountain steppes are good for only one crop of rice each year. They don't support fruit trees. The stall-owners sell no longan, rambuttan, or jackfruit. The market stinks of rotten old bananas and aged mushy pineapples. People cover their faces when they walk through it. Everyone looks very lean and fit.

They still greet each other beautifully, and the sun still shines on this glorious day.

It doesn't rain.

The amphitheater of paddies all around them echoes with the sound of labor—axes chopping stone, men grunting as they pump water, an argument because one man threw all his cleared pebbles into another man's field.

Kai himself has tiny new brown spots all over the back of his hand. "I'm getting old," he tells himself. "It is the natural way."

At the far side of the filthy market is one of the hastily constructed new houses, built from cast-off timber and tumbles of stone. Sons of Kambu are not used to building houses out of stone. They are not used to the winter wind that blows through the chinks.

Inside the house, a man is screaming in pain.

Hero Kai does not need to climb the ladder to see in. He can duck his head into the low shelter.

"Can I help?" he asks. He expects surprised pleasure at being visited by a Hero in the making. He imagines polite bowing and hands held up in prayer. A middle-aged woman whose swollen belly is popping the buttons of her shirt looks at him sullenly.

The old man, quivering, sits up. "No you can't!" he says. "Go away, go away and take my pain with you! May it eat your joints!"

Kai is taken aback. "I am so sorry you are ill."

The man shouts again. "I am not an opportunity for you to earn merit!"

Kai feels the blood in his cheeks prickle.

The man drops back. "Curse you, God, for accepting all my offerings and letting me die! Curse you, God, for creating pain. Go away, God, with all your high thoughts and sharp rocks. Blast every living slug, mosquito, spider, snake, civet, all of the thieving, biting things you created! Die, God! Like me! Die!"

Kai feels deafened by the words. He staggers back.

He turns and sees a ring of people around him. They are all grinning smugly. A young man with a particularly nasty smile starts to recite what sounds like a Chbap.

Oh great wise man with all your strength
Too big, you crush us like a mill
Too big, you soak up all our pride

Too strong, you sit on us like an ox.
Too clever, you take away all our comfort
Just because you do not need it.

The circle of people all chuckle. Kai reaches for his sword. He stops himself.

"I will think about what you say," he says. And waits for a respectful response.

"What will you *do?*" asks the smug young man.

Kai acknowledges that with a stiff shake of the head. He feels awkward and foolish as he walks away.

"Die, Big Man! Die!" screams the man in the house.

Kai draws Arun to one side and takes him for a walk out into the hills where spies can be easily seen.

"It is the way of the world, Arun. You offer people good things, but still they will always complain. To rule, you have to scare them as well as flatter them. We have not used fear. You and the Ten, go out among the town and drink some of these terrible fermentations people brew from the rotten fruit. Pretend to get drunk. Listen to who criticizes."

Kai sighs. "Then we will round them all up and pile stones on top of them."

Organized retreat is a form of advance

Another army pauses at the top of the fallen rubble.

Sunlight glints on metal. They are armored, and some of the armor is Kambu. Banners in the shape of flames flutter in the wind. Gongs and blaring trumpets signal some kind of advance.

The King sits cross-legged on the battlements consulting the Oracle, which of course no longer works here. The yarrow stalks clatter meaninglessly onto the paving. "It seems we have visitors," the King says, croaking and wheedling with an old man's voice.

Kai glares into the distance.

People have formed a long line along the rice terraces over the pass. They appear to be prizing free large sections of the cliff face. Huge flat plates of stone break away, land, rock, and settle.

Something like a staircase is being built down from the top of the dam.

This time the Neighbors know magic will not protect them. And they seem to have been joined by Kambu allies.

As he did two years ago, Kai keens like a eagle. It is the call to arms.

There is only silence. A baby wails somewhere.

He keens again and again. Likelihood remains still. Kai hears only wind in response.

The King chuckles and shakes his head.

Kai turns, and the King's courtiers block the ladder down. Kai looks at the beautiful superior cloth and imagines it sliced cleanly.

These are not soldiers. Kai puts his hand on the handle of one of his swords, and they flinch and step back. They will not fight him, but they are far from harmless. He walks forward and they step aside to let him through. He beheads them all anyway.

Then he saunters back to the King, hoists him to his feet, and jams a sword to this throat. "You have the benefit of one escape, because you are my King. But I don't respect you, and I have no use for you. Next time, you're dead."

The skinny old man quivers in his grasp bending backward over the edge of the wall.

Kai looks and counts. He sees the Neighbors whose helmets are round with a spike on the top, and he notes the lotus-blossom helmets of his own people. He counts them. Superior people outside Likelihood still depend on the King for their titles. They have come to get him, to take him back, to reclaim their superiority.

One thousand he counts. Estimate another thousand there. Three thousand?

There are more Kambu in this army than there are Neighbors.

He darts down the steps and into the Palace.

He can trust his secret police, most of them. He can trust the Ten. He needs nobody else with him.

Underneath the royal palace, on the slope amid its stilts, there hangs a chute for washing waste down over the hills. Kai called it the Tipping of the Balance, and it is the agreed meeting place in case of disaster.

The Ten are all there, with Arun.

Kai explains why they are not fighting. "We did not set out on this great scheme to become killers of the Sons of Kambu."

He is just a little surprised, just a little disappointed, when there is an urgent murmur of assent from even his most loyal.

"Go pack. Gather anyone you see along the way whom we have marked as Likely. Ask them to come with us, but do not wait. Our aim now is to be long gone by the time the new army gets here."

"But the Machine..."

Kai sighs and marvels at his own powers of acceptance. "The Machine is doomed."

All clatter away except for Arun. Arun says, "My only friend is you. The only person I respect is you. I will be with you until the end." The two men hug.

"Brother," declares Kai. This is a promotion.

They go back to the battlements, stepping over a few heads.

The wave of troops advances. They recite the Loyalty Chbap.

Respect the King, for the job of the King
Is to eat the country.
He eats the country so that it can be processed
Through his sacred alimentary canal.
It comes out rich fertilizer for us to live on.

Kai chuckles. "And the country is shit."

The loyal Ten come back, bringing, perhaps thirty Likely others with them.

"Enough," says Kai. And with measured pace they begin to climb.

From high in the hills, they look down on misty distance. Elephants have lumbered up and over the heap of stone, hauling a battering ram. Great silk-cotton logs slam repeatedly into the side of the Machine.

Kai can hear the breaking of the clay even from this great distance. A sparkling vapor dazzles its way out of the new mouth. It washes over the elephants, and they burn and shrivel. Their great legs twist, collapsing into heaps of ash.

Even on the high mountainside where the Ten stand, the air starts to buzz unpleasantly like a blow to the elbow.

Kai makes one sharp shrill cry. The fat under his skin seethes up and he burns again.

He contorts for a moment, stretching his neck, shoulders and arms. He shivers his way back into normal standing position, mastering himself and the fire.

"Now it's their turn to cheer," he says. He starts to climb again.

Only Arun can lay a comforting hand on his burning flesh.

Become evil to do good

A year later only the Ten are left.

They live in a cave, surviving on what they can hunt. They shiver in furs and spend the long dark hours in meditation. A hard life is what they have come to love, and despite all their virtues, they have become hard men. There are few words and no laughter between them.

Except for Arun. Curiously, he has learned how to laugh. He tells jokes to himself, the Ten, and sometimes even to Kai, when he can find him.

"Master, come back. We need you to warm the walls."

Kai has retreated into the high snows. He perches on icy crags, buffeted by howling winds. The snow sputters on his skin and melts in a perfect circle all around him. The rocks he sits on have the dull metallic look of stones in a steam bath. Trails of vapor hiss from them.

"At least you will be very clean," says Arun again. He crouches near Kai with a pot of stew. Already the stew is icy cold, which is how Kai likes it. It cools his throat as he swallows. Arun feeds him with a spoon he himself has chipped out of stone.

Arun sits in the shelter of Kai's warmth, and places the pot of stew on Kai's lap to heat it up. He tries to make conversation.

"You should come and burn the cave clean for us!" Arun says, but the gale drowns out his words.

"To tell you the truth, the Ten all think I am still a slave. I do all the work!" Still no response. Being with Kai now can be lonelier than being without him. Arun eats his boiling-hot stew.

The gray sky edges toward blue. Arun cannot be caught out on icy trails at night. Arun hugs Kai, though it sears his hides and makes them stink.

Kai looks pained and saddened, staring at something quite definite in all that swirling cloud and snow.

Arun stands up, shouts goodbye, gets no answer, and then turns and walks into the blizzard.

Kai sits alone. The wind drives the snow sideways. The world gets bluer, almost turquoise.

Then, swelling out of the storm and the hillside comes a giant stranger made of air and hardship, rock and salt, wind and sleet.

The Buddha was tempted by Mala, the World. Mala offered the Buddha kingship, and the power to do good in the real world.

"Well," says the World. "Here's a fine place for a Hero to end up. Happy in your work?"

"I know who you are," says Kai through broken teeth that glow like embers.

"I know a good dentist," says Mala. "I made him myself."

The World sits down and sighs in a showy, airy way. "Now what do I have here? Oh, cooling ices. They are made in a city called Baghdad. It's a desert town, quite sophisticated, fiercely hot. They have learned how to transport ice and make sweet delights from it that are colder even that this snow. Magic ices, that would soothe your fiery throat."

Kai chuckles, puffing out smoke and ash from his burnt windpipe. "Go to hell," he says.

"That's where I am. Hell is wherever you are, my friend," says Mala. "Freezing and burning for the rest of your life? Sounds familiar to me. Myself, I prefer comfort, the here and now, and if a little bit of magic gets us what we most desire, I, the World-as-it-actually-is, don't see any reason to forego it."

"It is not the will of God."

Mala sighs. "I have no idea what the will of God is. And, my would-be Hero, neither do you. By the way, you have not achieved Heroism."

"I know that."

"Think you'll find it in your navel?"

"Better place to look than up your ass."

"My my, we are sharp this morning, aren't we? A year of agony tends to do that to people. How about looking for Heroism in reality?"

"I do."

"Haven't found it, have you? Look, I'm the entire world and I have many places to be at once. So I'll say this once only and quickly. Your aim was *not* to destroy magic. Your aim was to free your kingdom from the Neighbors. I'm sorry to have to make this clear to you, but the only way to do that in the World is to destroy the Neighbors. So why not take the most direct and intelligent route? Destroy them through magic?"

Kai sits unmoved, eyes closed. "All I have to do is give up enlightenment."

The World's laughter melds with the sound of the storm. "You are so far from achieving enlightenment! You've killed too many people! You'll be lucky to reborn as a frog!"

Mala stands up, shaking his head. "You are a complete and total failure. I'll leave the ice cream here. Don't worry, it won't melt. Not up here."

In a particularly stinging blast of wind and snow, Mala leaves . . .

. . . Kai . . .

. . . alone.

He finally eats the ice cream.

He stands, and pauses for thought.

"Good?" asks the World.

Kai trots down the hill.

To Arun, he gives the power of wind, to freeze or dry or scorch. To the Likely Ten he gives in order:

- pestilence
- sudden rending of flesh

- blindness and deafness
- dazed stupidity and cretinism in all its forms
- sterility and impotence
- drought and famine
- age and the death of children
- disaster: flood, earthquake, accidents of all kinds
- depression and despair

He himself is already Fire, so he gives himself the power of kings to make things pretty.

Together with Mala, the Likely Ten descend howling on the Neighbors. Kai stands huge and billowing in flame over the capital city.

Fire torches all their wooden buildings, their finely carved palaces, and the beautiful verse inscribed on palm leaves.

The soldiers of the Neighbors fall where they stand, buboes swelling up and bursting under armpits or in their groins. Others are suddenly split into two. Their fathers go deaf and blind, their faithful wives become so stupid they cannot remember their own names. The young men will find they can't get it up. Their horses and elephants all have rabies, and the vaginas of their women blister with new and fatal contagious diseases. All—all—of their children under twelve die; a million children in one night.

Then the sea rises up to swamp their ports and sink their ships. Earthquakes shake their sacred temples into rubble.

Those few Neighbors who are left alive sit down and weep and surrender to dazed despair.

Kai flies on wings of fire and seizes hold of the King of Kambu. "Remember me?" he chuckles brightly.

He seals the body of the King in amber and uses it for his throne. He makes sure that none of the King's sons, cousins, wives, uncles, or nephews are left alive.

"No nonsense this time," Kai declares from his new and sad-eyed throne. "The Commonwealth of the Neighbors is no more. It is a happy part of the Kingdom of the Sons of Kambu. I am their King."

It is Mala, not Arun, who chuckles and pats his shoulder. No hurricanes blew during the conquest.

"We have swallowed you," Kai admits. "You should have considered the possibility when you tried to swallow us. Now, my dear friends and loyal subjects. It is your turn to build a railway."

All the Neighbors are enslaved.

Then do good to earn merit and undo harm

Women become pretty. The bones in their faces shift subtly and slowly at night. Their teeth straighten. They become pregnant, if they want to be.

Every afternoon, predictably, just before the children go to drive the oxen home, it rains. People finish their wholesome lunches listening to the pleasant sounds of rain on the roof.

The fruits on the market stalls are round, with perfect blushes of ripeness, firm enough but sweet. They scent the air.

Old people suddenly notice that they can stand up straight and that swinging their legs out of the hammock is easier. They find that standing first thing in the morning no longer hurts. They can dance for joy. They can work in the rice fields as the Chbap advise, and they call to their friends cheerily.

And most strangely of all, whenever they recite the Chbap, good things happen.

Kai chuckles to himself and confides in Arun. "I've given them all magic powers. What was wrong about magic was that it bent the rules unfairly for just a few people. Now, everyone has the power of magic. Everyone has the power to do good. They will realize it, but slowly."

"Whereas," says Arun, his smile a bit thin, "you have a monopoly on doing harm."

"Yes. But I don't have to use it."

"Much," says Arun.

Birds sing, the sun shines, people eat but don't get fat. The Neighbors see that Sons of Kambu have a superior way of life, and envy them. "Well, you know my grandfather was Kambu," they begin to say, as they stagger under the weight of railway ties. "I always put my superior good fortune down to that."

Kambu words sprinkle their speech. The Neighbors begin to recite the Chbap, and lo! Their backaches cease.

"We have a lot to learn from these Sons of Kambu," they agree.

Their few surviving daughters start to wear Kambu fashion. Their eyes follow noble Sons with alluring brightness.

And then the strangest thing of all comes to pass.

To earn merit, Kai orders the rebuilding of temples.

The stones are piled back more or less as they were. Kai is a follower of the Dharma, but he honors the gods that underlie that more clear-headed faith, as he sees it.

All the artisans of the Neighbors are now either dead or senile, so good Kambu craftsmen restore the temples to Vishnu, Siva, and even Brahma. The artists love doing this, for underneath the newer religion, the old gods survived in the hearts of the people. Fine new statues of the gods are made, and the monks who were the rivals of Kai are given new jobs. They get to enrobe and feed the statues.

The new enlarged kingdom smells of honey.

The old gods come back.

It starts quietly at first. Whispers are heard in cool stone galleries. The shawls and garlands of flowers that drape the statues flutter, with the wind surely, but as if the stone arm supporting them had moved.

Water poured over the linga and the yoni tastes delicious, poised between sweet and savory. The purified water has the power to restore even Neighbor slaves to health. All anyone has to do to receive a blessing is drink and swear loyalty to the gods and their earthly representative, King Kai the Merciful.

The temple oracles find that their ingenuity is no longer taxed. They no longer have to invent orotund but ambiguous answers to questions. Instead their heads are thrown back and a godlike voice whispers out of them. Sometimes their listeners look overjoyed by the answer, sometimes they are plunged into despair. But they no longer look baffled.

The Sons of Kambu never quite stopped believing in even older religions. For them, everything has a spirit—a house, a tree, or even a stone.

The food left in spirit houses is found suddenly eaten. The flowers in the beds stir and creep forward, conquering more waste ground. Roofs repair themselves and house fronts seem to adopt cheerful smiling faces.

Finally, at least to superior persons and Brahmins, the gods themselves begin to speak.

"More," the gods ask. They have a great way with simplicity in speech. More sweetmeats, more incense, more garlands, more rice. A little gold or a new temple would be appropriate.

"Well," sniffs Kai, to wealthy dependents. "You heard what the gods told you. Build them a temple."

It is good way to keep his nobles occupied and leave them no extra cash for private armies.

Suddenly there are hospitals and rest stations for travelers. New roads are built. The King is quick to point out to the gods that roads are necessary if worshippers are to bring offerings.

Roads are also necessary for trade.

A little grudgingly perhaps, the gods do some good. Strong trees, healthy rice, more wildlife to forage, fish in the sea, calm trade routes, and boats that do not leak. Things prosper even more.

"This is a really good deal for you," the gods point out to Kai.

"And for you." He smiles back.

Mala is happiest of all. "I surrender to the superiority of the gods," the World says and keeps himself in the background. The birds sing sweetly.

Heroism is completed by inaction

Late at night, Kai wakes up with Arun's sword at his throat.

A howling gale fills the room and pins Kai to his bed, pushing all his fire down onto the stone mattress.

Arun wants to talk.

He strokes Kai's flaming hair with one hand. "What," he asks Kai, "do you think you're doing? If you swallow the Neighbors, you need to consider the possibility that someone else will turn around and swallow you."

"Arun," says Kai in a tone of voice that embodies the realization that he should have expected this moment to come from him. "Of course I've considered it."

"Of course. But you take no action. You still have a problem taking action, after all these years. But only I know that." Arun lightly plants a kiss on Kai's fiery cheek. He waits for a response. Kai still takes no action.

Arun smiles at him. "Scared old man," he says affectionately. "Who do you think these gods are who are showing up wanting handouts and threatening to turn off the rain if they don't get it? How long do you think they will let you rule?"

"Until I die. They are gods and can afford to be patient."

"No, they can't. Nothing is more fragile than faith."

"Are you warning me of danger, or asking me to retire? Or just threatening to kill me?"

"All three," says Arun. "These gods of yours get bored. They do terrible things. They send plagues just to keep us in line, and make us pray and give more offerings."

"Sounds like the Ten."

"Oh, we are human. They are not. We can still sympathize. They consume. Poor people always get consumed."

"That is the way of the World," sighs Kai.

"Friend of yours, is he?" Arun asks.

"Yes."

Arun goes still. He strokes Kai's head. "You have been serving everything we are taught to shun. So have I."

"Well, there is no guarantee that what we were taught was true. How long can you lie on top of me with a sword at my throat?"

"Until we both die," says Arun, passion in his eyes.

Kai chuckles. "You are so like me when I was young."

Then he says it again in despair. "You are the closest thing I have to a son."

Arun says the obvious. "Then. Make me King."

Kai considers. "There is no such thing as an ex-King who is still alive. I have another proposal. I really like this idea, by the way. I make you Regent. You rule here. And I? I go on retreat and I try to recover a little bit of merit before I die. Enough to get me out of hell and perhaps be reborn as an insect or a slug."

"You will declare me your legitimate son, fathered in your youth. Your flesh and blood, your rightful heir. You will give me the title of Crown Prince."

"You're making demands, and all you have is a sword."

"No, Father. I have your love. And you don't want to be stuck in hell or reborn as a slug, and I don't want that for you either. I want to see Kai restored to himself."

They look at each other a moment, pat each other's arms, chuckle and sit up.

"What will you do as Regent?" Kai asks.

"I'll make us all Buddhists. But I'll let the worship of the old gods continue. I'll starve them slowly. And I'll make sure that dear old Mala is convinced that I will always give him his due."

"Like father, like son."

"Not always," says Arun.

The next day King Kai declares publicly that Arun is his natural son and heir. He makes him Crown Prince and announces his retirement from the capital. Arun will rule in his stead. Kai passes him the Sacred Sword. There is wild, ecstatic cheering at this delightful development.

There are some hours of light ceremonials, a bit of singing and dancing and drinking holy water. Then Arun mounts the dais. He looks down at the sad-eyed throne and says, "Get this terrible thing out of here and cremate it with honors."

Kai packs what he took with him on that first quest nine years ago. The Likely Ten, now terrible to behold, safely escort Kai to the gates of the royal precinct, just to be sure that he really has gone. With every step he chuckles.

He walks across the fields, toward the lake and across the kingdom. Everywhere people treat him with respect and kindness. This is due in part to a new Chbap that Arun commissioned and paid to have chanters repeat.

Imitate the wisdom of the Great King Kai
Know when to pass responsibility to your son
Depart in good cheer
For that quieter kingdom of the world
Where wisdom is found in small things.

Villagers recognize him, and beg him stay to chant at weddings. He does so in good cheer. No one accuses him of anything. Women who remember how handsome he once was place garlands of flowers around his neck and hold up their hands in prayer.

He finally arrives at the place where the paths wind back on themselves and the trees close over. "Undo!" he says again.

He finds the City of Likelihood, deserted and forlorn.

He goes to the simple house of unsteady stone in which another old man died in pain. Kai unrolls a mat and finds a forgotten bowl and spoon. Even after all these years with some of the dykes fallen, sparse rice still whispers in the thousand paddies. They climb toward heaven like stairs.

He gathers rice and stores it, some for seed, for there will be only one crop. The many deserted wooden houses will provide him with firewood. He takes the opportunity to prepare for death and accept the world as it is, and finds that there is surprisingly little to contemplate.

He draws in a breath, and goes down into the valley to carry out his plan.

He goes to the Machine. He is able to step through the breakage into its huge hollow coil. He climbs up the scaffolding and flaps the broken reed panels that once powered its engines. Some clay, some reed, some time—that will be all it needs.

The Machine was built in a dead whirlpool because of the centuries of sediment deposited there. Finding clay is easy. So is finding firewood. Kai hauls huge evergreens down from the hills and lets them dry until they are tinder. He touches them and they catch fire, for magic now rules everywhere, even in Likelihood. He bakes new sections of tube. He weaves the reed into new blades for windmills.

The Machine takes shape, the panels turn in the wind, and Kai sighs with satisfaction. He remembers the original inhabitants.

It's never properly been turned on.

Don't give him ideas!

Too late to avoid that, I'm afraid.

Kai once asked, "What would it do?"

"Buzz the world," said one old man.

Kai slides shut portal after portal. The old machine hums. Kai remembers the one bolted portal at the top that was left open.

Kai the warrior monk stands back and then runs up and over the round smooth sides.

Over the last open portal dances something that looks like stars. Kai, the man of magicked fire, reaches through them, pulls the bolt shut, and locks it. He survives the sparkling blast, where elephants could not. All it does is quench his fire like cooling water.

And all the World is deprived of magic.

Mala descends howling in rage and grief and betrayal, and Kai smiles at him. Just after his giant wings drop off, Mala melts harmlessly into the ground, personified no longer.

No more miracles.

In all the temples in the lands of Kambu, the voices of the gods whisper once like dust before being blown away. Then their halls are empty. The statues are wrapped, the oracles speak, but with voices that in their hearts they know are their own.

Kai is released for one last time from the fire in his body. He has changed the whole world forever. He made the world in which we now live. Which can hardly be called heroism completing itself through inaction.

Soon after, he gets sick and dies alone in agony in the tiny house of wood and stone.

GEOFF RYMAN

And what of heroism?

Well, the Rules don't understand it, but they sound good, and at least they don't say that you become a hero by being kind and doing your duty. Heroism consists of the moment that you are cheered by thousands. Heroism resides in the eyes of other people, and what you can get them to believe.

It can also be secret, without praise, and known to no one except you. That kind is a lot less fun.

Heroism, if you want it, resides nowhere, and everywhere, in the air, whether it buzzes with magic or not. In the hard, merciless world of Likelihood, there is no meaning, except in moments. There are also no Rules.

The old gods had been unstitched into ordinary molecules. The pretty magic of kings no longer worked. Kai's new railway, roads, and cities were an enticement.

Steamboats arrived from the West, bearing cannons and ambitious, likely people.

Birth Days

Today's my sixteenth birthday, so I gave myself a present.

I came out to my mom.

Sort of. By accident. I left out a mail from Billy, which I could just have left on the machine, but no, I had to go and print it out and leave it on my night table, looking like a huge white flag.

I get up this morning and I kinda half notice it's not there. I lump into the kitchen and I can see where it went. The letter is in Mom's hand and the look on her face tells me, yup, she's read it. She has these gray lines down either side of her mouth. She holds it up to me, and says, "Can you tell me why you wouldn't have the courage to tell me this directly?"

And I'm thinking how could I be so dumb? Did I do this to myself deliberately? And I'm also thinking wait a second, where do you get off reading my letters?

So I say to her, "Did you like the part where he says my dick is beautiful?"

She says, "Not much, no." She's already looking at me like I'm an alien. And I'm like: Mom, this is what you get for being NeoChristian—your son turns out to be a homo. What the Neos call a Darwinian anomaly.

Mom sighs and says, "Well I suppose we're stuck with it now."

Yeah Mom, you kinda are. Aren't you suppose to say something mimsy like, Ron honey you know we still love you? Not my mom. Oh no. Saying exactly what she thinks is Mom's way of being real, and her being real is more important to her than anything else. Like what I might be feeling.

So I dig back at her. "That's a shame, Mom. A few years later and I would have been embryo-screened and you could have just aborted me." Mom just sniffs. "That was a cheap shot."

Yeah, it was. NeoChristians are about the only people who *don't* abort homosexual fetuses. Everybody else does. What do they call it? Parental choice.

So Mom looks at me with this real tough face and says, "I hope you think you've given yourself a happy birthday." And that's all the conversation we have about it.

My little brother is pretending he isn't there and that he isn't happy. My little brother is shaped like a pineapple. He's fat and he has asthma and he's really good at being sneaky and not playing by the rules. I was always the big brother who tolerated stuff and tried to help Mom along. Her good little boy. Only now I'm samesex. Which to a NeoChristian Mom is like finding out your son likes dressing up as a baby and being jerked off by animals. Sometimes I think Neo is just a way to find new reasons to hate the same old things.

What really dents my paintwork is that Mom is smart. What she likes about Neo is that it's Darwinian. Last summer she's reading this article "Samesex Gene Planted by Aliens?" And she's rolling her eyes at it. "The least they could do is get the science straight," she says. "It's not one gene and it's not one part of the brain." But then she said, "But you gotta wonder, why is there a gene like that in the first place?"

My mom really does think that there's a chance that homos are an alien plot. Please do not fall over laughing, it hurts too much.

Ever since the Artifacts were found, people have been imagining little green men landing on this beautiful blue planet and just going off again. So people scare themselves wondering if the aliens are about to come back with a nice big army.

Then about five years ago, it turned out that the genes that control sexual orientation have some very unusual sugars, and all of a sudden there's this conspiracy theory that aliens created the samesex gene as some kind of weapon. Undermine our reproductive capacity. Even though when they landed we were all triblodites or whatever. Maybe having homos is supposed to soften us up for conquest. Hey, if the aliens invade, I promise, I'll fight too OK?

On my way to school I ring Billy and tell him. "Mom found out. She read your mail."

Billy sounds stripped for action. "Did she go crazy?"

"She went laconic. You could just hear her thinking: you gotta own this, Ronald, you did this to yourself, Ronald."

"It's better than crying."

Billy's in Comportment class. He believes all that shit. To be fair to him, that "you gotta own this" was me digging at some of the stuff he comes out with. That stuff pisses me off. In fact right now, everything pisses me off. Right now, it's like my guts are twisting and I want to go break something.

Comportment says you've got to own the fact people don't like you, own the fact you got fat hips, own the fact you're no good in math, own the fact that glacial lakes are collapsing onto Tibetan monasteries. Comportment says hey, you're complaining about the Chinese treatment of Tibet, but what have you personally done about it?

It's like: we'll make everybody who has no power feel it's their fault if stuff goes wrong, so the big people don't have to do anything about it.

My mom hates me being a homo. She likes being a big tough lady even more. So she, like, doesn't get all upset or cry or even say much about it. Being a tough lady is her way of feeling good about her son being an alien plot.

Billy is too focused on being Joe Cool-and-Out to cut me any slack. His stab at being sympathetic is "You should have just told her straight up, like I told you."

I say back to him in this Minnie Mouse voice, "I acknowledge that you are absolutely right." That's another line he's used on me.

He's silent for a sec and then says, "Well, don't be a bitch with me about it."

"It's my authentic response to an emotionally charged situation." Still sounding like Minnie Mouse.

I'm mad at him. I'm mad at him because he just won't unbend. Nobody unbends. It's bad comportment.

Billy comes back at me. "This is just you going back to being a baby. Only you don't have tantrums, you just whine."

"Billy. My NeoChristian Mom now knows I'm samesex. Could I have some sympathy?"

"Who's died, Ron? Anybody dead around here? Did you lose any limbs in the detonation? Or are you just getting all significant on my ass?"

"No. I'm looking for a friend. I'll try and find one, you know, someone who likes me and not my dick?"

And I hang up.

Like I said, I'm so mad.

I'm mad sitting here right now. I got my stupid kid brother who's been giggling all day, like it's such an achievement he likes pussy. I got my Mom doing the household accounts and her shares and her rollovers, and she's bellowing into the voice recognition and it's like: look at me having to do all the work around here. I'm realizing that I've probably screwed up my relationship with Billy and wondering if I really am the incredible wimp he thinks I am.

It's like everything all around me is Jell-O and it's setting into lemon-line, which I hate. I'm out. My brother knows and will try to give me a hard time, and if he does I'll slug his fat face. My Mom is being hard ass, and so I'm going to be hard ass back. I'm not an athlete, I'm not Joe Cool-and-Out, and I'll never go to Mom's Neo seminars.

I'm just sitting here all alone thinking: how can I win? What can I do?

I'll never be able to be a good little boy again. That is not an option. I'm not interested in being political about who I sleep with. I don't sign up to anything, I don't believe anything, and I don't like anybody, and I don't think anybody likes me.

Hey. A fresh start. Happy birthday.

So, twenty-six today!

I got up at 3:00 A.M. and holoed over to the Amazon to say hi to João. He looked so happy to see me, his little face was just one huge smile.

He'd organized getting some of his sisters to line up behind him. They all waved and smiled and downloaded me a smart diary for my present. In Brazil, they still sing Happy Birthday.

Love conquers all. With a bit of work.

I called João later and we did our usual daily download. His testosterone levels were through the roof, he's getting so stimulated by his new job in the Indian Devolved Areas. He's about to go off to Eden to start his diplomatic work. He looks so sweet in a penis sheath and a parrot's feather through his nose. Standard diplomatic dress for a member of the Brazilian Consular Team.

I love him I love him I love him I love him.

I am so god damned lucky. They didn't have embryo-screening on the Amazon. Hey! A fellow sodomite. We're an endangered species everywhere else. Must eliminate those nasty alien genes.

Then I had to go and tell him about how my project was going. And he looked glum.

"I know you don't like it," I told him.

"It feels wrong. Like genocide." He pronounces it jenoseed. "Soon they will be no more."

"But it's not genocide. The babies come out hetero, that's all. No more samesex, no more screening, just happy babies. And the adults who are left can decide for themselves if they want to be cured or not. Anyway, the Neos say that we're the genocide."

"You don't need to help them."

"João. Baby. It won't affect us. We'll still have each other."

"The Indians say it is unwise."

"Do they? That's interesting. How come?"

"They say it is good to have other ways. They think it is like what almost happened to them."

That rang true. So me and João have this really great conversation about it, very neutral, very scientific. He's just so smart.

Before the alien gene thing, they used to say that homos were a pool of altruistic non-reproducing labor. It's like, we babysit for our siblings' kids and that increases the survival potential of our family's genes.

Because genes that make it less likely that you'll have kids should have died out. So why was it still here?

João tells his usual joke about all the singers in Brazil being samesex, which is just about true. So I say, wow, the human race couldn't reproduce without Dança do Brasil, huh? Which was a joke. And he says, maybe so.

I say like I always do, "You know, don't you, baby?"

His voice goes soft and warm. "I know. Do you know?"

Yes. Oh yes, I know.

That you love me. We love each other.

We've been saying that every day now for five years. It still gives me a buzz.

It was a big day at the lab, too. The lights finally went on inside Flat Man.

Flat Man is pretty horrible, to tell you the truth. He's a culture, only the organs are differentiated and the bones are wafer-thin and spread out in a support structure. He looks like a cross between a spider's web and somebody who's been hit by a truck. And he covers an entire wall.

His brain works, but we know for a fact that it performs physical functions only. No consciousness, no narrative-of-the-self. He's like a particularly useful bacterial culture. You get to map all his processes, test the drugs, maybe fool around with his endomorphins. They got this microscope that can trail over every part of his body. You can see life inside him, pumping away.

Soon as I saw him, I got this flash. I knew what to do with him. I went to my mentor, wrote it up, got it out, and the company gave me the funding.

People think of cells as these undifferentiated little bags. In fact, they're more like a city with a good freeway system. The proteins get shipped in, they move into warehouses, they're distributed when needed, used up and then shipped out.

We used to track proteins by fusing them with fluorescent jellyfish protein. They lit up. Which was just brilliant really since every single molecule of that protein was lit up all the time. You sure could see where all of it was, but you just couldn't see where it was going to.

We got a different tag now, one that fluoresces only once it's been hit by a blue laser. We can paint individual protein molecules and track them one by one.

Today we lit up the proteins produced by the samesex markers. I'm tracking them in different parts of the brain. Then I'll track how genetic surgery affects the brain cells. How long it takes to stimulate the growth of new structures. How long it takes to turn off production of other proteins and churn the last of them out through the lysosomes.

How long it takes to cure being homo.

It's a brilliantly simple project, and it will produce a cheap reliable treatment. It means that all of João's friends who are fed up being hassled by Evangelicals can decide to go hetero.

That's my argument. They can decide. Guys who want to stay samesex like me... well, we can. And after us maybe there won't be any more homosexuals. I really don't know what the problem with that is. Who'll miss us? Other samesexers looking for partners? Uh, hello, there won't be any.

And yes, part of me thinks it will be a shame that nobody else will get to meet their João. But they'll meet their Joanna instead.

Mom rang up and talked for like seventeen hours. I'm not scared that I don't love her anymore. I do love her, a lot, but in my own exasperated way. She's such a character. She volunteered for our stem-cell regime. She came in and nearly took the whole damn program over, everybody loved her. So now she's doing weights and is telling me about this California toy boy she's picked up. She does a lot of neat stuff for the Church, I gotta say, she's really in there helping. She does future therapy; the Church just saw how good she is with people, so they sent her in to help people change and keep up and not be frightened of science.

She tells me, "God is Science. It really is, and I just show people that." She gets them using their Personalized Identity for the first time, she gets them excited by stuff. Then she makes peanut-butter sandwiches for the homeless.

We talk a bit about my showbiz kid brother. He's a famous sex symbol. I can't get over it. I still think he looks like a pineapple.

"Both my kids turned out great," says Mom. "Love you."

I got to work and the guys had pasted a little card to the glass. *Happy Birthday, Ron, from Flat Man.*

And at lunchtime, they did this really great thing. They set up a colluminated lens in front of the display screen. The image isn't any bigger, but the lens makes your eyes focus as if you are looking at stuff that's ten kilometers away.

Then they set up a mini-cam and flew it over Flat Man. I swear to God, it was like being a test pilot over a planet made of flesh. You fly over the bones and they look like salt flats. You zoom up and over muscle tissue that looks like rope mountains. The veins look like tubular trampolines.

Then we flew into the brain, right down into the cortex creases and out over the amygdala, seat of sexual orientation. It looked like savannah.

"We call this Flanneryland," said Greg. I guess you could say I have their buy-in. The project cooks.

I got back home and found João had sent me a couple of sweet little extra emails. One of them was a list of all his family's addresses ... *but my best address is in the heart of Ronald Flannery.*

And I suppose I ought to tell you that I also got an encryption from Billy.

Billy was my first boyfriend back in high school, and it wasn't until I saw his signature that I realized who it was and that I'd forgotten his last name. Wow, was this mail out of line.

I'll read it to you. *Ron,* it starts out, *long time no see. I seem to recall that you were a Libra, so your birthday must be about now, so, happy birthday. You may have heard that I'm running for public office here in Palm Springs*—well, actually, Billy, no I haven't, I don't exactly scan the press for news about you or Palm Springs.

He goes on to say how he's running on a Save Samesex ticket. I mean, what are we, whales? And who's going to vote for that? How about dealing with some other people's issues as well, Billy? You will get like two hundred votes at most. But hey, Billy doesn't want to actually win or achieve anything, he just wants to be right. So listen to this—

I understand that you are still working for Lumière Laboratories. According to this week's LegitSci News they're the people that are doing a cure for homosexuality that will work on adults. Can this possibly be true? If so could you give me some more details? I am assuming that you personally have absolutely nothing to do with such a project. To be direct, we need to know about this treatment: how it works, how long a test regime it's on, when it might be available. Otherwise it could be the last straw for an orientation that has produced oh, ... and listen to this, virtue by association, the same old tired list ... *Shakespeare, Michelangelo, da Vinci, Melville, James, Wittgenstein, Turing* ... still no women, I see.

I mean, this guy is asking me to spy on my own company. Right? He hasn't got in touch since high school, how exploitative is that? And then he says, and this is the best bit, *or are you just being a good little boy again?*

No, I'm being a brilliant scientist, and I could just as easily produce a list of great heterosexuals, but thanks for getting in a personal dig right at the end of the letter. Very effective, Billy, a timely reminder of why I didn't even like you by the end and why we haven't been in touch.

And why you are not going to get even a glimmer of a reply. Why in fact, I'm going to turn this letter in to my mentor. Just to show I don't do this shit and that somebody else has blabbed to the media.

Happy effin birthday.

And now I'm back here, sitting on my bed, talking to my diary, wondering who it's for. Who I am accountable to? Why do I read other people's letters to it?

And why do I feel that when this project is finished I'm going to do something to give something back. To whom?

To, and this is a bit of a surprise for me, to my people.

I'm about to go to sleep, and I'm lying here, hugging the shape of João's absence.

Today's my birthday and we all went to the beach.

You haven't lived until you bodysurf freshwater waves, on a river that's so wide that you can't see the other bank, with an island in the middle that's the size of Belgium and Switzerland combined.

We went to Mosquerio, lounged on hammocks, drank beer, and had cupu-açu ice cream. You don't get cupu-açu fruit anywhere else, and it makes the best ice cream in the world.

Because of the babies I had to drink coconut milk straight from the coconut . . . what a penance . . . and I lay on my tummy on the sand. I still wore my sexy green trunks.

Nilson spiked me. "João! Our husband's got an arse like a baboon!"

It is kind of ballooning out. My whole lower bowel is stretched like an oversized condom, which actually feels surprisingly sexy. I roll over to show off my packet. That always inspires comment. This time from Guillerme. "João! Nilson, his dick is as big as you are! Where do you put it?"

"I don't love him for his dick," says João. Which can have a multitude of meanings if you're the first pregnant man in history and your bottom is the seat of both desire and rebirth.

Like João told me before I came out here, I have rarity value on the Amazon. A tall *branco* in Brazil . . . I keep getting dragged by guys, and if I'm not actually being dragged, then all I have to do is follow people's eye lines to see what's snagged their attention. It's flattering and depersonalizing all at one and the same time.

The only person who doesn't do this is João. He just looks into my eyes. I look away, and when I look back, he's still looking into my eyes.

He's proud of me.

In fact, all those guys, they're all proud of me. They all feel I've done something for them.

What I did was grow a thick pad in Flat Man's bowel. Thick enough for the hooks of a placenta to attach to safely.

I found a way to overcome the resistance in sperm to being penetrated by other sperm. The half pairs of chromosomes line up and join.

The project-plan people insisted we test it on animals. I thought that was disgusting, I don't know why, I just hated it. What a thing to do to a chimp. And anyway, it would still need testing on people afterward.

And anyway, I didn't want to wait.

So I quit the company and came to live in Brazil. João got me a job at the university. I teach Experimental Methods in very bad Portuguese. I help out explaining why Science is God.

It's funny seeing the Evangelicals trying to come to terms. The police have told me, watch out, there are people saying the child should not be born. The police themselves, maybe. I look into their tiny dark eyes, and they don't look too friendly.

João is going to take me to Eden to have the baby. It is Indian territory, and the Indians want it to be born. There is something about some story they have, about how the world began again, and keeps re-birthing.

Agosto and Guillinho roasted the chicken. Adalberto, Kawé, Jorge and Carlos sat around in a circle shelling the dried prawns. The waiter kept coming back and asking if we wanted more beer. He was this skinny kid from Marajo with nothing to his name but shorts, flip-flops and a big grin in his dark face. Suddenly we realize that he's dragging us. Nilson starts singing, "*Moreno, Moreno...,*" which means sexy brown man. Nilson got the kid to sit on his knee.

This place is paradise for gays. We must be around four percent of the population. It's the untouched natural samesex demographic, about the same as for left-handedness. It's like being in a country where they make clothes in your size or speak your maternal language, or where you'd consider allowing the President into your house for dinner.

It's home.

We got back, and all and I mean all of João's huge family had a party for my birthday. His nine sisters, his four brothers, and their spouses and their kids. That's something else you don't get in our big bright world. Huge tumbling families. It's like being in a nineteenth-century novel every day. Umberto gets a job, Maria comes off the booze, Latitia gets over fancying her cousin, João helps his nephew get into university. Hills of children roll and giggle on the carpet. You can't sort out what niece belongs to which sister, and it doesn't matter. They all just sleep over where they like.

Senhora da Souza's house was too small for them all, so we hauled the furniture out into the street and we all sat outside in a circle, drinking and dancing and telling jokes I couldn't understand. The Senhora sat next to me and held my hand. She made this huge cupu-açu cream, because she knows I love it so much.

People here get up at 5:00 a.m., when it's cool, so they tend to leave early. By ten o'clock, it was all over. João's sisters lined up to give me a kiss, all those children tumbled into cars, and suddenly it was just us. I have to be careful about sitting on the babies too much, so I decided not to drive back. I'm going to sleep out in the courtyard on a mattress with João and Nilson.

We washed up for the Senhora, and I came out here onto this unpaved Brazilian street to do my diary.

Mom hates that I'm here. She worries about malaria, she worries that I don't have a good job. She's bewildered by my being pregnant. "I don't know, baby, if it happens, and it works, who's to say?"

"It means the aliens' plot backfired, right?"

"Aliens," she says back real scornful. "If they wanted the planet, they could have burned off the native life forms, planted a few of their own, and come back. Even our padre thinks that's a dumb idea now. You be careful, babe. You survive. OK?"

OK. I'm thirty-six and still good looking. I'm thirty-six and finally I'm some kind of a rebel.

I worry, though, about the Nilson thing.

OK, João and I had to be apart for five years. It's natural he'd shack up with somebody in my absence, and I do believe he loves me, and I was a little bit jealous at first ... sorry, I'm only human. But hey—heaps of children on the floor, right? Never know who's sleeping with whom? I moved in with them, and I quite fancy Nilson, but I don't love him, and I wouldn't want to have his baby.

Only ... maybe I am.

You are supposed to have to treat the sperm first to make them receptive to each other, and I am just not sure, there is no way to identify, when I became pregnant. But OK, we're all one big family, they've both ... been down there. And I started to feel strange and sick before João's and my sperm were ... um ... planted.

Thing is, we only planted one embryo. And now there's twins.

I mean, it would be wild, wouldn't it, if one of the babies were Nilson and João's? And I was just carrying it, like a pod?

Oh, man. Happy birthday.

Happy birthday, moon. Happy birthday, sounds of TVs, flip-flop sandals from feet you can't see, distant dogs way off on the next street, insects creaking away. Happy birthday, night. Which is as warm and sweet as hot honeyed milk.

Tomorrow, I'm off to Eden, to give birth.

Forty-six years old. What a day to lose a baby.

They had to fly me back out in a helicopter. There was blood gushing out, and João said he could see the placenta. Chefe said it was OK to send in the helicopter. João was still in Consular garb. He looked so tiny and defenseless in just a penis sheath. He has a little pot belly now. He was so terrified, his whole body had gone yellow. We took off, and I feel like I'm melting into a swamp, all brown mud, and we look out and there's Nilson with the kids, looking forlorn and waving good-bye. And I feel this horrible grinding milling in my belly.

I'm so fucking grateful for this hospital. The Devolved Areas are great when you're well and pumped up, and you can take huts and mud and mosquitoes and snake for dinner. But you do not want to have a miscarriage in Eden. A miscarriage in the bowel is about five times more serious that one in the womb. A centimeter or two more of tearing and most of the blood in my body would have blown out in two minutes.

I am one very lucky guy.

The Doctor was João's friend Nadia, and she was just fantastic with me. She told me what was wrong with the baby.

"It's a good thing you lost it," she told me. "It would not have had much of a life."

I just told her the truth. I knew this one felt different from the start; it just didn't feel right.

It's what I get for trying to have another baby at forty-five. I was just being greedy. I told her. *É a ultima vez.* This is the last time.

Chega, she said. Enough. But she was smiling. *É o trabalho do João.* From now on, it's João's job.

Then we had a serious conversation, and I'm not sure I understood all her Portuguese. But I got the gist of it.

She said: it's not like you don't have enough children.

When João and I first met, it was like the world was a flower that had bloomed. We used to lie in each other's arms and he, being from a huge family, would ask, "How many babies?" and I'd say "Six," thinking that was a lot. It was just a fantasy then, some way of echoing the feeling we had of being a union. And he would say no, no, ten. Ten babies. Ten babies would be enough.

We have fifteen.

People used to wonder what reproductive advantage homosexuality conferred.

Imagine you sail iceberg-oceans in sealskin boats with crews of twenty men, and that your skiff gets shipwrecked on an island, no women anywhere. Statistically, one of those twenty men would be samesex-oriented, and if receptive, he would nest the sperm of many men inside him. Until one day, like with Nilson and João, two sperm interpenetrated. Maybe more. The bearer probably died, but at least there was a chance of a new generation. And they all carried the genes.

Homosexuality was a fallback reproductive system.

Once we knew that, historians started finding myths of male pregnancy all over the place. Adam giving birth to Eve, Vishnu on the serpent Anata giving birth to Brahma. And there were all the virgin births as well, with no men necessary.

Now we don't have to wait for accidents.

I think Nadia said, You and João, you're pregnant in turns or both of you are pregnant at the same time. You keep having twins. Heterosexual couples don't do that. And if you count husband number three, Nilson, that's another five children. Twenty babies in ten years?

"Chega," I said again.

"*Chega,*" she said, but it wasn't a joke. Of course the women, the lesbians are doing the same thing now too. Ten years ago, everybody thought that homosexuality was dead and that you guys were on the endangered list. But you know, any reproductive advantage over time leads to extinction of rivals.

Nadia paused and smiled. *I think we are the endangered species now.*

Happy birthday.

VAO

Jazzanova wandered off again. He was out all night.

They tell me that they've found him up a tree. So I sit in his room and wait for him and I remember that he told me once that when he was a kid, he used to climb up pine trees in the park to read comics—*Iron Man, Dr. Midnight.* I guess he was a dreamy kind of kid. Then he came to Jersey and started to live it instead. That's when we met, in college.

They bring him back in. Jazza looks like a cricket that somebody's stained brown with tea. I hate his shuffling walk. His feet never leave the ground, like he's wearing slippers all the time. The backward baseball cap he always wears doesn't suit Alzheimer's, either. He shuffles off to take a leak and I hear him getting into a fight with his talking toilet.

The toilet says, "You've been missing your medication." It's probably sampled his pee.

Jazzanova doesn't like that. "Goddamit!" He sounds drunk and angry. He flushes the thing, to shut it up. He comes out, and his glasses start up on him. "Eleven-fifteen," his glasses say in this needling little voice. "You should have taken medication at 9:00 a.m. and 10:30 a.m. Go to the blue tray and find the pills in the green column."

They never let up on you. The whole place is wired. It's so full of ordnance you can hear it. Jazza's bedroom sounds like it's full of hummingbirds.

He blanks it all out and kinda falls back onto the sofa. His calipers aren't so hot on sitting down. Then he just stares for a couple of seconds. He's looking at his hands like they don't belong to him. Finally he says to me, "What say we get outa here for a beer, um..."

He's forgotten who I am again. I can see the little flicker in his glasses as it goes through photos and whispers my name at him. "Brewster," he says. Then he, like, shrugs and says, "It's all in the mix."

It's all in the mix. That's what he always says when he's pretending he's chilled out and not gaga. Jazza's still on planet Clubland, a million years ago. Maybe he's happy there.

But he can't pay his bills.

"Bar's not open," I tell him. I hold out his blue tray of pills. "Take one of these, man. Top buzz."

Instead of taking one, he fumbles up a whole handful and the tray says to him, "Nooooooo." It sounds like a bouncer outside a club.

"Shit," he says and takes five of the fuckers anyway.

Outside his big window, it's late summer, early morning, all kinda smoky. It's a nice view; I'll say that. Lawn, trees. The view is wired, too. Whole place is full of VAO—Victim Activated Ordnance. To protect us rich old folks.

Once I saw this kid who'd climbed over the wall. He was just a kid. He probably just wanted to play on the grass. The camera saw him and zapped him. They used pulse sound on him. He clutched his head and tried to run, but his feet kept wobbling. Each bullet is 150 decibels, and you can't really think. He stumbled down onto his knees, and he'd stand up, drop, stand up, drop down again until they came for him.

I used to make that stuff. I used to make the software that recognizes faces. Now it recognizes me.

I go back and my room smells like a trashcan. It's got gray hair in the corners. It pisses me off what I pay for this place. The least they could do is keep it clean. There's got to be some advantages to being an old vegetable.

I push the buzzer and I get no answer. I push again, and nothing happens so I go to the screen and start shouting. I tell 'em straight up, "I push your buzzer and you don't come, man. I could be dying of a heart attack up here. If I tell the papers, that'd blow your sales pitch. You don't answer my buzzer, I scorch your ass!"

About forty-five minutes later the Kid shows up moving real slow. He leans back against the wall, arms folded. I can't even remember what fucked-up country he's from, but I can read him. He's got that mean, sour look you get when nobody gives a fuck so why should you.

I feel pretty pissed off myself. "Next time I ring the buzzer you fuckin show up."

"Sorry, Sir." Kid says "Sir" like maybe it means "dog" in his own language.

"What the fuck is up with you?"

"Nothing, Sir."

I look for buttons to push. You know, like if someone blanks you out, you get them mad and maybe you find out what's going on?

I insult the Kid. "Can't you talk English?"

Nothing.

"It's a helluva way to get a tip. Or no tip. You want no tip?"

His arms snap open like a spring lock, his head swivels like armed CCTV, and his mouth spouts garbage like a TV in translation. I pushed his button all right.

When he stops swearing in Albanian or Mongolian or whatever, I finally hear him squawk. "I get no tip no how!"

So that's it. He's not getting his tips.

The assholes who run this place don't pay the staff. You gotta give the nurses tips, the cleaners tips, the doctors tips, the waiters tips. If the toilets get more intelligent we'll have to tip the toilets. And management makes sure you do it regular. That's one of the things about this dump I hate the most. They keep sending you little forms to fill in to debit your bank account. Those fuckin' forms show up on your computer, on your TV, on your microwave, on your specs. The forms have these horrible chirpy little voices. "I'm sure you want to express your appreciation for the staff."

It costs a hundred thousand a year to live here, and they call the tips discretionary. That's another hundred fifty a week. And I make sure I pay it, because I want these bozos to motor if I get sick or something.

I keep my voice cool 'cause I want to make sure I got this right. "No tips? I pay your tips, man."

I need this guy's name. You can't talk somebody down if you don't know their name. My eyeglasses are running through all the photographs of staff, and finally I see him. I click a bit of my brain, like I'm going to ask him his name. The glasses tell me.

The Kid is called Joao and he's from some part of Indonesia that speaks Portuguese.

"Joao?" I tell him. "I'm sorry. I am sorry. I pay. Really."

He stands there swelling up and down like he's pumping iron.

"Joao? I pay the tips. You don't get them?"

Kid's so mad his wires are crossed. He scowls and blinks.

"Lemme show you," I say.

I try to ease him to the machine, you know, I just touch his arm, and he throws it off, like this. For a second I think he's going to give me a Jersey kiss. So I keep my voice low and soft. "Hey, man, just be cool about it, OK? Lemme show you."

So I open up my records. See? I show him all that debit. All those tips going out just as regular as spam. I point to the money, there on the screen. Right out of my bank account.

The Kid blinks and rubs his whole face with his hands. I begin to wonder if they teach people to read in the country he's from.

Then suddenly he shouts. "I no get them!" He's throwing up his hands and wiggling his cheeks. But I can see. Now he's not mad at me.

I feel pretty sick myself, in my gut like my chicken was full of salmonella. I'm thinking, Oh fuck. We got ourselves a tips racket.

Somebody somewhere, probably one of the hotshot doctors who can't pay for his new swimming pool or his lawsuit insurance, is hacking out the cleaner's tips.

I could complain, and I could call in the law. But. I got reasons. Know what I mean?

"How long you not been getting your tips?" I ask him.

He tells me. Months. I can see why he isn't all that concerned about cleaning up my shit. I sit him down, pour him a whiskey. This will take a while, and I want him to know right in his balls who got him back his money. Me. Here. The Brewster.

I call up my contact. She's top dope, a tough old babe still on the outside called Nikki. She's got this great translation package. We have this audio conversation about her new bungalow which is a cover for a hack download. It comes in looking like a phone bill. It then runs a request from a nostalgia TV line. I load up and sit back and watch what looks like an old Britney Spears video.

It's not a video, believe me. I can't do anything that looks like a hack. The ordnance is always watching. They say it's in case we get ill, but hey, why do they snoop our keystrokes? If you want to hack here, it's a case of no hands. And everything has to look like something else.

I smile at the Kid and jerk my head at the cameras, glasses, TV, computer . . . all the surveillance. But hey, the Kid's cool. He can't speaka da English, but he gets what I'm doing. For the first time I get a smile out him. He chuckles and lifts up the whiskey glass. "Z24!" he says. Ah, that's Kidtalk.

"Banging!" I say back. That's my talk. "You're a Britney fan, huh?"

The Kid's sussed. He knows exactly what's going on. "Brit-ney . . . Whitney . . . all that old stuff." He chuckles and nods and shakes his head. "I big big fan!" I know what he's thinking. He's thinking, this old guy is into some shit. He's thinking, this old guy is hacking me back my tips.

The microwave pings like my dinner's ready, only it's not food that's cooking. I put on my glasses, and then put the transcoder on top of them and suddenly Britney is translated into the Corporation's accounts. But only if you are looking at 'em through my glasses.

I got a real good line on who's been stealing a little bit of the Kid's bandwidth.

My Medical Supervisor. My trusted Dr. Curtis. So I siphon out the dosh and siphon it into the Kid's corporate account. Ready for loading to his bank.

"Banging!" the Kid says.

Grand Dad House.

So then I call on Dr. Curtis. "You got a face like shit and your brains are all on your chin."

Dr. Curtis leans back and looks like someone who's just been told a real bad joke. Behind him is a wall of screens, some of them showing people's pumping insides.

You see, you get old, you end up in here, and that gives them the right to monitor every last act and word. You're a patient.

I'm one mad patient. "I may be eighty but I could still deck you!"

He leans back, with his eyebrows up and his eyes hooded. "I could always prescriptionize out all that aggressive testosterone. So unbecoming in the aged."

I hate him. Really. I can take most people, but if I could do Curtis an injury I would. Curtis has got hold of my pubic hair and can give it a twist whenever he wants.

"Look Curtis, you been hacking off our tips. Duh! Don't you think the staff kinda notice they're not getting paid? And I know we're all a bunch of senile old codgers, but even we can tell when we don't get our asses wiped 'cause the staff can't feed their kids. You leave our tips alone, asshole!"

The good doctor sniffs. "I'm afraid I have expenses."

"Yeah; and they all got tits."

"And I've only got one other source of income." He starts to smile. A nice long pause, like it's his close-up or something. He purses his lips into a little bitty kiss. "You."

He's such a drama student. He tells me, "If my account is empty, I'll hack it out of yours."

No, he won't. It won't be that easy. But he has got a point. It is the whole point, the underlying point. I gotta sit on that point everyday, and it goes straight up my ass.

I can't walk without help. My kid's poor. I gotta find a hundred thou a year.

So I take it out of other people's bank accounts, OK?

Curtis is my doctor. He knows everything I do. I have to give him a cut.

I have a dream. I put Dr. Curtis in rubber mask and backward baseball cap, and shove him out on the lawn at night so the cameras don't recognize him and he gets area-denied. He gets sound-gunned. He gets microwaved; his whole body feels like it's touching a hot lightbulb. His whole goddamned shaven tattooed trendy fat little ass feels what it's like to be poor and hungry and climbing over our wall just to activate some ordnance.

All this is before lunch. It's a well crucial day. Stick around, it's about to get even more crucial.

It's Saturday, and that's Bill's day to visit. I go to the Solarium and wait, and then wait some more. Today he doesn't show. I wait a little while longer. And then ring him up to leave a message. I don't want to sound whiney, so I try to sound up. "Hey, Bill, this your dad. Everything's cool. I hope it's under control for you, too."

Then I sit and hang out. I don't want to be some sad old fuck. I open up a newspaper. It tells me Congress wants to change tax rates, to ease the burden on younger taxpayers. Oh cool, thanks.

I go back to check out Jazza. It's the afternoon, but he's sleeping like a baby.

Jazza used to be so cool. It's good to have someone from your time, your place. Even if he doesn't remember who you are.

We wanted to send a rocket to Mars. We built it ourselves and called it Aphrodite and went to Nevada and launched it and it went straight up looking like 1969 and hope.

We made pretend-music; started our own company, developed a couple of computer games, called ourselves Fighting Fit and sold the company. We ran a pirate download and shared the same girlfriend for a while. After we lost all our money, we emptied the same accounts, too. Amateur spaceships don't pay for themselves. I decided to go mundane and went into security software. I went straight for a while. Jazza never did. He still hung out there. From time to time I gave him some freelance. When Bill went to college I went to check Jazza out. He was still at a mixing desk at fifty. He was wearing one of those shirts that keeps changing pictures or told the punters what toons he was pumping out.

I hack Jazza's bills as well. Otherwise, he'd be out on the street.

I sit there awhile, just making sure he's OK, if he wants anything. He snores. I give his knee a pat and leave. You get lonely sometimes.

I get to my room and there's a message. "Dad, you probably know this already, but Bessie was mugged. I'll be over tomorrow."

Bessie is my granddaughter. Never have a well crucial day.

The next morning we're doing Neurobics.

They found out that even old people grow new neurons. If they give you PDA, it goes even faster, but you got to use it or lose it. So they make us learn. They make us do crazy stuff. Like brush our teeth with the wrong hand. Or read stuff from a screen that is upside down. Sometimes they make us do really off-the-wall stuff, like sniff vanilla beans while we listen to classical music. They're trying to induce synaesthesia.

Today we were in VR. We're weightless in a burning space station. We got to get out through smoke and there is no up or down. What way does the lever on the door pull?

I get a tug on my arm. It's the Kid. He smiles at me real nice. "Mr. Brewster? I come find you. You son is here."

These days I walk like Frankenstein, on these fake little legs. They make your muscles work so they grow back. Nobody's supposed to hold me up. The Kid does, though. To him I guess I'm some old granddad and that is how you show respect.

So I introduce him to my son. Joao, this is my boy, Bill. Bill stands up and shakes the Kid's hand and thanks him for taking care of me. My boy is fifty years old. He's got a potbelly, but he still looks like a guy who never spent a day in an office.

Bill is real neat. I can say that. He's a neat kid; he just never made any money. He'd work in the summers as a diving instructor and in winter he'd go south. He went to teach primary school in the Hebrides. He did a stint putting chips in elephant's brains in Sri Lanka.

Today, though, his smile looks weirded out.

"How's Bessie?" I ask him.

Something happens to Bill's face and he sits down.

"Um. You didn't see the news? It was on the news."

"Bessie was in the news?" Oh shit. You don't get in the comics just for stubbing your toe.

Bill's voice rattles. "They did something to her face," he says. He takes out his paper and fills it, and lays it out on the table.

I tell him, "I didn't see anything about it. I think we're filtered. I think they filter our news."

"VAO. Only this time it really was a victim who got activated."

VAO protects banks, shopping malls, offices. Anything First World, or Nerd World, got VAO. It's supposed to zap thieves. For just a second I thought maybe Bessie had been on a job like maybe being a gangsta skips a generation or something.

Bill's newspaper fills up with an animated headline.

The headline says

V

A

O...

And the headline animates into

Very

Ancient

Offenders

And then, for your delectation and amusement, up comes my grand-daughter's mugging, caught on security camera and sold by the ordnance company to defray costs.

They run my granddaughter's mugging for laughs. Because the muggers are old.

Ain't dey cute, them old guys?

There's my Bessie, going out to her car. Slick black hair, skinny red trousers, real small, real sweet. Able to take care of herself, but you don't expect your own bolted, belted VAO parking lot to be the place where you get mugged.

These four clowns come lurching out at her. They're old guys like me. They're staggering around on calipers; they got the Frankenstein walk, but they stink of the street. One of them is wearing old trousers that are too small. The legs end up around his calves, and they're held up by a belt, they don't close at the front. There is a continent of dingy underwear on display.

Bill says, "Microwave. Somehow they turned it on her instead of them. But they didn't know what they were doing." Bill can't look at this, he's hiding his face.

And on the paper, Bessie is denied her own area.

The keys in her hand go hot, she drops them. Her own shiny hair goes hot and she clasps her head, and she crouches down and tries to hide under her own elbows.

Bill talks from behind his hand. "It's supposed to stop before two hundred and fifty seconds. After that it does damage."

These are old, old codgers. They shuffle. They forget to turn the fuckin' thing off. They pick up the car keys, and they're too hot and they drop 'em. Well, duh. Finally they shuffle round to some kind of switch.

We're at three hundred seconds, and Bessie's trousers are smoking, and the skin of her face is curling up.

"She'll need a cornea transplant," says Bill.

They pick up her purse and just leave her there. They get into the car. I get a look at them.

There's two ways you get old. One, you shrivel up. The other, you puff out like a cloud. One guy has a face like melted marshmallow in these dead-white hanging lumps.

"Old farts," I hear myself say. I'm so sick of feeling angry. I feel angry all the time, and there's nothing I can do about anything. There's nothing I can do about Bessie, nothing I can do for those old stupid jerks.

"She'll be OK," says Bill, and he's looking at me and for just a sec I'm his daddy again. I never was much of a daddy when he was a kid, always off on a job or working for the company. He ended up being the kind of guy who never stops looking for a father. Christ, Billy. I wanted to have enough money so that you would never have to work, to make up for not being around. But all my money goes into being old.

We latch hands. Bill's spent all his life helping people. Bill's just a better man than I am.

"I'm sorry, Billy," I say, and I mean for everything.

That night Jazza and I finally go for a beer at the bar in the Happy Farm, but J's in bad shape. He just sits staring. Neurobics make him dizzy. They got a new timed drug dispenser on his wrist. He does a little jump and groans when they dose him. We're hanging out with Gus.

Gus does this sweet little hippie routine. He says that he sold plankton to places like Paraguay so they could get carbon-reduction credits. Now. Everybody who was awake knows that it didn't work and nobody made any money at it. In fact they lost their shirts.

So I ask myself: Where does Gus's money come from? I mean, you got this greasy little dude who took too much whizz. His dialog is just too sussed for an eco-warrior.

"You heard about this VAO stuff?" he asks me.

"Only 'cause my granddaughter got mugged. I didn't know they filter our news."

"I got something that filters the filter," he says. "This is news we need to know."

"About my granddaughter?"

"No. Look me in the eye. The guys that do this are a crew. It's several crews all over the country, but they're all linked, and they're all old guys. And they're doing this kind of stuff a lot."

Suddenly, I am aware of the surveillance all around us. "So?"

"Kind of blows our story, doesn't it? Sweet little old guys playing computer games and taking physio." Gus's eyes are steady as a rock.

I knew it. Gus is a player.

I ask him, "How much are you, uh... *tipping* Curtis?"

His face and smile are less expressive than an armadillo's behind. "Too much," he says. His eyebrows do a little jump.

"Anybody else?" I ask him, meaning who are the other Players. It's nice to know that even at our age we can make new friends and acquaintances.

"Oh yeah," he says looking around. "You could start with The Good Fairies." The Good Fairies are a couple, been together fifty years. They look up from their table, and they look pretty mean to me.

"I'll get you that filter," says Gus.

Good as his word, I get mail. Takes me a while, because it downloads as dirty pictures. I try a couple of times and finally get the code. Load it up and I got a different personalisation on the news.

So I fill up my newspaper and I read the backstory. This crew has been at it for months. Old guys who hijack armed intelligent cameras, old guys who spray clubs with paralysis gas or shoot electricity through whole trainloads of commuters. They edit out every single last purse and wristwatch while the ordnance that is supposed to protect the punters is turned around on them.

There are zapped grannies, zapped babies, zapped beautiful teenage girls who should have been left to enjoy life. I never had any respect for direct-action crime. Money is magic, it's a religion. All you gotta do is just walk into the temple and help yourself and nobody gets hurt.

Not these geeks. For them, hurting people is part of the point. They're not even really crooks. Crooks want to be invisible. These guys are so stupid and vicious that they want everybody to know about them.

They got this crazy leader who calls himself Silhouette. Aw, Jesus, can you believe that? He probably grew up wanting to be Eminem or something. He still does that dumb thing with the splayed-open hands pointing down. Silhouette is skinny like a model. His knees are fatter than his thighs and ho-hum he's all in black and he has his whole face blanked out, just black, no eyes no mouth. Oh, Daddy Cool.

I take one look at this guy and I know just who he is. My generation, you know, we never fought a war. We grew up watching disasters on TV and worrying about our clothes. This guy is sitting there and he's holding his face so that we can see he's got killer cheekbones. The guy's probably eighty and he's worried about his looks.

And of course he's got a manifesto. He croaks it at me, in this real weird voice, until I figure out it's been recognition-masked. No voice-print. It makes him sound like he's talking underwater.

"You sniff money on old people, and just because we can't run and can't hurt you back you strip us naked. You leave us in cold-water flats and shut us up in expensive prisons you call Homes. You don't pay us the pensions you promised. When we get sick, you tell us our insurance that we paid for all our lives doesn't cover the cost of care. You want us to die. So. We'll die. And we'll take everything from you when we go."

You want to know the spookiest thing of all? I know where he's coming from. I know exactly what Silhouette means.

"Age Rage," he says and clenches a fist.

So the next day I'm back down in the bar with Gus. I got Jazzanova with me like he's my good-luck charm. Gus has his squeeze Mandy. Mandy used to be a lap dancer. She's still got a body, I can tell you.

She's also got a mouth and the brains to use it. Her cover is that she used to be in property development. Well yeah maybe. A certain kind of old babe has the hardest eyes you'll ever see.

Mandy says, "The trouble with that scum is they'll turn the heat up on all of us."

"Yup," says Gus. "We'll end up on the street."

"I'll take Curtis with me," I promise. "I got evidence on the guy."

Mandy's not impressed. "Good! You can share the same cardboard box. Hope it makes you feel better." We're too old for fear. We just turn our backs on it. If we get the fear at all, it takes us over and our legs don't work and we go little and frail and old. So we got to be like old dried leather. It used to be soft, but now it's as hard as stone.

The Good Fairies sit listening. They are as cerebral as fuck. I mean these guys are the only people I know who can tell their genitals what to do. They got married fifty years ago and they've only fucked each other since. I blame AIDs.

The Good Fairies sometimes talk in unison. It's like twins who've been locked up in the same closet since they were born. "We have to take out Silhouette."

Beat, as we cogitate. True. Beat. Us? Beat.

Then we all start roaring with laughter. Mandy coughs like a dog with its vocal chords cut out. Gus squeaks. I know I sound like gravel being milled. Jazzanova stares into outer space, and doesn't want to be left out, so he laughs at the strip lighting and then he swallows a chip off the table edge, thinking it's a pill.

Mandy is barking. "The Neurobics Crew!"

The Good Fairies sit holding hands, sipping their cigarettes, and they don't move a muscle.

Fairy One says, real calm, "It'll be real funny inside that cardboard box."

" 'Specially when it rains," says the other. This guy is five foot two with a dorky beard. He looks like a failed Drag King, but he calls himself Thug, which has to be some kind of joke.

"Yeah, but you guys," says Mandy. "I can hear where you're coming from, but what are you going to DO?"

Fairy One calls himself JoJo, but I bet he's really called George, and he says, "We ask him to stop."

"Oh yeah? Sure!"

"His position doesn't make sense. He says he does it because he's old. But it is the old he's hurting."

Mandy shakes her head. "He's in it for the money."

Thug disagrees. "He's in it for the showbiz. Money won't be enough."

JoJo says, "We show him how to get on TV and say something that makes sense for a change. I'm sure that most of us have something to say on the position of the old."

Mandy says, "How you gonna do that?"

JoJo says, "I used to make TV shows."

Thug says. "All we gotta do is find who Silhouette is."

And I get this real weird, sick feeling, and I don't know why.

Mandy jerks like she's laughing to herself. She flicks cigarette ash like it's going all over their pretty little dream. "You better get hacking," she says.

The next day my dear Dr. Curtis runs in to tell me we're all about to get a visit from the cops.

Curtis looks terrified. He looks sick. He leans against my door like they're going to hammer it down. Plump smooth-skinned pretty little doctor, he's got so much to lose.

"How's your system?" he asks, smiling like he's relearning how to use his facial muscles. He's got something he doesn't want to say in front of the ordnance.

I don't get it. "What's it to you?"

He makes a noise like someone's jammed a pin in his butt. His eyes start doing a belly dance toward the window. I look out and see that the front drive of the Happy Farm is stuffed like a turkey with police cars.

I just say, "A shape outlined against the light?"

I mean a silhouette. Curtis sorta settles with relief and nods yes. "You've been following the news."

I get it. The cops are here to find out if any of us nice old folks are funding Silhouette's reign of terror. That means that they'll be going through our accounts. For once Curtis and I have exactly the same self-interest.

I'm a thief and I've never been caught and that's not because I'm smart, but because I know I'm not. So I worry. So I prepare.

I got about ten minutes and that's all I need. I start running my emergency program. It looks like a rerun of pro golf. Curtis hangs around. He wants to see how I do this. I need to put on my specs, but I don't want him to know about the transcoder.

"Curtis, maybe you should go talk to our guests." I mean slow them down. I mean get out of here.

Then there's a knock. In comes the Kid. Maybe he's come to tell me about the cops, too. He sees Curtis, and I swear his eyes switch on with hate like lightbulbs.

"Joao, maybe you could take Dr. Curtis out to greet our guests." And that means: Joao help me get him out of here.

That Kid is sussed. "You," he says to Curtis, and punches the palm of his hand. Curtis understands that, too. Note. Not one of us has said anything that would sound bad in court.

I hear the door shut. Finally I put on my specs and the transcoder shows me data download on one eye lens and data upload on the other.

It's a fake I've had worked out for years. It'll cover my whole account and make it look like I'm some kind of gaga spendthrift, that I gamble a lot on a Korean site, lose my dosh, win some dosh. It matches, transaction for transaction, money in, money out.

That's what's uploading. On the other lens, I'm encrypting my old data. I got maybe five minutes now.

Just having some encrypted data on my system will be enough to make trouble. I'm ghosting the encrypted file, and then I go to get it off my disk. It starts to squirt into my transcoder.

I hear big heavy boots. I hear Dr. Curtis babbling happily. I hear a knock on the front door. Mine? No next door.

Six . . . five . . . four . . . stuff is still downloading. Three two one zero. Right, off comes the transcoder. It looks like one of the arms from my glasses. On my hard drive, iron molecules are being permanently scrambled. Sorry, Officer, I'm just this old guy and I've been having these terrible problems with my system.

I go take a shower. They monitor your heartbeat and video your keystrokes, but the law says they can't perve you in the shower.

And while I'm in the shower I take the transcoder and like I rehearsed a hundred times, I push it up the head of my penis.

The transcoder's long, it's thin. In an X-ray, it'll look like a sexual prosthetic.

When the knock on my door comes, I'm out, I'm dry, and I'm in my nice baggy shiny blue suit. I am the picture of a callipered, monitored neurobic modern Noughties Boy. With money of his own.

The Armament comes in. He looks like somebody who divides his time between weightlifting and V-games, hairy golden biceps, a smile like a rodent's and heavy-duty multipurpose specs. His manner is unfriendly. "You're Alistair Brewster. Hello. We've been wanting to talk to you."

"I don't see what's stopping you." I don't do polite even with Armament.

"Fine." He sits down without being asked. His specs have a little blinking light. Smile, you're on candid camera. "Mr. Brewster, you used to work for SecureIT Inc."

"Was that a question or a statement?"

He blinks. "You worked on the design of security systems."

There is no lie as effective as the truth. "That's how I made my money. I came up with some of the recognition software, the stuff that means the ordnance knows who it's dealing with." I try to make it sound rich.

He nods and pretends to be impressed. "I was wondering if you could help us understand some of the ways in which these safety checks could be subverted. During the recent spate of thefts."

Now, this is trouble. It's coming from an angle I was not expecting. They don't think I'm a thief. They don't think I'm a donor.

They think maybe I'm part of Silhouette's crew.

I stall for time. "Can I confirm your ID?"

"Sure."

"I'm not talking security until I know who you are."

"Very wise, Mr. Brewster."

"Not wisdom. Habit. You get by on habit at my age Mr. . . . ."

Secret Squirrel here won't give me his name, just a look at his dental work. So he leans forward, and my TV checks out his retinas. We share a polite, stone-cold silence as it chews over this for a while. Then out comes his stuff.

Secret Squirrel is thirty-six years old, has a tattoo on his right knee which sounds real romantic and is validated as Armament, Security Status Amber . . . oh, it takes me back to the good old days. It still won't give me his name. Psychological advantage.

I always hated Armament, for the same reason I hate Silhouette. They shoot people. Also, they never once gave SecureIT a clear brief. "OK, Secret Squirrel, shoot. I don't mean that literally, by the way. Feel free to make a few more statements you already know the answers to."

"Smart ass," says the Armament.

"Look, Squirrel, I'm rich, I'm happy, I don't have to take anything from anybody, and it was difficult getting to the point that I can say that with confidence. I didn't ask you in here, and I don't have to cooperate. In fact, I signed a nondisclosure agreement with SecureIT when I left. What they would prefer and what I would prefer is that you go talk to them instead of me. So. You want me to be nice to you, you start thinking nice thoughts about what a sweet old guy I am and how much you respect me."

"Age Rage," he says sweetly, calmly. "You're a suspect, Mr. Brewster, not an information source." He keeps smiling and waits for me to fall over in shock.

I just do Mr. Rich Disgusted. I roll my eyes. And hold up my hands like, I live in this place, so why would I have Age Rage?

He keeps his poker smile. "So, Mr. Brewster, it is in your own interests to cooperate fully. In the first place, Mr. Brewster, it is true that you came up with a lot of this stuff, and it is also true that it is all patented in the name of SecureIT and that you didn't get a bean. Isn't that so."

"I got paid," I say. "A lot. A lot more than you. And I'm smart with my money."

"Eighty percent, Mr. Brewster. Eighty percent of online crime is by employees or former employees. You fit the profile like a glove. Your profile is in neon lights all around your head."

I don't like his attitude. "First thing, I got nothing to do with all this crap. My own granddaughter just got her face burned off, so don't come here with some fairy tale about how I'm a big Age Rage freak."

He blinks. And I think: gotcha. I have no problems pressing my advantages. I go for it. "You dumb fuck, you didn't come here and not know that Elizabeth Angstrom Brewster is my granddaughter, did you? I mean you have read the files, I take it? Victims? Try 13705 Grande Mesa Outlook, apartment forty-one, Loma Linda, CA."

And for once Dr. Curtis does something smart. "It would be very difficult indeed for any of our guests to be involved in something unsavoury. You have to understand that for their own protection, our guests are monitored 24-7-365. We know every keystroke on their computers."

I play along. "Damn right. I can't even download any porn."

The Armament's face settles and his eyes narrow. He's mad. Somebody he relies on didn't add up Brewster and Brewster and come up with four. He coughs and blanks out his face. "How did they circumvent the recognition software?"

I answer him like I'm talking to a baby. "They . . . turned . . . it . . . off."

It was easy after that. I cooperated fully. I didn't know how it was done. You guys have been on the scene, what did you find there? He didn't wanna say, so I speculated, and I speculated for real. Infra red input, transcoding images? Not EMP, the stuff is hardened against that. Maybe they just broke the box and put their own software in. Maybe, yeah, it was an inside job.

When the Armament left he looked like there was some poor guy back in research was going to get a full-body electrolysis for free. We all shook hands.

I'd lucked out. That was all. I was one dumb fuck who'd lucked out. All this VAO uses my stuff. I should have known they'd think maybe I was part of it. I just didn't see it coming,

I'm getting old.

And something else.

It was very far from a dumb idea to check out SecureIT staff. I should have thought about it myself. Remember how I said I took one look at Silhouette and thought I knew him?

Well suddenly I realized that I did. I knew who he was, I could think how he used to talk, I knew he still had all his own hair.

I just couldn't for the life of me remember who he was or where I knew him from. So I'm gaga, too. I sat there and ran through every single face in my address book. Nothing. Who?

I am clearly going to spend much of my declining years with people's names on the tip of my tongue and no idea whether or not I've turned off the gas.

What I'm thinking is: I need something to get the Armament looking somewhere else. The best way to do that would be to ID Silhouette.

That night we're back in the bar, licking our wounds.

None of the Neurobics Crew got stung. But. The Armament got one old dear for illegal arms trading. She and her son on the outside were dealing in illicit ordnance. That lady had the biggest, highest, roundest widow's hump I'd ever seen, and I swear she was even more out of it than Jazza. It's kind of sad and sick and funny at the same time.

Mandy has no time for sympathy. "We're next."

Gus is reading the paper, and suddenly he drops it and says, "Holy shit. Have you seen this?"

He lays the paper out on the table. "It's another job," Gus says. *AGE RAGE ATTACK. VAOs use VAO again.*

The CCTV rerun shows the whole thing. The little label says: *Chase Manhattan Bank NYC, 1:00 a.m. this morning.*

You're looking at the inside of a vault and suddenly this iron door starts to rip. You see this claw widen the gap and then nip off some of the raggedy bits, and then they duck inside. This time my jaw drops.

This time they're wearing fireman's suits.

Walking exoskeletons that respond to movement pressure from the guys inside them. With training you can wear those things and walk through fire. You can lift up automobiles or concrete girders. You wear those things, you're Superman for the day.

The old codgers don't lurch anymore. Those suits weigh tons, but they dance. They duck and dive and ripple and flow. They shimmy, they hop, they look like giant trained fleas.

I'm saying over and over. "It's brilliant. It's fucking brilliant."

I worked on those things. You see, you can't send in rescue workers carrying hydrocarbon fuel or nuclear power on their backs, and even those suits can't carry enough ordinary batteries. So you beam the power at them. You beam microwaves. All you do if there is a disaster is you turn on your VAO, and the microwaves fuel the suits.

About the only people my software is programmed never to zap are rescue workers in exoskeletons.

Carte Blanche. We've given them Carte fucking Blanche and her sister Sadie, too.

All four of them move like fingers playing piano. They scamper up to rows of strong boxes and just haul them out of the wall.

The suits already have these huge blue tubs on their backs. Nobody likes to say, but they're for the body bags. The crew just dumps everything into them—heirloom jewellry and bearer bonds and old passports for new identities. Bullion or rare stamps. For the suits, it all just weighs a feather.

I say, "They're not going for virtual. They're going for atoms."

Mandy turns and looks at me like I'm a lizard. "Well, duh! That's why they call it burglary."

Just then the bank's security guards come running in. They're covered head to toe in foil, so they can't be area-denied. They start shooting.

You've never seen anything as beautiful as the movement in those mechanical arms. The old guys inside don't have to do a thing. The arms just weave magic carpets in the air. And they go ping ping ping like harps as the bullets hit off them, and they flash like fireworks.

Then the suits coil and spring, and one of them grabs a guard by his head and throws him three yards straight into the wall. The guard kinda hangs there for a second and starts to slide down it. Through the back of the silver suit, blood gets sprayed in a pattern like a butterfly. The guard hits the ground and stays sitting, his head dumped forward. He looks like the bridegroom after a stag party.

I don't see what happened to other guard, but it looked messier. He's nothing but a shape in the corner.

And then these beautiful suits turn to the cameras and wave like astronauts. They put a hand on each other's shoulders. And they dance off in line, like Dorothy and her tin men.

And Jazza is still staring at the strip lights.

I say, "This is one problem we gotta own."

Mandy barks a laugh. "Hell, I was thinking of running off and joining them. That looked like a lotta fun."

"Those guards got kids," says Gus. From the look on his face, I don't think he likes Mandy much right now.

I cut in. "We gotta get information, and we gotta get it to the cops. We all got to start hacking. I can get into SecureIT."

Gus is still in pain. He can't get the guards out of his head. "You reckon the company that sold that video will use any of the money to help their families?"

Thug says, "What do we hack?"

I got this one sussed. "They either bought those suits or they stole them. Either way there'll be a transaction or a report. The manufacturers are called..."

Great, I draw a blank. I hate this, I really hate this. Just before despair comes, I remember the name. "XOsafe. XOsafe Ltd. They're in Portland."

Mandy cuts in. "The first thing I'm doing is taking care of my own business so I have some money. That'll take a while." Suddenly she looks down and says in lower voice, "Then maybe I can look at who the guys in the crews are, OK?"

It's probably as close to an apology as Mandy can get. Since nobody ever apologised to her.

"Don't get your hopes up," she tells me and goes off.

I go and give Bessie a call. "How ya doing, babe?"

"Aw, Grandad," she says soft and faraway and grateful. She tries to sound like it's all covered, skin grafts, etc., but it can't be covered, it can never be covered. You see she was confident, she was sussed, and I'm scared. I'm scared it will make her timid and when she used to be so up front.

All I can say is, "Baby, I'm so sorry."

"Hey, you're the Brewster. Nothing gets you down."

"We're going to get him for you, babe," I promise.

I retrieve my transcoder, which is a more delicate operation than sticking it was. I get my glasses back and go to Jazza's room because I want to use his station to hack. Never put an old hack back from the same place. I go to his room, but he's not there. I keep the lights low and make like I'm loading my pro golf program onto his machine. Money starts flowing back into my account but from a different source this time.

After a while I ask: Where is Jazza?

I go back to the bar. My crew's not there. Neither is Jazza. Oh god, he's wandered again.

I get worried; I turn on his terminal to trace his bracelet. It's pumping out signals. It's coming from the shower. But there's no shower running.

GEOFF RYMAN

At our age, you're always thinking in the back of your head: Who's going to go next? And I'm thinking maybe this time it's Jazza. I can just about see him crumpled up on the floor. So I go to that shower with everything in my chest all shrivelled shut like a fist. I turn on the light, and there's no Jazza there.

Just his bracelet on the shower floor.

Oh fuck. I push the buzzer. It seems to take an age. They've done these experiments that show why we always think a second is longer than it really is. The brain is always anticipating. It starts measuring time from the thought, not the vision. So I cling on to the buzzer, saying come on, come on.

I think of all those times I check Jazza's buzzer before going to bed. Jazza nice and secure in his bed, it shows, or Jazza happy in the shower.

Has he done this before? You see Alzheimer's, they wander off, they try to buy ice cream in the middle of the night in a suburb or they pack a couple of telephone directories and go catch a plane. They don't understand, they feel trapped, sometimes they get frustrated and start to punch. They disappear and leave you to worry and grieve and hope all at the same time.

"We find him, don't worry, Mr. Brewster," says the Kid.

So I see them, on the lawn, with flashlights. A light little feather-duster of a thought brushes past me: the ordnance is turned off. The lights dance around the trees. The bricks in the wall are lit from underneath like a Halloween face.

Nothing.

I haul myself off to bed, and the calipers are really doing it to the side of my knees, scraping the skin, and I'm old and I just don't sleep. Here in the Happy Farm aren't even passing car lights on the ceiling to look at. There's only walls, and what's up ahead, closer now. At night.

When you're old you got a few things left and one of them is your promises. You can keep a promise as slow as you like, and as fast as you can, just so long as you don't give up. I promised Bessie. I turn on my machine and hack.

84

Who knows SecureIT like me? Well, it's been a few years. I get to work through a whole new bunch of stuff, but I do get into the Human Resource files. I mean, who would want to hack personnel, right? Just everybody.

And I go through every name, every face, every voiceprint recording. I see a face, I know it, but only sort of. I know that girl, sort of. She went and got a patent out on a new polymer, then joined. Real scholarly, real pretty, real nice legs. And I realize hell, she'll be forty now. She left years and years ago. After I did.

I see some old guy like me, pouchy cheeks and glasses and I can't place him at all, except there's a weird sensation in my chest, like I'm a time traveler. I used to say hi to that face every day.

One after another after another. Who are these people being replaced?

One guy I knew now heads up a department. What? He was nothing. He was a plodder. Guess what? That's who becomes head of department.

I look at a skinny, hollow staring scared face and I suddenly realize, shoot, that's Tommy. Tommy was a nice young kid who taught himself to program; he had talent. Now he's staring out at me wide-eyed with creases round his mouth like he's been surprised by something. Like failure, like going nowhere. It makes me want to get in there and sort it out, and tell them, no you got it wrong, this guy's got talent, you're supposed to use it for something!

It makes me want to show up again every day at 8:00 a.m., and work my butt off, and take the kids out for a drink. It makes me want to make something happen again, even if it's just in some little job in an office.

And I look at face after face and there is no Silhouette. There just is no Silhouette.

And then I find my own record. I see my own face staring out at me. Hey, maybe that guy's Silhouette.

First time I saw that photograph I couldn't take it, I thought that's not me, that's not the Brewster, who is that old, double-chinned geezer? Now, I look and I've got most of my hair and it's black, and I think how young I look.

And I read my record, and it tells the story of a middle manager who got a couple of promotions. It doesn't say I came up with loop recognition iterations. It doesn't say I was the first guy to use quantum computers on security work. It doesn't say I was the guy who first told the CE about ISO 20203 and that getting registered to that standard got us Singapore and Korea and finally China.

What it does have is my retirement date. And then it says down at the bottom. "Left without visible security compromises. No distinguishing features."

No fucking distinguishing features. What was I expecting, a thank you? A corporation that tried to credit its employees? I guess I was expecting that since I did some pretty extraordinary stuff for them, big stuff, stuff that got a whole congress of my peers on their feet and applauding, I guess I somehow thought I'd made some kind of mark. But they don't want you to make a mark. They want that mark for themselves. But they don't get it, either.

We just all go down into the dark.

And I feel the fear start up.

Oh, you can blank out the fear. You can turn and walk away from it. Or you can let it paralyse you. The one thing you can't do is what you would do with any other fear. You can't just turn and walk right at it. It won't go away. Because this fear is the fear of something that can only be accepted.

The only thing you can do with death is accept it, and if you do that at our age, it's too close to dying. You accept it, and it can come for you.

You get something like angry instead. You do what you do when you're trapped. You writhe.

I can't stay still. I go lolloping and limping like I'm stoned and drunk at the same time, because my room is like a coffin and the dark is like my eyes will never open. I go off down the corridor bobbling and jerking like some kind of goddamn puppet that something else is making move. I'm slamming my ribs against the wall and I don't care.

And then I see a light under Mandy's door. I don't have my shirt on, but what the fuck. I'm scared. And I can't afford to let myself stay scared. I knock on her door.

"Kinda early for socialising," she says. She checks out my sagging pecs. "Are you inviting me for a swim?"

She still has her makeup on, she looks sussed, she looks great, she looks like it's a big bright beautiful Saturday.

For me, everything starts to fall back down into normal. "I...I just need to talk. Do you mind?"

"Not much. I hate nights as well." She walks off and leaves her door open.

Her room smells of perfume. On the bed there are about eight stuffed toys...puppy dogs, turtles. On the shelf there is a huge lavender teddy bear, still wrapped in cellophane with a giant purple bow.

"I got nothing," she says, and flings her fake fingernails at the TV screen. For a second I think she means nothing in her life. Then I get it: she's been hacking. On the screen are eight old faces and the photo of the guy who mugged my granddaughter.

I take a chair, and I start to feel strong again. "Me neither," I say, meaning I got nothing out of SecureIT. "I'm...uh...kinda surprised that you're doing this so openly."

"Are you kidding? We're doing our bit to catch Silhouette. I want any brownie points that are going."

That TV is pointed straight at the surveillance. I gotta smile.

"You're smart," I say.

"Oh, wow, really? Like I didn't know that without you telling me." She looks at me like I'm bumwipe.

I like her. "So, has anybody else said you're smart recently?"

She nods. She accepts. "Most people don't give a fuck what you are so long as you can pay."

"You got any family?" I lean forward, into the conversation. I want to hear.

"No," she says, just with her lips, no sound. She breathes out though her nose. "I got property instead."

"For real." I understand. I flick my eyebrows. It's like: So why do you have to hack, then?

She gets it. She answers the question without having to hear it.

"Keeps the brain in gear," she says. "Beats talking to teddy bears."

"At least you got one smart person to talk to."

"Who?" She turns around and she's dripping scorn, expecting some egotistical-guy kind of remark.

I lean forward again. "You."

"Oh." She looks down and finally smiles. "Yeah, OK, I'm smart. Thanks. You want a whiskey while you're sitting there?"

"That'd be great."

"Just a few more months in Neurobics and a six-month course of PDA will replace the neurons you're destroying."

And I say, "Maybe I'll die first." It's not such a joke.

She turns with the glass. "I hope not. Here."

Mandy tells me about how she bought land in Goa and sold it for a dream. She talks about investing in broadband pipes while she was in her twenties so she could get out of lap dancing. She really did lap dance. The only other thing I get out of her is that she lived with her mother in a trailer until her mom met a car dealer and they settled into a little bungalow in Jersey. "I'd go into my room and run shootemups on my video. I kept pretending I was shooting him."

Finally I say, "I better go and see if they found Jazza."

She nods, and we both get up. And she says to me, "It's real cool they way you still look out for him after all these years."

I say, "He's part of my crew."

"Come off it," she says. "He's the only crew you got." But she says it in a real sweet way.

The next morning, I got a mail on my TV.

It's from the Kid. They've found Mr. Novavita on a Greyhound bus going south to Maryland. Jazza hasn't lived in Maryland since he was a kid and his parents moved to Jersey. How the hell did he do that?

They bring him back in about noon, and he looks like the night has been beating him up: purple cheeks, brown age spots, clumps of thick greasy gray hair. It wasn't the night: this is how Mr. Novavita looks now and I keep forgetting that. But he still climbs trees.

"He'll be OK. He'll sleep," says the Kid.

I see his glasses on the table, and there's another feather-duster thought. "He was wearing these?"

I put them on. There's a transcoder, but it's built right into the arm. High tech. Higher than mine. There's glowing fire all along the Kid's arm. Heat vision. For night?

"Fancy glasses," I say.

I go down to my crew. We're all hacked back, so we're sorted for cash flow. Thug has done some work on the suits. He has this little radio he plays, so they can't snoop our dialogue.

Thug says, "XOsafe's iced solid. So we hacked into the police files."

"What!" My voice sounds like an air pump on arctic ice.

"We have a plant on the police computer," says JoJo. "Tells us whenever we're mentioned. We added Brewster. Got a lot. They reckon Silhouette could be you.

"What, ME?"

Mandy just barks, and waves at the smoke like she's waving away the dumbest thing she's ever heard.

I'm still stuck in high gear. "They think I'm Silhouette!"

"You were the prime suspect. Until your own granddaughter got it."

I'm outraged. "Dumb shits!"

JoJo says: "Not so dumb, apparently. There's a line they've been following, right into the Happy Farm."

Mandy barks. "Oh, I don't believe it. This place?"

I take a look at her cheekbones. There's this funny tickle in my head. It's recognition. Of something. All of a sudden it's like I'm hearing someone else ask her, "Is it you?"

Only it's me that said it. The room goes cold. The radio plays dorky lounge. "Mandy. I asked are you Silhouette?" What I mean by this is strange: I really want to tell her don't worry, we'll protect you if you are. I kind of feel like I've said that. But that's not what's coming out. Actually, I'm just not in control. Because, as you will see, there's something else going on here.

Mandy's face kind of melts. All the lines in it sag, like she holds them up by constant effort. Her eyes go hollow and suddenly you see how she would look if she let herself become a little old lady. Hurt, confused. She shakes her head and the jowls go in different directions. She stands up and her hands are shaking. "Dumb old fucks."

I get a feeling like I've just been real mean to somebody who I shouldn't be mean to. And I don't know why.

Gus shouts after her. "You haven't exactly shown much concern about the people they hurt."

I go galumphing after her in my calipers. "C'mon, Mandy, nothing personal." She just shows me her back. "Mandy?"

She spins around, and she's got a face like a cornered porcupine. "Space off!"

"Mandy, the cops think there's a line out on this stuff from here and they're not dumb."

Her eyes point toward the floor. She's talking to the air. She's talking to her entire life. "Every time I think maybe, just maybe, there's somebody who has any idea . . . who just . . . SEES! ME! That's when I get kicked in the teeth again." She looks up with eyes like a mother tiger, and she's sick and mad. "Just space off back to your little crew. Go play your little-boy games." Her voice goes thin like mist. "I don't have time."

None of us have.

"I'm sorry."

She stays put, staring out through the gray window onto the lawn.

"Mandy. I'm sorry. You know why I asked? It's because I know I know that face under the black stuff. I'm sure I know who it is, if I could just remember. I just flashed . . . hey. Who says Silhouette is a guy? I just said it, the minute I thought it. I'm sorry."

She turns and looks back at me. Unimpressed. Tired. "I found something out," she says. "I was so proud of myself. I actually thought, Brewster'll be pleased." She sniffed and pulled in some air. "I got the faces of the guys in the suits, and the guys who mugged your granddaughter. I kept running 'em through, all night long. The cops must know this. But."

She looks so tired. She looks like she's going to fall asleep standing up.

"All those guys have Alzheimer's."

I let that sink in. Mandy didn't move. It was as if her whole body was swelling up to cry. She just kept staring out the window.

"Alzheimer's?"

"Yeah. It's kind of like *Attack of the Zombies*. We lose our minds and they send us in to steal. We're just bodies, meat. They won't need us for even that soon."

The gray light through the gray window, on her nose, on her cheeks. It made her beautiful.

I thought of the glasses on the bed, with built in transcoders. The glasses will tell you who your friends are. They'll tell you it's time to take your pill. They'll tell you that you have a plane to catch, and how to get out of the Happy Farm, and where the pick-up point is.

I think cheekbones. I think a shriveled cricket's face.

"Oh, shit," I say, like my stomach's dropping out. "Oh, SHIT!" Already I'm walking.

"Brewst?" Mandy kind of asks. Goddamn calipers. I'm bobbling up and down like a fishing cork. I'm trying to run, and I can't.

"Brewst. What is it?" Hey, you know, tears are streaming down my face. I suddenly feel them. My elbow kind of knocks them off my face. Those bastards, those bastards are making me cry.

"Brewster? Wait."

Mandy's tripping after me.

And all I can think is: Jazza. Jazza, you're worth so much more than that. You used to design things, mix music, girls would look at you with stars in their eyes. Ahhhcccceeeeed! Dancing with your shirt off on the brow of a bridge, young and strong and smart and beautiful. Jazza.

You're not just a meat puppet, Jazza. I hope.

I'm still crying, and I'm bumping into things because I can't see.

Back in his room Jazza is sitting up on the edge of his bed staring, looking at the corners of the ceiling like he can't figure them out. I sit and stare and look at the flesh that's as shriveled as his life tight all around his wrists, his ankles, his skull, his cheeks.

I'm aware that Mandy's standing next to me.

I put on Jazza's glasses. I try a couple of passwords: Age Rage, Silhouette. Nothing. Then I take at stab at something else:

Iron Man.

And then his glasses say to me. "Where did you read comics as a boy?" I say back. "Trees."

And there's a flash of light, brighter than the sun, up into my eyes, into my head. And I know for certain then. It's checking my retinas.

Then it all goes dark. I'm not Jazza. So the program won't open, but hey, it doesn't need to open.

I look at the face again, just to be sure.

"Mandy," I croak, and I'm real glad she's there. "Meet Silhouette."

And the only thing I'm feeling is gratitude. I'm just glad that Jazza was more than a zombie. I'm just glad that he was more than that. I still can't quite see, my eyes inside are dappled by the retina check. I'm thinking of all the times he did freelance for me: on the software, on all that VAO. He worked on it, he would know how all the ordnance cooked.

And I get it.

You see, you're this smart guy. You've buzzed all your life, but there's no money, and you're losing your mind. Maybe you get told by some young stuck-up intern doing time on the social programs that he's real sorry that your insurance won't pay for the drugs. You're poor so you get to loose your marbles. So you get mad. You get mad at everybody, at the world, at God. You turn all your brain onto one final thing. You plan ahead, for when you're gaga and beyond being charged or convicted. You invent Silhouette and store him up, and set the bugs loose to search for a new kind of crew.

You get your revenge.

Mandy takes my arm and shakes it. "Brewst. Brewster," she says. All she can see is some sad old fuck dissolving into tears. She can't understand that I'm crying because I'm happy. I can't understand it, either.

I just know in my butt: Jazza thought of this.

"He was Silhouette," I say, and breathe in deep.

"How?" demands Mandy. Hand on hip, Mandy won't buy just any fairy story.

I feel reasonably cool again as well.

"Silhouette's not a person, it's a program, a series of programs that all work on the same algorithms. The programs take you over, tell you what to do, how to do it. Maybe what to say. Maybe you get to be Silhouette for a while and if you're gaga enough you won't even know it. So trace Silhouette then. One week he's in Atlanta, the next he's in L.A., the next week he's in New York. They'll be hacked into the glasses. The glasses and the terminals and the crude little chips in your head."

I go to Jazza's machine. And look for the files. I won't be able to open any of them, of course, but of course there is a whole directory. Anything encrypted is enough to get you. The directory is called Aphrodite. What we called our spaceship to Mars. Everything in it's encrypted, and the file sizes are huge. That ain't no banking hack.

"That's it," I say. "That's the masterplan."

I look back at Jazza. He looks like a little boy in a bus station waiting for his Mom to show up before the bus goes.

I open up the email package and start keying in. I shop Jazza. It's painless. Just an email to Curtis, to the Armament. Over in two minutes. And all the while I'm doing it, I feel proud. Proud of him.

"Sorry, Jazza." I tell him. I take hold of his hands. That makes me feel better. "They'll wipe the program. That's all. No more trips to Maryland."

He looks back at me like a baby. He's not sure who I am, but he trusts me.

Five minutes later, the Kid slips in.

"Sorry, Mr. Brewster," he says quietly. "Sorry it was your friend."

The Kid comes from a country where people are still human. The sorrow is upfront in his eyes.

I ask him. "What's Curtis doing?"

"Damage limitation." It's the kind of jargon you learn early in our part of the world. It eats your soul. "He worry about the Home."

"His own ass," corrects Mandy.

The Kid can't help but smile. But he sticks to the point. "You do right thing, Mr. Brewster."

Isn't it great how people can still care about each other? Isn't it some kind of miracle sometimes?

This time the cops show up in a plain car, and this time it's IT specialists not Armament. They start going through Jazza's station. Jazza starts to sing to himself, some dumb old toon about everybody being free, it's all love, let's just party down. Did we really think that was all it took?

He lets them take away his machine, and he just curls up on the bed, back to us all. I say something corny like "Sleep well, old friend."

And the Kid says, "I watch him for you, Mr. Brewster."

Mandy and I slump off to the bar and the Neurobics are all there but before we can say anything Gus jumps us and says, "You guys gotta see this!"

Mandy says, "Do we?"

The whole crew are leaning over the newspaper. "I'll rerun it," says Gus.

"Fasten your seat belt," says Mandy, and she gives me a long look like: I'm tired of these bozos.

On the newspaper is a wall of people, and the label says:
Latest VAO attack SHUTZE STADIUM 8:35 p.m. last night.

The whole thing looks like diamonds, huge overhead lights, flashing cameras, halfway through a night game. Gus has plugged in his speakers, so we get the TV announcer too and the sound of the crowd. The camera moves to a big guy on the mound chewing gum, thumping the ball into his mitt, and looking pissed off.

Over the stands a kind of rectangle just hangs in midair. It looks like it should be there, just part of the stadium, you have to blink to realize it's hovering. It's a rescue platform, designed for getting people out of tall buildings in midair. It looks as small as a postage stamp, only it's crowded with exoskeletons.

On all the tall cathedral lights, red lights start flashing and sirens rouse themselves.

One announcer says, "That's the fire alarm, John."

"Yup, and those are firemen. Though I have to say right now, I can't see any sign of a fire."

"If there is, John, official figures estimate that it takes fifteen to twenty minutes to clear the stands here at Shu Tze Stadium."

On the field the players stand morose and still, hands on hips. Their show is over.

Firemen stumble off the platform. It bobs. Close up, the platform is more unstable than a rowboat. The suits hop down, straighten up and start to jog up the steps through the stands. You can see it now that there's a lot of them together: the suits move in unison.

On the field one of the fat little umpires is running as fast as he can. A police car comes driving straight onto the diamond.

"Certainly something is happening here at Shu Tze, Marie, but it may not be a fire. That's Lee van Hook, manager of the Cincinnati Reds getting out of the police vehicle. And he's waving his hands, yes, he's waving the players off the field!"

You hear a crunching. It's a nasty goose-stepping sound, and the camera blurs back to the stands. All the suits have raised automatic weapons at once. And they're jammed straight at the crowd.

Speakers crackle and feedback whine shoots round the stadium.

And a voice like Neptune bubbling out of the sea says, "This is a public service announcement."

Announcer cuts in. "John, reports are saying this is a VAO attack."

"You are going to help the aged. You will pass all valuables, watches, wallets, and jewellry to the men and women with the guns."

"Just to repeat that, we are witnessing a VAO attack here live at Shu Tze Stadium."

The digital gurgle goes on. "For your own safety please remember that some of the people with the guns will die soon and have nothing to lose. Many of them cannot think for themselves and so will shoot anyone who resists."

A kind of roar is spreading all through the crowd.

"You won't pay taxes. You won't let us into your houses. We save and plan and invest and insure and in the end that still is NOT enough. What you should do is love us. It's too late for love, now. Now is the time for money. What you are doing to do now is give us your wallets."

Some fat guy in a baseball cap is shouting. An exo arm is raised. The suit is like a metal cage around some ancient old dear, and you can see that she's blinking and confused. I realize all the CCTV is on, and they've edited it later. That's entertainment.

The gun goes off. The fat man ducks and yelps, but his hat has already spun off his head. Those suits can aim to within a fraction of millimeter.

"That's one move he won't pull again in a hurry," says announcer John. He chuckles, like it's a wrestling match. This stuff, you react to it like a movie. It performs the same function.

All along the rows, a gentle sideways motion flows toward the suits, like a rippling river. It all looks so gentle and calm. On the field police cars pull up and rub noses like it's a BBQ on a bank by a river on a summer day.

The announcers can only tell us what we can see for ourselves. But you know, it becomes more real when they say it. "John, it looks like the police on the field are conferring with both the team heads and stadium security managers."

"It's a real problem for them, Marie. How can they apprehend the VAO without injuring any of the fans?"

The great burbling voice begins again. "What do you think of, when you see us? Do you think getting old is something we did to ourselves? Do you think it won't happen to you? Do you think you won't get ugly, sick, and weak? Do you think health foods, gyms, and surgery are going to stop that? We're going to go now. But just remember. Your kids are watching you. And learning. What you do to us, your kids will do to you."

The crowd is kind of silent, no motion, just a kind of hush, as if the sea had decided to be still. The siren goes round and round, but you have the feeling no one's listening. The suits march the old guys inside them back down from the stands toward the rescue platform.

The weirdest thing: some kid in a foilsuit helps one of the VAOs up. And I realize that they understand. They're halfway there, all these people in this stadium, with their soyaburgers and beer and team shirts. They're halfway there to being on our side.

You got to them, Jazza.

And the platform snores itself awake and coughs and whirs, and sort of tilts a bit getting up, like all of us old stereotypes. But once it's steady, it soars straight up.

And Jazza stands. Just stands still. The program has given him nothing to do, but i's also like he's finished. He looks up to the sky, like he always does now, up at nothing. He stands like a king on the prow of his ship praying to heaven, and sails away.

And oh god I'm leaking again. Mandy can't look at me. Her mouth does a bitter little twist and she says, "Silhouette was Jazza."

Gus says, "What?"

I don't want to hear it. I don't want explain or talk or do anything at all, but I can't sit still, either. I feel sick. I feel messed up. I feel angry. I stand up and lurch out of there. Gus calls after me. "Hey, Brewst, what is this? Brewst?"

I'm walking, and I don't know where or why. I walk into the Solarium and walk into the gym, and walk into the garden, and I go to the library but that only has books, and in the end, there's only one place to go.

I go back to Jazza's room. The Kid is still there, like he said he would be. "Scram," I tell him.

I really look at Jazza. I think that maybe he was going back to Maryland for one last time. Maybe he was going to climb a tree and just stay there.

I'm thinking how we lose everything. Everything we were, everything we made ourselves into. If you were strong, that goes; if you were smart, that goes; if you were cool, that goes.

Jazza's face is brown and blue like a map. He's sitting up, but his head has dropped backward, so he's staring up at the ceiling with his mouth pulled open. His blue eyes go straight through me to nowhere, like he's looking for an answer but forgot the question.

And that's when I finally say to myself. He's gone. Jazza leaked away a long, long time ago. There's been nothing left of Jazza for months. So I let him go.

I'm not too clear about the whole show after that.

Armament comes back and tries to sound like they're going to be tough on my ass. Secret Squirrel keeps asking the same questions over and over. The message is: if we find you had anything to do with this, we'll still get you.

The Armament looks at me. "We know about your hacks. That'll have to stop."

Curtis stands there watching, and he starts to squirm a bit and look in my direction.

"Given that you cooperated, we may take a tolerant view of that. But only if you continue to cooperate, only if the attacks stop."

What I do next is deliberate. I turn to Curtis and shrug and apologise with my eyes. That's all it takes. Secret Squirrel snaps his head round at Curtis and narrows his eyes.

"24 by 7 by 365, huh?" Armament says in a quiet little voice.

He's got it. I shrug an apology to Curtis again, just to drive my point home.

Curtis goes edgy, jumpy, mean. "Well. Well, if that means what I think it does, you cannot continue to be a guest here, Mr. Brewster."

After that things moved quick.

I told Bill about the hack and the police and it was decided. I would go and live with my boy. It's just a beaten-up old bungalow on the Jersey side. Like the kind of house I grew up in, when computers were new and cool, and everything was new and cool from shoes to playing cards and you had takeaway pizza for dinner. Even Mom was cool with headphones. Hot in summer with screen doors for the flies, and dry and warm in winter.

I'm on the phone to Bill and I say, "At least I'll get out of this goddamned dump."

There's a minute silence, and then Bill says, "Dad. They've worked miracles for you."

And I think about the neurobics and how my legs are learning to walk, and I have to acknowledge that. So I guess I can lose being mad at the Farm. I guess I can feel I got a pretty good deal.

I go see Mandy. I fill her in. She says, "You're the only man here with any cool whatsoever." She's got a face like the badlands of Arizona. And I don't know why, but right now that's as sexy as fuck.

Remember that transcoder jammed into my dick? Found a new use for it.

So I'm lying there with all the teddy bears and the scent of Miss Dior and I say to Mandy. "Come to Jersey with me."

She looks down and says, "Oh boy." Then she says, "I gotta think."

I ask her, "What's to think?"

"Baby. If I wanted a bungalow in Jersey, I could have had it. Here, I got a Solarium, I got quiet, I got my own room."

"You dumb cluck. You'll be alone."

I see her looking at different futures. I see her get the fear. It makes all the skin of her face sag like old chamois leather. I hold her and hug her and kiss the top of her dyed conditioned perfumed hair. I try to open up things for her. "Come and be part of my family, babe. Bill's a great kid. He'll let us stay up late drinking whiskey. We'll watch old DVDs. They'll be people round at Thanksgiving."

And her head is shaking no. "I'll be stuck in one tiny bedroom, with someone else's family. That's where I started out."

She grunts and slaps my thigh. "I can't do it." She sits up and lights a cigarette and then she lets me have it straight.

"I danced for fat old men. I'd get into a bath with other women, and they'd look at our cunts through a pane of glass. I was that far from being a whore. I took the money and I got smart with it, and I kept it. Even though asshole after asshole man tried to take it away from me. This, here, fancy-pants Happy Farm, is my reward."

She takes a breath and says. "I'm too scared to go to Jersey."

"I'll come and see you," I say. She doesn't believe me, and I'm not entirely sure I do, either.

So suddenly I'm standing outside the Happy Farm and thank God they're not currently microwaving anybody, and I'm saying goodbye to the place and, you know, I think I'll miss it. Mandy isn't there. Gus is there, which is big of him, and he shakes my hand like maybe he thinks he'll get

Mandy back. But I can see. His arms are thin like sucked-on pens, and his tummy is big like a boil. Gus isn't going to be with us long.

The Kid comes, and he brings his sweet tiny little wife with him. She's rehearsed something to say in English. She says it with her eyes closed and giggles afterward. "Thank you very much, Mr. Brewster, you have been so good to my Joao." And then she holds up her beautiful new baby daughter for me to see.

Life goes on. And then it doesn't. It doesn't mean anything. Which means that death doesn't mean anything, either. It means that while you're here you can do what the hell you want.

I took off the calipers. I wanted to show them that I could do it. I walked for all of us old farts with no money, all the way to the bus. Bill caught me and helped me up the steps.

I looked around for Jazzanova, but he wasn't there, and never will be.

One thing those bastards don't know about is the hack that pays Jazza's bills. It's a one-off on the bank's system. It's not on my machine or on Jazza's. Curtis doesn't know that, and the Armament doesn't know that. We're gonna keep Jazza cared for.

And all I'm feeling is one solid lump of love. I give the Farm one last wave goodbye and go home.

Total buzz.

The Future of Science Fiction

Print. Hard Copy.

It sure sounded like it. The printer hammered outside Alex's head, punctuating the Sibelius within it. The hammering turned the *Karelia Suite* into Static (rigid, hard, fast, new dance music, SF clue).

This fucking book. Alex hated it. There was a mistake on page 307. Well, more of an omission. To correct it, Alex would have to add three paragraphs.

Three extra paragraphs would have a knock-on effect on all fifty-seven remaining pages of chapter 3a. Alex would have to reprint all fifty-seven pages of chapter 3a. And renumber the full four hundred and twenty-seven pages of chapters 3b, 3c, 3d, 3e. Probably by hand since he didn't want to reprint. That'll teach him to be so fucking clever. Alex had a headache.

His agent was pushing him to finish. Alex's agent was called Knockers. It was a kind of nickname, and it probably cost Alex £10,000 on every sale. Knockers kept sending messages to a window on Alex's screen, big handwritten scrawl. HOW'S IT GOIN? CAN YOU SEND FIRST CHAPTERS NOW? The deadline was as hard as the copy. Hard and fast. Static.

They needed the basic Hard Copy to go Soft. Going Soft meant the publisher brought in a sampling agency. They would sample the Encyclopedia Titanica—botany, archaeology, anthropology, history of stage costuming—to flesh out his world. That way people could navigate, rather than just read. I mean, why would people who found real botany boring want to know about Rhodopsin photosynthesis on a postmodern, rust-eating Mars? They did.

Alex was part of a genre called Adult Sampling. He sampled psychological research models and used them as part of the characterization. So people could play games with his anorexic heroines, his mother-fixated heroes. It was like Adult Westerns. Like Adult Westerns, it was the shooting and not the characterization that kept people watching.

Heigh ho. After going Soft, they (meaning the hundreds of people who produced his book) then had to arrange the tour. For each book, Alex put on a stage show.

The next book would sample Edinburgh Castle. It would appear holographically on stage as Alex read. Music too, mixing Beethoven, Glass, Tallis and a Turkish popular singer called Bulent who was a lady but used to be a man. Lights, music, dancing, both live and simulated, and finally, in person and in imaging, Alex Clarke, reading.

Alex was quite a charismatic performer when he wasn't exhausted. You had to be charismatic if you were an SF writer. Alex was doing a Con in April. It was Eastercon, the only one big enough to afford his fees. Con was the right word for it. World Premiere of his next book, staged in Wembley Stadium. Fortunately Alex had a deep voice and actorish good looks—after plastic surgery, liposuction, and stimulated growth. Along the way he had become addicted to surgery.

There was the tour, the Bookman version with games and music, the Virtual version, and finally, somewhere, something printed on paper.

At night Alex dreamed of letters on a screen. All the curves, if you looked carefully enough, moved up in steps, and in his dreams people were being carried up them, helplessly, as on escalators. They couldn't get off. They were waving to him. Their arms, their fingers were escalators and on those as well, little people were...

Two weeks later Alex took an electric carving knife and sawed off his own penis. He had a tiny little hole through which he peed, just over his swelling testicles. They made him a new penis out of a section of his leg. It worked, and was bigger and more sexually satisfying than his first one had been. He burned off his corneas and replaced them with better ones. He became a star of *The British Journal of Plastic Surgery*.

Alex was becoming a legend. But not for his books.

In the heat of the battle, He-roch-che moved with the deliberation of a machine, hanging back from the blow. He wore armour; each careful step had a metallic ring to it. The muscles on his arms were round like melons. The ache in them, bearing up the lance, felt good. The lance had a hook at the bottom, spearhead at the top, axehead just below that.

He-roch-che fought piggyback style, a partner on his back. His name meant Real War Eagle. His partner was called Tha-in-ge and her name, in a different language, meant Persimmon. Tha-in-ge was a child template and she rode him, firing tiny arrows. The tiny arrows hissed, trailing smoke. They were chemical weapons. In the middle distance, enemies swelled and burst like fruit. All across the horizon, there were fires.

Tha-in-ge fought long and middle distance. He-roch-che defended at close quarters. Another piggyback couple faced them, two of the Perverse, all lace and souvenir bones. He-roch-che circled the carrier. He-roch-che's smile was a snarl. He loved this. He loved bashing enemies into eternity with the cheerfulness of a schoolboy. He had never grown up. He had a dim idea that he was as complicated as an animated cartoon.

The Perverse lunged. He-roch-che grinned and dodged, his earrings swinging, the crest of his glossy orange hair whipping about his head, and he parried and whipped up the hooked base of the lance. It caught, he pulled, and God's richness spilled, purple-veined and glossy, intestines and organs. They gushed out of his enemy. The enemy, surprised, fell to his knees. He-roch-che still backed away from him. His feet slipped slightly under him. Blood.

He-roch-che was intelligent enough to know he was Virtual, a tangle of samples that could think, feel, smell. He knew he could not die. He knew thousands of people watched him, somewhere. He played up to it, tossing his head like a wild horse.

"Ah!" said Tha-in-ge, pointing. Someone else to kill.

He-roch-che reared up and jogged toward them. Another piggyback Perverse, but these two were exhausted, slow. Tha-in-ge kicked He-roch-che with her spurs, drawing blood.

Knockers sat on the beautifully clean, folded corner of Alex's hospital bed. It was very embarrassing having Knockers there. Knockers was altogether too old for his particular schtick.

Knockers was a middle-aged man who had had a Mole job—molecular level genetic tampering. Mole jobs were extravagant, unpredictable, dangerous. Alex always saw a mole tunneling through you like a little gentleman in a brown waistcoat. They stripped your DNA and gave you a sample of someone else's.

Knockers had grown huge breasts, which he proudly displayed, attached to each other with chains. He had had cosmetic surgery on his name as well, to match them. When he wasn't stoned, Knockers could still be a very professional agent. Right now his eyes were crossed and his speech was slurred. The woman in the next bed had drawn curtains between them.

"Zuh book'ssh late, Alexssh. It'ssh too fuckin late, man."

Alex lay on his bed in a private ward, recovering. He had bought himself a better heart. It had double chambers, beat twice as fast, producing a smoother flow of blood. His enhanced heart fluttered in his chest like birds. His cheeks felt hot. All his skin was bright pink and the top of his head felt like a metal hat that was about to pop off. He could feel oxygen sizzle through his cortex like champagne.

"Tell them to cut out some of the sampling," said Alex. Knockers seemed to float as if underwater, his smile, his eyes, unfocused. It was if he were so stoned that he had managed to derange the very light around him. Had Knockers understood?

"Knock, knock. Anybody home?" Alex asked. "I said, they can cut out some of the geo sampling. I told you, the place is Scotland. Same rocks, same ground cover, same hills, same little bays, just lift it as it is— or was—and stick it onto a continent instead of England and find a way for the land crabs to survive."

"It'ssh late. They really asshed…" Knockers burped and farted at the same time. How could an intelligent man allow himself to become quite so uncouth? "You know how long it took to find some Early Lithuanian Music?"

Alex grinned. He had thought it might take a while. "I also knew," he said, "that there was no existing lexicon for the Kaw Indians."

Knockers guffawed. "We got Indians wearing kilts in Schcotland, only it's attached to France and has some land crabs." He liked the idea. "How we gone have the Indians talk?"

"I'll tell them for an extra twenty thou," said Alex and grinned. He had smart teeth. He could use them for credit.

Why should he make it easy for them?

Why was he so bored?

He-roch-che watched land crab soaking in a dead man's helmet. The flesh of the crabs was black and had to be soaked for a week in salt water before it was eatable. Otherwise it tasted of burnt rubber. Scum floated on the surface of the water in thick, gray bubbles. Gray clouds, mingled mist, and smoke were reflected on them.

He-roch-che was sitting on a beach. Somewhere behind him was the comforting hush of surf. Sand in the air stung his naked arms, tufts of long gray grass stirred in the same wind that moved He-roch-che's kilt.

By flipping, He-roch-che could access the structure of the grass blades. He could flip his vision in degrees until he saw the grass as a giant quilt of cells. He could access its composition, the structure of cellulose, the movement of protein and sugars. At the same time the systems of high and low pressure that made the wind, made the clouds, isobarred through his constructed mind.

I'm a boat, he thought. People ride me, navigating by charts or by whim.

Tha-in-ge hunted. She crouched, keeping still. The light caught her lycra suit like sunlight on sea seen from miles above.

Tha-in-ge had tied together two thigh bones with tanned gut, and there was a net of gut all around a hump in the seashore sand. She prodded the hump with He-roch-che's lance.

Suddenly there was a belching of dust, and sand hissed, spilling in slithery currents. Giant claws were unveiled. Tha-in-ge pulled on the criss-crossing of gut. The net tightened. With a lurch, something huge and leathery tried to lunge toward her. One free claw came for her. She threw the two thigh bones. With a whirling sound they spun around each other, caught the claw, entangled it.

Tha-in-ge used the lance to pole vault onto the crab's back. It was the size of the shell of a sea turtle. She pulled the reins tighter.

She had harnesses ready. Her people trained the crabs and rode on their backs.

"Zetanzaw," said He-roch-che. It was one of the few words remaining from the speech of the Kaw Indians. It meant big. He meant big crab. He-roch-Che thought in English but could only speak in the few surviving words of the Kaw.

"Tuh" said Tha-in-ge, and tossed black hair out of her eyes. She despised He-roch-che's people. She spoke another language of the Sioux, with a full lexicon. She was a person of the Heaven and the Earth. He was one of the People of the Wind.

He-roch-che accessed memories of home. He saw in his mind domes of earth, houses on which horses grazed. The doorways had to point toward the stars of particular gods. The houses were from the wrong tribe, but close enough. You had to sample from somewhere. Even He-roch-che's thick hands, with their veins and sleek, yellow-brown skin were samples. Whose hands were they really?

Pulling on the reins, Tha-in-ge made the crab scuttle forward. Her people trained them as carriers. She started to sing in a throaty voice that had once belonged to a Turkish popular singer.

Bus tires still made that delicious, squishing noise on wet roads. You could hear the tread pushing water out of the way, channelling it out, leaving a track behind.

Alex stood in the rain looking at tire tracks. Funny the things you held on to. The main effect of his new heart was that he couldn't stop thinking. His data bills were enormous, he kept thinking of things to access. Government, astrophysics, oral literature. A Niagara of information. All he wanted now was silence.

He looked up into the sky. It was low and gray, mist and mingled smoke.

What he really wanted, what he would really like, would be to know, really know, what the future would be. He could write about it then, even if he didn't know how it all came about, even if he couldn't explain it. And one hundred years later, people would say, he got it RIGHT, how did he KNOW that? Jeez, reproduction by multicellular division, human beings just splitting in half, who would EVER have thought that would happen? How did he KNOW?

Unless, of course, it turned out that he made it happen by imagining it.

Or prevented it happening by imagining it.

The trouble with intelligent, enhanced humanity, Alex thought, is that we are just a little too far from the primaeval swamp. We have drives, drives toward ends that no longer exist.

I want, thought Alex, I want something so badly it tastes in my mouth like oranges accidentally soaked in garlic. I want it so badly that my eyes have swollen with it and are now wilting like leaking balloons after a party. I want, I need, and I don't know what it is.

A drink? A woman? A poodle that I can shave into strange poodle shapes?

That's why I keep cutting my body.

I could sample myself. Sample myself, yeah, and take the sample to one of those Chaos guys. I could find out what I want. They could use the N constant to predict the surface turbulence. The surface turbulence of the self, the Fluid Dynamics of my emotions. Find out my needs, predict their ends. Maybe I would end up being a fractal of everyone else. I would be an image of the pain in these dark streets and in those dark, hissing, crowded cars. The people in them were shadows.

He felt lighter hearted. So simple. They have an answer for everything these days. There was even one of those Chaos joints just around the corner. What was it called?

CRUNCH YOUR NUMBERS said the sign.

Alex got a butterfly graph of his soul.

"You need," said the Chaos Man, "to think of something new. You are bored with your work."

"Thanks a lot," said Alex. For this he had cashed in a smart tooth?

"You are bored," the Chaos Man continued, "because you lack integrity."

It had the ring of truth.

Outside, it had stopped raining, and the sun seemed to swell orange in the puddles, huge, overripe. The sky was misted over with dusk, streaked with blue and purple cloud that rolled back to pinkish grey. There was a hint of green in the sky, somewhere.

I have been false, thought Alex. Where? I want to write about the future. How is that dishonest?

He had known all along of course. The future could not be sampled. It was not there to be sampled. The future would not be, could not be, a patchwork quilt of things that were past, stale whimsy and other people's books. The future would be truly new.

He was smiling. The future would be new and clean, thrilling. I don't want any more screens, any more data banks, he thought. And I don't want to sit alone anymore, either, trying to dredge up something new from nowhere. Speculating with a few spare ideas like fruit left too long in the bowl. Using surrealism like cinnamon to spice it up. Stealing, lying to myself.

All that's over now. Transfixed on the pavement, Alex saw a way ahead. The tires still hissed.

He-roch-che marched toward the final battle.

There was a castle on a rock. Ringed round it were the enemy, still some distance away. Tha-in-ge rode him, encased in armour. She was like an armadillo, all in spines. The spines would blow free in flashes of light and powder. They shot out into dusk, seeking life. Drawn to it, the missiles destroyed life from a distance.

Tha-in-ge had a tiny harp and played sweet sad songs of killing for the Unending War.

In the air all around them, came the sound of massed bagpipes, tart, bitter, sweet all at once. And underneath that, somehow low and sad, there was an Indian war chant. Hey ya hey hey, Hey ya hey hey.

They marched through the remains of a park. There were clipped hedges in concentric patterns, around a Stonehenge temple. The grass was pockmarked with humps of earth dug by moles and the hooves of the temple goats and oxen. The two armies advanced.

Anachronism, thought He-roch-che, having no Indian word for it. I fight with giant battle-axe while Tha-in-ge fires intelligent rockets from her back. A sinuous symbolic pattern wound its way through his imagination—a summary of this constructed world and how it came to have its mixed technology.

Lies. He-roch-che felt anger.

Ahead of him were the Army of the Perverse. They wore scarves of translucent fabric, lace as well as metal. Their armour showed genitals, they mocked the more lumpen mass of soldiery that followed the Ambition. The Perverse wanted the world to end in pleasure.

The Ambition wanted to rule it, and He-roch-che shared that Ambition.

Why? Because he had been so constructed. And who had made him, to live a life through him? He-roch-che addressed his audience directly. My life is as real to me as yours is to you.

I could have made me better, thought He-roch-che. I am some blunt, dull idea—big muscles, murderous intent, a crest of hair, a skull earring. I would have made me slimmer, sleeker, faster. I could have created more animals, more birds. I would have made my life with Tha-in-ge more tender. I would have had nothing second hand, nothing stale, nothing second rate.

He-roch-che hated his creator.

Our blood will coat this green field to depth of my ankles, he thought, for you.

Suddenly loudspeakers behind him sputtered. They spoke in false, tinny voices. "Pi-sing!" they cried, a last remaining Kaw word meaning Game. The bagpipes ceased, the Ambition Army charged.

He-roch-che feinted a blow that would have left his midriff exposed, pulled back, and used the hook to grapple and disarm. Then his axeblade came down on the neck, seeking the weak point of his enemy's armour. He felt Tha-in-ge above him exchange blows. She was not meant for hand-to-hand. In panic, she fired spines in all directions.

His lance was stuck between plates of metal on his enemy's shoulder. Another cohort of the Perverse came at him, sword drawn. With a wrench, He-roch-che was able to swing his first victim into the path of the blow. Metal rang on metal. Lubricated by blood, his axe slipped free and swung into the face of the second cohort.

Tha-in-ge screeched.

An axe—from where—had buried itself in He-roch-che's arm. The weight of it was dazing, numbing. The edges of He-roch-che's torn armour dug into the wound. He brought his own axe up and despatched his third Perverse that day.

Racing, his mind reflected. I am the hero, he thought. I cannot die.

Oh really? In this world, the knowledge of medicine had been driven out by the war. In this world, with a wound like that, he was already dead. It might take time, weeks perhaps, throbbing with infection and fever. But he was already, mathematically at least, dead.

He flipped in closer to the wound, explored its depths. He had been cut to the bone. The bone itself had been cut. Blood welled, like the seasons, unstoppable.

There was nothing to do, but go on fighting. Some part of his constructed mind resolved a problem for itself. Now he knew why people, real people in history, had gone on fighting.

He-roch-che flipped out of the wound, back to battle, he flipped far far back from it, viewed it mistily from far away, the beautiful castle on the rock, the beautiful green garden. Real War Eagle flew.

There was a word from his own language he could use.

Wah-kon-dah, he thought. The word in both his and Tha-in-ge's language was said to mean God. It actually meant Great Mysterious Spirits.

"Wah-kon-dah!" He-roch-che said, to the people watching, listening, enjoying. Mysterious Spirits, feel this. Feel what it is like to kill someone for sport.

Somewhere through the screen of his virtual reality, beyond the sunset with its orange sun, its blue and purple clouds, its hint of green, there was another world where people watched him die for fun.

He flipped back. It was raining blood from Tha-in-ge's severed back. With a howl, He-roch-che launched himself at a writhing, mocking wall of the Perverse, and he cut and slashed and cut and slashed, trying to cut his way through the screen of his virtual world. He was trying to cut his way through the fiction.

The tires hissed past. There was a clicking of heels as a woman in fish-net tights and Carmen Miranda hat walked around Alex with a cheerful nod. "Rain's over," the woman murmured. She was taking her dog, and enhanced Watchhound, for a walk.

"Have a nice day," said the dog.

Alex was still riveted by his idea. No sampling. But no staring into nothing, either.

How about a genuine, scientific excavation of the future? Surely the most complex surface turbulence of any system was social interaction. But if there was an N constant, couldn't it predict the sudden shifts, the irrational responsiveness of the world? Could Chaos predict when the Muslim Alliance might break apart, when the New Age islands could finally cohere into a political system? A fiction that was actually a form of research, with testable hypotheses, building, building a virtual construct of the future, to be tested, refined each month, improved.

And sure, monthly updates on what the model was doing, that would be news in itself.

This surely, he thought, was the future of science fiction.

A shopping Priority Board was at hand, on the panel of the shelter of the bus stop. It was a way of helping people consume. He keyed in his password, coded the service he wanted, Scientific Theory and Modelling, asked for a ballpark estimate of cost, no upper limit but with possible financing alternatives to be displayed. He wanted to build a team of scientists.

He waited as the machine resolved his priorities. There was a stirring of air in his face.

He looked at the Shopping Board, its rounded edges, its high resolution display, the ratta-tat-tat Static music it played. How sweet, he thought, how quaint, how redolent of this decade.

He looked at the street, its brick frontages, the too typical billboards. One of them was very familiar, made famous by an old photograph, a billboard that had a tendency to show up in every construct of the period.

What? Oh. Alex remembered that he was part of a series, *Lives of the Great Artists.* He remembered and then forgot it. Self-conscious constructs helped navigate through a fantasy, but now verisimilitude was all.

Realism had come back into fashion.

Omnisexual

There were birds inside of her. Was she giving birth to them? One of them fluttered its wings against the walls of her uterus. He felt the wings flutter, too. He felt what she felt in a paradise of reciprocity, but she was not real. This world had given birth to her, out of memory.

A dove shrugged its way out of her. Its round white face, its surprised black eyes, made him smile. It blinked, coated with juices, and then, with a final series of convulsions, pulled itself free. The woman put it on her stomach to warm it, and it lay between them, cleaning itself. Very suddenly, it flew away.

He buried his face in her, loving the taste of her.

"Stay there," she told him, holding his head, showing him where to put his tongue.

And he felt his own tongue, on a sensitive new gash that had seemed to open up along the middle of his scrotum.

She was delivered of fine milky substance that tasted of white chocolate. It sustained him through the days he spent with her.

She gave birth to a hummingbird. He knew then what was happening. DNA encodes both memory and genes. Here, in this other place and time, memory and genes were confused. She was giving birth to memories.

"Almost, almost," she warned him, and held his head again. The hummingbird passed between them, working its way out of her and down his throat. Breathing very carefully, not daring to move in case he choked, he felt a wad of warm feathers clench and gather. He felt the current of his breath pass over its back, and he swallowed, to help it.

It made a nest in his stomach. Humming with its wings, it produced a sensation of continual excitement. He knew he would digest it. The walls of its cells would break down, giving up their burden of genes. He knew they would join with his own. Life here worked in different ways.

He became pregnant. All over his skin, huge pale blisters bubbled up, yearning to be lanced. He clawed at them until they burst, with a satisfying lunging outward of fluid and new life.

He gave birth to things that looked like raw liver. He squeezed them out from under the pale loose skin of the broken blisters, and onto the ground. They pulled themselves up into knots of muscle and stretched themselves out again. In this way, they drew themselves across the ground, dust sticking to each of them like a fine suede coat.

They could speak, with tiny voices. "Home," they cried. "Home, home, home," like birds. They wanted to go back to him. They were part of him, they remembered being him, they had no form. They needed his form to act. They clustered around him for warmth at night, mewling for reentry. In the end, he ate them, to restore them. He could not face doing anything else.

Their mother ate them, too. "They will be reborn as hummingbirds," she told him. She gave birth instead to bouquets of roses and things that looked like small toy trains.

He did not trust her. He knew she was collecting his memories from them. She collected people's memories. She saw his doubt.

"I am like a book," she said. "Books are spirits in the world that take an outward form of paper and words. They are the work of everyone, a collection. I am like that. I am communal. So are you."

Her directness embarrassed him. His doubts were not eased. He walked through the rustling tundra of intelligent grasses. The hairs on the barley heads turned like antennae. The grass was communal too.

When he came back to the woman who was not real, she had grown larger. She lay entwined in the grass and hugged him; she opened up and enveloped him. Warm flesh, salmon pink with blue veins, closed over him moist and sheltering, sizzling like steak and thumping like Beethoven. He lived inside her.

Prying ribbons explored him gently, opened him up. They nestled in his ears, or crept down his nose, insinuated their way past his anus, reached needle thin down the tip of his penis. They untied his belly button, to feed him. Flesh was a smaller sea in which, for a time, he surrendered his independent being.

What conjunction could be more complete than that? When he emerged after some months, he was a different person. He had a different face. It had grown out of him, out of his old one. He looked into her eyes and saw the reflection of his new face. It was a shock. This was the face of a conqueror, a hero, older, like a head on a Roman coin.

Her eyes looked back at him, amused and affectionate. "You will go away now," she told him. "You have become bored. You should always listen to boredom or disgust. It is telling you that it is time to move."

On the other world, the world he had come from, there had been a fluorescent sign outside his window.

BUILDING TOMORROW, the sign had read, WITH THE PEOPLE OF TODAY.

It did not seem to him that this was possible.

Rain would pimple the glass of the window, breaking up the red light from the sign, glowing red light drops of blood. And he would listen to the wind outside, or fight his way along the blustery streets under clouds that were the color of pigeons.

Everything was covered over by concrete. There were no trees; the buildings had been cheaply made and were not kept clean. The people were the only things that were soft.

People lived where they worked, crawling out from under their desks in the morning, sleepy, embarrassed, polite, smelling of body processes, wearing faded robes to blanket the smells, shuffling off to the toilets to wash. Their breasts, their buttocks, were wrapped and hidden. Disease was a miasma between them, like some kind of radiant ectoplasm. He would rove the blustery streets, dust in his eyes, looking at the young people. He could not believe the beauty of their faces and bodies, and he ached for them, to think that they would grow old, and he wanted to hold them and to touch them, so that the beauty would not go unacknowledged or hoarded by only one or two others. He ached to think of them losing their beauty here.

He saw them losing it. He saw what they would become. The people he worked with had tiny cookers under their desks, and they made tiny meals. Everything in the office smelled of cabbage. Their faces went lined and apologetic and pale, sagging eventually into permanent pouchy frowns. Loss provoked a longing within him. He wanted the old. He wanted to reach out for and soothe the ghosts of their younger selves and make what was left of their bodies bloom. He wanted the young, who were doomed.

They didn't have to live this way. They could choose freedom. He did. He had a vocation, a vocation to love. To have a vocation, it is necessary to give up ambition and normality. He went to live in another place, where love was allowed because life there worked differently, and disease, and procreation. Those who went there could love without risk and come back clean. He did not want to come back. He gave up his desk and the smells of cabbage. He was called a whore.

This is not a story of other planets. It is a story of being driven from within. He was driven to a different place and a different time. Visitors came there to be loved, and he loved them. It was a paradise of politesse. There were the approaches, elegant or shy; and the jokes; and the fond farewells; and the mild embarrassment of separation when it did not work, and the kindly stroking of the hair that meant—this has been nice and now it is at an end. Some of them never believe he was not doing it for the money. They left, believing that.

The man began to see that he had set himself an unending task. You could not touch all human beauty, not unless you flung yourself in threads across the space between the worlds and stitched all the people and planets together in one sparkling cobweb. You could not do it, give or receive enough, unless you ceased to be human. A paradise of politesse was not quite enough.

His tastes began to change. He wanted to go in and not out, to stay with one person. He met the woman who was not real. He realized that this world had given her birth. Why she had chosen him, he did not know. Could she read his mind from his semen? First his tastes, and then his body had changed, from love and viruses.

And now he was bored with that, too.

He left the woman who was not real and walked across the austere tundra. His body had gone crazy. A steady stream of new life poured out of him, small and wet and sluglike, vomiting out of his mouth or dropping from the tip of his penis. He grew a pouch on his belly, to keep them warm. They would craw up his stomach on batwings or hooks that looked like a scorpion's sting. Others darted about him like hummingbirds. His nipples became hard and swollen, and they exuded a thick, salty, sweaty paste. His humming children bit them to force out food. The others hung on to the hair of his chest or on to each other, mouthing him.

Berries grew on bleak and blasted shrubbery. He ate them and the fleshy protuberances that popped, like mushrooms, out of the earth. As he ate them, he knew that genetic information was being passed on to him, and through his breasts, on to his strange children. His body grew crazier.

Then autumn came and all his children dropped from him like leaves.

After the first snow, he built himself a hollow in the snow drifts. He licked the walls and his spittle froze. He lived in the hollow, naked, warming it with his body heat. He would crawl up the warm and glassy tunnel and reach out of the entrance to gather the snow. It was alive. It tasted of muesli and semen. He was reminded then of people, real and unreal.

Why had he come here at all, if it were only to huddle alone in a room made of spit? He began to yearn for company. He began to yearn for the forest, but a forest untouched by fantasy. He was a contradiction. Without simplicity, it is difficult to move. He stayed where he was.

Until he began to see things moving on the other side of the spittle wall and tried to call to them. He could see them moving, within the ice.

Then he realized that they were only reflections of himself. He threw on his clothes and left the burrow in the middle of winter.

The snow was alive and it loved him. It settled over his shoulders and merged into a solid blanket of living matter that kept him warm. As he walked he turned his mouth up open to feed. Again the taste of semen.

The world was ripe with pheromones. It was the world that drew him, with constant subliminal promises of sex or something like it, of circumstance, of change. What use was an instinct when its end had no distinct form or shape? It was form or shape that he was seeking.

The snow fertilized his tongue. It grew plump and heavy. It ruptured as he was walking, spilling blood over his chin and down his throat. He knelt over the ice to see his reflection, holding out his tongue. It was covered with frantically wiggling, burrowing white tails. He sat down and wept, covering his face. It seemed that there was no way forward, no way back.

He broke off a piece of the ice and used it like a blade to scrape his tongue. The white things squealed and came free with peeling, suction-cup sounds. He wiped them onto the snow. The snow melted, absorbing them, pulling them down into itself.

He ate the ice. The ice was made of sugar. It was neutral, not alive, secreted by life, like the nuggets of sugar that had gathered along the stems of his houseplants back home. He still thought of the other world as home. He spurned the snow and survived the winter on ice.

He trudged south. Even the rays of light were sexual. They came at him a solid yellow. They shot through him, piercing him, making his flesh ache. They sent a dull yearning along the bones of forearm and thighs. His bones shifted in place with independent desire. They began to work their way loose, like teeth.

His left thigh broke free first. It tore its way out of his leg, pulling the perfect, cartilage-coated ball out of its socket with a sound like a kiss. The bone fell and was accepted by the snow, escaping. As he tried to find it, the bone above his right elbow ripped through his shoulder and followed, slipping out into the living snow. It too was lost. He was lame. He drank his own blood, to save his strength. He walked and slept and grew new children. They were new arms, new legs, many of them, but they would not do what he wanted. They had a will of their own. They pulled back the flesh of his face while he dozed, peeling back his lips so that he gave birth to his own naked skull. His bones wanted to become a coral reef. They did not let him move. The plates of his skull blossomed out in thin calcium petals, like a flower made of salt. He waited, wistful, patient, resting, hopeless.

The spring came. The snow grew into a fleshy forest, pink and veined. There were fat, leathery flowers, and wattle-trees that lowed like cattle. Pink asparagus ran on myriad roots, chattering. His bones grew into dungeons and turrets, brain-shaped swellings, spreading fans, encrusted shrubberies. His body lurked in hidden chambers and became carnivorous again. It would lunge out of its hiding like moray eels, to seize capering scraps of flesh, dragging them in, enfolding them in shells of bone with razor edges.

Finally he became bored. Bored and disgusted and able to move.

The coral reef stirred. With its first shifting, delicate towers crumbled and fell. They smashed the fantastic calcium spirals and bridges. They broke open the translucent domes of bone. The whole mass began to articulate, bend. He pulled himself free, slithering out of its many rooms.

He no longer resembled a human being. He lay on his back, unable to right himself. It was the first night of summer, warm and still. Lying on his back, he could see the stars. He tried to sing to himself, and his many mouths sang for him. The forest swayed slightly, asleep, in the wind.

He loved the world. He finally, finally came to it. Semen prised its way out from under his thousand eyelids, scorching his eyes. It flowed from his moray mouths, from his many anuses, and from his host of genitals, a leaping chorus the color of moonlight. The scrota burst, one after another, like poppy pods. He was no longer male. He slept in a pool of his own blood and sweat and semen.

By morning it had seeped away, given to this living world. The soil around him rippled, radiating outward. Everything was alive. Rain began to fall, washing him clean. Where he had touched the coral, he was stung and erupted in large red weals.

One of his children came to its father. It was no particular shape or gender. It had a huge mouth and was covered in lumps like acne. It was still an adolescent.

It found his real arms and legs, found the ones that were lame, and mumbled them, warming them. Deftly, with the tip of its tongue, it flicked bones out of itself and pushed them through the old wounds back into place. Then it pruned him, biting, cutting him free from his accretion of form, into an approximation of his old shape.

"Ride me," his child whispered. Exhausted, he managed to crawl onto its back. Hedgehog spines transfixed his hands and feet, holding him on to the back of his child. The thorns fed him, pumping sugar into his veins. As he rested, growing fat, he was carried.

His desires hauled him across the world. Staring up at the changing sky, he had opportunity to reflect. He could fly apart and pull himself together. His DNA could carry memory and desire into other bodies. DNA could combine with him, to make his living flesh behave in different ways. Was it only power that pushed him? To make the world like himself? Or was it that the world was so beautiful that the impulse was to devour it and be in turn devoured?

His child set him down in a cornfield. Great thick corn leaves bent broken-backed from their stalks like giant blades of grass and moved slightly in a comfortable breeze. He had never seen a cornfield, only read about them. He and this world together had fathered one.

"You have grown too heavy," said his child. Its speech was labored, the phrases short and punctuated with gasps for air. "How long do I have to live?"

"I don't know," he said. It blinked at him with tiny blue eyes. He kissed it and stroked the tuft of coarse hair on the top of its head. "Maybe I will grow wings," it said. Then it heaved its great bulk around and with sighs and shifting began its journey back.

The cornfield went on to the horizon. He reached up and broke off an ear of corn. When he bit into the cob, it bled. There was a scarecrow in the field. It waved to him. He looked away. He did not want to know it if were alive.

He walked along the ordered rows, deeper and deeper into the field. The air was warm, heavy, smelling of corn. Finally he came to a neatly cultivated border on top of the bank of a river. The bank was high and steep, the river muddy and slow moving.

He heard a whinnying. Rocking on its way back and forth up the steep slope came a palomino pony. Its blond, ragged mane hung almost down to the ground.

It stopped and stared at him. They looked at each other. "Where are you from?" he asked it, gently. Wind stirred its mane. There was bracken in it, tangled. The bracken looked brown and rough and real. "Where did you get that?" he asked it.

It snorted and waved its head up and down in the air, indicated the direction of the river.

"Are you hungry?" he asked. It went still. He worked an ear of corn loose from its stalk, peeled back its outer leaves, and held it out. The pony took it with soft and feeling lips, breaking it up in its mouth like an apple. The man pulled the bracken out of its mane.

It let him walk with it along the river. It was hardly waist-high and its back legs were so deformed by rickets that the knee joints almost rubbed together when it walked. He called it Lear, for its wild white hair and a crown of herbs.

They walked beside the cornfield. It ended suddenly, one last orderly row, and then there was a disorder of plants in a dry grassland: bay trees smelling of his youth, small pines decorated with lights and glass balls, feathery fennel, and mole hills with tiny smoking chimneys. Were they all his children?

They came to a plain of giant shells, empty and marble patterned. Something he had wished to become and abandoned. The air rustled in their empty sworls, the sound of wind; the sound of the sea; the sound of voices on foreign radio late at night, wavering and urgent.

All the unheard voices. The river became smaller and clearer, slapping over polished rocks on its way from the moors. The clouds were low and fast moving. The sun seemed always to be just peeking out over their edge, as if in a race with them.

They came to bracken and small twisted trees on spongy, moorland soil. There, Lear seemed to say, this is where I said I would take you. This is where you wanted to be. It waved its head up and down, and trotted away on deformed legs.

The man knelt and ate the grass. He tore up mouthfuls of it, flat, inert, and tasting only of chlorophyll and cellulose. It seemed to him to be as delicious as mint.

He walked into the water. It was stingingly cold, alien, clean. He gasped for breath—he always was such a coward about going into the water. He half ran, half swam across the pond and came up in the woodland on the opposite shore. Small, old oaks had moss instead of orchids. Rays of sunlight radiated from behind scurrying small clouds. The land was swept with light and shadow. Everything smelled of loam and leaf mold and whiplash hazel in shadow.

He sat down in a small clearing. There was a beech tree. Its trunk was smooth and sinuous, almost polished. The wind sighed up and down its length, and the tree moved with it. The soil moved, and out of it came his children, shapeless, formless, brushing his hand to be petted. "Home," they mewed.

Everything moved. Everything was alive in a paradise of reciprocity. The man who was real had fathered the garden that had fathered him.

The woman came and sat next to him. She was smaller, flabbier, with the beginnings of a double chin. "I'm real now," she said. They watched the trees dance until the four suns had set. All the stars began to sing.

Home

There was another one of them this morning, by Waterloo Station. He was a young lad. About a month ago, he had asked me for money. He said it was to feed his dog. He kept the animal inside his jacket, and it poked its head out. I remember thinking it looked too gentle a creature to live out on the street. The dog leaned out and tried to lick my hand.

"I'm sorry," I told him. "I only have twenty pence."

He had some sort of regional accent, rather pleasant actually. "Ach, I cannot take a man's last twenty pee."

"Take it, take it, I've got credit cards." Why do they beg for change when no one carries money anymore? Finally I got him to take it. The tips of his fingers were yellow.

He lived with others of his kind under a railway arch that had canvas across its mouth and a painted board over the top that announced that it was a Homeless Peoples' Theatre Group. Rather enterprising I thought, and I would have gone, except that they never put anything on. Sometimes when I walked past, there would be a fire behind the canvas and a few chords from a guitar. That took me back, I can tell you, just try to hear a guitar anywhere these days.

Someone had crucified him. He was hanging on a wire-mesh fence in front of a demolition site. A crowd of people were gawking at him, as though they were slightly but personally embarrassed by something. I think they were feeling a bit silly, grinning at each other, rather like they used to look when they lined up to see the Queen. Actually, I couldn't imagine what they were feeling.

Very suddenly all the boys, none of the girls, just the boys, began to dance in unison, a sort of gloomy square dance. Well, that was just too much for me, I couldn't make it out at all, I turned to an older woman who looked rather sensible. By older, I mean about thirty-five, and I said to her, "He had a dog. Has anyone seen his dog?"

She tutted. "They would have killed that too." She said it in the most extraordinary way. I simply could not understand her tone of voice. I think she felt it would have been a botched job if they had not killed the dog.

"You oughtn't to be allowed out," she said with a kind of crooked smile. Her intent may even have been kindly, to warn me. But there was a glint about it that I did not like. It is obviously going to be my fate from now on to understand every word that anyone says to me, but not a single sentence. I couldn't find the dog.

And I couldn't face the wait on the train platform either. I do hate stepping over sleeping bags, especially when they're full of person. I indulged and took a taxi.

"Steady, old boy, let me help you in," said the driver.

"Thank you," I said, trying to settle myself in, but my coat had twisted itself about me in the most uncomfortable way. "It's good to know that human beings are not an entirely extinct species."

He was looking at me in his mirror by now, his face closed up like a shop. I evidently was an old codger.

"There's just been another one of those killings," I said. "All these people smirking at the poor boy just as though someone had told a bad joke. Nobody trying to get the poor lad down from where they'd strung him up."

"Uh," he said. "Yeah." Yes. I was a boring old coot, and I was going to go on being boring.

"It's not decent. There wasn't a shred of acknowledgment that killing people is wrong."

The taxi driver shrugged. "Some people think it keeps the streets clear."

"Well, there's a lot of old people too. I suppose you'll be saying they ought to start on us next."

He roared with laughter. He nodded. I think he agreed.

I got out and watched him drive off, and it was only then that I realized I'd forgotten to get my coffee. Coffee, I'll have you know, was the whole reason for going to Waterloo in the first place. There used to be a little shop near me that sold coffee, nice young person ran it, rather old-fashioned, you know, dungarees and no makeup. I could talk to her. Now the only place left is near Waterloo, where they sell it to Frenchmen. It's like going into a sex shop. All nudges and winks and some sort of coffee-fiend argot. And I do resent being held up as some sort of laboratory specimen proving the harmlessness of caffeine.

"There you go," says the man behind the counter, and points to me. "He's still with us. Didn't do him any harm, did it?"

"I drink coffee because I like the taste," I say, and they all roar with laughter. Well, it's nice to find yourself a continual source of amusement to others.

I live in fear. I can't carry groceries, they're too heavy for me. Not that anyone knows what you mean when you use the word groceries. They send these food kits. You know, yeast tablets, vitamin E capsules. And the persons who deliver them are more terrifying than anything you'll see around Waterloo. They wear these tribal-mask things over their faces. I asked one of them once if it was something to do with air pollution. His response was to repeat the words "air pollution" several times over, at increasing volume. I think everyone imagines they're having to shout at people who are wearing headphones.

And I don't like those Home Help things. How is a computer supposed to know what's good for you? Bloody fascist health freaks. Always trying to replace a good cuppa with Hibiscus or Rose Hip— they all sound like plump women. I refuse to have my eating habits monitored by a machine. I'll eat and drink what I like, thank you very much.

———

I finally succeeded in getting my front door open, and there was my niece and her friend with their boots on my sofa. I can't say I like the way she drops in and uses my house, but you can't be an old stick all the time, can you. My niece is called Gertrude and her friend is Brunnhilde. Who gives people these names? They all sound like characters in grand opera.

"Tough time, Grumps?" Gertrude bellows. It's like trying to hold a conversation in the middle of a rugby pitch.

"You'll get marks on my sofa," I tell her.

"Not marks. Bloodstains," said Brunnhilde going all bug-eyed like a horror movie. Something else they don't have these days. Both girls are huge, vast, like something out of the first issue of *Superman*, you know, lifting vehicles single handed. I, in the meantime, am getting into a wrestling match with my coat and scarf. My coat and scarf are winning. Even my clothing is insolent these days.

"Here, let me do it for you," says Gertrude and takes them from me. "Wossa ma-ah, Grumps?" Her speech is interrupted by more glottal stops than a Morris Minor in need of a service.

"I saw another one of those bodies," I said.

"You weren't down Wa'ahloo, again, were you?" she said.

"It's where I get my coffee from," I said. "Or rather, used to."

"Coffee," says Brunnhilde and makes a moue of disgust the size of a bagel. "I'd rather drink paint stripper."

"Wa'ahloo is where all the dossers hang out, Grumps. Issa bloody wossa butcher shop."

Brunnhilde is rubbing her thighs in a way that I take to be sarcastic. "Maybe he likes a bit of excitement."

Gertrude giggles at the idea, and smoothes down my coat. For her, it lies still. I tell you the thing is alive and has it in for me. "Look, Grumps. Do yourself a favour. Stay north of the river. You don't know where the safe passages are."

"I refuse to accept that there are parts of this city where I must not walk."

"You don't go for a stroll down the middle of the motorway, do you? Come on, sit down."

I do as I'm told, but I'm still upset. My hands are shaking. They are also lumpy and blue and cold. "Why do they do it?" I say.

"Why do we do it, you mean," says Gertrude, plumping up a pillow.

"You do it?"

"Well, yeah. We all do it, Grumps. It's game. There's too many of them on the streets. If you know what you're doing, you don't get hurt. You know. You're out with your mates, you're in a gang, you see another gang. You leave each other alone."

"And go for the defenceless. Well, that is brave of you!"

Brunnhilde explains the rationale for me. "They're killing themselves with all that booze and fags." I remembered the yellow tips of that boy's fingers.

"Then let them do it in peace, you don't have to help them."

Oh dear. I'm shocked again. I can't accept that nice young people on a date will kill someone as part of the evening's entertainment. In my day, you felt racy if you fell down in the gutter. Stoned was lying on your back upside down and realizing you were trying to crawl across the sky.

"They're just using up resources," says Brunnhilde, and she stands up, and starts to case the joint. Her upper lip is working as her tongue runs back and forth over her teeth. It looks as though she has a mouthful of weasels. "You live here all alone, then?" she asks.

"I was married," I say.

"Nice place. Aren't you a bit scared living here all alone? With all this stuff?" She is fingering my Yemeni dagger. A souvenir of a very different time and place.

"Some of it must be worth a packet. Don't you feel unprotected?"

"Yes," I say. "All the time."

"Yeah. You could be here all alone and someone come in." She's taken the dagger out of its decorated sheath. It's curved and it gleams. It's not very sharp. It would hurt.

"In the end, it's all just things," I say.

"Oh, can I have some of them, then?" she asks, and giggles. I'm rather pleased to report that I was not frightened, simply aware of what was going on.

"Look at the poor old geezer," said Brunnhilde. "Using up space. Using up food." She looked at Gertrude. "Let's put him out of his misery."

"Honestly, Brum, you're such a wanker!" Gertrude said, and threw a pillow at her. "I mean, your idea of sport is to pitch into my old Grumps? Well, you do like a pulse-pounder, don't you?"

Brunnhilde looked downcast, as though she had failed to be elected Head Girl.

Gertrude was on her feet. "Come on, let's get you out before Grumps does you some collateral. Honestly. You can be so naff sometimes."

"All right then!" said Brunnhilde, biting back rather ineffectively. "Social work is not my forte anyway." She took a final slurp of my fruit juice. As she held the glass, she curled her little finger delicately away from it. Then Gertrude bundled her toward the door.

"See you later, Grumps. I'll take this wild woman off your hands."

"I wasn't frightened, you know." I said. I wanted her to know that.

"Course not. You're the hard type that goes to Waterloo." They both laughed, and the door closed. I heard Gertrude say outside. "S'all right. I'll get it all when he dies anyway."

I'm reasonably certain that Gertrude saved my life, but I don't think she thought that was very important. She did it rather as one might stop someone putting his greasy head on the antimacassars. I am so grateful for small favours.

But at least I understood what was happening.

I miss Amy, of course. I sometimes wonder if things would be any different if we'd had children, grandchildren. They would have turned out like Gertrude, I expect. Strangers, complete strangers, no matter how often I talked to them.

So, I bolted my door, and I went Home.

It is vaguely embarrassing. I expect I smiled to myself, slightly guilty, slightly ashamed, like those people gawking at corpses. Rigging myself up in all the gear, as though I were auditioning for a part in *Terminator II*. Better than the muck they put on these days, it's all like old Shirley Temple movies to me. I slip on the spectacles and I put on the boots and the gloves, and then I'm off Home.

Village near Witney, Oxfordshire, 1954. Church bells. The elms have not all died of disease, so there are banks of them, huge, high, billowing like clouds and squawking with rookeries. And all the Cotswold stone houses are lined up with thatched roofs and crooked windows in which sit Delft vases, and the Home Service is playing music so sensible it almost smells of toasted white bread. There used to be a country called England. I'm not the one who remembers this, though I was there. My bones remember it.

And I knock on a door and say, "Good morning, Mrs Clavell, is Kimberly there, please?" and then out comes my friend Kim.

Same age as me. We've taken recently to looking as we actually are, old fools. Kim has some snow-white hair left and his cheeks are mapped with purple veins. But we're wearing shorts and we can climb trees. We can climb to the pinnacle of the old ruined abbey, and there is no one guarding it and no one charging admission. No *son et lumière* for Japanese tourists. And do you know? Hardly even a ritual killing. It's ours.

Kim moved to California, and became both rich and poor at the same time as is the way in California, always about to make a film. He's even worse off than I am now, in some home, without another friend in the world, in someone else's country. But he's Home now.

We take the short cut, through the fields, past the hall. Here, the safe passages are ours, all the way to the river.

Warmth

I don't remember the first time I saw BETsi. She was like the air I breathed. She was probably there when I was born.

BETsi looked like a vacuum cleaner, bless her. She had long carpeted arms, and a carpeted top with loops of wool like hair. She was huggable, vaguely.

I don't remember hugging her much. I do remember working into that wool all kinds of unsuitable substances—spit, ice cream, dirt from the pots of basil.

My mother talked to BETsi about my behaviour. Mostly I remember my mother as a freckled and orange blur, always desperate to be moving, but sometimes she stayed still long enough for me to look at her.

"This is Booker, BETsi," my mother said at dictation speed. "You must stay clean, BETsi." She thought BETsi was stupid. She was the one who sounded like a robot. "Please repeat."

"I must stay clean," BETsi replied. BETsi sounded bright, alert, smooth-talking, with a built-in smile in the voice.

"This is what I mean, BETsi: You must not *let* Clancy get you dirty. Why do you let Clancy get you dirty?"

I pretended to do sums on a pretend calculator.

While BETsi said, "Because he is a boy. From the earliest age, most boys move in a very different, more aggressive way than girls. His form of play will be rougher and can be indulged in to a certain extent."

Booker had programmed BETsi to talk about my development in front of me. That was so I would know what was going on. It was honest in a way; she did not want me to be deceived. On the other hand, I felt

130

like some kind of long-running project in child psychology. Booker was more like a clinical consultant who popped in from time to time to see how things were progressing.

You see, I was supposed to be a genius. My mother thought she was a genius, and had selected my father out of a sperm bank for geniuses. His only flaw, she told me, was his tendency toward baldness. BETsi could have told her: baldness is inherited from the maternal line.

She showed me a picture of herself in an old *Cosmopolitan* article. It caused a stir at the time. *"The New Motherhood,"* it was called. *Business women choose a new way.*

There is a photograph of Booker looking young and almost pretty, beautifully lit and cradling her swollen tummy. Her whole face, looking down on herself, is illuminated with love.

In the article, she says: I know my son will be a genius. She says, I know he'll have the right genes, and I will make sure he has the right upbringing. *Cosmopolitan* made no comment. They were making a laughing stock out of her.

Look, my mother was Booker McCall, chief editor of a rival magazine company with a £100 million-a-year turnover and only fifteen permanent employees, of which she was second in command. Nobody had a corporate job in those days, and if they did, it was wall-to-wall politics and performance. Booker McCall had stakeholders to suck up to, editors to commission, articles to read and tear to pieces. She had layouts to throw at designers' heads. She had style to maintain, she had hair to keep up, shoes to repair, menus to plan. And then she had to score whatever she was on at the time. She was a very unhappy woman, with every reason to be.

She was also very smart, and BETsi was a good idea.

I used to look out of the window of the flat, and the outside world looked blue, gray, harsh. Sunlight always caught the grime on the glass and bleached everything out, and I thought that adults moved out into a hot world in which everybody shouted all the time. I never wanted to go out.

BETsi was my whole world. She had a screen, and she would show me paintings, one after another. Velasquez, Goya. She had a library of picture books—about monkeys or fishing villages or ghosts. She would allow me one movie a week, but always the right movie. *Jurassic Park, Beauty and the Beast, Tarzan on Mars.* We'd talk about them.

"The dinosaurs are made of light," she told me. "The computer tells the video what light to make and what colours the light should be so that it looks like a dinosaur."

"But dinosaurs really lived!" I remember getting very upset. I wailed at her. "They were really really real."

"Yes, but not those, those are just like paintings of dinosaurs."

"I want to see a real dinosaur!" I remember being heartbroken. I think I loved their size, their bulk, the idea of their huge hot breath. In my daydreams, I had a dinosaur for a friend and it would protect me in the world outside.

"Clancy," BETsi warned me. "You know what is happening now."

"Yes!" I shouted, "but knowing doesn't stop it happening!"

BETsi had told me that I was shy. Did you know that shyness has a clinical definition?

I'd been tested for it. Once, BETsi showed me the test. First she showed me what she called the benchmark. On her screen, through a haze of fingerprints and jam, was one fat, calm, happy baby. Not me. "In the test," BETsi explained, "a brightly coloured mobile is shown to the child. An infant who will grow up to be an outgoing and confident adult will tend to look at the mobile with calm curiosity for a time, get bored, and then look away."

The fat happy baby smiled a little bit, reached up for the spinning red ducks and bright yellow bunnies, then sighed and looked around for something new.

"A shy baby will get very excited. This is you, when we gave you the same test."

And there I was, looking solemn, two hundred years old at six months, my infant face crossed with some kind of philosophical puzzlement. Then, they show me the mobile. My face lights up, I start to bounce, I gurgle with pleasure, delight, spit shoots out of my mouth. I get over-excited, the mobile is slightly beyond my grasp. My face crumples up, I jerk with the first little cries. Moments later I am screaming myself purple, and trying to escape the mobile, which has begun to terrify me.

"That behaviour is hardwired," BETsi explained. "You will always find yourself getting too happy and then fearful and withdrawn. You must learn to control the excitement. Then you will be less fearful."

It's like with VR. When they first started making that, they discovered they did not know enough about how we see and hear to duplicate the experience. They had to research people first. Same here. Before they could mimic personality, they first had to find out a lot more about what personality was.

BETsi had me doing Transcendental Meditation and yoga at three years old. She had me doing what I now recognize was Alexander Technique. I didn't just nap, I had my knees up and my head on a raised wooden pillow. This was to elongate my back—I was already curling inward from tension.

After she got me calm, BETsi would get me treats. She had Booker's credit-card number and authorization to spend. BETsi could giggle. When the ice cream was delivered, or the new CD full of clip art, or my new S&M Toddler black-leather gear, or my Barbie Sex-Change doll, BETsi would giggle.

I know. She was programmed to giggle so that I would learn it was all right to be happy. But it sounded as though there was something who was happy just because I was. For some reason, that meant I would remember all by myself to stay calm.

"I'll open it later," I would say, feeling very adult.

"It's ice cream, you fool," BETsi would say. "It'll melt."

"It will spread all over the carpet!" I whispered in delight.

"Booker will get ma-had." BETsi said in a sing-song voice. BETsi knew that I always called Booker by her name.

BETsi could learn. She would have had to be trained to recognize and respond to my voice and Booker's. She was programmed to learn who I was and what I needed. I needed conspiracy. I needed a confidant.

"Look. You melt the ice cream and I will clean it up," she said.

"It's ice cream, you fool," I giggled back. "If it melts, I won't be able to eat it!" We both laughed.

BETsi's screen could turn into a mirror. I'd see my own face and inspect it carefully for signs of being like Tarzan. Sometimes, as a game, she would have my own face talk back to me in my own voice. Or I would give myself a beard and a deeper voice to see what I would look like as a grown up. To have revenge on Booker, I would make myself bald.

I was fascinated by men. They were mythical beasts, huge and loping like dinosaurs, only hairy. The highlight of my week was when the window cleaner arrived. I would trail after him, too shy to speak, trying to puff myself up to the same size as he was. I thought he was a hero, who cleaned windows and then saved people from evil.

"You'll have to bear with Clancy," BETsi would say to him. "He doesn't see many men."

"Don't you get out, little fella?" he would say. His name was Tom.

"It's not safe," I managed to answer.

Tom tutted. "Oh, that's true enough. What a world, eh? You have to keep the kiddies locked in all day. S'like a prison." I thought that all men had South London accents.

He talked to BETsi as if she was a person. I don't think Tom could have been very bright, but I do think he was a kindly soul. I think BETsi bought him things to give to me.

"Here's an articulated," he said once, and gave me a beautifully painted Matchbox lorry.

I took it in silence. I hated myself for being so tongue-tied. I wanted to swagger around the flat with him like Nick Nolte or Wesley Snipes.

"Do men drive in these?" I managed to ask.

"Some of them, yeah."

"Are there many men?"

He looked blank. I answered for him. "There's no jobs for men."

Tom hooted with laughter. "Who's been filling your head?" he asked.

"Clancy has a very high symbol-recognition speed," BETsi told him. "Not genius, you understand. But very high. It will be useful for him in interpretative trades. However, he has almost no spatial reasoning. He will only ever dream of being a lorry driver."

"I'm a klutz," I translated.

Booker was an American—probably the most famous American in London at the time. BETsi was programmed to modulate her speech to match her owners. To this day, I can't tell English and American accents apart unless I listen carefully. And I can imitate neither. I talk like BETsi.

I remember Tom's face, like a suet pudding, pale, blotchy, uneasy. "Poor little fella," he said. "I'd rather not know all that about myself."

"So would Clancy," said BETsi. "But I am programmed to hide nothing from him."

Tom sighed. "Get him with other kids," he told her.

"Oh, that is all part of the plan," said BETsi.

I was sent to Social Skills class. I failed. I discovered that I was terrified without BETsi, that I did not know what to do or say to people when she wasn't there. I went off into a corner with a computer screen, but it seemed cold, almost angry with me. If I didn't do exactly the right thing it wouldn't work, and it never said anything nice to me. The other children were like ghosts. They flittered around the outside of my perceptions. In my mind, I muted the noise they made. They sounded as if they were shouting from the other side of the window, from the harsh blue-gray world.

The consultants wrote on my first report: Clancy is socially backward, even for his age.

Booker was furious. She showed up one Wednesday and argued about it.

"Do you realize that a thing like that could get in my son's record!"

"It happens to be true, Miss McCall." The consultant was appalled and laughed from disbelief.

"This crèche leaves children unattended and blames them when their development is stunted." Booker was yelling and pointing at the woman. "I want that report changed. Or I will report on you!"

"Are you threatening to write us up in your magazines?" the consultant asked in a quiet voice.

"I'm telling you not to victimize my son for your own failings. If he isn't talking to the other children, it's your job to help him."

Talking to other kids was my job. I stared at my shoes, mortified. I didn't want Booker to help me, but I half wanted her to take me out of the class, and I knew that I would hate it if she did.

I went to BETsi for coaching.

"What you may not know," she told me, "is that you have a natural warmth that attracts people."

"I do?" I said.

"Yes. And all most people want from other people is that they be interested in them. Shall we practice?"

On her screen, she invented a series of children. I would try to talk to them. BETsi didn't make it easy.

"Do you like reading?" I'd ask a little girl on the screen.

"What?" she replied with a curling lip.

"Books," I persisted, as brave as I could be. "Do you read books?"

She blinked—bemused, bored, confident.

"Do . . . do you like *Jurassic Park*?"

"It's old! And it doesn't have any story."

"Do you like new movies?" I was getting desperate.

"I play games. *Bloodlust Demon*." The little girl's eyes went narrow and fierce. That was it. I gave up.

"BETsi," I complained. "This isn't fair." Booker would not allow me to play computer games.

BETsi chuckled and used her own voice. "That's what it's going to be like, kiddo."

"Then show me some games."

"Can't," she said.

"Not in the program," I murmured angrily.

"If I tried to show you one, I'd crash," she explained.

So I went back to Social Skills class determined to talk and it was every bit as awful as BETsi had said, but at least I was ready.

I told them all, straight out: I can't play games, I'm a klutz, all I can do is draw. So, I said, tell me about the games.

And that was the right thing to do. At five I gave up being Tarzan and started to listen, because the kids could at least tell me about video games. They could get puffed up and important, and I would seep envy, which must have been very satisfying for them. But. In a funny kind of way they sort of liked me.

There was a bully called Ian Aston, and suddenly one day the kids told him: "Clancy can't fight, so don't pick on him." He couldn't stand up to all of them.

"See if your Mum will let you visit," they said, "and we'll show you some games."

Booker said no. "It's very nice you're progressing socially, Clancy. But I'm not having you mix just yet. I know what sort of things are in the homes of parents like that, and I'm not having you exposed."

"Your mum's a posh git," the children said.

"And a half," I replied.

She was also a drug addict. One evening she didn't collect me from Social Class. The consultant tried to reach her PDA, and couldn't.

"You have a Home Help, don't you?" the consultant asked.

She rang BETsi. BETsi said she had no record in her diary of where Miss McCall might be if not collecting me. BETsi sent round a taxi.

Booker was out for two weeks. She just disappeared.

She'd collapsed on the street, and everything was taken—her handbag, her shoes, her PDA, even her contact lenses. She woke up blind and raving from barbiturate withdrawal in an NHS ward, which would have mortified her. She claimed to be Booker McCall and several other people as well. I suppose it was also a kind of breakdown. Nobody knew who she was, nobody told us what had happened.

BETsi and I just sat alone in the apartment, eating ice cream and Kellogg's Crunchy Nut Cornflakes.

"Do you suppose Booker will ever come back?" I asked her.

"I do not know where Booker is, Kiddo. I'm afraid something bad must have happened to her."

I felt guilty because I didn't care. I didn't care if Booker never came back. But I was scared.

"What happens if you have a disk fault?" I asked BETsi.

"I've just renewed the service contract," she replied. She whirred closer to me, and put a carpeted arm around me.

"But how would they know that something was wrong?"

She gave me a little rousing shake. "I'm monitored all day so that if there is a problem when your mother isn't here, they come round and repair me."

"But what if you're broken for a real long time? Hours and hours. Days?"

"They'll have a replacement."

"I don't want a replacement."

"In a few hours, she'll be trained to recognize your voice."

"What if it doesn't work? What if the contractors don't hear? What do I do then?"

She printed out a number to call, and a password to enter.

"It probably won't happen," she said. "So I'm going to ask you to do your exercises."

She meant to calm me down, as if my fears weren't real, as if it couldn't happen that a machine would break down.

"I don't want to do my exercises. Exercises won't help."

"Do you want to see *Jurassic Park*?" she asked.

"It's old," I said, and thought of my friends at Social Class and of their mothers who were with them.

There was a whirring sound. A panel came up on the screen, like what happened during a service when the engineers came and checked her programming and reloaded the operational system. CONFIGURA-TION OVERRIDE the panels said.

When that was over, BETsi asked, "Would you like to learn how to play *Bloodlust Demon*?"

"Oh!" I said and nothing else. "Oh! Oh! BETsi! Oh!"

And she giggled.

I remember the light on the beige carpet making a highway toward the screen. I remember the sound of traffic outside, peeping, hooting, the sound of nightfall and loneliness, the time I usually hated the most. But now I was playing *Bloodlust Demon*.

I played it very badly. I kept getting blown up.

"Just keep trying," she said.

"I have no spatial reasoning," I replied. I was learning that I did not like computer games. But for the time being, I had forgotten everything else.

After two weeks, I assumed that Booker had gotten bored and had gone away and would never be back. Then one morning, when the hot world seemed to be pouring in through the grimy windows, someone kicked down the front door.

BETsi made a cage around me with her arms.

"I am programmed for both laser and bullet defence. Take what you want, but do not harm the child. I cannot take your photograph or video you. You will not be recognized. There is no need to damage me."

They broke the glass tables, they threw drawers onto the floor. They dropped their trousers and shat in the kitchen. They took silver dresses, Booker's black box, her jewellry. One of the thieves took hold of my Matchbox lorry, and I knew the meaning of loss. I was going to lose my truck. Then the thief walked back across the carpet toward me. BETsi's arms closed more tightly around me. The thief chuckled under his ski mask and left the truck nearby on the sofa.

"There you go, little fella," he said. I never told anyone. It was Tom. Like I said, he wasn't very bright. BETsi was programmed not to recognize him.

So. I knew then what men were; they could go bad. There was part of them that was only ever caged up. I was frightened of men after that.

The men left the door open, and the flat was a ruin, smashed and broken, and BETsi's cage of arms was lifted up, and I began to cry, and then I began to scream over and over and over, and finally some neighbours came, and finally the search was on for Booker McCall.

How could an editor-in-chief disappear for two weeks? "We thought she'd gone off with a new boyfriend," her colleagues said, in the press, to damage her. Politics, wall to wall. It was on TV, the Uncaring Society they called it. No father, no grandparents, neighbours who were oblivious— the deserted child was only found because of a traumatic break-in.

Booker was gone a very long time. Barbiturates are the worst withdrawal of all. I visited her, with one of the consultants from my Class. It got her picture in the papers, and a caption that made it sound as though the consultants were the only people who cared.

Booker looked awful. Bright yellow with blue circles under her eyes. She smelled of thin stale sweat.

"Hello, Clancy," she whispered. "I've been in withdrawal."

So what? Tell me something I didn't know. I was hard-hearted. I had been deserted; she had no call on my respect.

"Did you miss me?" She looked like a cut flower that had been left in a vase too long, with smelly water.

I didn't want to hurt her, so all I said was: "I was scared."

"Poor baby," she whispered. She meant it, but the wave of sympathy exhausted her and she lay back on the pillow. She held out her hand.

I took it and I looked at it.

"Did BETsi take good care of you?" she asked, with her eyes closed.

"Yes," I replied, and began to think, still looking at her fingers. She really can't help all of this, all of this is hardwired. I bet she'd like to be like BETsi, but can't. Anyway, barbiturates don't work on metal and plastic.

Suddenly she was crying, and she'd pushed my hand onto her moist cheek. It was sticky and I wanted to get away, and she said, "Tell me a story. Tell me some beautiful stories."

So I sat and told her the story of *Jurassic Park*. She lay still, my hand on her cheek. At times I thought she was asleep; other times I found I hoped she loved the story as much as I did, raptors and brachiosaurs and T Rex. When I was finished, she murmured, "At least somebody's happy." She meant me. That was what she wanted to think, that I was all right, that she would not have to worry about me. And that, too, I realized, would never change.

She came home. She stayed in bed all day for two more weeks, driving me nuts. "My life is such a mess!" she said, itchy and anxious. She promised me she would spend more time with me, God forbid. She raged against the bastards at BPC. We'd be moving as soon as she was up, she promised me, filling my heart with terror. She succeeded in disrupting my books, my movies, my painting. Finally she threw off the sheets a month early and went back to work. I gathered she still went in for treatment every fortnight. I gathered that booze now took the place of barbies. The smell of the flat changed. And now that I hated men, there were a lot of them, loose after work.

"This is my boy," she would say with a kind of wobbly pride and introduce me to yet another middle-aged man with a ponytail. "Mr. d'Angelo is a designer," she would say, as if she went out with their professions. She started to wear wobbly red lipstick. It got everywhere, on pillows, sheets, walls, and worst of all on my Nutella tumblers.

The flat had been my real world, against the outside, and now all that had changed. I went to school. I had to say goodbye to BETsi, every morning, and goodbye to Booker, who left wobbly red lipstick on my collar. I went to school in a taxi.

"You see," said BETsi after my first day. "It wasn't bad was it? It works, doesn't it?"

"Yes, BETsi," I remember saying. "It does." The "it" was me. We both meant my precious self. She had done her job.

———

Through my later school days, BETsi would sit unused in my room—most of the time. Sometimes at night, under the covers, I would reboot her, and the screen would open up to all the old things, still there. My childhood was already another world—dinosaurs and space cats and puzzles. BETsi would pick up where we had left off, with no sense of neglect, no sense of time or self.

"You're older," she would say. "About twelve. Let me look at you." She would mirror my face, and whir to herself. "Are you drawing?"

"Lots," I would say.

"Want to mess around with the clip art, Kiddo?" she would ask.

And long into the night, when I should have been learning algebra, we would make collages on her screen. I showed surfers on waves that rose up amid galaxies blue and white in space, and through space there poured streams of roses. A row of identical dancing Buddhas was an audience.

"Tell me about your friends, and what you do," she asked as I cut and pasted. And I'd tell her about my friend John and his big black dog, Toro, and how we were caught in his neighbours' garden. I ran and escaped, but John was caught. John lived outside town in the countryside. And I'd tell her about John's grandfather's farm, full of daffodils in rows. People use them to signal spring, to spell the end of winter. Symbol recognition.

"I've got some daffodils," BETsi said. "In my memory."

And I would put them into the montage for her, though it was not spring any longer.

I failed at algebra. Like everything else in Booker's life, I was something that did not quite pan out as planned. She was good about it. She never upbraided me for not being a genius. There was something in the way she ground out her cigarette that said it all.

"Well, there's always art school," she said and forced out a blast of blue-white smoke.

It was BETsi I showed my projects to—the A-level exercises in sketching elephants in pencil.

"From a photo," BETsi said. "You can always tell. So. You can draw as well as a photograph. Now what?"

"That's what I think," I said. "I need a style of my own."

"You need to do that for yourself," she said.

"I know," I said, casually.

"You won't always have me to help," she said.

The one thing I will never forgive Booker for is selling BETsi without telling me. I came back from first term at college to find the machine gone. I remember that I shouted, probably for the first time ever. "You did what?"

I remember Booker's eyes widening, blinking. "It's just a machine, Clancy. I mean, it wasn't as if she was a member of the family or anything."

"How could you do it! Where is she?"

"I don't know. I didn't think you'd be so upset. You're being awfully babyish about this."

"What did you do with her?"

"I sold her back to the contract people, that's all." Booker was genuinely bemused. "Look. You are hardly ever here—it isn't as though you use her for anything. She's a child-development tool, for Chrissakes. Are you still a child?"

I'd thought Booker had been smart. I'd thought that she had recognized she would not have time to be a mother, and so had brought in BETsi. I thought that meant she understood what BETsi was. She didn't, and that meant she had not understood, not even been smart.

"You," I said, "have sold the only real mother I have ever had." I was no longer shouting. I said it at dictation speed. I'm not sure Booker has ever forgiven me.

Serial numbers, I thought. They have serial numbers, maybe I could trace her through those. I rang up the contractors. The kid on the phone sighed.

"You want to trace your BETsi," he said before I'd finished, sounding bored.

"Yes," I said. "I do."

He grunted and I heard a flicker of fingertips on a keyboard.

"She's been placed with another family. Still operational. But," he said, "I can't tell you where she is."

"Why not?"

"Well, Mr. McCall. Another family is paying for the service, and the developer is now working with another child. Look. You are not unusual, OK? In fact this happens about half the time, and we cannot have customers disturbed by previous charges looking up their machines."

"Why not?"

"Well," he chortled; it was so obvious to him. "You might try imagining it from the child's point of view. They have a new developer of their own, and then this other person, a stranger, tries to muscle in."

"Just. Please. Tell me where she is."

Her memory has been wiped," he said abruptly.

It took a little while. I remember hearing the hiss on the line.

"She won't recognize your voice. She won't remember anything about you. She is just a service vehicle. Try to remember that."

I wanted to strangle the receiver. I sputtered down the line like a car cold-starting. "Don't... couldn't you keep a copy! You know this happens, you bastard. Couldn't you warn people, offer them the disk? Something?

"I'm sorry, sir, but we do, and you turned the offer down."

"I'm sorry?" I was dazed.

"That's what your entry says."

Booker, I thought. Booker, Booker, Booker. And I realized; she couldn't understand, she's just too old. She's just from another world.

"I'm sorry, sir, but I have other calls on the line."

"I understand," I replied.

All my books, all my collages, my own face in the mirror. It had been like a library I could visit whenever I wanted to see something from the past. It was as if my own life had been wiped.

Then for some reason, I remembered Tom. He was fat and forty and defeated, a bloke. I asked him to break in to the contractor's office and read the files and find who had her.

"So," he said. "You knew then."

"Yup."

He blew out hard through his lips and looked at me askance.

"Thanks for the lorry," I said, by way of explanation.

"I always liked you, you know. You were a nice little kid." His fingers were tobacco-stained. "I can see why you want her back. She was all you had."

He found her all right. I sent him a cheque. Sometimes even now I send him a cheque.

Booker would have been dismayed—BETsi had ended in a resold council flat. I remember, the lift was broken and the stairs smelled of pee. The door itself was painted fire-engine red and had a nonbreakable plaque on the doorway. The Andersons, it said amid ceramic pansies. I knocked.

BETsi answered the door. Boom. There she was, arms extended defensively to prevent entry. She'd been cleaned up, but there was still rice pudding in her hair. Beyond her, I saw a slumped three-piece suite and beige carpet littered with toys. There was a smell of baby food and damp flannel.

"BETsi?" I asked and knelt down in front of her. She scanned me, clicking. I could almost see the wheels turning, and for some reason, I found it funny. "It's OK," I said. "You won't know me, dear."

"Who is it, Betty?" A little girl came running. To breathe the air that flows in through an open door, to see someone new, to see anyone at all.

"A caller, Bumps," replied BETsi. Her voice was different, a harsher, East End lilt. "And I think he's just about to be on his way."

I found that funny too; I still forgave her. It wasn't her fault. Doughty old BETsi still doing her job, with this doubtful man she didn't know trying to gain entry.

There might be, though, one thing she could do.

I talked to her slowly. I tried to imitate an English accent. "You do not take orders from someone with my voice. But I mean no harm, and you may be able to do this. Can you show me my face on your screen?"

She whirred. Her screen flipped out of sleep. There I was.

"I am an old charge of yours," I said—both of us, me and my image, his voice echoing mine. "My name is Clancy. All I ask you to do is remember me. Can you do that?"

"I understand what you mean," she said. "I don't have a security reason not to."

"Thank you," I said. "And. See if you can program the following further instructions."

"I cannot take instruction from you."

"I know. But check if this violates security. Set aside part of your memory. Put Bumps into it. Put me and Bumps in the same place, so that even when they wipe you again. You'll remember us."

She whirred. I began to get excited; I talked like myself.

"Because they're going to wipe you BETsi, whenever they resell you. They'll wipe you clean. It might be nice for Bumps if you remember her. Because we'll always remember you."

The little girl's eyes were on me, dark and serious, two hundred years old. "Do what he says, Betty," the child said.

Files opened and closed like mouths. "I can put information in an iced file," said BETsi. "It will not link with any other files, so it will not be usable to gain entry to my systems." Robots and people: these days we all know too much about our inner workings.

I said thank you and goodbye, and said it silently looking into the eyes of the little girl, and she spun away on her heel as if to say: I did that.

I still felt happy, running all the way back to the tube station. I just felt joy.

So that's the story.

It took me a long time to make friends in school, but they were good ones. I still know them, though they are now middle-aged men, clothiers in Toronto, or hearty freelancers in New York who talk about their men and their cats. Make a long story short. I grew up to be one of the people my mother used to hire and abuse.

I am a commercial artist, though more for book and CD covers than magazines. I'm about to be a dad. One of my clients, a very nice woman. We used to see each other and get drunk at shows. In the hotel bedrooms

I'd see myself in the mirror—not quite middle-aged, but with a pony tail. Her name is some kind of mistake. Bertha.

Bertha is very calm and cool and reliable. She called me and said coolly, I'm having a baby and you're the father, but don't worry. I don't want anything from you.

I wanted her to want something from me. I wanted her to say marry me, you bastard. Or at least: could you take care of it on weekends? Not only didn't she want me to worry—it was clear that she didn't want me at all. It was also clear I could expect no more commissions from her.

I knew then what I wanted to do. I went to Hamleys.

There they were, the Next Degradation. Now they call them things like Best Friend or Home Companions, and they've tried to make them look human. They have latex skins and wigs and stiff little smiles. They look like burn victims after plastic surgery, and they recognize absolutely everybody. Some of them are modeled after *Little Women*. You can buy Beth or Amy or Jo. Some poor little rich girls started dressing them up in high fashion—the bills are said to be staggering. You can also buy male models—a lively Huckleberry, or big Jim. I wonder if those might not be more for the mums, particularly if all parts are in working order.

"Do you…do you have any older models?" I ask at the counter.

The assistant is a sweet woman, apple cheeked, young, pretty, and she sees straight through me. "We have BETsis," she says archly.

"They still make them?" I say, softly.

"Oh, they're very popular," she says, and pauses, and decides to drop the patter. "People want their children to have them. They loved them."

History repeats like indigestion.

I turn up at conventions like this one. I can't afford a stand but my livelihood depends on getting noticed anyway.

And if I get carried away and believe a keynote speaker trying to be a visionary, if he talks about, say, Virtual Government or Loose Working Practices, then I get overexcited. I think I see God, or the future or something and I get all jittery. And I go into the exhibition hall and there is a wall of faces I don't know and I think: I've got to talk to them, I've got to sell to them. I freeze, and I go back to my room.

And I know what to do. I think of BETsi, and I stretch out on the floor and take hold of my shoulders and my breathing and I get off the emotional roller-coaster. I can go back downstairs, and back into the hall. And I remember that something once said: you have a natural warmth that attracts people, and I go in, and even though I'm a bit diffident, by the end of the convention, we're laughing and shaking hands, and I have their business card. Or maybe we've stayed up drinking till four in the morning, playing *Bloodlust Demon*. They always win. They like that, and we laugh.

It is necessary to be loved. I'm not sentimental: I don't think a computer loved me. But I was hugged, I was noticed, I was cared for. I was made to feel that I was important, special, at least to something. I fear for all the people who do not have that. Like everything else, it is now something that can be bought. It is therefore something that can be denied. It is possible that without BETsi, I might have to stay upstairs in that hotel room, panicked. It is possible that I would end up on barbiturates. It is possible that I could have ended up one of those sweet sad people sitting in the rain in shop doorways saying the same thing in London or New York, in exactly the same accent: any spare change please?

But I didn't. I put a proposition to you.

If there were a God who saw and cared for us and was merciful, then when I died and went to Heaven, I would find among all the other things, a copy of that wiped disk.

Everywhere

When we knew Granddad was going to die, we took him to see the Angel of the North.

When he got there, he said: It's all different. There were none of these oaks all around it then, he said, Look at the size of them! The last time I saw this, he says to me, I was no older than you are now, and it was brand new, and we couldn't make out if we liked it or not.

We took him, the whole lot of us, on the tram from Blaydon. We made a day of it. All of Dad's exes and their exes and some of their kids and me aunties and their exes and their kids. It wasn't that happy a group to tell you the truth. But Granddad loved seeing us all in one place.

He was going a bit soft by then. He couldn't tell what the time was anymore and his words came out wrong. The mums made us sit on his lap. He kept calling me by my dad's name. His breath smelt funny but I didn't mind, not too much. He told me about how things used to be in Blaydon.

They used to have a gang in the Dene called Pedro's Gang. They drank something called Woodpecker and broke people's windows and they left empty tins of pop in the woods. If you were little you weren't allowed out cos everyone's mum was so fearful and all. Granddad once saw twelve young lands go over and hit an old woman and take her things. One night his brother got drunk and put his fist through a window, and he went to the hospital, and he had to wait hours before they saw him and that was terrible.

I thought it sounded exciting meself. But I didn't say so because Granddad wanted me to know how much better things are now.

He says to me, like: the trouble was, Landlubber, we were just kids, but we all thought the future would be terrible. We all thought the world was going to burn up, and that everyone would get poorer and poorer, and the crime worse.

He told me that lots of people had no work. I don't really understand how anyone could have nothing to do. But then I've never got me head around what money used to be either.

Or why they built that Angel. It's not even that big, and it was old and covered in rust. It didn't look like an Angel to me at all, the wings were so big and square. Granddad said, no, it looks like an airplane, that's what airplanes looked like back then. It's meant to go rusty, it's the Industrial Spirit of the North.

I didn't know what he was on about. I asked Dad why the Angel was so important and he kept explaining it had a soul, but couldn't say how. The church choir showed up and started singing hymns. Then it started to rain. It was a wonderful day out.

I went back to the tram and asked me watch about the Angel.

This is me watch, here, see? It's dead good isn't it, it's got all sorts on it. It takes photographs and all. Here, look, this is the picture it took of Granddad by the Angel. It's the last picture I got of him. You can talk to people on it. And it keeps thinking of fun things for you to do.

Why not explain to the interviewer why the Angel of the North is important?
Duh. Usually they're fun.

Take the train to Newcastle and walk along the river until you see on the hill where people keep their homing pigeons. Muck out the cages for readies.

It's useful when you're a bit short, it comes up with ideas to make some dosh.

It's really clever. It takes all the stuff that goes on around here and stirs it around and comes up with something new. Here, listen:

The laws of evolution have been applied to fun. New generations of ideas are generated and eliminated at such a speed that evolution works in real time. It's survival of the funnest and you decide.

They evolve machines, too. Have you seen our new little airplanes?

They've run the designs through thousands of generations, and they got better and faster and smarter.

The vicar bought the whole church choir airplanes they can wear. The wings are really good, they look just like bird's wings with pinions sticking out like this. Oh! I really want one of them. You can turn somersaults in them. People build them in their sheds for spare readies, I could get one now if I had the dosh.

Every Sunday as long as it isn't raining, you can see the church choir take off in formation. Little old ladies in leotards and blue jeans and these big embroidered Mexican hats. They rev up and take off and start to sing the Muslim call to prayer. They echo all over the show. Then they cut their engines and spiral up on the updraft. That's when they start up on "Nearer My God to Thee."

Every Sunday, Granddad and I used to walk up Shibbon Road to the Dene. It's so high up there that we could look down on top of them. He never got over it. Once he laughed so hard he fell down, and just lay there on the grass. We just lay on our backs and looked up at the choir, they just kept going up like they were kites.

When the Travellers come to Blaydon, they join in. Their wagons are pulled by horses and have calliopes built into the front, so on Sundays, when the choir goes up, the calliopes start up, so you got organ music all over the show as well. Me dad calls Blaydon a sound sandwich. He says it's all the hills.

The Travellers like our acoustics, so they come here a lot. They got all sorts to trade. They got these bacteria that eat rubbish, and they hatch new machines, like smart door keys that only work for the right people. They make their own beer, but you got to be a bit careful how much you drink.

Granddad and I used to take some sarnies and our sleeping bags and kip with them. The Travellers go everywhere, so they sit around the fire and tell about all sorts going on, not just in England but France and Italia. One girl, her mum let her go with them for a whole summer. She went to Prague and saw all these Buddhist monks from Thailand. They were Travellers and all.

Granddad used to tell the Travellers his stories, too. When he was young he went to Mexico. India. The lot. You could in them days. He even went to Egypt, my granddad. He used to tell the Travellers the same stories, over and over, but they never seemed to notice. Like, when he was in Egypt he tried to rent this boat to take him onto the Delta, and he couldn't figure why it was so expensive, and when he got on it he found he'd rented a car ferry all to himself by mistake. He had the whole thing to himself. The noise of the engines scared off the birds which was the only reason he'd wanted the boat.

So, Granddad was something of a Traveller himself. He went everywhere.

There's all sorts to do around Blaydon. We got dolphins in the municipal swimming pool.

We dug it ourselves, in the Haughs just down there by the river. It's tidal, our river. Did you know? It had dolphins anyway, but our pool lured them in. They like the people and the facilities, like the video conferencing. They like video conferencing, do dolphins. They like being fed and all.

My dad and I help make the food. We grind up fish heads on a Saturday at Safeways. It smells rotten to me, but then I'm not an aquatic mammal, am I? That's how we earned the readies to buy me my watch. You get everyone along grinding fish heads, everybody takes turns. Then you get to go to the swimming.

Sick people get first crack at swimming with the dolphins. When Granddad was sick, he'd take me with him. There'd be all this steam coming off the water like in a vampire movie. The dolphins always knew who wasn't right, what was wrong with them. Mrs Grathby had trouble with her joints, they always used to be gentle with her, just nudge her along with their noses like. But Granddad, there was one he called Liam. Liam always used to jump up and land real hard right next to him, splash him all over and Granddad would push him away, laughing like, you know? He loved Liam. They were pals.

Have a major water-fight on all floors of the Grand Hotel in Newcastle.

Hear that? It just keeps doing that until something takes your fancy.

Call your friend Heidi and ask her to swap clothes with you and pretend to be each other for a day.

Aw Jeez! Me sister's been wearing me watch again! It's not fair! It mucks it up, it's supposed to know what I like, not her and that flipping Heidi. And she's got her own computer, it's loads better than mine, it looks like a shirt and has earphones, so no one else can hear it. It's not fair! People just come clod-hopping through. You don't get to keep nothing.

Look this is all I had to do to get this watch!

Grind fishfood on 3.11, 16.11, 20.12 and every Sunday until 3.3
Clean pavements three Sundays
Deliver four sweaters for Step Mum
Help Dad with joinery for telecoms outstation
Wire up Mrs Grathby for video immersion
Attend school from April 10ᵗʰ to 31 July inclusive

I did even more than that. At least I got some over. I've saving up for a pair of cars.

Me and me mates love using the cars. I borrow me dad's pair. You wear them like shoes, and they're smart. It's great fun on a Sunday. We all go whizzing down Lucy Street together, which is this great big hill, but the shoes won't let you go too fast or crash into anything. We all meet up, whizz around in the mall in a great big serpent. You can pre-programme all the cars together, so you all break up and then all at once come back together, to make shapes and all.

Granddad loved those cars. He hated his stick, so he'd go shooting off in me dad's pair, ducking and weaving, and shouting back to me, Come on, Landlubber, keep up! I was a bit scared in them days, but he kept up at me 'til I joined in. He'd get into those long lines, and we'd shoot off the end of them, both of us. He'd hold me up.

He helped me make me lantern and all. Have you seen our lanterns, all along the mall? They look good when the phosphors go on at night. All the faces on them are real people, you know. You know the ink on them's made of these tiny chips with legs? Dad's seen them through a microscope, he says they look like synchronized swimmers.

I got one with my face on it. I was a bit younger then so I have this really naff crew cut. Granddad helped me make it. It tells jokes. I'm not very good at making jokes up, but Granddad had this old joke book. At least I made the effort.

Let's see, what else. There's loads around here. We got the sandbox in front of the old mall. Everybody has a go at that, making things. When King William died all his fans in wheelchairs patted together a picture of him in sand. Then it rained. But it was a good picture.

Our sandbox is a bit different. It's got mostly real sand. There's only one corner of it computer dust. It's all right for kids and that or people who don't want to do things themselves. I mean when we were little we had the dust make this great big 3D sign Happy Birthday Granddad Piper. He thought it was wonderful because if you were his age and grew up with PCs and that, it must be wonderful, just to think of something and have it made.

I don't like pictures, they're too easy. Me, I like to get stuck in. If I go to the sandbox to make something, I want to come back with sand under me fingernails. Me dad's the same. When Newcastle won the cup, me and me mates made this big Newcastle crest out of real sand. Then we had a sandfight. It took me a week to get the sand out of me hair. I got loads of mates now, but I didn't used to.

Granddad was me mate for a while. I guess I was his pet project. I always was a bit quiet, and a little bit left out, and also I got into a bit of trouble from time to time. He got me out of myself.

You know I was telling you about the Angel? When I went back into that tram I sat and listened to the rain on the roof. It was dead quiet and there was nobody around, so I could be meself. So I asked me watch, OK then. What is this Angel? And it told me the story of how the Angel of the North got a soul.

There was this prisoner in Hull jail for thieving cos he run out of readies cos he never did nothing. It was all his fault really, he says so himself. He drank and cheated his friends and all that and did nothing with all his education.

He just sat alone in his cell. First off, he was angry at the police for catching him, and then he was angry with himself for getting caught and doing it and all of that. Sounds lovely, doesn't he? Depressing isn't the word.

Then he got this idea, to give the Angel a soul.

It goes like this. There are eleven dimensions, but we only see three of them and time, and the others are what was left over after the Big Bang. They're too small to see but they're everywhere at the same time, and we live in them, too, but we don't know it. There's no time there, so once something happens, it's like a photograph, you can't change it.

So the prisoner of Hull said what means is that everything we do gets laid down in the other dimensions like train tracks. It's like a story, and it doesn't end until we die, and that does the job for us. That's our soul, that story.

So what the prisoner in Hull does, is work in the prison, get some readies and pay to have a client put inside the Angel's head.

And all the other computers that keep track of everyone's jobs or the questions they asked, or just what they're doing, that all gets uploaded to the Angel.

Blaydon's there. It's got all of us, grinding fish heads. Every time someone makes tea or gets married from Carlisle to Ulverton from Newcastle to Derby, that gets run through the Angel. And that Angel is laying down the story of the North.

My watch told me that, sitting in that tram.

Then everyone else starts coming back in, but not Dad and Granddad, so I go out to fetch them.

The clouds were all pulled down in shreds. It looked like the cotton candy that Dad makes at fêtes. The sky was full of the church choir in their little airplanes. For just a second, it looked like a Mother Angel, with all her little ones.

I found Dad standing alone with Granddad. I thought it was rain on my dad's face, but it wasn't. He was looking at Granddad, all bent and twisted, facing into the wind.

We got to go, Dad, I said.

And he said, In a minute, son. Granddad was looking up at the planes and smiling.

And I said, it's raining, Dad. But they weren't going to come in. So I looked at the Angel and all this rust running off it in red streaks onto the concrete. So I asked, if it's an Angel of the North, then why is it facing south?

And Granddad says, Because it's holding out its arms in welcome. He didn't want to go.

We got him back into the tram, and back home, and he started to wheeze a bit, so me stepmum put him to bed and about eight o'clock she goes in to swab his teeth with vanilla, and she comes out and says to Dad, I think he's stopped breathing.

So I go in, and I can see, no, he's still breathing. I can hear it. And his tongue flicks, like he's trying to say something. But Dad comes in, and they all start to cry and carry on. And the neighbours all come in, yah, yah, yah, and I keep saying, it's not true, look, he's still breathing. What do they have to come into it for, it's not their granddad, is it?

No one was paying any attention to the likes of me, were they? So I just take off. There's this old bridge you're not allowed on. It's got trees growing out of it. The floor's gone, and you have to walk along the top of the barricades. You fall off, you go straight into the river, but it's a good dodge into Newcastle.

So I just went and stood there for a bit, looking down on the river. Me granddad used to take me sailing. We'd push off from the Haughs, and shoot out under this bridge, I could see where we were practically. And we'd go all the way down the Tyne and out to sea. He used to take me out to where the dolphins were. You'd see Liam come up. He was still wearing his computer, Liam, like a crown.

So I'm standing on the bridge, and me watch says: go down to the swimming pool, and go and tell Liam that Granddad's dead.

It's a bit like a dog I guess. You got to show one dog the dead body of the other or it will pine.

So I went down to the pool, but it's late and raining and there's nobody there, and I start to call him, like: Liam! Li-am! But he wasn't there.

So me watch says: he's wearing his computer: give him a call on his mobile.

So me watch goes bleep bleep bleep, and there's a crackle and suddenly I hear a whoosh and crickle, and there's all these cold green weaves on the face of my watch, and I say Liam? Liam, this is me, remember me, Liam? My granddad's dead, Liam. I thought you might need to know.

But what is he, just a dolphin, right, I don't know what it meant. How's he supposed to know who I am. You all right then, Liam? Catching lots of fish are you? So I hung up.

And I stand there, and the rain's really bucketing down, and I don't want to go home. Talking to yourself. It's the first sign, you know.

And suddenly me watch starts up again, and it's talking to me with Granddad's voice. You wanna hear what it said? Here. Hear.

Hello there, Landlubber. How are ya? This is your old Granddad. It's a dead clever world we live in, is it? They've rigged this thing up here so I can put this in your watch for when you need it.

Listen, me old son. You mustn't grieve, you know. Things are different now. They know how it works. We used to think we had a little man in our heads who watched everything on a screen and when you died he went to heaven not you. Now, they know, there's no little man, there's no screen. There's just a brain putting everything together. And what we do is ask ourselves: What do we think about next? What do we do next?

You know all about those dimension things, don't you? Well, I got a name for them. I call them Everywhere. Cos they are. And I want you to know, that I'm Everywhere now.

That's how we live for ever in heaven these days. And it's true, me old son. You think of me still travelling around Mexico before I met your Mamby. Think of me learning all about readies to keep up with you lot. Think of me on me boat, sailing out to sea. Remember that day I took you sailing out beyond the Tyne mouth? It's still there, Landlubber.

You know, all the evil in the world, all the sadness comes from not having a good answer to that question: What do I do next? You just keep thinking of good things to do, lad. You'll be all right. We'll all be all right. I wanted you to know that.

I got me footie on Saturdays, Granddad. Then I'm thinking I'll start up school again. They got a sailing club now. I thought I'd join it, Granddad, thought I'd take them out to where you showed me the dolphins. I'll tell them about Everywhere.

Did you know, Granddad?

They're making a new kind of watch. It's going to show us Everywhere, too.

No Bad Thing

Job interview

I thought he was just a sweet addled little vampire who lost his shoes. A lot of them are like that—brain dead, traumatised.

But this one had sparkling brown eyes, an amused smile, and thick black hair. You have to be careful around vampires. They've learned how to be appealing, and they do it so that they can eat you.

"I...notice the date of birth," I say, looking at his application. 1879.

"It's easier these days to be honest." He says it in a humble, weary kind of way, with a Mittel European accent. He's taking off his shoes in the middle of a job interview and they go clump clump on the floor. The tips of his socks wriggle like octopus tentacles looking for food. One sock is red, the other green.

"We don't see many of, uh, you, uh, Virally Affected Revenants up here in Canada. We're not a very good bet with our ozone layer problems."

"But you have very early sunsets." He bats his eyelids at me.

"You've left the name blank," I say.

"Yes. We don't like names."

"I'm sorry, but I do need a name if you are to work at the lab."

He sighs. "Albert Einstein." It gives him pain to admit it.

"Just...just to check. *The* Albert Einstein?"

"Oh, I think so. It's hard to tell. So many memories over so long a period. You should hire me. V.A.R.s make very good scientists, you know. Our brains go young again and in theory we have centuries of work in us."

He laughs and shakes his head. "In life, I was so against quantum theory. It offended my ideas about God." He smiles ruefully, charmingly. "That's less of a problem for me now, God not being high on the Vampire Top Ten."

My tongue is buzzing because I'm nervous. "Thhhhhhhhhhhhhhhhhhis is a biology lab."

He nods approvingly. "You're exploring radiation resistance in plants, particularly quinoa. Also the transfer of genetic material from quinoa to other plants, such as food crops. This is something I find very, very interesting. I've been doing work on it myself." He hands trace something in the air. "Maybe I should grow a coat and hat of quinoa for myself."

I have no idea what he's talking about.

"Duh... do you have any qualifications?"

He nods. "The Nobel Prize."

"Dooooooooooo...uh...you have any experience in biology?" I'm finding him very distracting.

The man is beautiful. Cuddly with button eyes. Albert Einstein, you're a knockout, especially when you're young, with cut, combed hair, no wrinkles and dressed all in black.

"I have a degree in biology now. Night courses." Was that another joke? He smiles and shrugs. "I had good reason to learn biology." I see no joke and I get no meaning.

"What, what reason?"

"Well! You wake up in a mortuary cold box and you realise that you are not breathing, but you are moving and thinking. You're wondering: How will I explain this to the person who opens the drawer? How can I be dead and alive at the same time? It becomes a very interesting question."

Then he adds, "I have solved it." He looks like a little boy with a new toy.

Finally I get it. "Oh! Radiation! Sorry, of course, ultraviolet. You're interested in resistance to sunlight. You really will be making quinoa into hats and coats."

"Exactly," he says. When he smiles, his eyebrows slant as if everything is life is a comforting joke.

He thanks me for scheduling such a late interview, and I suddenly realise I'm shaking hands with a predator. He leaves, walking out onto icy pavements wearing only odd socks. He's forgotten his shoes.

Almost without realising it, I've given him the job.

Bar talk, early evening

If Albert Einstein applies for a job at your lab, you hire him, right?

You have to watch him, because he is very, very charming and polite. If I'm working late, he brings me a cup of coffee and asks me about the kids and Henny, and if we're planning to have any more children. He just seems to love the idea of kids. You have to keep thinking: if this guy gets hungry...

Yeah, I'll have another Carling, thanks.

Oh he's bright, yeah, he's a genius. Just the other day, he was explaining what ultraviolet does to vampire cells.

Sunlight breaks the sugar-phosphate backbone of a vampire's DNA. It can make two thymine bases next to each other join up. They get these burn marks and the cancer tissue just goes wild, growing all over the place.

He says to me—and this is how he talks—"I haf two friends, zey look like potatoes!"

According to him, vampires are tumours, organised tumours in the shape of a human being. "But ze toomor has differhezeeated into zpezific tissues. Like all toomorz, it iz immortal."

Legal Surveillance keeps CCTV footage on everybody, and I just have to watch his every day, which is terrible of me I know, but every day he does something wacky.

Albert Einstein, leaving his hand over a Bunsen burner. Albert Einstein getting his nose slammed by test tubes in a centrifuge. Genius at work.

He can't feel it. Their nerves don't quite work. Like lepers, but unlike lepers, they heal, and boy do they heal quickly. The next day, the burn is all gone. He says it's because they can undifferentiate their tissue at will. So you can also think of them as a bunch of stem cells walking around.

Cheers thanks, it's my round next.

He has hundreds of fans. They call him Einstein, Dark Lord of the Undead. They hang around the lab waiting for him.

They look normal enough so long as they don't smile. Some of them don't even move; they just stand for hours like they're posing for a statue. Since they can't feel any pain. They twist their heads up to look at the moon and leave them like that. If water melts and re-freezes on top of their heads, they just leave it there. Snow stays on their shoulders.

One of them waited outside all night in the cold with his bare hand on our front gates. He turned around and left his hand behind, stuck to the metal. The new shift came in and found it there and refused to open up.

OK, if you insist. Another Carling, cheers.

A couple of nights ago, Albert comes up to me, just as I'm leaving, and there must be fifty vampires in our parking lot. They're all chanting "Albert, Albert." He says, "I'm so sorry. I hope you don't find this intimidating."

So I say, yes, actually, it is very intimidating.

"Oh dear," he says. "They have strict instructions to harm no one from the lab."

So I say, "Uh. Do they always follow instructions?"

And he says, "They love me. I am their father. They cannot disobey." And he smiles, but there are these two little pinprick fangs, and you think, ho boy, is there a lot of power there.

Vampires are so hierarchical. Every one of them has a title; everybody has some kind of line manager, and they sit around tracing who gave birth to who. And of course, all these vampires are all trying nowadays to make as many of themselves as they can so that they can have fans too. It's like the old days when your salary was based on how many people worked for you, so you kept hiring more people?

Oh, it's a terrible health and safety issue!

Some companies make V.A.R.s use separate entrances, even separate elevators, but my God, the expense! It was bad enough having to rebuild for wheelchair access.

We just give the day staff medication. Well, Janula holds the patents on anti-vampirals; if we can't get treatment, who can?

Oh spare me! You can't catch being Mexican or gay, it's entirely different. This is a disease; you can't have a political argument with a disease. Even if they don't feed on us, they're constantly shedding viral loads.

Of course corporations love them! They don't need pensions and they are really useful for 24 x 7, which is why Janula hires so many of them. I mean these...things...they have lifetimes! They get one degree after another, have all that experience. I mean how would you justify NOT hiring someone with a Nobel Prize? If you don't hire them, they call the Commission down on your head for discrimination! You practically have to get into an argument to hire a real person!

As a member of a threatened population, I can tell you: they really will miss us when we're gone.

I mean what are they going to eat, right?

Here's to the ozone hole.

Just between you and me: I hate those creeps.

Preliminary hearing

When did I first notice that Albert Einstein was doing something outside his job description?

Well, your Honour, as I've said, he did work in a very odd way. I think the court has seen some of the CCTV footage? I think the worst was when he knocked the on-switch of the dry-ice fire extinguisher and was deep-frozen.

Sorry, your Honour. No, I did not notice anything to indicate he was working on other research until I got a call from our Legal Surveillance team. They said that they had found about 100 frozen human embryos, and they didn't know what they were. I was completely mystified. Janula Micromed does not do any research on human embryos as a matter of policy. We don't even do any research using animals. All of our research is on plants.

Einstein just admitted it. He said, "Oh, I was doing that." He took responsibility, and told everybody that I had nothing to do with it. He said that he didn't want to me to get into any trouble.

Yes, of course I knew we had legal obligations in this area. I said Albert, you can't do that, unlicensed human cloning is illegal.

Yes, I did ask him what he was using them for, and he said, to test if the quinoa plant might in some way prevent radiation damage to humans.

No, your Honour, I didn't realise the implications of that statement at the time. I don't usually think of V.A.R.s as human beings. And I had absolutely no idea that genetic modification had taken place in the embryos themselves. I thought he meant he was working on fabric made from quinoa or some kind of treatment and perhaps wanted to use the embryos to test that.

We did have a huge problem about what to do with the embryos. Legal Surveillance was very concerned about future grant funding or licensing if we let anybody else have them. In any case, the original donors had made it plain that the embryos should not be used for any other research, so we couldn't. I should just say how helpful Professor Einstein was. He had permissions from the original donors for a range of options. For example, ah, we had the permission to put the embryos out for adoption and normal pregnancy, but only if the donors were allowed to know who the surrogate parents were. The difficulty was that we did not have 100 adoption opportunities. It was the Professor who then got us the clearance for ordinary burial.

Our PR partners loved the idea. We had an internment ceremony at St. James' Cemetery near Parliament Street. It was very moving. Even the evangelical watchdog bodies found that it was an appropriate thing to do and sent representatives.

Yes, that was unfortunate, the attempt to stake Professor Einstein, and I make no apologies in that regard for helping him to escape.

Well, now that you mention it, he had the donor permissions for the burial ready in advance, that's true.

I suppose there is a possibility that he planned it, yes.

No, we had no idea that all the donours were all Virally Affected Revenants.

Partly it's because nobody has even been able to take a tissue sample successfully from a V.A.R. The sample immediately reverts to something like an undifferentiated tumour. It becomes a not very useful biopsy sample in a petri dish. So it never occurred to us that someone would have cracked cloning vampires. It was light-years beyond what we believed to be possible.

I got a call at home about 3:00 a.m. It was from our PR Department. In some distress. They, they just said that they were getting reports of human embryos moving along the Bloor St. Viaduct. Snapping at people, yes.

I have no idea how the embryos came to be there. But I imagine that they rose from the dead. Undead embryos are not something we've had to deal with before, in fact, at Janula Micromed.

Of course, we were very concerned. I should point out that immediately, at once, Janula Micromed stepped up to the plate. I myself and members of the PR and Legal sections went out at once to try to round up the little devils. We called out pest-control agencies to help with the cleanup, we paid for public-service announcements. From the beginning we offered anyone who had been in the Viaduct area free anti-vampiral drugs.

Too lenient with Professor Einstein? Well, he is a very distinguished man, and...

We fired him, of course. As soon as we found out about the illicit cloning. I said, I'm terribly sorry Herr Professor Doctor Dark Lord Einstein, but you will have to leave the premises.

He thanked me for giving him a job.

Yes, I have to suppose that he planned... planned for the embryos to rise from the dead.

You, you, you, you will have to talk to someone other than myself about the the the the legal side of uhhhhh any damages.

How many of the embryos did we collect? I'm not entirely sure. You'd have to talk to the people in charge of the cleanup operation, but I think it was very few. Yes, there's a possibility that some of them are still out there. But, uh, in their state of immaturity and helplessness if they stayed out in the Canadian sun, they in all likelihood are now dead.

No, no, no, I meant to say Re-dead. Actually still. Unmoving. Burnt to a crisp.

Incompetent? I, I, I wouldn't say I'd been incompetent, no. I, I, I would say that I treated Albert Einstein with great respect and kindness. Undue kindness? Yes.

I apologise for repeating everything you say, your Honour. Bad habit. When I'm nervous.

Have you ever known a vampire? A vampire who needed something from you?

Reminiscence

Einstein came back to show me his baby.

I was sitting outside on a bench at night, nothing to do, and there was a wuffling sound, and suddenly, there he was—Albert, sitting next to me. He bounced the baby up and down on his lap. It looked just like any other baby only bigger, healthier, very pink. Adorable. Even with the fangs. And the muzzle.

"He's beautiful," I said. I thought that Albert had come to take me with him.

"Of course he's beautiful; he's me," said Albert. He turned and smiled, and—oh God!—the light, the joy, seemed to surround him like a halo. "Do you want to hold the baby? He'll try to bite, but he's perfectly safe."

He handed over the child, and our hands touched. How can someone's hand be moving? It was soft and warm, so warm, feverish with life, constantly burning with the virus. Their eyes glow with it. So did the baby's. I wanted to offer the baby my neck.

"He can walk out into the sunlight," Albert said, with love. "If you gave him a pressure suit, he could ride outside a spaceship and the radiation would do him no harm. He will be well placed to survive all the coming catastrophes. We all will be, all us vampires, thanks to you."

I kept hoping, hoping that he'd offer.

He asked me about Henny.

"I told her about you. I didn't—I couldn't—hide it. I just said, I've fallen in love with a guy at work. And he's a vampire. Maybe she could have handled a guy. But a vampire? I think she worried about the virus around the kids. So. She left."

"Ah! I'm so sorry."

"I don't have a job. I guess I'm lucky not to be in jail. Sometimes at night I can't stop shaking."

He still didn't invite me. He told me a story, instead. "When I was young, I was a Patent Clerk in Berne, and I had no money, and my first child was born and I had to beg my boss for a raise, and when I got it, it was so small. It seemed to me then that all life was against me, and that those things were the most important things in the world. Now that little baby is not even an old man. He's dust, and I can't remember Mileva's maiden name. Everything passes. You must be ruthless about what to forget and what to remember." His eyes suddenly looked hard.

I think he was saying, forget me.

I finally asked, "Can I come with you?"

He looked sad, and didn't answer. He took back the baby. "For all the talk of viruses, there is still something supernatural in this. We don't take blood only. We take what is most precious about you. Life, certainly, but also beauty, mathematics, the ability to tap dance. We leave you drained, but we shine. Or, if you are a genius, we recruit you." He stroked my face. "There's nothing precious about you."

I loved him and he was going to leave and I would be left with nothing.

"I muh-make great pancakes." I meant I could make a beautiful life, full of sunny mornings.

He knew that. "Find someone," he counselled. He stood up, and put his hat on backward. Then he paused.

"We don't just take," he said. His face was so full of kindness and wisdom, you'd think he was seeing God. "We give, too. We can give back small things, or everything. This little fellow here? I'm going to give him my identity. He will look like me, smell like me, and reason as I do. He will have all my memories. I'll let him drain this body entirely, of everything. I'll drop it like an old shoe. And he'll walk with all of his kind, into the future. A sunlit future."

The baby had a beautiful laugh.

"But there is a little something I can spare for you," he said.

He touched my hand, and this time I felt a kind of Halloween sparkler dazzle inside my head. "I'm sorry you must suffer," he said. He took his hand away, and it was as if he was tearing a spider's web of love.

"How far ahead does your plan go?" I asked him.

"To the stars," he said. "Fifty-year voyages in deep space make sense if you're a vampire. We'll have to take care of you, too. You are so short-sighted and destructive and bound up in ideas of goodness. We will love you and tend you like farmers love their cattle."

I mooed like a cow as a joke.

"In about fifteen years time, you might see Einstein again, but be extremely careful, because it won't be me, it will be this little fellow here. He may be hungry and kill you."

"I'll try to remember."

"He won't let you join us. Even if he says that he will. When a population cannot die, you have to be very sparing about the number of births."

Then he excused himself, gathered up the baby, and walked away, still wearing odd socks with no shoes.

I still have his shoes. They are as empty as he will be by now.

My wife has the house. I managed to buy a small apartment. Ex-housing project, but at least it has hot water in winter. I'm left with my memories. One of them isn't mine.

I'm in the back of a limousine with Charlie Chaplin and it's 1928. Charlie is beautiful; his body language seems to skip, and reel and rhyme, heartbreaking and witty at the same time. It seems to promise a better world.

I'm famous now too. I mean "genius" to people, kindly intelligence.

Together we roll out of the Hotel Grande in Geneva and thousands of people are waiting for us. They call our names, his and mine. They press their hands against the windows.

I am confounded by it; I don't know why they are shouting or what they want. I look to Charlie in dismay. "Mr. Chaplin, what does it all mean?"

He leans back and chuckles with affection. Charlie Chaplin is charmed by me. "Professor," he says. "It means absolutely nothing."

They will rule us.

Perhaps it's no bad thing.

Talk Is Cheap

It's first thing and I'm already out Walking and listening for Jinny.
I dream of Jeannie ref Stephen Foster *19ᵗʰ century composer in* Minstrel
tradition. *Jin as in* cotton gin, Eli Whitney. Gin, *prohibition, speakeasies, the*
pansy craze, *the 18ᵗʰ amendment . . .*

A blizzard of links, and none of them from her. Culture bores me,
but I added it to my Priorities because of Jinny.

She's a continual stream of beautiful little visual notes, flowers with
sheep's heads or entire false catalogues for museums of anachronisms.
Bakelite handsets on *Flash Gordon* spaceships (*produced three serials, the first
being in 1936, etc., etc.*). *Collab music 2030 craze of different flavours from different eras.*

I love it that Jinny wants to share so much with me, with everyone.
She shares continually, even when she's working, sometimes when she's
sleeping, through her Turing. I always have my Turing turned off.

I love Jinny's teeth. Yes, I know, that's the bacteria gnawing away—
no links, please. I just love her bright white teeth. They protrude and
gleam so that Jinny always looks as though she's smiling.

Her Turing seems to touch my arm and the touch feels like sunlight. Everything out here is brushed by sunlight, still cool, a delicate rose
colour, not at all like sunset or the bleaching white light of noon. I'm
walking out of our little town through scant agriculture modelled on that
of the Mayans . . . wide-planted corn and beans under shade. I'm going
to check our river.

The Turing and I walk together, she in my head. It's monitored that
something's bothering me, and sends me one of Jinny's little packages, a

history of charitable acts, all folded, crisp and delicious like a spring roll:

the refusal of the UK to retaliate for the bomb
the Bill Gates bequest and its long history
the arrival of Concurrency as a medium of exchange
the abolishing of copyright.

If you prioritise charity, caritas and acts of breathtaking neutrality, you also apparently tend to prioritise effectiveness, weightlessness, spoons, weeds, ants and old gramophone recordings. How Jinny gets that I don't know, but I can see the files weave. It works. She just does it, mixes things, makes things.

I can't keep up. The packet keeps blossoming out, laced with all kinds of daffy Jinny things. They make me smile; they make me despair because I would like to keep her, like to stay part of her world. But I don't do this, make all those gifts of info.

"It's not content, it's the act that's important," I say. It sounds grumpy even to me.

"Of course," the Turing answers. "But projecting is an act too." Of a kind, and there is so much of it at so little cost to anyone. Talk is cheap.

"What is she really doing now?" I ask.

"I . . . I could wake her if you like," says the Turing.

"No, no," I say. I want Jinny to sleep. I can imagine her, all soft and warm and dreamy. I love that image of her; my heart pines, sinking again.

I walk naked in our beautiful desert sun, and I smell sage and dust all around me. Wind sweeps along the arroyo.

For years since my Joey died, I've been putting out feelers for other people. An old guy like me. Even to me it's like I'm peeking out of my snail shell, oozing out soft antennae, hoping to find love. Yuck.

I must have reccied seven hundred people. Jinny was one of the few who reached back. She said our profiles matched. They didn't, but we kept talking. We kept almost meeting. That "almost" makes my heart sore. It makes me think that she's just being polite; she's just being friendly; I'm an embarrassment, she wants me to go away but won't say so.

The Turing hears me think that. "That's not true." The thing touches me again on the arm, invisible but soothing. "She especially wants me to talk to you."

It's a strange situation. Both of us want me to win her love. But neither of us has succeeded. I have this numbing idea that she can't really respect or like me, but that there is, or may be only at times, something simple about me that she likes, and I feel very lucky and very sad, because this simple something is probably quite fragile. It could blow away.

She's a Doctor for heaven's sake. Only Infotechs get more respect and that's kind of a branch of medicine, and anyway she freelances as one of those as well.

Me, I'm only a Walker. I go places, confirm that reality matches our models, that all our balanced and merged Priorities are being met.

I'm following an irrigation canal, the sun growing stronger on my skin. I feel photosynthesis kick in, to power the tech that inhabits me. My body and my tools are fuelled by the same sugars, the same blood. And my feet grow their own shoes.

"Oh," people say when I tell them who I am. "Well you must be strapping fit." They don't know what else to say; they're embarrassed. A necessary task, but not really dazzling, is it? It's not healing people, or advancing the genome. It's not combining information. The Techs engineer info like mutant DNA. It keeps re-combining. *Hi! I'm a mutant idea!*

In all the Fictions that whiz by so entertainingly these days, the walking is all done by robots. That's how automatic people think my work is. Only, guess what, dream on fellow travellers, there is no A.I. There are just us Walkers, alone, on our appointed rounds.

A few days ago she said, the real Jinny not her Turing, "I want to go with you on one of your walks." This was imaginative and sweet and careful of my feelings, as if what I do were interesting, as if we might share insights as we stroll.

"Do you have the right shoes?" I asked her.

She giggled and barraged me with a million files on shoes prioritized by Uselessness.

The most Useless shoes she indexed were made out of chocolate. They melt or crumble and stain the floor.

"You made those up!"

"No, no, they're real!" she protested, "The Sybarites really made delicious shoes you could eat!"

She kept on linking and projecting, and I didn't know if she was joking or not, a whole range of hopping, useless shoes:

shoes that obey simple heurirstics to spin spiderwebs as you walk,

shoes that sing

shoes that know all the constellations

shoes that sail the seven seas all by themselves out of interest; sweet except that they love making sea turtles abort their egg sacs

shoes with delicious new recipes tickertaping across their soles,

shoes that calculate values of pi

shoes that suck up anything with a positive charge

shoes that keep scuttling away from you the moment you take them off.

"Stop!" I laughed. Creativity scares me. I always think it's going to run away with us. My real Priority is rectitude.

I'm at the edge of our creek, standing on a rock shelf that's gray with dead lichen.

I try and put it off. I kneel down and sip water from my cupped hand and it's cool and tastes of granite, and the sensors understand its qualities. The water is just as people want it. The Joshua trees stand around me like friends, holding up their arms as if to show that they're honest. I smell sage and dust all around me. Today is the day I scheduled months ago to test levels once again, now when the snows upstream are supposed to melt.

I wade in, my legs reading the depth and flow.

Yep. Welp. Here it is.

The water may be delicious, but we're using too much of it. Current and projected population; water usage average preferred and necessary all rattle past me.

Soon we won't have enough water. Soon as in say five years.

Nothing is simple, except for reality. Reality is a tiny white stable dot in the middle of all this info. Everything else, all the talk, is piled up sky-high, prioritised, processed, and offered back.

Mr. Cranky, my old mean streak, would say that folks could just as easily test the water themselves. They could all take turns confirming.

Later Jinny, the real Jinny, connects to whisper that tomorrow she wants to join me on my Walk.

She shows up in reality. I see her coming and I can feel my arms tense up, specifically my arms for some reason. For her I'm wearing shorts, how old-fashioned. I worry about the creases age has made across my skinny stomach.

It's cool dawn. The sunlight catches her sideways. Her skin has a perfect pink glow, her smile is ready on her face like she's come back from a future where everything works. And she's wearing serious shoes.

She says hi, I say hi. Our PAs do a quick exchange to look at the day's tasks. If she was in any doubt before, Jinny will now know for sure that I'm the bottom of the social heap. Everybody sets Priorities together and I just check them out. I guess she wants to see what that's like.

So she's going to do air-quality analysis for me, and keep track of wind direction, humidity, acidity, all that stuff as it changes over time and distance. I'm going to do street semiology, traffic absence, and basic demographics. There's numbers, and there's graphs, but what counts is being able to say how all of this will land for people with very different Priorities. Oh, and here's another thrill: I'm checking for termites.

Me, I'm a Dog man. Really, that's what I'm now called. People with my nest of Priorities get called Dogs because we value faithfulness, trust, and constant grooming. We like repetition but we want to get to know things, too, so we like to go out sniffing and snooping. I'm in the perfect job.

Oops, I've been telling her all that. She nods, looking slightly glazed and distracted. "How's your gout?"

She means the pains in my feet. She remembers stuff.

"Medication. Little critters are eating up those crystals."

"You should have come to me for that!"

If she can't love me, then maybe we can still be friends. I can use friends, too. I feel an idiot grin on my face, just to have her near me, and I can't think of anything to say.

She's not just a doctor. Naw, that wouldn't occupy her. She runs a business on the side as a Bespoke Prioritiser. She probably needs a whole lake of homeopathic info to store her credits. I want to ask her dumb questions such as: Do you rank for anybody who's well crucial? I don't ask, but she answers anyway.

"Naw, not really. Most of mine are overseers needing to find balance. One of them wanted every single thing about the Buddha itemized, ranked, and prioritised around something "innovative." He didn't say what, just something, anything zazzie and chic. Do you know how complicated Buddhism is? All those different Ways? Minayana, Therevada, Zen ..."

"Not as big as Hinduism."

She laughs lazily, and I don't know if it's because what I said was charmingly irrelevant or not. I was, of course, being entirely serious. She touches my arm again, grooming. "I gave him a package centered on the need to keep records as the main criteria." Maybe she sees her job as part of the same hazy joke. "Buddhism as an aid to bureaucracy."

We're alone outside, the streets press in close around us. It's not a particularly nice day and the village is still asleep. Who walks except Walkers?

Our streets wind, houses close together, friendly, with shared doorways between them, rooftop pathways across them, and all around us on the slopes, turbines white as doves that turn in our arroyo winds. On some roofs, fleshsails catch the sun and make sugar.

Folks still have to have things in reality. Paint which adjusts to temperature and heats the rooms. The grafts which grow some of the houses, or the mud bricks baked in kilns, or the wires and circuits that also work like spiders to spin more wires and circuits. Some houses are made of flowers, growing. Some are made of laterite for people who love the miracle of mined dirt oxydizing into stone; others are stacked shitcakes dried and sterilized. Those match people who value self-sufficiency. Plenty of those still since the time of the troubles.

"Semiologizing," Jinny says and chuckles.

"We're about to metastasize," I say. Our village will split, probably along Predator/Herbivore lines. I guess the Predators will make us poor Herbivores move again.

"Dogs aren't Herbivores," she reminds me. But there is a glow of agreement coming off her. Like me, she's clocked this crowding of styles, the closely packed fabric of the town almost not quite on the edge of mismatch, conflict.

Partition they tell us is fun, good. New birth is always good. "Water's the problem," she says. And I wonder, how did she get hold of that?

"Didn't you report that yesterday? We're running out of water."

We make our own sugar from the sun; our gut makes a lot of our protein. Our own bodies fuel the information which now lives as part of us. In the right climate, we could live without anything else, for a time at least. Except for water.

"Not run out so much as just that it will trigger the breakup."

Our home. It will go.

We walk, I watch her. She's not just confirming, she's filtering, scanning her takes through all kinds of Priorities from government diaries to chaotic monitors. She's making something interesting out of my boring job.

"This is fun," she says. "It's reassuring. It all works." The movement of her hands takes in our settlement, the network as a whole, the desert landscape in cool morning. The soft pink light on the ridges, the deep kindly mauve in the canyons.

"For now," I say.

She looks at the streets that coil about us. "I want to go inside the houses and swap with people."

"You don't need to go inside to do that."

"I mean for real, one-to-one like us now." She starts to giggle and footnote all kinds of sociologies. "Come on, keep up the semio."

I riff. "Deeply social creatures needing each other for physical shelter and to keep at bay a sense of threat to their highly complex culture. Being dependent on weather, they are also frightened and resentful of it. Spaces are designed to minimize the impact of sun, wind, rain, cloud, night, day. Needlessly, in some ways, as they are actually more independent of the environment than at any point in human history. They love info, they value preservation of it, but they have a low Priority for actual experience, thus the low Priority for physical transport. Me, I want to walk through the Rockies. Beyond that, fearful of a loss of a single member, driving a mix of socialisation and isolation caused by the intimacies of info."

"None of that footnotes." She looks distracted. I feel inside her that a thesaurus of names from Saussure to Tamagocuchi is flurrying past with no matches.

"None of that was a quote." She means it's harder to put in a tree. She blurts out a chuckle. "I'll just have to quote you!"

That's why she likes me: because I say new things. I'm flattered.

On a flat roof, sunbathers. Jinny wants to eyeball them. She calls hello. Silence. They remain on their soft roof, naked, sleeping in sunlight.

"Conflicting Priorities for communication and independence," I remind her. It's a joke. She doesn't laugh, she grimaces. She waves. She jumps up and down and calls. I just know she's buzzing them with feelers. She sends them and me a gift of niche Priorities, a lovely lavender suggestion for emphasising open-plan living and geneswapping as a substitute for reproduction.

The people on the roof behave like plants. I mistake them for Herbivores. One of them finally says aloud, not looking up, "I'm not really here."

"We're Dolphins," murmurs the other and they share a sarky smile. They are both identical, which means they've morphed. Into each other. Yuck.

"They're Sharks," Jinny says downturning her mouth quickly to mean, let's get out of here. Sharks prioritize winning and making good use of you. This new astrology of Priority. It really works.

"What are you?" the two Predators ask in unison.

Jinny bursts out laughing and shakes her head. "I'm a Hamster!" The absurdity of a Hamster facing Sharks. "No, really. I prioritise . . ." She shakes her head cos it's all too silly.

"Activity," I say for her. I'm a bit surprised that she's something, well, so humble and sweet.

"Running in circles," she chuckles again. Already we are walking away from the Sharks and talking only for each other.

I list a few other Hamster priorities for her. "Functional feeding only. Clear goals."

I have to admit it does sound slightly comic, this lean yet nourished looking woman taller than I am calling herself a Hamster. "Hamsters are harmless," she says. "Harmless and delighted."

So you like Dogs because we're harmless too. I'm thinking that maybe Jinny likes old guys, tall lanky old guys because everybody else is round and soft. She's done comfort, she's done fast, she's done young and handsome. She's lonely. How did she end up lonely? Long story. I hope to hear it.

Next job, we confirm bacteria and virus levels and then spend the rest of the day counting numbers of beneficial insects and useful information retroviruses. *All's Quiet on the Western Front, Remarque* . . . I actually start producing footnotes from Priorities of my own. I feel like I'm flying.

"We couldn't do medicine without Walkers," she says.

The next day and there's nothing from her. I was expecting all kinds of links, packages, even conclusions. I was quite proud of some of the stuff I gave her. Shitcakes as a marker of independence, itself a marker of fear. I really had given of my best. Nothing came of it, apparently. She'd been smiling in order to keep a distance, was that it? *How nice he is and how desperately dull, really.*

Again, it's happening again.

My stomach sinks, I feel despair. There is no poetry that footnotes when really nice women don't call back. Was she just pretending then, to be nice? The way you placate an embarrassing link-partner who runs out of material, or a genepooling that bellyflops?

I do get a call from Spotty Derek. He really is terribly spotty, something to do with his mitochondrial communications, but he's deeply sweet. After all, we're both Walkers. He's skinny as a toothpick, though there's something sheeplike in his gaze that makes him button-cute so that people forgive his being smart and an overseer at eighteen.

"Watchinit," he twerps at me. "You landed one yesterday. FRD. QED. Whoa!" I think he means my date. If that is what it was. He looks pleased for me. I wait, because he'll have a comment. He starts to chuckle. "Shitcakes as what? A bit tenuous."

"I thought it was OK."

"Yeah, but your job is to Confirm, not invent. Whose Priorities were those?"

Mine, I realize. My Priorities. Nobody gives a shit about those. My priorities might skew the measure. I'm not paid to confirm things that are important to me.

And what do I want to have confirmed?

That I have a heart, have a soul? I really thought she wanted to please me, I really thought she wanted me. Good at faking I guess. All that bedside-manner stuff, all that selling her gift priorities to the higher-ups, I guess it makes you professionally pleasant, effortlessly charming.

Derek is still chuckling, and gives me a hug by feeler. "You can move in with me if you like." He doesn't mean it. He's very kind. And very bossy. The amount of understanding it takes to be like him takes my breath away and intimidates me a bit. His authority creeps up on you. You don't notice it at first. He looks like Sam out of *Pickwick Papers*, and please keep the footnote.

He's a Madonna. Priorities: power and nurturing. And yeah, I'd do a trans for him in a second and have his babies, which he knows, and likes, but will never do anything about, except to use that underlying warmth to make me like him and do what I'm told.

"You—uh—should reconfirm those figures on water," he says. Before we all panic, he means. We're all so low-key and calm.

"Yeah," I say as if he'd said, weather's nice today.

"Ahhh watchinit...," he says, all I get is a strong blast of something hearty, cheerful and dismissive. I give him a blast of something else.

"Just wait til it gets political. Just wait til you try to separate us by Priority, by info type. And you lose your wife, or your brother refuses to talk to you, or it all gets tense and nasty, and out of nowhere, suddenly nice-enough people become thugs. Very quiet, very smiling, neighbourly thugs, and if it's not you who move out, it will be over your dead body. Not theirs!"

"Sorry," he says and something gentle and distant like the sound of surf washes out from him.

"You weren't there!" I relent a bit. "You're too young."

So I head out again to the creek. Today I'll check downstream as well. But I'm all unwanted downloads, spam, reccies like wasps. Everybody else is scattered. *Water, we can't do without water. Is that Walker nuts or something?* I just don't care.

So I do what I promised myself I would not do. I send out feelers again to Jinny.

Where are you, what system you in? Did you enjoy reality? Nice Walk, wasn't it? Did you think so? Did it measure up, or was it all a bit dull and lifeless?

Nothing.

Oh for heaven's sake, I tell myself, give it a rest.

I really am a Dog, I really do need to be petted and stroked. I promised myself I'd let potential lovers come to me. Only if they wanted to and when they wanted to, so I would know they meant it. Just let someone else do the chasing and the chancing for a change.

But I really thought yesterday had been good. It felt so good to be with her, just to talk or not to talk, just to walk, see some bricks, taste some air and let her prattle on, dumping all this wonderful stuff. She's fine for me. She'll do. I don't want anything else. I just want her to touch me back. I just want her to want me.

So I'm walking through the village and at that exact moment, I see her, outside for real. She's on that flat roof. She's huddled under a blanket with the two Sharks, smoking weed.

I'm angry.

I stomp on ahead. I project something-anything and for some reason all that comes out is: *Neither snow nor rain nor heat nor gloom of night stays these couriers from the swift completion of their appointed rounds* ... What am I doing? Pony Express? Do I really have a major priority to make an idiot of myself?

"Faithful," Jinny says, aloud. She smiles hazily to her Predator friends, shrugs off the blanket, and crouches down on the edge of the roof. "As you see, I connected." She means with the Sharks.

"Yeah, I can see."

"It was a lot of work." I think she means she went back and spent a lot of time eyeballing them. She either has a lot to share with me or a lot she can't be arsed to share.

"More of a challenge than someone it's easy to connect with." I'm trying not to look disappointed. No, I'm trying not to look hurt.

No, I am trying not to cry. In the street. If there is a single particle of cruelty in her, it will come out now.

Those gnawing teeth highlight the downturning of her mouth. Somehow she's suddenly flipped down from the roof onto the ground

"Don't be like that," she says.

"Like how?" The words swell out of my throat like knocked elbows.

"Angry," she says. "Look, come on, let's walk."

Mr. Cranky says, "You're not wearing anything, it's early, it's windy."

"Well, yeah, so we better walk to warm up. Come on." She flicks her fingers towards herself. "Come here." She puts an arm around me, and pulls. "The Sharks don't want to push the Herbivores out this time. They want to move. After all, they're Sharks, they have to keep moving to breathe."

I taste our dust in the air; it's spicy, the taste of home.

She gives me a little shake. "They're the kind of people who wanted to go to the stars. The Bears, the Pumas, the domestic Cats..."

Then she footnotes how Dogs are really wolves, noble beasts who care for their own and live in packs, the most sociable of creatures, how they keep each other warm. Jinny's arms are cold, so I hold her and her shoulders and arms feel smooth and soft. I chafe them a bit, and we start to walk, bouncing files back and forth between us. And all around us, the fleshsails fill with sunlight, the windmills turn, our purple skins seethe with sugars fueling the eyes, the implants, the GMs, the receiving bones, all that information babbling powered away.

"Anyway we're not Herbivores or Predators anymore. That's just leftover emotional garbage." She smiles again. "We're more like plants."

Sometimes it all comes right. Sometimes something like love is possible. We come to the edge of the town.

I feel humorous. "I'd just like to confirm that rampant fancying combined with a kind heart are possible."

"Then," she says, "the future's good."

Days of Wonder

L eveza was the wrong name for her; she was big and strong, not light. Her bulk made her seem both male and female; her shoulders were broad but so were her hips and breasts. She had beautiful eyes, round and black, and she was thoughtful; her heavy jaws would grind round and round as if imitating the continual motion of her mind. She always looked as if she were listening to something distant, faraway.

Like many large people, Leveza was easily embarrassed. Her mane would bristle up across the top of her head and down her spine. She was strong and soft all at once, and kind. I liked talking to her; her voice was so high and gentle; though her every gesture was blurting and forlorn.

But that voice when it went social! If Leveza saw a Cat crouching in the grass, her whinnying was sudden, fierce and irresistible. All of us would pirouette into a panic at once. Her cry was infallible.

So she was an afrirador, one of our sharpshooters, always reared up onto hind quarters to keep watch, always carrying a rifle, always herself a target. My big brave friend. Her rear buttocks grew ever more heavy from constant standing. She could walk upright like an Ancestor for a whole day. Her pelt was beautiful, her best feature, a glossy deep chestnut, no errant Ancestor reds. As rich and deep as the soil under the endless savannah.

We were groom-mates in our days of wonder.

I would brush her, and her hide would twitch with pleasure. She would stretch with it, as it were taffy to be pulled. We tried on earrings, or tied bows into manes, or corn-rowed them into long braids. But Leveza never rested long with simple pleasures or things easily understood.

Even young, before bearing age, she was serious and adult. I remember her as a filly, slumped at the feet of the stallions as they smoked their pipes, played checkers, and talked about what they would do if they knew how to make electricity.

Leveza would say that we could make turning blades to circulate air; we could pump water to irrigate grass. We could boil water, or make heat to dry and store cud cakes. The old men would chuckle to hear her dreaming.

I thought it was a pointless game, but Leveza could play it better than anyone, seeing further and deeper into her own inherited head. Her groom sister Ventoo always teased her, "Leveza, what are you fabricating now?"

We all knew that stuff. I knew oh so clearly how to wrap thin metal round and round a pivot and with electricity make it spin. But who could be bothered? I loved to run. All of us foals would suddenly sprint through long grass to make the ground thunder, to raise up the sweet smells of herbs, and to test our strength. We had fire in our loins and we wanted to gallop all the way to the sun. Leveza pondered.

She didn't like it when her first heat came. The immature bucks would hee-haw at her and pull back their feeling lips to display their great white plates of teeth. When older men bumped her buttocks with their heads, she would give a little backward kick, and if they tried to mount her, she walked out from under them. And woe betide any low-grade drifter who presumed that Leveza's lack of status meant she was grateful for attention. She would send the poor bag of bones rattling through the long grass. The babysquirrels clutched their sides and laughed. "Young NeverLove wins again."

But I knew. It was not a lack of love that made my groom-mate so careful and reserved. It was an abundance of love, a surfeit of it, more than our kind is meant to have, can afford to have, for we live on the pampas and our cousins eat us.

Love came upon Leveza on some warm night, the moon like bedtime milk. She would not have settled for a quick bump with a reeking male just because the air wavered with hot hormones. I think it would have been the reflection of milklight in black eyes, a gentle ruffling of upper lip, perhaps a long and puzzled chat about the nature of this life and its consequences.

We are not meant to love. We are meant to mate, stand side by side for warmth for a short time afterward, and then forget. *I wonder who fathered this one?*

Leveza knew and would never forget. She never said his name, but most of us knew who he was. I sometimes I caught her looking toward the circle of the Great Men, her eyes full of gentleness. They would gallop about at headball, or talk seriously about axle grease. None of them looked her way, but she would be smiling with a gentle glowing love, her eyes fixed on one of them as steadily as the moon.

One night, she tugged at my mane. "Akwa, I am going to sprog," she said, with a wrench of a smile at the absurdity of such a thing.

"Oh! Oh Leveza, that's wonderful. Why didn't you tell me, how did this happen?"

She ronfled in amusement, a long ruffling snort. "In the usual way, my friend."

"No, but . . . oh you know! I have seen you with no one."

She went still. "Of course not."

"Do you know which one?"

Her whole face was in milklight. "Yes. Oh yes."

Leveza was both further back toward an Ancestor than anyone I ever met, and furthest forward toward the beasts. Even then it was as if she was pulled in two directions, Earth and stars. The night around us would sigh with multiple couplings. I was caught up in the season. Sex was like a river, washing all around us. I was a young mare then, I can tell you, wide of haunch, slim of ankle. I plucked my way through the grass as if it were the strings of a harp. All the highest-rankers would come and snuffle me, and I surprised myself. Oh! I was a pushover. One after another after another.

I would come back feeling like a pasture grazed flat; and she would be lumped out on the ground, content and ready to welcome me. I nuzzled her ear, which flicked me like I was a fly, and I would lay my head on her buttock to sleep.

"You are a strange one," I would murmur. "But you will be kind to my babes. We will have a lovely house." I knew she would love my babies as her own.

That year the dry season did not come.

It did go cooler, the afternoon downpours were fewer, but the grass did not go gray. There was dew when we got up, sparkling and cold with our morning mouthfuls. Some rain came at nighttime in short, soft caresses rather than pummeling on our pavilion roofs. I remember screens pulled down, the smell of grass, and warm breath of a groom-mate against my haunches.

"I'm preggers too," I said some weeks later and giggled, thrilled and full of butterflies. I was young, eh? In my fourth year. I could feel my baby nudge. Leveza and I giggled together under our shawls.

It did not go sharply cold. No grass-frost made our teeth ache. We waited for the triggering, but it did not come.

"Strangest year I can remember," said the old women. They were grateful, for migrations were when they were eaten.

That year! We made porridge for the toothless. We groomed and groomed, beads and bows and necklaces and shawls and beautiful grass hats. Leveza loved it when I made up songs; the first, middle, and last word of every line would rhyme. She'd snort and shake her mane and say, "How did you do that; that's so clever!"

We would stroke each other's stomachs as our nipples swelled. Leveza hated hers; they were particularly large like aubergines. "Uh. They're gross. Nobody told me they wobble in the way of everything." They ached to give milk; early in her pregnancy they started to seep. There was a scrum of babysquirrels around her every morning. Business-like, she sniffed and let them suckle. "When my baby comes, you'll have to wait your turn." The days and nights came and went like the beating of birdlike wings. She got a bit bigger, but never too big to stand guard.

Leveza gave birth early, after only nine months.

It was midwinter, in dark Fehveroo when no one was ready. Leveza pushed her neck up against my mouth for comfort. When I woke she said, "Get Grama for me." Grama was a high-ranking midwife.

I was stunned. She could not be due yet. The midwives had stored no oils or bark-water. I ran to Grama, woke her, worried her. I hoofed the air in panic. "Why is this happening now? What's wrong?"

By the time we got back, Leveza had delivered. Just one push and the babe had arrived, a little bundle of water and skin and grease on the ground behind her rear quarters.

The babe was tiny, as long as a shin, palomino, and covered in soft orange down so light that he looked hairless. No jaw at all. How would he grind grass? Limbs all in soft folds like clouds. Grama said nothing, but held up his feet for me to see. The forelegs had no hoof-buds at all, just fingers; and his hind feet were great soft mitts. Not quite a freak, streamlined and beautiful in a way. But fragile, defenseless, and nothing that would help Leveza climb the hierarchy. It was the most Ancestral child I had ever seen.

Grama set to licking him clean. I looked at the poor babe's face. I could see his hide through the sparse hair on his cheeks. "Hello," I said. "I'm your Groom-Mummy. Your name is Kaway. Yes it is. You are Kaway."

A blank. He couldn't talk. He could hardly move.

I had to pick him up with my hands. There was no question of using my mouth; there was no pelt to grip. I settled the babe next to Leveza. Her face shone love down on him. "He's beautiful as he is."

Grama jerked her head toward the partition; we went outside to talk. "I've heard of such births; they happen sometimes. The inheritances come together like cards shuffling. He won't learn to talk until he's two. He won't walk until then, either. He won't really be mobile until three or four."

"Four!" I thought of all those migrations.

Grama shrugged. "They can live long, if they make it past infancy. Maybe fifty years."

I was going to ask where they were now, and then I realized. They don't linger in this world, these soft sweet angelic things.

They get eaten.

My little Choova was born two months later. I hated childbirth. I thought I would be good at it, but I thrashed and stomped and hee-hawed like a male in season. I will never do this again! I promised. I didn't think then that the promise would come true.

"Come on, babe, come on, my darling," Leveza said, butting me with her nose as if herding a filly. "It will be over soon, just keep pushing."

Grama had become a friend; I think she saw value in Leveza's mindful way of doing things. "Listen to your family," she told me.

My firstborn finally bedraggled her way out, tawny, knobbly, shivering and thin, pulled by Grama. Leveza scooped my baby up, licked her clean, breathed into her, and then dandled her in front of my face. "This is your beautiful mother." Choova looked at me with intelligent love and grinned.

Grama whinnied the cry that triggers Happy Birth! Some of our friends trotted up to see my beautiful babe, stuck their heads through the curtains. They tossed their heads, chortled, and nibbled the back of her neck.

"Come on, little one. Stand! Stand!" This is what the ladies had come to see. Leveza propped Choova up on her frail, awkward, heartbreaking legs, and walked her toward me. My baby stumbled forward and collapsed like a pile of sticks, into the sheltering bay of my stomach.

Leveza lowered Kaway in front of Choova's nostrils. "And this is your little groom-brother Kaway."

"Kaway," Choova said. Our family numbered four.

We did not migrate for one whole year. The colts and fillies would skitter unsteadily across the grass, safe from predators. The old folk sunned themselves on the grass and gossiped. High summer came back with sweeping curtains of rain. Then the days shortened; things cooled and dried.

Water started to come out of the wells muddy; we filtered it. The grass started to go crisp. There was perhaps a month or two of moisture left in the ground. Our children neared the end of their first year, worthy of the name foal.

Except for Leveza's. Kaway lay there like an egg after all these months. He could just about move his eyes. Almost absurdly, Leveza loved him as if he were whole and well.

"You are a miracle," she said to Kaway. People called him the Lump.

She would look at him, her face all dim with love, and she would say her fabricated things. She would look at me rapt with wonder.

"What if he knows what the Ancestors knew? We know about cogs and gears and motors and circuits. What if Kaway is born knowing about electricity? About medicine and machines? What he might tell us!"

She told him stories, and the stories went like this:

The Ancestors so loved the animals that when the world was dying, they took them into themselves. They made extra seeds for them, hidden away in their own to carry us safely inside themselves, all the animals they most loved.

The sickness came, and the only way for them to escape was to let the seeds grow. And so we flowered out of them; the sickness was strong, and they disappeared.

Leveza looked down at her little ancestral lump. Some of us would have left such a burden out on the plain for the Cats or the Dogs or the scavenging oroobos. But not Leveza. She could carry anything.

I think Leveza loved everyone. Everyone, in this devouring world. And that's why what happened, happened.

The pampas near the camp went bald in patches, where the old and weak had overgrazed it. Without realizing, we began to prepare.

The babysquirrels gathered metal nuts. The bugs in their tummies made them from rust in the ground. The old uncles would smelt them for knives, rifle barrels, and bullets. Leveza asked them to make some rods.

She heated them and bent them backward and Grama looked at them and asked, "What kind of rifle is that going to make, one that shoots backward?"

"It's for Kaway," Leveza replied. She cut off her mane for fabric. I cut mine as well, and to our surprise, so did Grama.

Leveza wove a saddle for her back, so the baby could ride.

Once Grama had played the superior high-ranker, bossy and full of herself. Now it was, "Oh, Leveza, how clever. What a good idea." And then, "I'm sorry for what I said, earlier." She slipped Leveza's inert mushroom of a boy into the saddle.

Grama had become kind. Grama being respectful about Leveza and Kaway set a fashion for appreciating who my groom-mate was. Nobody asked me any more why on Earth I was with her. When the Head Man Fortchee began talking regularly to her about migration defenses, a wave of gossip convulsed the herd. Could Leveza become the Head Mare? Was the Lump really Fortchee's son?

"She's always been so smart, so brave," said Ventoo. "More like a man," said Lindalfa, with a wrench of a smile.

One morning, the Head Man whinnied over and over and trod the air with his forelegs.

Triggered.

Migration.

We took down the pavilions and the windbreaks and stacked the grass-leaf panels in carts. We loaded all our tools and pipes and balls and blankets, and most precious of all, the caked and blackened foundries. The camp's babysquirrels lined up and chattered goodbye to us, as if they really cared. Everyone nurtured the squirrels, and used them as they use us; even Cats will never eat them.

It started out a fine migration. Oats lined the length of the trail. As we ate, we scattered oat seed behind us, to replace it. Shit, oat seed, and inside the shit, flakes of plastic our bellies made, but there were no squirrels to gather it.

It did not rain, but the watering holes and rivers stayed full. It was sunny but not so hot that flies tormented us.

In bad years your hide never stops twitching because you can't escape the stench of Cat piss left to dry on the ground. That year the ground had been washed and the air was calm and sweet.

We saw no Cats. Dogs, we saw Dogs, but fat and jolly Dogs stuffed to the brim with quail and partridge which Cats don't eat. "Lovely weather!" the Dogs called to us, tongues hanging out, grins wide, and we whinnied back, partly in relief. We can see off Dogs, except when they come in packs.

Leveza walked upright the whole time, gun at the ready, Kaway strapped to her back.

"Leveza," I said, "You'll break your back! Use your palmhoofs!"

She grunted. "Any Cat comes near our babies, and it will be one sorry Cat!"

"What Cats? We've seen none."

"They depend on the migrations. We've missed one. They will be very, very hungry."

Our first attack came the next day. I thought it had started to rain; there was just a hissing in the grass, and I turned and I saw old Alez; I saw her eyes rimmed with white, the terror stare. I didn't even see the four Cats that gripped her legs.

Fortchee brayed a squealing sound of panic. Whoosh, we all took off. I jumped into a gallop, I can tell you, no control or thought; I was away; all I wanted was the rush of grass under my hands.

Then I heard a shot and I turned back and I saw Leveza, all alone, standing up, rifle leveled. A Cat was spinning away from Alez, as if it were a spring-pasture caper. The other Cats stared. Leveza fired again once more and they flickered like fire and were gone. Leveza flung herself flat onto the grass just before a crackling like tindersticks came out of the long grass.

The Cats had guns, too. Running battle. "Down down!" I shouted to the foals. I galloped toward them. "Just! Get! Flat!" I jumped on top them, ramming them down into the dirt. They wailed in panic and fear. "Get off me! Get off me!" My little Choova started to cry. "I didn't do anything wrong!"

I was all teeth. "What did we tell you about an attack? You run, and when the gunfire starts you flatten. What did I say! What did I say?"

Gunsmoke drifted; the dry grass sparkled with shot, our nostrils shivered from the smell of burning.

Cats prefer to pounce first, get one of us down, and have the rest of us gallop away. They know if they fire first, they're more likely to be shot themselves.

The fire from our women was fierce, determined, and constant. We soon realized that the only gunfire we heard was our own and that the Cats had slunk away.

The children still wailed, faces crumpled, tears streaming. Their crying just made us grumpy. Well, we all thought, it's time they learned. "You stupid children. What did you think this was, a game?"

Grama was as hard as any granny. "Do you want to be torn to pieces and me have to watch it happen? Do you think you can say to a Cat very nicely please don't eat me and that will stop them?"

Leveza was helping Alez to stand. Her old groom-mother's legs kept giving way, and she was grinning a wide rictus grin. She looked idiotic.

"Come on, love, that's it." Leveza eased Alez toward Pronto's cart.

"What are you doing?" Pronto said, glaring at her.

Levesa replied, "She's in no fit state to walk."

"You mean, I'm supposed to haul her?"

"I know you'd much rather leave her to be eaten, but no thanks, not just this once."

Somehow, more like a Goat than a Horse, Alez nipped up into the wagon. Leveza strode back toward us, still on her hind legs.

The children shivered and sobbed. Leveza strode up to us. And then did something new.

"Aw, babies," she said, in a stricken tone I had never heard before. She dropped down on four haunches next to them. "Oh darlings!" She caressed their backs, laying her jaw on the napes of their necks. "It shouldn't be like this, I know. It is terrible, I know. But we are the only thing they have to eat."

"Mummy shouted at me! She was mean."

"That's because Mummy was so worried and so frightened for you. She was scared because you didn't know what it was and didn't know what to do. Mummy was so frightened that she would lose you."

"The Cats eat us!"

"And the crocodiles in the river. And there are Wolves, a kind of Dog. We don't get many here, they are on the edge of the snows in the forests. Here, we get the Cats."

Leveza pulled back their manes and breathed into their nostrils. "It shouldn't be like this."

Should or shouldn't, we thought, that's how it is. Why waste energy wishing it wasn't?

We'd forgotten, you see, that it was a choice, a choice that in the end was ours. Not my Leveza.

The Head Man came up, and his voice was also gentle with the colts and fillies. "Come on, kids. The Cats will be back. We need to move away from here."

He had to whinny to get us moving; he even back-kicked the reluctant Pronto. Alez sat up in the cart looking cross-eyed and beside herself with delight at being carried.

"Store and dry cud," Fortchee told us.

Cudcakes. How I hate cudcakes. You chew them and spit them out on the carts to dry and you always think you'll remember where yours are and you always end up eating someone else's mash of grass and spit.

Leveza walked next to the Head Man, looking at maps, murmuring and tossing her mane toward the east. I saw them make up their minds about something.

I even felt a little tail-flick of jealousy. When she came back, I said a bit sharply. "What was that all about?"

Leveza sounded almost pleased. "Don't tell the others. We're being stalked."

"What?"

"Must be slim pickings. The Cats have left their camp. They've got their cubs with them. They're following us." She sighed, her eyes on the horizon. "It's a nuisance. They think they can herd us. There'll be some kind of trap set ahead, so we've decided to change our route."

We turned directly east. The ground started to rise, toward the hills, where an age-old trail goes through a pass. Rocks began to break through a mat of thick grasses. The slope steepened, and each of the carts needed two big men to haul it up.

The trail followed valleys between high rough humps of ground, dovetailing with small streams cut deeply into the grass. We could hear the water, like thousands of tongues lapping on stone. The most important thing on a migration is to get enough to drink. The water in the streams was delicious, cold and tasting of rocks, not mud.

My name means water, but I think I must taste of mud.

We found ourselves in a new world, looking out on waves of earth, rising and falling and going blue in the distance. On the top of distant ridge a huge rock stuck out, with a rounded dome like a skull.

Fortchee announced, "We need to make that rock by evening." It was already early afternoon, and everyone groaned.

"Or you face the Cats out here on open ground," he said.

"Come on, you're wasting breath," said Leveza and strode on.

The ground was strange; a deep rich black smelling deliciously of grass and leaves, and it thunked underfoot with a hollow sound like a drum. We grazed as we marched, tearing up the grass and pulling up with it mouthfuls of soil, good to eat but harsh, hard to digest. It made us fart, pungently, and in each others faces as we marched. "No need for firelighters!" the old women giggled.

In places the trail had been washed away, leaving tumbles of boulders that the carts would creak up and over, dropping down on the other side with a worrying crash. Leveza stomped on, still on two legs, gun ready. She would spring up rocks, heel-hooves clattering and skittering on stone. Sure-footed she wasn't. She did not hop nimbly, but she was relentless.

"They're still here," she muttered to me. All of us wanted our afternoon kip, but Fortchee wouldn't let us. The sun dropped, the shadows lengthened. Everything glowed orange. This triggered fear—low light means you must find safe camping. We snorted, and grew anxious.

Down one hill and up the other: it was sunset, the worst time for us, when we arrived at the skull rock. We don't like stone, either.

"We sleep up there," Fortchee said. He had a fight on his hands. We had never heard of such a thing.

"What, climb up that? We'll split out hooves. Or tear our fingers," said Ventoo.

"And leave everything behind in the wagons?" yelped one of the men. "It'll be windy and cold."

Fortchee tossed his head. "We'll keep each other warm."

"We'll fall off...."

"Don't be a load of squirrels," said Leveza, went to a cart, picked up a bag of tools, and started to climb.

Fortchee amplified, "Take ammo, all the guns."

"What about the foundries?"

He sighed. "We'll need to leave those."

By some miracle, the dome had a worn hole in the top full of rainwater and we drank. We had our kip, but the Head Man wouldn't let us go down to graze. It got dark and we had another sleep, two hours or more. But you can't sleep all night.

I was woken up by a stench of Cat that seemed to shriek in my nostrils. I heard Leveza sounding annoyed. "Tuh!" she said, "Dear oh dear!" Louder than a danger call—bam!—a gun blast, followed by the yelp of a Cat. Then the other afriradors opened fire. The children whinnied in terror. Peering down into milklight I could see a heaving tide of Cat pulling back from the rock. They even made a sound like water, the scratching of claws on stone.

"What fun," said Leveza.

I heard Grama trying not to giggle. Safety and strength came off Leveza's hide like a scent.

She turned to Fortchee. "Do you think we should go now or wait here?"

"Well, we can't wait until after sunrise, that'll slow us down too much. Now."

Leveza really was acting like Head Mare, and there had not been one of those in a while. She was climbing into the highest status. Not altogether hindered by having, if I may say so, a high-class groom-mate.

The afriradors sent out continual shots to drive back the last of the Cats. Then we skittered down the face of the rock back toward the wagons.

At the base of the cliff, a Cat lay in a pool of blood, purring, eyes closed as if asleep. Lindalfa scream-whinnied in horror and clattered backward. The Cat rumbled but did not stir.

Muttering, fearful, we were all pushed back by Cat-stench; we twitched and began to circle just before panic.

Leveza leaned in close to stare.

"Love, come away," I said. I picked my way forward, ready to grab her neck and pull her back if the thing lunged. I saw its face in milklight. I'd never seen a Cat up close before.

The thing that struck me was that she was handsome. It was a finely formed face, despite the short muzzle, with a divided upper lip which seemed almost to smile, the mouthful of fangs sheathed. The Cat's expression looked simply sad, as if she were asking Life itself one last question.

Leveza sighed and said, "Poor heart."

The beast moaned, a low miserable sound that shook the earth. "You ... need ... predators."

"Like cat-shit we do," said Leveza, and stood up and back. "Come on!" she called to the rest of us, as if we were the ones who had been laggard.

The Cats were clever. They had pulled out far ahead of us so we had no idea when they would attack again. Our hooves slipped on the rocks. Leveza went all hearty on us. "Goats do this sort of thing. They have hooves, too."

"They're cloven," said one of the bucks.

"Nearly cousins," sniffed Leveza. I think the light, the air, and the view so far above the plain exhilarated her. It depressed me. I wanted to be down there where it was flat and you could run and it was full of grass. The men hauling the wagons never stopped frothing, eyes edged white. They were trapped in yokes and that made them easy prey.

We hated being strung out along the narrow trail, and kept hanging back so we could gather together in clumps. She would stomp on ahead and stomp on back. "Come on, everyone, while it's still dark."

"We're just waiting for the others," quailed Lindalfa.

"No room for the others, love, not on this path."

Lindalfa sounded harassed. "Well, I don't like being exposed like this."

"No, you'd far rather have all your friends around you to be eaten first." It was a terrible thing to say, but absolutely true. Some of us laughed.

Sunrise came, the huge white sky contrasting too much with the silhouetted earth so that we could see nothing. We waited it out in a defensive group, carts around us. As soon as the sun rose high enough, Leveza triggered us to march. Not Fortchee. She urged us on and got us moving, and went ahead to scout. I learned something new about my groom-mate: the most loyal and loving of us was also the one who could most stand being alone.

She stalked on ahead, and I remember seeing the Lump sitting placidly on her back, about as intelligent as a cudcake.

A high wind stroked the grass in waves. Beautiful clouds were piled up overhead, full of wheeling birds, scavengers who were neither hunters nor victims. They knew nothing of ancestors or even speech.

Then we heard over the brow of a hill the snarl of Cats who have gone for the kill and no longer need stealth.

Leveza. Ahead. Alone.

"Gotcha!" they roared in thunder-voices. We heard gunfire, just a snapping like a twig, and a Cat yelp, and then more gunfire and after that a heartfelt wail that could not have come from a Cat, a long hideous keening, more like that of a bird.

Fortchee broke into a lurching, struggling gallop. He triggered me and I jumped forward into a gallop, too, slipping on rocks, heaving my way up the slope. It was like a nightmare where something keeps pulling you back. I heaved myself up onto the summit and saw Leveza, sitting on the ground, Fortchee stretching down to breathe into her ears.

She was staring ahead. Fortchee looked up at me with such sadness.

Before he could speak, Leveza turned her heavy jaws, her great snout toward the sky and mourned, whinnying now a note for the dead.

"They got the Lump," said the Head Man, and turned and rubbed her shoulders. Her saddle-pack was torn. The baby was gone. Leveza keened, rocking from side to side, her lips forming a circle, the sound coming from far back and down her throat.

"Leveza," said Fortchee, looking forlornly at me.

"Leveza," I agreed, for we knew that she would not forget Kaway soon. The rest of us, we lose a child, we have another next year; we don't think about it; we can't afford to. We're not strong enough. They die, child after child, and the old beloved aunties, or the wise old men who can no longer leap away. We can hear them being eaten. "Remember me! I love you!" they call to us, heartbroken to be leaving life and leaving us. But we have to forget them.

So we go brittle and shallow, sweet and frightened, smart but dishonest.

Not Leveza. She suddenly snarled, snatched up her rifle, rocked to her feet, and galloped off after the Cats.

"She can't think that she can get him back!" I said.

"I don't know what she can think," said Fortchee.

The others joined us and we all stood haunches pressed together. None of us went to help, not even me, her beloved groom-mate. You do not chase prides of Cats to rescue anyone. You accept that they have been taken.

We heard distant shots, and the yelping of Cats. We heard hooves.

"She's coming back," whispered Grama and glanced at me. It was as if the hills themselves had stood up to stretch to see if things looked any different. A Horse had been hunting Cats.

Leveza appeared again at the top of the hill, and for a moment I thought she had wrought a miracle, for her child dangled from her mouth.

Then I saw the way she swayed when she walked, the dragging of her hooves. She baby-carried a tiny torn head and red bones hanging together by tendons and scraps of skin. Suddenly she just sat on the ground and renewed her wailing. She arched her head round and looked down at herself in despair. Her breasts were seeping milk.

She tried to make the bones drink. She pushed the fragments of child onto her dugs. I cantered to her, lost my footing, and collapsed next to her. "Leveza. Love. Let him be."

She shouted up into my face with unseeing eyes. "What am I supposed to do with him?"

"Oh Leveza," I started to weep for her. "You feel things too much."

"I'm not leaving him!"

You're supposed to walk away. You're supposed to leave them to the birds and then to the sun and then to the rains until they wash back into the earth.

To come again as grass. We eat our grandmothers, in the grass. It shows acceptance, good will toward the world to forget quickly.

Leveza began to tear at the thin pelt of ground that covered the rocks. She gouged at it, skinning her forefingers, broke open the sod, and peeled it back. She laid the scraps on the bare rock, and gently covered what was left of him as if with a blanket. She tucked him in and began to sing a soft milklight song to him.

It simply was not bearable. If a child dies through sickness, you take it away from camp and let the birds and insects get to it. Then later you dance on the bones, to break them up into dust to show scorn for the body and acceptance of fate.

The Head Man came back and bumped her with his snout. "Up, Leveza. We must keep moving."

Leveza stroked the ground. "Goodnight, Kaway. Sleep, Kaway. Grow like a seed. Become beautiful Kaway grass."

We muttered and murmured. We'd all lost people we love. Why should she keen and carry on, why should she be different?

"I know it's hard," said Lindalfa. Unspoken was the "but."

Love can't be that special. Love must not cost that much. You'll learn, Leveza, I thought, like all the others. You'll finally learn.

I was looking down at her in some kind of triumph, proved right, when Leveza stood up and turned everything upside down again.

She shook the tears out of her eyes and then walked away from me, shouldering past Fortchee as if he were an encumbrance. Tamely we trooped after her. She went to a wagon and reloaded her gun. She started to troop back down the hill in the direction of the rock.

"That's the wrong way, isn't it?"

"What's she doing?"

Fortchee called after her, and when she didn't answer, he looked deeply at me and said, "Follow her."

I whinnied for her to wait and started to trot down the hill. Her determined stomp became a canter, then, explosively, a kind of leaping, runaway gallop, thundering slipshod over stones and grass, threatening to break a leg. I chortled the slow-down cry but that checked her only for a moment. At the foot of the rock she slid to a halt, raising dust.

She leveled her gun at the head of the wounded Cat. A light breeze seemed to blow her words to me up the slope. "Why do we need predators?" The Cat groaned, its eyes still shut. "The Ancestors destroyed the world."

I reached them. "Leveza, come away," I nickered.

The Cat swallowed heavily. "They killed predators." All her words seemed to start with a growl.

Leveza went very still. I flanked her, and kept saying, leave her, come away. Suddenly she pushed the gun at me. "Shoot her if she moves."

I hated guns. I thought they would explode in my hands, or knock me backward. I knew carrying a gun made you a target. I didn't want the gun; I wanted to get us back to safety. I whinnied in fear.

She pushed on back up the hill. "I'm coming back," she said over her shoulder. I was alone with a Cat.

"Just kill me," said the Cat. The air was black with her blood; everything in me buzzed and went numb. Overhead the scavengers spiraled, and I was sure at any moment other Cats would come. *Climb the rock!* I told myself, but I couldn't move. I looked up at the trail.

Finally, finally Leveza came back with another gun and a coil of rope.

"Don't you ever do that to me again!" I sobbed.

She looked ferocious, her mane bristling, teeth smiling to bite out flesh. "You want to live, you put up with this," she said. I thought she said it to me.

"What are you fabricating now?" I hated her then, always having to surprise.

She bound the Cat's front paws together, and then the back, and then tied all four limbs to the animal's trunk. Leveza seized the mouth; I squealed and she began to wrap the snout round and round with rope. Blood seeped in woven patterns through the cord. The Cat groaned and rolled her eyes.

Then, oh then, Leveza sat on the ground and rolled the Cat onto her own back. She reached round and turned it so that it was folded sideways over her. Then she turned to me. "I don't suppose there's any chance of you giving me a hand?"

I said nothing. All of this was so unheard of that it triggered nothing, not even fear.

Slowly, forelegs first, Leveza stood up under the weight of the Cat. The Cat growled and dug in those great claws, but that just served to hold her in place. Burdened, Leveza began to climb the hill, her back beginning to streak with blood. I looked up. Everyone was bunched together on the brow of the ridge. I had no words, I forgot all words. I just climbed.

As we drew near, the entire herd, every last one of them, including her groom-mother Alez formed a wall of lowered heads. *Go back, get away.* I think it was for the Cat, but it felt as if it were for us. Leveza kept coming. Hides started to twitch from the smell of Cat blood carried on the wind. Leveza ignored them and plodded on. The men had also come back with the carts. Old Pronto in harness tried to move sideways in panic and couldn't.

"Think," she told him. "For a change."

He whinnied and danced in place on the verge of bolting with one of our main wagons.

"Oh for heaven's sake!" She plucked out the pin of his yoke with her teeth and he darted away, the yoke still on his shoulders. He trotted to a halt and then stood there looking sheepish.

Leveza rolled the Cat onto the wagon, tools clanking under the body. Brisk and businesslike, she picked up pliers and began to pull out one, by one, all of the Cat's claws.

The poor beast groaned, roared, and shivered, rocking her head and trying to bite despite her jaws being tied shut. The Cat flexed her bloodied hands and feet but she no longer had claws. It seemed to take forever as the air whispered about us.

Undirected, all of us just stared.

When it was over, the Cat lay flat, panting. Leveza then took more rope, tied it tight round the predator's neck, lashing the other end to the yoke fittings. She then unwound the rope from her jaws. The Cat roared and rocked in place; her huge green fangs smelling of blood. Leveza took a hammer and chisel, and began to break all the Cat's teeth.

Fortchee stepped forward. "Leveza. Stop. This is cruel."

"But necessary or she'll eat us."

"Why are you doing this? It won't bring Kaway back." She turned and looked at him, the half wheel of her lower jaw swollen.

"To learn from her."

"Learn what?"

"What she knows."

"We have to get moving," said the Head Man.

"Exactly," she said, with flat certainty. "That's why she's in the cart."

"You're taking her with us?" Everything on Fortchee bristled, from his mane to his handsome goatee.

She stood there, and I think I remember her smiling. "You won't be able to stop me." The entire herd made a noise in unison, a kind of horrified, wondering sigh. She turned to me with airy unconcern and asked, "Do you think you could get me the yoke?"

Pronto tossed it at her with his head. "Here, have it, demented woman!"

I started to weep. "Leveza, this won't bring him back. Come, love, let it be, leave her alone and let's go."

She looked at me with pity. "Poor Akwa."

Leveza pulled the wagon herself. Women are supposed carry guns; men haul the wagon, two of them together if it is uphill. I tried to walk with her. No one else could bear to go near the prickling stench of Cat. It made me weep and cough. "I can't stay."

"It's all right, love," she said. "Go to the others, you'll feel safer."

"You'll be alone with that thing."

"She's preoccupied." Unable to imagine what else do, I left.

We migrated on. All through that long day, Fortchee did not let us sleep, and we could sometimes hear Leveza behind us, tormenting the poor animal with questions.

"No," we heard her shout. "It's not instinct. You can choose not to eat other people!"

The Cat roared and groaned. "Sometimes there is nothing else to eat! Do you want us to let our children die?"

Leveza roared back. "Why take my baby then? There was no..."
She whinnied loud in horror, and snorted in fury. "There was no meat
on him!"

The Cat groaned. She was talking, but we couldn't hear what she
said. Leveza went silent, plodding on alone, listening to the Cat. She fell
far behind even the rear guard of afriradors who were supposed to protect stragglers. Already it was slightly as though she did not exist.

The light settled low and orange, the shadows grew long. I kept
craning behind us, but by then I could neither see nor hear Leveza.

"They'll attack her! She'll be taken!" I nickered constantly to Grama.

She laid her head on my neck as we walked. "If anyone can stand
alone against Cats, it's her."

We found no outcropping. On top of a hill with a good view all
around, Fortchee lifted himself up and trod the air, whinnying. The men
in the carts turned left and circled. "Windbreaks!" called the Head Man.
We all began to unload windbreak timbers, to slot down the sides of the
carts, to make a fortress. I kept looking back for Leveza.

Finally she appeared in the smoky dusk hauling the Cat. Froth had
dried on her neck. She looked exhausted; her head dipped as if chastened.

Fortchee stepped in front of her. "You can't come into the circle
with that cart."

She halted. Burrs and bracken had got tangled in her mane. She
stared at the ground. "She's tied up. She's very weak."

Fortchee snorted in anger and pawed the dirt. "Do you think anybody could sleep with a Cat stinking up the inside of the circle?"

She paused, blinked. "She says the other Cats will kill her."

"Let them!" said Fortchee. Without answering, Leveza turned and
hauled the cart away from the camp. Fortchee froze, looked at her, and
then said, "Akwa, see to your groom-mate."

Something in that made Grama snort, and she came with me. As we
walked together toward the cart, we pressed together the whole length of
our bodies from shoulder to haunch for comfort.

Grama said, "She's reliving what happened to Grassa."

"Grassa?"

"Her mother. She saw her eaten, remember?"

"Oh yes, sorry." I did the giggle, the giggle you give to excuse forgetting, the forgetting of the dead out of embarrassment and the need to keep things light. "Anyway," I said, "you made things hard enough for her when she was young."

Grama hung her head. "I know." Grama had tried to bully Leveza until she'd head-butted her, though two years younger.

It's not good to remember.

Leveza had already climbed up into the cart without having watered or grazed. Her eyes flicked back and forth between me and Grama. "Grama, of course, how sensible. Here." She threw something at me and without thinking I caught it in my mouth. It was a bullet, thick with Cat blood, and I spat it out.

"Fortchee wouldn't thank you for that. He's always telling us to save metal. Grama, love, do you think you could bring us bark-water, painkillers, thread?"

Grama's hide twitched, but she said, "Yes, of course."

Leveza reached around and tossed her a gun. "Watch yourself. I'll keep my gun ready, too."

Grama picked up the bullet, then trotted back through the dusk. I felt undefended, but I could not get up into the wagon with that thing. Leveza stood on hindquarters, scanning the camp, her gun leveled. As Grama came back with a pack, Leveza's nostrils moved as if about to speak.

"They're here," she said.

Grama clambered up into the cart. I couldn't see the Cat behind the sideboards, but I could see Grama's eyes flare open, her mane bristle. Even so, she settled on her rear haunches and began to work, dabbing the wounds. I could hear the Cat groan, deep enough to shake the timber of the cart.

Leveza's tail began to flick. I could smell it now: Cat all around us, scent blowing up the hillside like ribbons. The sunset was full of fire, clouds the color of flowers. Calmly Grama sewed the wound. Leveza eased herself down, eyes still on the pasture, to feel if Grama's gun was loaded.

"Her name's Mai, by the way," said Leveza. Mai meant Mother in both tongues.

The Cat made a noise like Rergurduh, Rigadoo. Thanks.

Leveza nickered a gentle safety call to me. I jumped forward, and then stopped. The smell of Cat was a wall.

"Get up into the cart," said Leveza in a slow mothering voice.

It was the Terrible Time, when we can't see. Milklight fills the night, but when the sky blazes and the earth is black, the contrast means we can see nothing. Leveza reached down, bit my neck to help haul me up.

I was only halfway into the cart when out of that darkness a deep rumble formed words. "We will make the Horses eat you first."

Leveza let me go to shriek out the danger call, to tell the others. I tried to kick my way into the cart.

"Then while you cry we will take their delicious legs."

I felt claws rake the back of my calves. I screamed and scrambled. A blast right by my ears deafened me; I pulled myself in; I smelt dust in the air.

Leveza. How could she see? How could she walk upright all day?

She touched a tar lamp, opened its vent, and it gave light. "Aim for eyes," she said.

We saw yellow eyes, narrow and glowing, pure evil, hypnotizing. Ten, fifteen, how many were there, trying to scramble into the wagon?

Grama shot. Leveza shot. I had no gun and yearned to run so stamped my feet and cried for help. Some of the eyes closed and spun away. I looked at Mother Cat. She had folded up, eyes closed, but I was maddened and began to kick her as if she threatened my child. The sun sank.

Finally we heard a battle-cry and a thundering of hooves from the circle. Leveza bit my neck and threw me to the floor of the cart. My nostrils were pushed into a pool of Cat juices. I heard shots and metal singing through the air. Our mares were firing wildly at anything. Why couldn't they see?

"Put that lamp out!" shouted Fortchee. Leveza stretched forward and flicked it shut. Then in milklight, our afriradors took more careful aim. I felt rather than heard a kind of thumping rustle, bullets in flesh, feet through grass. I peered out over the sides of the wagon and in milklight I saw the Cats pulling back, slipping up and over rocks, crouching behind them. I lay back down and looked at Mother Cat. She shivered, her eyes screwed shut. A Cat felt fear?

We could still smell them, we could still hear them. Fortchee said, "All of you, back into the circle. You too, Leveza."

She snuffled from weariness. "Can't!"

I cried, "Leveza! Those are real Cats, they will come back! What you care about her?"

"I did this to her," Leveza said.

Fortchee asked, "Why do other Cats want to kill her?"

A deep voice next to me purred through broken teeth. "Dissh-honour." Chilled, everyone fell silent. "Alsho, I talk too much," said Mother Cat. Did she chuckle?

I pleaded. "Choova misses you; she wants her groom-mummy; I miss you; please, Leveza, come back!" Fortchee ordered the men to give her a third gun and some ammo.

Grama looked at me with a question in her eyes I didn't want to see. As far as I was concerned, Fortchee had told us to pull back. I was shaking inside. Grama wasn't the one who had felt claws on her haunches.

All the way back, Grama bit the back of my neck as if carrying me like a mother.

We nestled down under a wagon behind the windbreak walls. Choova worked her way between us. None of us could sleep even the two hours.

We paced and pawed. I stood up and looked out, and saw Leveza standing on watch, unfaltering.

At dawnsky when she would have most difficulty seeing, I heard shots, repeated. I fought my way out from under the wagon, and jerked my head over the windbreak between the carts where there are only timbers.

Blank whiteness, blank darkness, and in the middle a lamp glowing like a second sunrise. I could see nothing except swirling smoke and yellow dust and Leveza hunching behind the sides of the wagon suddenly nipping up to shoot. Someone else glowed orange in that light, firing from the other side.

Leveza had given a gun to the Cat.

I saw leaping arms fanning what looked like knives. Everything spiraled in complete silence. The Cats made no sound at all. I was still rearing up my head over the windbreak to look, when suddenly, in complete silence, a Cat's head launched itself at my face. All I saw was snout, yellow eyes, fangs in a blur jammed up close to me. I leapt back behind the windbreak; the thing roared, a paralyzing sound that that froze me. I could feel it make me go numb. The numbness takes away the pain as they eat you.

I couldn't think for a long time after that. I stood there shaking, gradually becoming aware of my pounding heart. Others were up, had begun to work; the sun was high; dawnsky was over. I heard Choova call me, but I couldn't answer. She galloped out to me, crying and weeping. Grama followed, looked concerned, and then began to trot.

It showed in my face. "Did one of them get in here?" she asked.

I couldn't answer, just shook my head, no. Choova cried, frightened for me. "It climbed the wall," I said and realized I'd been holding my breath.

"Leveza's not in the wagon," said Grama. We reared up to look over the wall. The slope was grassy, wide, the day bright. The wagon stood alone, with nothing visible in it. Grama looked at me.

Maybe she'd gone to graze? I scanned the fields and caught motion from the slopes behind me, turned and my heart shivered with relief. There was Leveza slowly climbing toward us.

"What's she doing down there, that's where the Cats are!"

She held something in her mouth. For moment I thought she'd gone back again for Kaway. Then I saw feathers. Birds? As she lowered herself, they swayed limply.

"She's been hunting," said Grama.

"She's gone mad," I said. "I fear so."

We told Choova to stay where she was, and Grama and I trotted out to meet her.

"Is that what I think it is? Is it?" I shouted at her. I was weepier than I would normally be, shaken.

Leveza reared up and took the dead quail out of her mouth. "She needs to eat something," said Leveza. She was in one of her hearty,

blustering moods, cheerful about everything and unstoppable. She strode
on two legs. She'd braided her mane and then held it on top of her head
with plastic combs, out of her eyes.

Grama sighed. "We don't take life, Leveza. We value it."

She looked merry. She shook the quail. "I value thought. These
things can't think."

"That's a horrible thing to say!"

She swept past us. "You'd rather she ate us, I suppose. Or maybe
you want her to die. How does that show you value life?"

She trooped on toward the cart. Grama had an answer. "I'd rather
the Cat hunted for herself."

"Good. I'll give her a gun then."

I was furious. "She had a gun last night!"

"Oh. Yes. Well. She was a welcome addition to our resources."
Leveza smiled. "Since I was otherwise on my own." She looked at me
dead in the eye, and her meaning was plain enough.

"If they value life so much, why did they take Kaway then?" I was
sorry the instant I said it. I meant that I'd heard her ask the Cat that and
I wanted to know the answer, too, just like she did.

"Because I broke the bargain," she said, so calmly that I was almost
frightened.

I wanted to show her that I was outraged at what they'd done.
"What bargain?"

She lost some kind of patience. "Oh come on, Akwa, you're not a
child. The bargain! The one where they don't take children so they grow
up nice and fat for them to eat later and we let them take our old and
sick. They get to eat, and we get rid of people whose only use is that they
are experienced and wise, something Horses can't use, because of course
we know everything already. So we don't shoot Cats except to scare them
off, and they don't shoot us." Her eyes looked like the Cats' reflecting our
lamps. "That bargain."

"I . . . I'm sorry."

"I shot them when they took the old. They saw I was the leader, so
I was the target."

Grama and I looked at each other. Grama said with just a hint of a smile, "You...?"

"Yes, me. The Cats can see it even if you can't."

Grama pulled back her lips as if to say, oops, pushed her too far that time. As we followed her Grama butted me gently with her head. *It's just Leveza fabricating.*

Leveza strode ahead of us, as if she didn't need us, and it was uncomfortably like she didn't.

Once at the cart, Leveza took out a knife and began to butcher the quail. I cried and turned away. She pushed the meat toward the Cat, who opened her eyes but did not move. The creature had had to relieve herself in the cart so the stink was worse than ever.

Leveza dropped onto all fours and trotted to the neck of the cart. "Help me into the yoke?"

"You've not asked me about Choova."

"How is she?" She picked up the yoke by herself.

"Terrified and miserable. She saw the empty cart and thought you were dead." Grama helped settle the yoke, slipping in the pin. At once Leveza started to drag the cart forward.

"You're going now?" The camp was not even being dismantled.

"Stragglers get taken. Today I intend to be in front. We start going downhill."

"Let's go!" I said to Grama, furious, but she shook her head and walked on beside the cart.

"I've got a gun," she said. "We should guard her."

I should have gone back to take care of Choova, but it felt wrong somehow to leave someone else guarding my groom-mate. I shouted to Choova as we passed the camp. "Groom-mummy is fine, darling; we're just going with her to make sure she's safe."

All of us walked together, the cart jostling and thunking over rocks.

"So tell them, Mai. Why does the world need predators?"

I looked into the wagon and saw that the Cat had clenched about herself like fingers curled up inside a hoof. I could sense waves of illness coming off her. I saw the horrible meat. She hadn't touched it. She looked at me with dead eyes.

"Go on, Mai; explain!"

The Cat forced herself to talk, and rolled onto her back, submissively. "'ere wasssh a ribber...," she said, toothlessly. "There was a river and there were many goats and many wolves to eat them." Her voice sounded comic. Everything came out sssh wvuh and boub, like the voices we adopt when we tell jokes. "Verh whuh whvolbss...there were wolves, and the Ancestors killed all the wolves because they were predators."

It was exactly as though she were telling a funny story. I was triggered. I started to laugh.

"And then the rivers started to die. With nothing to eat them, there were too many goats and they ate all the new trees that held the banks together."

I shook my head to get rid of the laughter. I trembled inside from fear. I wanted to wee.

The Cat groaned. "Issh nop a zhope!" *It's not a joke.*

Leveza craned her neck back, looking as though she was teaching me a lesson, her eyes glinting at me in a strange look of triumph and wonder. "What Memory Sticks do Cats have?"

The Cat said, "We know about the seeds, the seeds inside us."

Grama's ears stood straight up.

Leveza's words kept pace with her heavy feet, as if nothing could ever frighten her or hurry her. "Cats know how Ancestors and beasts mingled. They understand how life is made. We could split us up again, Horse and Ancestor. We could give them something else to eat."

It was all too much for me, as if the Earth were turning in the wind. I was giddy.

Grama marched head bowed, looking thoughtful. "So...you know what the other peoples know?"

Leveza actually laughed aloud too. "She does! She does!"

"What do Dogs know?" Grama asked.

The Cat kept telling what sounded like jokes. "Things that are not alive are made of seeds too. Rocks and air and water are all made of tiny things. Dogs know all about those."

"And goats?"

"Ah! Goats know how the universe began."

"And electricity?" Grama actually stepped closer to the Cat. "Everything we know is useless without electricity."

"Bovines," said the Cat. "I've never seen one. But I've heard. You go south and you know you are there because they have lights that glow with electricity!"

"We could make a new kind of herd," Leveza said. "A herd of all the peoples that joins together. We could piece it all together, all that knowledge."

The Cat rolled on her belly and covered her eyes. Grama looked at her and at me, and we thought the same thing. Wounded, no food, no water—I felt nausea, the Cat's sickness in my own belly. Why didn't Leveza?

Grama said, almost as if defending the Cat, "We'd have to all stay together though, all the time. All of us mixed. Or we'd forget it all."

The Cat rumbled. "The Bears have something called writing. It records. But only the big white ones in the south."

"Really!" Leveza said. "If we could do that, we could send knowledge everywhere."

"I've thought that," the Cat said quietly. "Calling all of us together. But my people would eat them all."

It was one of those too-bright days which cloud over, but for now, the sun dazzled.

"The Dolphins in the sea," murmured the Cat as if dreaming. "They know how stars are made and stay in the sky. They use them to navigate."

Sun and wind.

"Sea turtles understand all the different elements, how to mix them."

Grama said, "She needs water."

Leveza sniffed. "We've crossed a watershed. We're going downhill; there'll be a stream soon."

We marched on, toward cauliflower clouds. Grama and I took over pulling the wagon for a time. I don't know what hauling it uphill is like, but going downhill, the whole weight of it pushes into your shoulders and your legs go rubbery pushing back to stop it rolling out of control.

It's worrying being yoked: you can't run as fast; you're trapped with the cart. I looked back round and saw Leveza in the cart fast asleep, side by side with a Cat.

I found myself thinking like Leveza and said to Grama, "I can't aim a gun. You better keep watch."

So I ended up pulling the cart alone, while Grama stood in the wagon with a gun, and I didn't know which one of us was the biggest target.

The slope steepened, and we entered a gully, a dry wash between crags. The wind changed direction constantly, buffeting us with the scent of Cat.

"They're back," I said to Grama.

The scent woke up Leveza. "Thank you," she said. "The two of you should go join the others." She dropped heavily down out of the cart. She searched me with her eyes, some kind of apology in them. "Choova's alone."

Grama's chin tapped me twice. Leveza was right. As we climbed together uphill toward the herd, I said, "Cats don't go out of their territory."

"They're following Leveza. They want Mai, they want her." In other words, Leveza was pulling the Cats with her.

"Don't tell the others," I said.

The wall of faces above us on the hill opened up to admit us, and then closed again behind. We found Choova, who had been having fun with playmates. She'd forgotten Cats, Leveza, everything, and was full of giggles and teasing, pulling my mane. As we walked, the herd gradually caught up with Leveza, and we could hear her and the Cat murmuring to each other.

"What on earth to they find to talk about?" said Raio, my cousin.

"How delicious horseflesh is," said Ventoo.

Choova scowled. "Everybody says that Leveza is bad."

I stroked her and tried to explain it and found that I could not. All I could say was, "Leveza wants to learn."

The trail crossed a stream and Fortchee signaled a break. Leveza still in harness was reaching down to drink. The trickling sound of safe, shallow water triggered a rush. We crowded round the creek, leaning down and thrusting each other's head out of the way. Grama trotted up the hill to make room and found herself the farthest one out, the most exposed. I was about to say, Grama get back.

Three Cats pounced on her. The entire herd pulled back and away from her, swiftly, like smoke blown by wind. Two Cats gripped her hind legs; one was trying to tear out her throat. She was dead, Grama was dead, I was sure of it. I kept leaping forward and back in some kind of impulse to help. Then came a crackle of gunfire. The two Cats on her hindquarters yowled and were thrown back. One spun away and ran; one flipped over backward and was still.

Then one miraculous shot: it sliced through the Cat in front without touching Grama. I looked back in the cart and saw that Leveza had been held down in harness, unable to stand up or reach for her gun.

In the back of the wagon, head and rifle over the sides, was Mother Cat.

Grama shook and shivered, her whole hide twitching independently from the muscles underneath, her eyes ringed round with white. She wasn't even breathing, she was so panicked. I knew exactly how awful that felt. I ronfled the comfort sound over and over as I picked my way to her, touched her. She heaved a huge, painful-sounding breath. I got hold of the back of her neck. "Come on darling, come on baby," I said through clenched teeth. I coaxed her back downstream toward the others. Her rattling breath came in sobs.

There were no sympathy nitters. The other Horses actually pulled back from us as if we carried live flame. Grama nodded that she was all right and I let her go. She still shivered, but she stepped gently back and forth to test her torn rear legs. I lifted the healer's pack from her shoulders and took out the bark-water to wash her.

I was angry at the others and shouted at them. "It's all right, all of you, leave her be. Just leave her alone. She's nursed you often enough."

Fortchee stepped toward us, breathed in her scent to see how badly hurt she was.

Then he looked over in the direction of the Cat, who still held the gun. He calmly turned and walked toward the cart. Leveza had finally succeeded in slipping out of the yoke and begun to climb the hill back toward him.

I tried to coax Grama back to our wagons, but she firmly shook her head. She wanted to listen to what Fortchee said.

I couldn't quite hear him, but I certainly could hear Leveza. "She has just as much reason to escape them as you do!"

Fortchee's voice went harsher, giving an order.

"No," said Leveza. He said something else, and Leveza replied. "It seems she's done a good job of protecting us."

His voice was loud. "Out, now! You or her or both of you."

"I'm already out. Haven't you noticed?" She stepped back toward the long neck of the cart and slammed back on the yoke. "I don't need you, and I don't have you!"

She wrenched herself round, almost dragging the cart sideways, turning it down to follow the stream itself. Fortchee shouted for a break. "Afriradors, guard everyone while they drink." To my surprise, Grama began to limp as fast as she could after Leveza's wagon.

I couldn't let her go alone, so I followed, taking Choova with me. As we trooped down the hill, we passed Fortchee trudging up the slope, his head hanging. He ignored us. A Head Man cannot afford to be defied to his face too often.

I caught up to Grama. We hobbled over rocks, or splashed through shallow pools. Choova rubbed her chin against my flank for comfort. Leveza saw us behind her and stopped.

"Hello, darling," Leveza called back to Choova, who clattered forward, glad to see her. They interlaced their heads, breathed each other's breath. I pressed in close, and felt my eyes sting. We were still a family.

Grama stuck her head over the sides of the wagon. "Thank you," she told Mai.

"You nursed me," said the Cat.

"Mai?" said Leveza. "This is my groom-daughter, Choova."

"Choova," said the Cat and smiled, and crawled up the wagon to be nearer. "I have a boy, Choova, a little boy." Choova looked uncertain and edged back.

"Is he back ... with the pride?" Leveza asked.

"Yesh. But he won't want to know me now." Mai slumped back down in the wagon. "Everything with us is the hunt. Nobody thinks about anything else." She shrugged. "He's getting mature now, he would have been driven off soon anyway."

Leveza stopped pulling. "You should drink some water."

As slow as molten metal, the Cat poured herself out of the cart, halting on tender paws. She drank, but not enough, looked weary, and then wove her unsteady way back toward the wagon. She started to laugh. "I can't get back in."

Leveza slipped out of harness, and we all helped roll Mai onto Leveza's back. Grama sprang back up into the cart and helped pull up the Cat.

"Good to be among friends," Mai whispered.

Leveza stroked her head. "Neither one of us can go back home," she said, staring at Mai with a sad smile. Then she looked at me with an expression that seemed to say, *I think she's going to die.*

I wanted to say, I'm supposed to care about a Cat?

"Don't you get pushed out, too," she said to me, and jerked her head in the direction of the herd. She asked us to bring her lots of lamp fuel, and Grama promised that she would. As we walked toward the others, I couldn't stop myself saying in front of Choova. "She's in love with that bloody Cat!"

That night, Choova, me and Grama slept together again beneath a wagon, behind the windbreak wall.

In the middle of the night, we heard burrowing and saw claws, digging underneath the timbers, trying to get in. We jammed little stakes into the tender places between their toes. I cradled Choova next to me as we heard shots from overhead and Cat cries. We saw flickering light through the boards and smelled smoke.

Fortchee stuck his head underneath the wagon. "Leveza's set the hillside on fire! We have to beat it back." He looked wild. "Come on! There's no more Cats, but the camp's catching fire!" He head-butted Ventoo. "We need everyone!"

Light on the opposite hillside left dim blue and gray shadows across our eyes. Fire rained slowly down, embers from the grass, drifting sparks. Ash tickled our nostrils; we couldn't quite see. We had fuel and firestarters on the wagons; if those caught alight we'd lose everything.

"That bloody woman!" shouted Ventoo. Blindly, we got out blankets and started to beat back the grass fire, aiming for any blur of light. The men stumbled down the stream with buckets to fill, stepping blindly into dark, wondering if Cats awaited them. The ground sizzled, steamed, and trailed smoke. We slapped wet blankets onto the gnawing red lines in the wood.

It was still milklight, and the fire had not burnt out, when Fortchee called for us to pack up and march. Blearily, we hoisted up the windbreak walls, only too happy to move. The smell of ash was making us ill. I glanced up and saw that Leveza had already gone.

Butt her! I thought. My own milk had given out on the trek, and Choova was hungry. What do you have a groom-mate for if not to help nurse your child? "You'll have to graze, baby," I told her.

We churned up clouds of ash. I wandered though something crisp and tangled and realized I had trodden in the burnt carcass of a Cat. Later in the grass we saw the quail that Leveza had shot, thrown away, the meat gone dark and dry. The Cat still had not eaten.

"I want to see if Mai's all right," said Grama.

In full milklight, we trotted ahead to the wagon to find the Cat asleep and Leveza hauling the wagon on two legs only, keeping watch with the rifle ready. She passed us the gun and settled down onto all fours and started to haul again. Her face and voice were stern. "She says it would be possible to bring Horses back, full-blooded Horses. Can you imagine? They could have something else to eat, all of this could stop!"

"What? How?" said Grama.

"The Ancestors wanted to be able to bring both back. We have the complete information for Horses and Ancestors, too. We still carry them inside us!"

"So . . . what do we do?" Grama asked.

"Bee-sh," said a voice from the cart. The Cat sat up with a clown's expression on her face. She chuckled. "You could carry them forever, and they wouldn't come out. They need something from Bees."

For some reason, Leveza chuckled, too. She was always so serious and weighty that I could never make her laugh.

"It's called. . . ." The Cat paused and then wiggled her eyebrows. "Ek-die-ssshone." She paused. "That-ssh a word. I don't know what it mean-sh, either. It's just in my head."

That Cat knew her toothless voice was funny. She was playing up to it. I saw then how clever she was, how clever she had been. She knew just what to say to get Leveza on her side.

"Bee-sh make honey, and bee-sh make Horshes."

"So you give the seed something from bees, and we give birth to fullbloods?" Everything about Grama stood up alert and turned toward the Cat.

"Not you too," I moaned.

Finally I made Leveza laugh.

"Oh Akwa, you old chestnut!"

"No," said the Cat. "What gets born is much, much closer to Horses. It's a mix of you and a full-blooded Horse, but then we can. . . ."

"Breed back!" said Grama. "Just pair off the right ones."

"Yup," said the Cat. "I've alsway-sssh thought I could do it. I jussht needed lotsh of Horshes. My pridemates had sschtrong tendenshee to eat them."

There was something deadly in Leveza's calm. "We could bring back the Ancestors. Imagine what they could tell us! Maybe they have all the Memory Sticks, all together."

The Cat leaned back, her work done. "They knew nothing. They had no memory. Everything they knew, they had to learn. How to walk. How to talk. All over again each time. So they could forget. But they could learn."

Overhead the stars looked like a giant spider's web, all glistening with dew.

"They wanted to travel to the stars. So they thought they would carry the animals and plants inside them. And they were worried that all their knowledge would be lost. How, they asked, can we make the information safe? So they made it like the knowledge every spider has: how to weave a web."

"Kaway," said Leveza, in a mourning voice.

I felt as though I had gone to sleep on the ground all alone instead of sleeping on my feet to watch. This was madness, just the kind of madness to capture Leveza. I will keep watch now, I promised myself.

"Maybe one day the Ancestors will sail back." Leveza arched her neck and looked up at the stars.

All the next day, as we headed east, they talked their nonsense. Nowadays, I wish that I had listened and could remember it, but all I heard then was that the Cat was subverting my Leveza. I knew it was no good pleading with her to let all of this madness alone, to come home, to be as we were. How I wanted that Cat to die. I've never felt so alone and useless.

"Don't worry, love," said Grama. "It's Leveza's way."

I was too angry to answer. The stream dipped down through green hills which suddenly fell away. We stopped at the top of a slope, looking out over a turquoise and gray plain. We had made it to the eastern slopes facing the sea. The grass was long and soft and rich, so we grazed as we walked, and I hoped my milk would come back. The foals, Choova included, began to run up and down through the meadows as if already home. We'd made it; we would be fine.

Fortchee kept pushing us, getting us well out of the Cats' range. Still, it was strange; this was flatlands, full of tall grass. Why were there no other Cats? I kept sniffing the wind, we all did, but all we smelled was the pure fresh smell of grazing.

It was not until near sunset that Fortchee brayed for camp. Grama and I went back, and I kicked the grass as I walked. Grama chewed my mane and called me poor love. "She's always loved ideas. The Cat is full of them."

"Yes, she wants us to make new children to feed to her!" I pulled Choova closer to me and nuzzled her.

We camped, grazed, and watered, but I couldn't settle. I paced round and round. I went back to our wagon, slumped down, and tried to feed Choova again. I couldn't. I wept. I was dry like old grass, and I had no one to help me and felt alone, abandoned. I heard Leveza start to sing! Sing, while sleeping with a Cat. She was blank, unfeeling, something restraining had been left out of her. She didn't love me, she didn't love anything. Just her fabrications. And she'd pulled me and used me up and left me alone.

Choova was restless too. For a while, getting her to sleep occupied me. Finally her breathing fell regular, soft and smelling of hay, sweet and young and trusting, her long slim face resting on my haunches.

I lay there and heard Leveza sing the songs about sunrise, pasture, running through fields, the kinds of songs you sing when you are excited, young. In love.

Sleep wouldn't come, peace wouldn't come. I turned over and Choova stirred, Grama groaned. I was keeping them awake. Suddenly I was determined to bring all of this to a stop. I was going to go out there and get my groom-mate back. So I rolled quietly out from under the wagon. Everything was still; even birds and insects—no stars, no moon. Yet I thought I heard . . . something.

I reared up to look over the windbreaks and saw light over the horizon, and drifting white smoke. I thought it was the last of the fire, then realized it was in the wrong direction. Did I hear shots? And mewling?

I was about to give the danger call when Fortchee stepped up to me. "Fuhfuhfoom," he said, the quiet call. "That's Cat fighting Cat. The ones chasing us have strayed into another pride's territory."

I felt ice on our shoulders. We stood and watched and listened, and our focusing ears seemed to pull the sound closer to us.

A battle between Cats.

"We can sleep on a little longer in safety," he said. "I had to tell Leveza to stop singing."

I started to walk. "I need to talk sense to that woman."

"Good luck." He pulled a cart aside to make a gap for me. "Be careful anyway."

As I walked toward the wagon the sound grew, a growling, roaring, crying, a sound like a creeping wildfire. It was as if all the world had gone mad along with me.

I slipped down the track, silently rehearsing what I would say to her. I would tell her to come back to Choova and the herd and let the Cat do what it could to survive. I would tell her: you choose. Me or that Cat. I would force her to come back, force her to be sensible.

I got halfway down the track, and clouds moved away from the moon, and I saw.

At first I thought Leveza was just grooming her. That would have been enough to make me sick, the thought of grooming something that smelt of death, of blood.

But it wasn't grooming. The Cat had not eaten for days, was wounded and hungry, and Leveza had leaking tits.

I saw her suckling a Cat.

The Earth spun. I had never known that such perversion existed; I'd never heard of normal groom-mates doing such a thing. But what a fearful confounding was this, of species, of mother, of child? While my Choova starved, that Cat, that monster, was being fed, given horsemilk as if by a loving mother.

I gagged and made a little cry and stumbled and coughed, and I think those two in the wagon turned and saw me. I spun around and galloped, hooves pounding, and I was calling over and over, "Foul, foul, foul!"

I wailed, and I heard answering shouts from inside the camp. Ventoo and Lindalfa came hobbling out to me.

"Akwa, darling!"

"Awka, what's wrong?" They were mean-eyed. "What's she done now?" They were yearning for bad news about Leveza.

I wept and wailed and tried to pull myself away. "She won't feed Choova but she's feeding that Cat."

"What do you mean, feed?" I couldn't answer. "Hunting! Yes we saw! Killing for that thing!"

"Foul, yes, poor Akwa!"

I hauled in a breath that pushed my voice box the wrong way.

"It's not hunting!" I was frothing at the mouth, the spittle and foam splayed over my lips and chin. "Uhhhhh!"

I wished the grass would slash her like a thousand needles. I wanted hot embers poured down her throat, I wanted her consumed, I wanted the

Cats to come and make good all their terrible threats. Yes, yes, eat your Cat lover and then be eaten too. Call for me and I will call back to you: *you deserve this!*

Grama was there. "Akwa, calm down. Down, Akwa." She ronfled the soothing noise. I blew out spittle at her, rejecting the trigger from my belly outward. I shriek-whinnied in a mixture of fear, horror, and something like the sickness call.

"She's suckling the Cat!"

Silence.

Someone giggled. I head-butted the person I thought had laughed. "Suckling. An adult. Cat!"

Grama fell silent. I shouted at her. "Heard of that before, Midwife?" My eyes were round; my teeth were shovels for flesh; I was enraged at everything and everyone.

Grama stepped back. Fortchee stepped forward. "What is all this noise?"

I told him. I told him good, I told him long. Ventoo bit my tail to keep me in place; the others rubbed me with their snouts.

"Poor thing! Her groom-mate."

"Enough," said Fortchee. He turned and started to walk toward their wagon.

"Too true there!" said Ventoo. Old Pronto grabbed a gun.

We all followed, making a sound like a slow small rockslide, down toward the cart.

Leveza stood up in the wagon, waiting. So did the Cat.

"Give us your guns," said Fortchee.

"We can't...."

"I'm not asking, I'm ordering."

Leveza looked at him, as if moonlight still shone on his face. She sighed, and looked up at the stars, and handed him her gun.

"The Cat's, too."

Silently Leveza held it out to him.

"Now get down out of that cart and rejoin the herd."

"And Mai?"

Such regret, such fondness, such concern for blood-breathed Cat.

The spittle curdled; the heart shriveled; I tasted gall, and I said, "She's taken a Cat for a groom-mate. I don't want her! I don't want her back!"

Her head jerked up at me in wonder. "All her fabricating!" I felt myself rear up in the air, and I bucked. I bucked to get away from my own heart, from the things I'd seen, for the way I'd been stretched. I was tired, I was frightened, I wanted her to be as we had been. Our girlhoods when we galloped beribboned over the hill.

"She'd feed my child to that bloody Cat!"

Reared up, wrenching, I made a noise I had never heard before, never knew could be made.

It was like giving birth through the throat, some ghastly wriggling thing made of sound that needed to be born, and it came out of me, headless and blind. A relentless, howling pushing-back that flecked everything with foam as if I were the sea.

Triggered.

Even Fortchee. All.

We all moved together, closing like a gate. Our shoulders touched and our haunches. We lowered our heads. We advanced. I saw Leveza look into my eyes and then crumple. She knew what this was, even if I did not, and she knew it had come from me.

We advanced and butted the cart. We pushed all our heads under it and turned the cart over. Leveza and the Cat had to jump out, clumsy, stumbling to find their feet.

The Cat snarled, toothless. Leveza shook her head. "Friends...."

We were deaf. We were upon them. We head-butted them. Leveza slipped backward, onto her knees. Fortchee reared up and clubbed her on the head with his hooves. She stood up, turned. Fortchee, Ventoo, Raio, Pronto, all bared their teeth and bit her buttocks hard. Feet splaying sideways, she began to run.

The Cat bounded, faster in bursts than Leveza was, and leapt up onto her back. Leveza trotted away, carrying her. Her tail waved, defiant. Then milklight closed over them as if they had sunk. We heard light scattering sounds of stones for a while, then even her hoofbeats faded into the whispering sound of spaces between mountains.

Without a word, Grama sprang after them. I saw her go, too. There were no Cats on the plain to seize them as the horizon burned.

The herd swung to the left in absolute unison, wheeling around, and then trotted back to the camp. We felt satisfied, strangely nourished, safe and content. I looked back under the cart. Choova raised her head. "What was that, Mummy?"

"Nothing, love, nothing," I said.

Fortchee told us quietly that we should get moving now while the Cats were occupied. We dismantled the windbreaks and packed the tools. Some of the men turned Leveza's cart upright, and Old Pronto went back to his post in harness. Never did we pack with so little noise, so swiftly, calmly. Nothing was said at all, no mention of it. The horizon burned with someone else's passion.

Choova ran out to graze, her mane bobbing. She never asked about Leveza or Grama, not once, ever. A soft glowing light spread wide across the pampas.

We followed the stream to the sea and then migrated along the sand. It got between our fingers. We did see the Turtles. I would have asked them about acids, especially the acids in batteries, but they were laying eggs and would have been fearful.

Fortchee led us to a wonderful pasture, far to the south, on a lake next to sea, salt and fresh water so close, beside tall sudden cliffs that kept Cats at bay. Oats grew there year round; the rains never left. By digging we found rust shoals, thick layers of it, enough to make metal for several lifetimes. There was no reason to leave. We waited for the trigger to leave, but year in, year out, none came.

Fortchee had us build a stone wall across the small peninsula of land that connected our islet to the mainland, and we were safe from Cats. When he died, we called him our greatest innovator.

On top of a high hill we found the fallen statue of an Ancestor, his face melted, his arms outstretched. As if to welcome Ancestors back from the stars. No one came to me in the night to comfort me or bite my neck and call me love. I suppose I'd been touched by something strange and so was strange myself. I would have taken a low-rank drifter, only they did not get past the wall. Still, I had my Choova. She brought me her children to bless, and then her grandchildren, though they never really recognized what I was to them. Their children had no idea that I still lived. My loneliness creaked worse than my joints, and I yearned for a migration to sweep me numbly away.

Not once did anyone speak of Leveza, or even once remember her. Our exiled groom-brothers would drift by, to temporarily gladsome cries, and they told us, before moving on, of new wonders on the prairie. But we blanked that, too.

Until one dusk, I saw the strangest thing picking its way down toward our lagoon.

It looked like a fine and handsome young girl, beautifully formed though very, very long in the trunk. She raised her head from drinking, and her mane fell back. The top of her face was missing, from right above the eyes. It was terrible to see, someone so young but so deformed. She whinnied in hope and fear, and I ronfled back comfort to her and then asked her name. But she couldn't talk.

A horse. I was looking at a full-blooded horse. I felt a chill on my legs and wondered: Did they bring the Ancestors back, too?

"Leveza?" I asked it, and it raised and lowered its head, and I thought the creature knew the name. It suddenly took fright, started, and trotted away into the night, as someone else once had.

Then there was a sound like thousands of cards being shuffled, and a score of the creatures emerged from the trees. They bent their long necks down to drink. Their legs worked backward.

A voice said softly, "Is that Akwa?" Against a contrast sky, I saw the silhouette of a monster, two headed, tall. Then I recognized the gun.

She had trained one of the things to carry her, so she would always sit tall and have her hands free. I couldn't speak. Somewhere beyond the trees carts rumbled.

"Hello, my love," she said. I was hemorrhaging memory, a continual stream; and all of it about her—how she spoke, how she smelled, how she always went too far, and how I wished that I'd gone with her too all those years ago.

"We're going south, to find the Bears, get us some of that writing. Want to come?" I still could not speak. "It's perfectly safe. We've bought along something else for them to eat."

I think that word "safe" was the trigger. I did the giggle of embarrassment and fear. I drank sweet water and then followed. We found writing, and here it is.

You

You switch on your lifeblog for the first time, and your eyes feel bigger, heavier. Your eyes are your portal to both worlds, real and virtual. You blink, and see your own present life, as if through the eyes of a fish, rounded, clear and smooth.

You see your own hands. To occupy them, you are knitting, blue yarn with biowires sparkling in it.

That number to the right is a date and time. No, inside your eye. Focus on the middle distance. See it?

The little glowing virtual anatomy is you. That one there, bottom middle. Your physiome. It shows us if you are in pain, under stress or ill. It has a series of recognized emotional states. Right now you are in A: very alert, interested—alive, we would say.

Everything you see and hear is recorded and shared. That graph on the left shows how much data has been saved, compared to the amount published on your social server.

You wear the computer and the computer wears you. In a sense your lifeblog is you. It's who you are socially. Trimmed, edited, it's how people see you.

Most of us talk over our lifeblogs, explain as we live like we're telling a story. In a sense who you are has always been a story that you told to yourself. Now your self is a story that you tell to others.

So small, so light, so capacious, the appliance that you now call your blog not only records but lets you live in other lifeblogs. You can share the day of a celebrity. Share the day of someone long since dead.

So. The lights go on, in someone else's life.

————

You're looking at soil, red soil bare of plants.

You look up, and falling away in layers of tan, ochre, and bronze are the silhouettes of cliffs, one growing out of another, going farther and farther back. There's a small and misty sunset scattered through dust. The shadows are long and cold.

See the date? See the identifier? JoyAnna Haven. Her physiome shows perfect heart and lung capacity, though her age is thirty-nine. She's been in training.

This is JoyAnna on Mars.

The sky is the colour of tarnished copper saucepans, and the frozen ground underfoot crackles with a thin noise. That's the ice as JoyAnna walks. Numbers dance in her eyes; something is feeding data all the time.

Someone else says, right up close to your ear, "You know, we never would have the funding for this without you."

"Naw," says JoyAnna. "It's Assumpta Ciges you want to thank."

All of you start to walk determinably. You see something like a white tent ahead, but it doesn't flap.

JAH: "She's the one who cracked all this for us."

"We wouldn't know that but for you."

"Me? I was just a little info-digger. I didn't even do the basic Software Archaelogy to retrieve it. All I knew was that she'd done some work on the cylinders. So I got a grant to go through her blogs. I thought I'd just blip through at high speed, see what was there." JoyAnna's chuckle sounds pained. "I was very young."

You come to the entrance of the tent, duck and push aside layers of plastic that seal the entrance. Then you look down in a dimmer light.

A pit has been dug into the Martian surface, its sides supported by plastic battens. A ramp of earth slopes to the floor of the dig, which is perfectly level, though slightly rippled like the floor of a sea. Thousands of tiny objects, a bit like bullets, are arranged in the form of a giant spiral with arms, like a galaxy.

JoyAnna says, "She'd have loved to see this. She died, you know, 2030, right in the middle of the big storm. I've got an edited version of her blog stored, if you'd like to go through it."

The other woman says, "Yes please." She sits down cross-legged on the mat.

Blip.

You see a street. It's white: the pavements, the asphalt, the roof-tops—everything is white, with seamless blue above it, no clouds.

Numbers dance. That's the temperature. It's twenty-nine celsius, a beautiful summer's day. The air is full of misted light. Find the date. See it? This is 2027. That indicator on the left? JAH to JAH to AC?

That means you're looking at JoyAnna's blog from 2073, but she's looking at her own blog from 2058. And that's the one who is looking at the lifeblog of Assumpta Ciges.

You're seeing Manchester, as it was, one hundred years ago. Next to you is some kind of park—grass, trees, all a livid green. The software archaeologists have done a superb job, resolution, colour, 3D, and sound, all just superb. The eye-camera is rocking from side to side. Assumpta Ciges walks with a limp. See? Six physiomes. Yours. Mine. Assumpta's with her arthritis and replacement hip, two of JoyAnna's, and of course the woman listening on Mars.

That's why they call this vortexing. You just spiral down through layers of other people's lives.

A young voice says, "Trees! Look at those trees, they're huge!"

The same voice when old says, "This is so embarrassing!"

JAH: "I'm looking at private trees. People had trees of their own. It's all so green that it hurts my eyes. And the houses, and the roadway, everything, it's all painted white! I thought it was snow. But access has just told me, it's paint, they painted everything white, I guess that's to reflect sunlight, increase albedo. And it's so clean, everything. Nothing on the pavements, no horse manure anywhere. Ow! What's that?"

It's a bus. It roars past you all. There is an interesting sign on its side, *Fueled by biotechnology.* It creaks to a stop and waits rumbling at a shelter.

JAH: "Whatever it is, it looks medieval, like some kind of war machine, only so blue and polished, bluer than the sky. And look at the clothes. I mean, I don't know what I was expecting. I guess stupid extravagance, but these are really nice clothes. I mean if it's this warm, they're going to be wearing light stuff, but look, it's all printed in colours. They're functional but also so, so pretty. Why shouldn't things be pretty as well? And all those bicycles, and funny shoes I don't know what they're made of, and the white is just blinding, against the blue. Everything white, blue, green and then pink, red, yellow on the people, and all the bells from the bicycles. Oh! She's getting onto it, it's like a huge car!"

The eye-cameras lurch and sway, and Assumpta's hand holds up a blue card. You can see the sleeve of her coat: it looks as thin and light as leaves. She swings round into a seat, and the camera begins a light continual shiver that makes everything shimmer in white light. Rows of old brick buildings jolt past. Biolumescent signs with look in daytime like green lichen. Rows of stalls and carts, and all along the eaves, the rooftops, thousands of tiny buzzing windmills.

The bus stops. The cameras limp off it, one step at a time. An Asian gentleman helps her down.

Assumpta says to him, to his crumpled face and his neat gray beard. "Oh thank you so much!"

JoyAnna old: "All those beautiful people. Dead."

Blip.

You're looking at red soil again.

JoyAnna old: "So this is when Assumpta got time with the robot on Mars."

From Assumpta or one of the JoyAnnas, from someone's life Handel's *Water Music* is playing.

JAH: "Outgoing messages to the bot take nine minutes and the answer takes nine minutes so we're on an eighteen-minute cycle. Right now, Assumpta is waiting for the bot to respond."

All of you wait looking at soil. Handel adorns.

JAH: "I don't think Assumpta talks enough. She's telling us hardly anything, so just to fill you in, this is just over five years since the cylinders were found. A bot took a core sample, baked it as usual, only it turned out to be full of perfect little cylinders. All with marks on them, in a spiral going round it like a piano roll."

Someone shows you one of them. Inside your eyes, a cylinder turns. It's tiny, two centimetres long, burned black, flat at both ends. Spiralling round it are recurring patterns, swoops and swirls.

JAH: "They look a bit like Arabic, don't they? Everybody was hoping that they were a *cultural artifact*." She has a horrible regional accent and slices those last two words up into precise little tranches.

Something pings, and with a sudden smoothness, the bot on Mars lifts up its head. Inside Assumpta's eyes, then JoyAnna's and yours, the image comes to life. Broken rocky ground out to a very near horizon, and looming over that bronze cliffs looking just like Utah, a bronze sky, that's dust, but deep purple just overhead. The bot rolls toward a small crane, printed from scratch out of poly on Mars. It's a rough lattice of material.

Assumpta says, "Rendition."

JAH: "*Chren-dee-shon.* I love the way she talks. I didn't expect her to sound so Spanish. That's the order to the bot to scan the excavation site. They'll make a laser print of it, so it can be printed in poly back on Earth. We won't begin to see that for eighteen minutes. I hope nobody minds if we skitter ahead."

JoyAnna old: "Oh no, why would anyone want the experience of walking with a botblog on Mars? We'd much rather hear you, JoyAnna." Handel skips and jumps; images skitter.

JAH: "It's a rendition bot. So it will take a laser impression from different angles for the printout. After that, infrared for compositional analysis. Then we'll get ground-penetrating radar just to confirm that there is nothing else below the one level. Then X-rays to stimulate ultra-violet and other light emissions to help with dating. And EXAFS for structural detail. It's amazing what they were able to do."

The bot looks down into the trench at a small intelligent digger. Nothing reenforces the sides; the dig is open to elements. The Spiral opens up its arms to you in natural light. There is a buckling sound from behind the bot, thin in the Martian air.

Suddenly the bot is hoisted up and swings out over the dig. It hangs suspended over it, the cylinders in a neat arrangement, like stars.

There is a blast of light, blanking out the cameras. Colour swirls. Handel plays.

People in those days thought of time as straight. For you now, time spirals.

Blip.

And a room trills suddenly into place.

One of the JoyAnna's says, "This is Assumpta's house, that evening."

Electric lights blaze. They look like miniature suns. Assumpta has a big box, *Refrigerator* access tells you, and the floor is covered in red, fired tiles. Assumpta's hand pours a whiskey rather unsteadily into a glass and she passes it to a man. He's her age, and wearing some kind of absorbent sportswear, though he doesn't look like he runs much.

JAH: "This is just after the botshare with Mars. The gentleman is Assumpta's client, Tomas Schelling. He paid for the botshare. He's Director of the University's Meridiani Crescent project. Assumpta was already Professor Emeritus at this stage; so she's working for him on a contractual basis."

Two glasses clink together. Assumpta says, "The surrounding clay has iron it. The cylinders do not. I don't know if that is significant."

Assumpta swivels in her chair, to look at a screen on the kitchen table. They were still using terminals. She points to an image of a cylinder, a series of marks at one end of the spiral. Suddenly the marks are highlighted, gold against black.

AC: "Marks like these appear at one end of all the cylinders."

Schelling: "Some kind of starting point?"

"Assuming that the marks are indeed deliberate. I think they're numbers."

"Oh."

JAH. "He's sounding so unsurprised. His face is absolutely still."

AC: "Here, look. They differ each time in a very regular way."

TS: "You've been able to translate them?"

JAH: "That's a very careful sip of whiskey that Tomas is taking."

AC: "Well. The first is a single mark of a kind I'll call a twirl. And another twirl and below that, two twirls close together. It could show us one plus one equalling two. The next cylinder in the sequence should be, and yes it is: two plus two equalling four!"

JoyAnna when young makes a coarse little laugh. "Look at his eyes. It's love. His risky little commission has just come up trumps."

TS: "Then they're not numbering the cylinders?"

AC: "No, but they may be establishing mathematical patterns."

Tomas Schelling tosses back his head and drains his glass in one.

There is a thin sound of wind and ice. An older JoyAnna says, "I was privileged to live through Assumpta Ciges's first great mistake. Establishing numerical patterns is what Americans did on the bronze plates on Voyager. That was to show that the plate was a cultural artifact. And because that's what we'd done, we expected something similar from aliens."

On the screen the cylinder turns, the marks spiralling.

JAH: "Mysterious little buggers, aren't they?"

Blip.

The same kitchen, only now with the sound of rain on windows.

JAH old: "After that she worked on them for about seven or eight months. Mostly from home, she wasn't very mobile. She drank way too much. It's not a fun blog. I'll just show you this part. Though it always makes me sad."

Assumpta is feeding sliced chorizo to a tortoiseshell cat. It winds itself around her legs. She looks up, cuts a slice from the dried sausage for herself. On a plate, mozzarella, some lettuce. She eats with her fingers.

In her eyes a cylinder turns.

JAH: "She's just called up the forty-seventh cylinder again, turning it over and over in her eyes. Now she's calling CGIs to help visualize tools that might have made those marks."

On the kitchen terminal, you suddenly see something like a metal corkscrew.

But it's far too inflexible. It obliterates any chance for the more narrow strokes that follow.

So now Assumpta calls up a kind of pen with a soft tip. It flips bits of wet clay, which would account for the prickly-pear nodes that appear on the surface sometimes. She's comparing them. Yes, there's an approximate match.

And for the first time, she's trying to imagine what might hold a pen. So, she's finally begun to imagine aliens, if that's what they are, and how they work. There's a kind of mouth holding the cylinder still, and she's pulling the image like taffy, to create a kind of tentacle that holds the pen.

And now she's laughing at herself. She gives up and just shows a pair of hands. She knows she's come up with a tool for two-handed bipeds. Us.

So she makes the corkscrew flexible. She shows it stretching, thinning, shortening, and fattening. How flexible does it have to be? In the end, she has to make it as flexible as mist, fitting the curlicues.

Assumpta makes it more solid, and it looks like a worm.

JoyAnna old: "This is as far as we'd known for certain that she got. I feel very strange. I really want her to get it, I want her to solve it. She deserves to. But not yet."

Assumpta twists the worm and shows it grasping the cylinder at one end and turning it like a corn cob. The other end bites out a mark, then turns it, shifts, and bites out the next.

Assumpta turns off the CGI. She's magnifying an image of a cylinder to microscopic scale.

You see the marks at almost nanoscale. The bites are smooth with gliding streaks in them, but nothing like tooth marks or cuts. It's like they've been sucked out of the clay.

Assumpta calls up a CGI of a mouth, and she's now making it fit the streaks and smears. She pulls back, and there we have it.

A worm with a mouth.

Assumpta's turned off all imaging. Her physiome shows her bowing. She's put her head in her hands. She says, "The possibility is that the marks are simply a trace of something eating the clay. The nodes left on the surface are probably just faeces."

Assumpta tries to laugh. The sound seems to be coming out of the bottom of a well.

JoyAnna young almost shouts. "Except for the numbers! Assumpta! The numbers. She can't hear me."

Numbers flip up, tones bleep. That is Assumpta calling up a blog share. Access tells you that that is the Shelling's blog ID. She's calling him.

"Dear Tomas."

She sounds as though she is sending condolences for a funeral.

"I will of course be writing a full report. But as you will see from readings and images attached, I am fairly certain that the marks are simply the result of something feeding on the clay cylinders, probably for the iron content. So the marks are repeated probably because they tended to scoop the clay in a limited number of ways. I wish I had something more satisfactory for you. But I think we can consider the consultancy at a close. As always, it has been a pleasure. I hope you won't mind, but I will continue working on the problem, and if there is anything further, I will be sure to let you know. A hard copy will follow for your records, along with my last invoice and record of expenses, which in any case will not be large. Yours as ever, Assumpta Ciges."

The cat mews, unseen, rain prickles windows, Assumpta stares. Her breath wreathes in the cold.

They were so isolated. They only had one self.

Blip.

And then all you see is a floor. Poured concrete, and a sleeping bag full of knees, and next to that a bowl.

Can you guess where you are? Look at the indicator, it says JAH, nothing else, so this is just one level of one blog. Look at the date: 2048. And Handel is playing.

JoyAnna is inside a sleeping bag, and venturing a chill hand out to a bowl of soy crisps. You hear them crunch and a mug goes up to her lips. If this were a modern blog you could at least taste it. From JA's physiome, she's drinking some kind of homemade hooch. Maybe she thinks being slightly tipsy is a good way to get into Ciges's mindset. She looks up: a bare room, with what look like charcoal drawings direct onto a wall. There are windows, that at first glance look like pixelated screens. That odd popping sound is actually the clucking of hens.

JAH: "I'm freezing cold. Even with the sun out. They call this our summer. There's a cloud of mosquitoes outside. They just kamikaze into my window screens."

The windows have a fine mesh across them, and we can see mosquitoes swirling around outside. Some kind of alert flashes inside JoyAnna's eyes.

"My cows' lifeblogs are calling me. They need milking. Their virts usually herd them back from the park to my stable, but I think there's a glitch in their eye receivers and they're not being triggered to hook themselves up to the milking machines. That's not such a huge problem. I just need to get up and walk to the stables. I need to feed my hens, too; the feed is in my backpack. I should just haul it over there and TCB. But I don't want to."

Her physiome shows a clear X state. JoyAnna in despair. She sits in silence. You look hungrily at the uneaten soycrisps, out of your reach by eighty years.

Then she says just one word. "Mystery."

You're probably thinking, well the young JoyAnna was such a little gold digger. She'll just do a search, blip to the end, find the solution, and go off and make her fortune. You haven't been paying attention.

No. She goes back inside, to be with Assumpta.

Blip.

She goes right back to the end of that phone call.

Assumpta strokes her cat and slowly finishes the chorizo.

"Yes, Bertie, yes, I shall feed you in moment."

She heaves herself up from the table, finds the cat food, cuts off a slug of it, and lumps in onto a plate.

Then Assumpta thumps upstairs. Rain on the roof. Stockings peel off wearily. She rolls under the covers and finds her book.

JoyAnna young coughs to clear her throat. "The Professor Emeritus and ex-President of the British Academy spends her nights reading fanfic gardening slash."

Young JoyAnna is content to read with her.

> **Love in a Changing Climate**
> *Denim's eyes were still fixed on her, as Julie squatted to feel in the soil for potatoes. She knew her jeans were too tight and rode down at the back. It was a bit shameless of her. In the cleft of her exposed butt, a tattoo spelled out the word in Samoan that only Denim could read: LOVE.*
>
> *"Come on, you're supposed to be helping me dig," she said, and only then realized that it sounded like an innuendo.*
>
> *Denim's glossy, long black hair whisked against her cheek as he crouched beside her. His great thighs were as smooth as her own. She could smell him, a mixture of sweat and spice and something delicious all his own.*
>
> *"Do you miss home?" Julie asked.*

JoyAnna whispers, "My husband left me, too, Assumpta. I've got too many keys myself, all in my eyes, for the stables, the dispensary, my files, my grant ID. I don't spend hours on the phone talking to friends like you do. We don't have phones. And I've let your friends become my friends. I sometimes think they're still with us. I want to know if your nephew got his scholarship or if your students found jobs. It's like I could turn a corner, and find all the roadways painted white."

She starts to read again. You're the one who wants to blip now. You try to push Assumpta's blog, can't, then locate the right version of Joy-Anna's. OK we can blip.

———

It's a rickety table in a forecourt on a sun-flecked day. Assumpta is lowering a tray full of cake and coffee. Her physiome is in an almost even gray: you feel as though she's in a moment of respite from everything unlovely and harsh. Under her trousers, electric bandages filamented with wires keep her ligaments warm and give her muscles a neurological boost. The camera motion shows that she no longer limps.

At the table sits a much younger man: Asian, handsome, with black hair, black eyes. He is cherubically plump, and he moves like a little boy, shrugging with pleasure. "Assumpta, you are lovely. Lovely, lovely." He tucks into his cake.

Assumpta sweeps into her chair and watches him eat. His cheeks bulge with cream. He swallows. She asks, "Now?"

Then everything swims unfocussed, and in your eyes physiomes line up—yours, JAH's, Assumpta's, and now the male's. A report is offered. It flowers open, full of details.

JoyAnna says "They've just descraped privacy."

His name is Gudu and he's forty-two. And he will be able to see that Assumpta is sixty-eight, suffers from arthritis and a hereditary heart condition. She is of course no longer fertile. He on the other hand has what Access tells you is an extraordinarily high sperm count. A small article starts to explain: reduced pollution is improving male fertility. He has a slight predisposition to baldness. Self-cured of appendicitis and... what is this? Damage to the frontal lobe. All of your physiomes seem to thump in unison.

Gudu says, "Oh, all of that is lovely."

JAH:, "I'm tempted to say of course he doesn't want a child. I mean, he wouldn't want a rival, would he?"

Numbers flow into a grid, and Gudu says, "Now this is my equivalent. An Indian horoscope."

JAH: "He's explaining, and I'm talking over him and I feel bad about that, but I can't be bothered. Assumpta, I have to say, selfishly, that I'm dreading that I'll have to spend the rest of our time together with this man. My mother's lifeblog is just the same, full of an annoying twit online."

The numbers boil down to a very high fraction.

"That means we are very compatible." Gudu beams. "I remember when I was young my parents tried to marry me, though the incompatibility was high, and sure enough, we didn't get on from the moment we met."

Assumpta chuckles. "That is reassuring."

The last of the cake crumbs pinched together, Gudu puts his hands down flat on the table.

"The Financial Advisers Guild needs to see that I have twenty thousand euros in my account before they will let me register. Would you be able to transfer that sum into my account?"

Assumpta's physiome pulses once. It lights up, red blue yellow, and continues to coruscate.

JAH: "Don't give it to him!"

"I will pay you right back the moment they see it."

JoyAnna rails, "If he had a brain in his head, he would have waited six months until you couldn't live without him. A brain in his head and he wouldn't need the twenty thousand. And he wants to give people financial advice?"

The whole image seems to twist in harness, and Assumpta draws a deep breath. "It really is very difficult." Her voice creaks like leather being stretched. "I really don't have a spare twenty thousand."

"Oh! You have time. You can think about it." He's still smiling and he waves everything else away. "Thank you."

JAH: "It sounds like what he says to all the old women who turn him down. Old men as well, I reckon. You'll recall, Assumpta, that he did like a finger up his arse."

You live through Assumpta paying for the coffee, and kissing him on the cheek, and then the bus ride from the Northern Quarter. Would it be so very bad, you wonder. Buying someone? When you're sixty-eight and alone?

White Manchester, green trees, bicycles, home.

JAH: "I want to hug you and I can't."

Assumpta gets home; she allows herself to limp and she goes straight back to that box of a computer. She takes down her dating profile. She enters codes and webcams her retina to the bank. She waits looking at her own reflection on the screen.

."You fool. You idiot." The cat springs up onto her lap and hides his head under her forearm, as if sheltering from the overhead light.

Blip.

The lifeblog tells you this is summer, a year later. You see a marble floor. Assumpta has apparently twisted round her bare foot so that she can see the sole. It's dusted with fine white powder.

Someone, another aged female you can't see, says something in Spanish. Access tells you: Asumpta's sister, Bella. This is Barcelona. Someone's blog, yours or JoyAnna's, translates. The voice has said, "I wish you would wear shoes! You're not a child!"

Assumpta is humming a childish song; you've heard it before. She looks up to a sink full of water and plunges her hands into it. "This marble is beautiful. It really does cool down the house."

The sister's voice echoes, "Not if you keep opening windows."

Assumpta still does not look at her. Instead she holds up a soup plate. Light reflects on its moulded edges, which are a faded green with gold. A bubble slides down it.

Up from Access comes an image of a Meridiani cylinder. Assumpta is thinking of work.

AC: "These beautiful plates."

Bella says, "We need to talk about Mother's legacy."

AC: "Of course."

Assumpta slots the plate into a rack full of crocks and cutlery. She shakes the water from her hands and walks out of the kitchen, looking at the pattern on the rug in the hall. She goes into a parlour or sitting room and strokes the polished surface of a mahogany table and admires heavy candlesticks with cherubim.

"Assumpta! Assumpta, where are you going?"

She limps across the room, opens the French windows, pushes back the shutters. Noise from the street floods in. Barcelona booms, crackles, wheezes, clatters. Summer solstice, thirty-two degrees, St. Joan's Day. In the street below, children are setting off firecrackers. They're crouching under long-needled pine trees that run straight down the middle of the medieval road.

"Assumpta, Assumpta, please! They're setting off rockets! They fly in through the windows!"

Assumpta grunts.

Bella's voice sounds querulous and old. "One of the apartments across the road was set on fire last year! This is too much, too much!"

The image jerks. The sister is perhaps trying to pull her back inside. Someone who may be JoyAnna makes a piteous sound. You glimpse Bella's black trousers and shirt; you see Assumpta's hands pushing her away.

AC: "All right! You close the shutters. I'll watch from outside."

The image pulls back from the French doors, its attention fixed on the cracks that run around the edge of the balcony. The shutters thunk shut, and the green handle turns as if by itself.

Assumpta looks out; the rooftops are now dark, street lights shining. There is a fizzing from below. Children scatter and a rocket squeedles like a mouse, shooting up into the trees. It gets stuck in the branches. It sprays glitter and then suddenly the image blanks out with a boom. When the cameras adjust, the tree is on fire, burning like a torch.

Assumpta says to herself, "Car paint. So. Peels. Some fades. Lately all gray, perhaps puritan. No one wants to look fancy, though more intelligent than their owners. We preserve, the trees root us too in the old shapes. Firewood in winter."

Something wrong with the translation? Cars, those ancient monstrosities, still swollen and polished, line the street.

And JoyAnna says as all of you watch, "Why is the past glamorous? I mean, it was everyday to them. But I love all those shiny things, and the beautiful cloth, it looks just like coloured fog, it's that thin. It makes everything here look gray and cold. I am so sick of digging in cold mud. Your trees and sunsets aren't really that much more beautiful than mine. Except to me."

A particularly huge rocket bursts overhead, its dancing light, its illuminated smoke for a moment imitating a nebula.

"This is what books only aimed to do and never could. Give you the glint of someone else's sunrise, what living is really like, you get old and it hurts to bend your elbow; your friends start to die, you can't get fresh fruit in the shops."

All of you watch in silence until the fireworks die.

The cylinders turn.

JoyAnna no longer sounds quite so young.

Blip.

Autumn 2030. Assumpta has a phone call in her head. It rings with the sound of blackbirds singing. A name comes up in the eye: Magda Parentes.

JAH: "Oh no! It's the Horrible Serb!"

A new voice says, "Assumpta, my dear, are you very busy? Can you talk?" She sounds polite, sugary.

AC: "Yes, of course."

MP: "You must feel so dreadful. So sad."

"Must I?"

Assumpta summons up one of the cylinders, the usual one, number forty-seven, the one that begins with sixteen.

MP:"Well, with Tomas not there any longer."

The walls and ceiling seem to nod. Assumpta pauses only briefly but sails on. "Well, I finished my work on that over a year ago, so though it's sad..." She lets her voice trail away in what sounds like wisps of relative unconcern, but the physiome shows her heart is thumping.

"You're being very brave. But still. It must rankle just a touch to have someone take over your work on the cylinders. At the 3D print. And for it to be Herr Kurtmeier?"

Assumpta's voice manages to chuckle and be icy at the same time. "Which is the point of your call, obviously."

"You don't mean to say you didn't know?"

JoyAnna hisses. "Lie, Assumpta. Tell her they consulted you. Tell her that you and Kurtmeier patched up the quarrel."

MP: "Personally, I've never cared for Kurtmeier, but his work isn't bad. And people so want to be told that the artifacts are cultural, don't they? They'll keep hiring people till they find someone who will."

AC: "Are you working on them as well? If you don't mind my asking."

Magda sighs. "Well, yes, actually. I hope I can keep his fantastical streak in check."

"So kind of you to call."

"Well, you were always so good to me in the past."

End.

Her physiome roils. She calls Tomas. His Turing answers sounding just enough like him to be maddening. Hearty. "He's away on holiday. How are you, Assumpta?"

"You can tell him that I'm not well. That I'm sorry he's lost his post. He must feel dreadful. I'm mystified that no one had the grace to tell me what is going on. Have him call me."

She paces the house.

JoyAnna says, "I wish I could get you to just let it go. Of course other people will want a chance to work on them, but there's nothing to stop you doing something as well."

Assumpta stands up with a sniff. "Yes."

She scrapes her chair toward the terminal and the keyboard. There is a ping. Her newsfeeds automatically begin to chime: a story about the salt pump and the Gulf Stream. Assumpta switches it off, muttering. "Get out of my head."

Something disappears from your array. Your date, JoyAnna's date are both there, but the blogdate for Assumpta is missing. You want to ask JoyAnna: What day is this?

AC: "Earthworms subsist on rich organics in soil. But there is no loam or hummus on Mars. So why no other finds of cylinders if they are the remains of food? Otters leave heaps of abalone shells, Neanderthals leave gnawed bones. But there is no other similar find." Assumpta makes her rustling, breathing-out sound. "Not even the faeces."

She steadies her nerves with a small sherry.

AC: "All right. Then we must assume it is some other kind of purposeful activity other than feeding and look at it again."

She makes a lunch out of cheese and salad, but doesn't eat it. She reads papers and listens to taped lectures on earthworms and cuttlefish, then a very bad popular book on possible alien biologies.

She turns her newsfeeds back on. It talks to her as she works. It's a blog from a young Reservist overseeing the evacuation of Phoenix. He's heard gunfire getting out of town. Vehicles are running out of electricity while idling in the jam; people are walking in the heat toward California; there's no water. JoyAnna's blog offers her the option of following the Reservist's lifeblog instead.

Assumpta's date comes back on. JoyAnna goes still. A file opens, flowers, showing research-grant application, and its summary with a date. JoyAnna's voice quavers. "Twenty-third December? You only have five days left!"

Ping.

Assumpta receives an RSS report. The newly established dates from the Martian mass extinction match those of the cylinders. The Spiral and the climate tipped at the same time.

The English have been picking raspberries in December. That night Assumpta reads two gardening romances.

The next morning, Assumpta wakes up hungover and immediately begins to do housework. She has a long-handled feather duster to reach up into the corners to get the cobwebs. She then washes dishes and the eight soup-bowls that arrived from Spain. Her physiome shows she is dehydrated.

She gets herself a whiskey. Sitting at the table she says, "The only thing I have is the numbers. If that is indeed what they are. If I can understand why they are not in sequence, then I will understand something at least."

JoyAnna starts to talk and you realize that she's been silent for hours. "I think Assumpta's understood that lifeblogging counts as publication. If she makes a discovery and it's logged, she'll get the credit."

The flickering stops, once again at cylinder forty-seven, where the Spiral gets stuck on the number sixteen.

The cylinders move in order inside Assumpta's eyes.

First cylinder forty-seven in which there are four groups of four. Is that indeed a representation of sixteen?

Cylinder forty-eight starts off with two sequences of eight swirls, also sixteen.

Forty-nine repeats that but follows it with several prickly-pear nodes.

Assumpta then stops, and orders a system check and special backup. *Ping.* The blog has been published, but also backed up.

JAH: "Good girl. I was right. She's in a race and she's making sure the blog is being backed up, saved, and registered. She's got it."

Fifty shows sixteen individual swirls piano-rolling the length of the entire cylinder.

Fifty-one repeats that pattern and follows it with a single very large node.

And Assumpta begins to laugh.

At first she laughs like Oliver Hardy, everything bouncing up and down, her hands patting the table in unison. Then a happy, gentle sound, through teeth, like rain.

"Ssh ssh ssh ssh It's . . . a . . . ha . . . ha . . . TURD! They *shat* to hoo hoo hoo say NO!"

Assumpta stands up to do a little dance. Her hips roll in a perfect figure eight and her feet trace a samba.

JoyAnna laughs aloud a hearty, British, baying laugh, and that knocks her back into blogging mode. "That's a samba." Thanks, you think. "Assumpta lived in Brasil for a while, taught at the State University of Para in Belem, right on the mouth of the Amazon."

The arthritis intervenes, Assumpta stumbles, goes ooooh, and then finds that funny as well. She starts to sing a song in Portuguese. It's a laughing song, the chorus consists of the sound of laughter. Translated the title is "Who's Laughing Now?" Aha-ha-HAH-HAH-HAH.

She calls Schelling. The Turing says, "Sorry, Assumpta, but he's away for Christmas now."

She chuckles. "Just tell him I have something to report on the cylinders."

The cylinders with their numbers flutter back and forth. "Well, my darlings. What were you up to?"

Then she says. "Hmm. It's chilly in here."

The cylinders dance all day long. Assumpta keeps pouring herself a whiskey to celebrate. By six p.m. it's dark, and she is asleep.

Day three starts very late. The blog records snores, then the slow waxing of light on the walls. But Assumpta is not conscious to see it.

Up come the feeds with news from Bangladesh, and the American Southwest, and now trouble on the border between India and China.

Assumpta groans, then stomps her way out the bed and goes downstairs to the refrigerator. She surveys it for a moment before taking out the sherry, but what she says is, "Nothing can survive just eating iron in clay. What else did they eat? They must have eaten something!"

Still in her nightie, she puts in a round-robin call to biologists in her network. She magnifies the signs again, to see how they were made.

AC: "All right. I think we can say that the worms definitely did not have teeth."

She has a continental breakfast of cheddar cheese, oatcakes and raisins. She calls on the CGI package. "So let's just try to imagine what they were like."

She tries to imagine the worms in a colony. She pastes them onto a Mars whose surface is not red, but streaked with ice and tiny melted puddles. In the end it looks like grass, a lawn of worms, reaching up toward the light.

"They photosynthesized." That's JoyAnna. "Rhodopsin. It's protein in the human eye, it photosynthesizes, and it's red, like Mars."

And Assumpta says, "Yes, that's it."

And it takes you a moment to realize that the two of them cannot be in discussion.

AC: "If they photosynthesized they might eat clay only when suffering iron deficiency. So we might not find any other cylinders. They wouldn't need them that often."

She checks to make sure the lifeblog is still saving and registering. She goes upstairs, puts the blog on block. Presumably she showers.

When it comes back on the time is 15:37 and the sky has gone ominously dark. Assumpta is bundling herself up in sweaters and a coat, and goes outside. She has difficulty opening her French doors, steps outside and gasps. The air looks like solidified crystal. The sky overhead is clear pale blue, except for a bank of cloud to the north that is being pulled over it like a blanket.

You see the outside temperature is minus fifteen degrees. Assumpta's breath sidles out of her nostrils like thick steam. She shivers her way to the clothesline and starts unpegging a shirt. Her hand shakes and fumbles it. A solid sheet of cotton, the shirt tumbles to the paving.

And shatters like china. It lies in shards.

AC: "What is going on?"

She turns and hobbles, quivering, back inside. She closes the French doors and then, lumbering, rolls up the kitchen rug against the lower edge of the door. She collects bread and bananas, a tub of yogurt, all the food in the house, and then retreats into the sitting room. She rolls up rugs against the doors there too, and turns on the heater at full blast.

Then she checks to make sure that the lifeblog is continuing to save.

"I'm afraid we are having some unusual weather."

She goes back to the CGI. As she uses the blog to tell the University computers what she wants. Worms, two centimetres long. Photosynthesizing. Capable of movement. The CGI system goes to work.

Turings begin to call, delivering automatic Christmas greetings. *Hello (slight pause) Assumpta, Ted's calling to wish you a merry season!* She turns them all off.

Overhead, the sky begins to make an ominous grinding sound, like pepper being milled.

JoyAnna suddenly yelps. "Shit! The date of your death is actually the day they found you. But you'd been lying dead for two days. This is it. It's now. You're going to die now."

The worm resolves as an image.

AC: "For the sake of neatness. Make them the same size as the cylinders."

The machine takes over, and the worm is there, wrestling with a cylinder in clay, and it is clear: one is a simulacrum of the other.

Assumpta breathes out. "Of course."

The sky grinds. The heat blows.

"Any system of writing must mimic the original kind of communication." Then she says to her system, "Make them both worms."

Two worms roll together, mouthing each other's bodies.

"They communicated by touch. By kissing the lengths of their bodies. And the cylinders tried to record that process of whole-body touching. We'll never translate that language without a Rosetta stone. But why the debate over numbers?"

She calls up a gathering of worms and then superimposes the Spiral. A Spiral of worms.

They are passing the cylinders along its length. Passing them out, passing them back.

AC: "The definition of writing is that which preserves information across both space and time."

The worms seethe, the university pseudo-AI starts to improve the image. You see a Martian sky, slightly blue from the presence of water vapour; you see the congress.

AC: "They were trying to invent writing. They started with numbers. The Spiral was a debate about how to write numbers. Todd told me they couldn't be intelligent, their whole body size would not allow the brain complexity. But what if they had some kind of neural interface when they touched?"

"What if it started to go cold and dry? They knew they needed to measure that?"

And she starts to cry. It must be all that booze at work. "Deaf dumb blind. But they could feel the cold!"

JoyAnna says, "You don't have to feel that we are like them."

Two of the worms dance together, turning each other, kissing in spirals.

Then, with a soft click, all the lights go out. You can hear the blow heater die. The room is as dark as the inside of the brain. Assumpta's physiome fluxes in panic. She yelps, stands up, thumps against furniture. She checks if the lifeblog was being saved.

JAH: "It's all right, Assumpta, the Library has its own generators, it has saved all of this. It is saving it!"

A clumping of furniture. No light at all. Garments rustle and slither. A clatter in the dark, a fumbling, and finally a battery-operated torch snaps on. Assumpta now wears an overcoat.

Her front corridor is spotlit all around us. She steps outside her front door, and her breath is pulled out of her, making a noise like the counterstroke of a cello. The numbers for temperatures rattle through her eyes. She tries to call Tomas.

NO NETWORK COVERAGE.

The phone system is down.

Outside there is only driving snow, like stars shooting past at warp speed. They swallow up all the light; there is nothing beyond. Gasping for breath, Assumpta tries to advance, but the wind is extraordinary, pushing her back. From somewhere up the street, peoples' voices echo, shouting. Assumpta tries to shout, too, but it is too cold; she can't.

A voice echoing from down the street says, "The radio says to stay inside!"

Assumpta turns and the wind harries her back. Hinges squeal as the front door opens. They resist being closed against the gale. The lock won't click shut. She rams her body against it. Her knee gives away and she cries aloud, but she falls against the door and it finally closes. On the floor, she pushes the welcome mat against the lower edge of the doorway and crawls along the corridor.

"Stupid!" She'd left the sitting room door ajar, and much of its saved heat will have been sucked up the staircase. As if praying, on her knees, she pushes the sitting room door shut behind her. She crawls across the floor onto the sofa and pulls the sofa cushions on top of herself, and curls up. To save the batteries, she turns off the flashlight.

The air outside growls like a wounded beast. She sits chill in the dark. She calls Schelling again, gets his Turing again.

"Hello, Tomas. Things are pretty serious here; there really is the most terrible storm. All the lights and power are out, and of course I have no heating. Please call."

She rings Bella, but her sister has put her on block.

She waits in the dark.

JoyAnna says, "How did your pretty little sister, the one everyone adored, the one you used to dress up, how did she get so mean? Maybe it's better never to be adored, like us. Momma never called me pretty; I could see I wasn't pretty. I'd go to the movies and pray for the lights to go down so that people wouldn't see what a dump I was, and that I had to go to movies alone. I was too brainy, I brought in my files to the class and showed my favourite saved things: planets and starfish and Persepolis, and that popular girl tossed her hair and said what's so interesting about all of that stuff? Papa said I would have to get by on my brains."

Still no image, except for three glowing physiomes and lots of numbers, so many numbers and icons that they almost crowd out the world.

Her voice constrained, Assumpta calls up a number code and clearance information. She turns on the torch and points it into her eye, and the darkness disappears in light.

JAH: "You've just retinaed Mars. Can that work?"

Nine minutes to wait. The image of the worms comes back. The worms turn each other like corncobs, talking in a spiral.

Then they begin to make love.

JoyAnna murmurs, "You spent the last quarter century trying to find love. You believed in progress, too, I bet, the advancement of science. The world is folding in on itself. Your Martians died just as they invented culture.

"Our world isn't dying, Assumpta. I know it feels like that now. Because of Gudu, your sister, your work, everything that's on the news, but it isn't the same as those little bits of brain on Mars. We already have writing and numbers; we have more than writing. We have wireless and blogging; we can reason; we didn't fight a war, we won't; we're all still here, Assumpta."

The flashlight snaps on. The temperature in the room is still above freezing. Assumpta opens a wooden cabinet, and gets out the whiskey, and starts to drink. Alcohol is a food. But it opens the circulation system near the skin and speeds freezing. Assumpta climbs back into her shelter of sofa cushions. She puts all her mailing list on autodial.

NO NETWORK CONNECTION.

The power for the network is down. Only military channels are open now. You have those because of your contract: to the Rylands Library. To Mars.

JAH: "Assumpta, can you sense me in the future, sitting next to you, reading with you, drinking with you, hell, even peeing with you. You got love, Assumpta. Me."

Wind batters the roof.

"You might still have been alive after I was born. I might have met you as a little girl. I could have sat on your lawn, or looked at your twenty-thousand books and said, 'Why would anyone want so many books? Just keep 'em on your pod.' I could have called you Aunty."

Assumpta sits up again and reads out new parameters for her blog.

JAH: "She's trying to make this last sequence have a wider distribution; it will be stored in a different inbox than usual. That's one of the reasons it wasn't noted. Also, nobody thought that anybody's blog was saved with the power down. It's the military channels."

Assumpta says, to the lifeblog, her audience, her people, "The Spiral is a record of a process of invention. It was an attempt to turn a system of communication through touch into a system of writing. They photosynthesized but ate clay for mineral content. They wrote with their mouths. They did not finish developing their system of numbering and writing. The Spiral was a debate about how to record numbers and something like words. We now know climate change comes quickly. It tips. This change happened in four Martian years, as it is coming upon us.

"Record and post."

ENTRY POSTED.

Ping.

And suddenly, there is a bronze plain, bronze sky. All three of you now stand on Mars, with the bot. Assumpta tells it, "Please show me the Spiral."

Nine minutes to receive, nine minutes to answer. The image is frozen. Somewhere Handel plays.

All three of you sit and wait.

Assumpta says, "All my books are upstairs."

Her physiome shows pains around her chest. There's a burble, and she looks down; she's coughed up whiskey.

JAH: "I bet it's like this for angels. They just have to stand by and watch it happen as we make a mess of everything. Mouth useless, God's love useless, freedom useless. Freedom is the enemy, it just lets us make mistakes. *Love in a Changing Climate.* Love without words. Love as angels love beyond comprehension, outside words, beyond hope or any objective correlative. You don't know I'm here, but I'll stay here and I'll keep listening. I'll keep watch."

The cold sinks in. The physiome starts to shut down. Time rolls down, the numbers decrease.

"Your blog still keeps going on. Your eyes still get data. The blog's still there. And me. For a while."

Elsewhen, on Mars, JoyAnna when old has finished her tale, and is being buckled in. There is a jerk, and she is swept up, swung out over the dig. The Spiral opens its arms wide.

"Rendition," she says, with the accent of Assumpta Ciges. The cameras blank and you, and me, and they and us, we hang with her in the very centre of the light.

K is for Kosovo
(or, Massimo's Career)

I like the Serbs. My friend Vesna is Serbian. We used to come here all the time, drink together, talk about luxury brands: Vuitton, Gucci, Hugo Boss. You do that in our job.

She's a trained UNHCR interviewer. Mostly our job was to get the Kosovo refugees back home. We follow the principle of durable solutions. If it's not possible for them we would settle them somewhere else, another country willing to take them. Our job was to go over their testimonies, interview them separately, verify the basics from whatever state records were left. And spot inconsistencies.

We had a family of gypsies, *Roma.* They were from Mitroviça. The Roma Mahala district is mostly destroyed now, the big houses gone or occupied. Mostly the Roma live in barracks on the north side side of the railway. It's not good, but we still try to get them home.

This family said their daughter had been raped by the Kosovo Liberation Army. Well, you know, the Albanians had been through it as well and they think gypsies sided with the Serbs. We briefed the family on what was going to happen and why, but they showed up wanting to be interviewed all together.

In Italy, we think gypsies are dark; some say they are really Asian. It's not that different here. The old omen cover their heads, even the Christians. They wear brown and yellow and smell of wood smoke. They're tiny. The men look like plump little sad eyed dolls.

The father brought his accordion. He played it in the reception area as they waited. Perhaps he was working. You know, busking.

They spoke a little Italian, but Serbian was their second language. I speak some Serbian, but not so well so Vesna did the talking. *No, no, no, you must go back to the centre and be interviewed separately, I'm sorry those are the rules.* That time the mother was the unhappy one. I never saw crying like it, her face calm, but tears constant and smeared all over her cheeks . Somehow we got her to understand what we meant, but she still said, "I go in with my daughter."

Vesna said for me, *"Don't be worried by this man here, he won't be with us."*

I said in my bad Serbian, "It will just be this lady and Servette." So, after a while, the mother stayed outside.

Servette was twelve. She had huge black hair and a tiny sad face. Her sweater had a zip and collar and button-down pockets. It looked, you know, stylish, till you saw the little balls of wool all over it.

The story was that a gang of Albanians, 15 of them, held her down and raped her in front of her family. Before the interview, Servette looked composed and pretty, but also very fragile. You could see how big strong men away from home might want her.

I stayed with Mrs Paçaku,who sat in her head scarf, composed and silent, ankles crossed like she was waiting to catch a train The girl came back out after an hour, looking like one of those Polaroid photographs that melt. The mother started shouting at us her face fat and pink; I couldn't tell what she was saying. Vesna stood there, hugging her stomach, looking away. We got the mother to go and I said nothing, just pointed to our office. As soon as we were inside, Vesna spun around and said, "That was terrible! The poor child didn't want to say a thing. I just had to keep asking her over and over." Then Vesna told me that the daughter said that the mother had been raped too.

So we had to interview Mrs Paçaku. In she came, and started just where she'd left off the previous day. Her eyes burned, she was furious. How could we ask such questions of a child!

I kept saying, "I'm sorry, this is a procedural necessity."

Vesna said, "Please just tell us what happened and then this will be over."

The mother said, "You have the truth, we told the truth, this is rape all over again!"

"We just need to make sure the stories match." And so on.

Suddenly she told us, snap in a sentence. Yes, she'd been raped too, in front her husband.

So we had to ask the rest of the questions. Was the girl first or her? The girl was first. Good, thank heavens, the stories added up. How many were there?

She flared up at us again. "How many? What difference can it make, how many?"

"We need to know in case any charges can be brought."

She chewed the inside of her cheek. Then she dismissed it, a trifle with the wave of her hand. "All fifteen."

Military rape is about terror and subjugation; it's about hollowing the heart out of an enemy people. It's strategy, nothing more. But you have to wonder about the men who do it. OK, you rape a beautiful girl, but how can you keep it up, frankly, when it's an old woman and your second time? What was going on inside their heads?

"Then they did the boy," said the mother, with another snap, of the hand, the mouth. She looked defiant.

Vesna and I went very still, kept our faces and ran our fingers up and down the notes. Those beautiful notes we keep. Otherwise you know, they all bleed into each other. The boy? The son? Which son?

"Skender." Alexander. A gypsy boy with an Albanian name.

"We have nothing in our records about that."

"Ah! You see? You don't have everything in your records."

We had to talk to the daughter again. I wasn't there, but the questions would have been: Who else was raped? Was anyone else in your family raped?

Vesna came out and said nothing, just stood there, only the tips of her fingers shivering. Her wedding ring was still. I sent the mother and daughter back. Vesna sat down on one of the visitors chairs. She looked at her nails and told me, "I had to ask the direct question. Was Skender raped too? Then she said yes."

The direct question invalidated the evidence.

"Do you have any doubt they were raped?" Vesna asked me.

"Let it go," I said. "Just say ... Just say the stories matched."

Next day we called in the son.

He was a little thing for fifteen, skinny, black eyes like a squirrel. Half his hair had been dyed blond. He didn't sit down. He said he didn't like to sit. Something I learned for next time.

So he stood and we asked questions. Did the men do anything? How many? What did they do? What did they do next? How many? Who was first? How did they hold your sister down? Who was next? How many? You have to keep asking the same question over and over.

The boy kept shifting one foot to the other. "Please sit down," Vesna said.

He said, "It hurts too much."

Then he told us. All fifteen.

Were they possessed by devils? What does a man who goes home to his family, to his wife, a man who procreates, what does he think when he remembers he penetrated a young boy after ten other men? Is it comradeship, like a football team? Is that military life suppresses them? Or all that killing stimulates them? Where do they recruit, gay discos?

The poor little fellow wet himself. A stain across the trousers, across the floor, but he wouldn't let us clean him up. He just suddenly started to talk. He talked and talked, strands of spittle between lips, and we had to sit there taking notes so neatly. Vesna's face swelled up; pushing down tears. I felt sorry for her, but you have to stay detached. You do want to comfort them, give them a hug, but it's not professional.

He remembered every last detail. One of the men was still chewing rotten salami. One of them had beautifully clean, polished boots.

Then he took a deep breath and said something I couldn't understand. Vesna dropped the pen, and pushed her forehead down onto her hands. "He's just told us the father was raped as well."

We would have to interview them all, all over again. The wife refused. She sat there popping pieces of apple into her mouth, shaking her head. Vesna begged her. "Look! It is in your interests if all the evidence works together."

"The boy tells stories. He's too ashamed. He wants everyone to be ashamed. Nothing else happened. Isn't what happened bad enough for you?" She had very few, very yellow teeth. "I shall take him and I shall beat him."

"Don't do that," Vesna asked her.

"What else am I to do?" the mother answered.

I was the senior officer, so I said, "Vesna, we'll just talk only to the father. Corroborate as much as we can."

He came in with his accordion. We could hear him outside the front door playing it. He brought it into the interview room with him, and smiled, as if we were all inside a bar. He kept it on his lap, ready to play. He was smiling with one silver outlined tooth, and unlike his wife looked young for his age.

The questions back forth and over again, the same ground. He perched forward, eyebrows arched as if straining to say *nothing is wrong;* his manner straightforward, as though he understood that we were trying to help. *Da, da,* firm downward strokes of the head. Yes they held my daughter down, and turned her so that I had to see what they did. Yes, they did that to her as well. Yes, my poor Shemsije, she was next. What do you think they did? Almost a chuckle. The usual thing. Like in barnyard. Son? Yes.

It was like he was discussing sporting results.

Did they assault anyone else?

No.

No one else was assaulted?

No.

Mr Paçaku, it is necessary that all the stories match.

Da, yes, downward stroke.

That went on for about an hour. I nodded to Vesna. *Go ahead, ask.*

"I'm sorry, Mr Paçaku, but your son says that other people were raped."

"Yes, poor boy. He is ashamed, it's his way of spreading it around."

"It wasn't anyone in your family's fault. None of you have done anything to be ashamed of. But we do need the basic facts."

"Ah! The facts! If you want the facts. We used to help on a farm you know?"

He starts to tell us stories about some lost golden age, when he worked on a farm, and his family didn't have to beg. Then he tells us about his wedding. It was a real Romany wedding in summer, wildflowers on the bed. The women gave his wife gold, it went on all day, guns shooting into the air. He starts to play the wedding music on his accordion.

We have to stop him. "Mr Paçaku? Please. Mr Paçaku. That's very nice but we still have to ask you some questions."

He told us about his cousin's new car. He told Vesna about how he hid Muslims. He must think she is a Muslim, maybe he knows she lives south of the river. Nobody ever says where they live, their lives depend on it. He tells us about gypsy arts and crafts, how to carve, how to read fortunes, how his aunt predicted her own death. Sometimes in this job you have to let them see you are prepared to wait.

"Mr Paçaku.. We need to know who else was raped."

We really want to help him. I go outside and tell the clerk to send everybody else home, and to get us more water and some food. We give him noodles.

He starts to talk about recipes, about the kindness of the Kosovars before the war. Everybody live in peace, everybody happy. He tells us about his brother's prowess as a bare-knuckles boxer. He starts to cry, he mops his tears with the bread. He's smearing butter on his cheeks and he's crying about lost animals, his father's animals. They stole my pigs and ducks! He tells us a story about how the pig died of a broken heart because it lost its favorite duck. Suddenly it's dark outside. Vesna looks beside herself.

"Just ask him directly," I tell her.

She does. He blows up. "Do you think I would let such a thing happen to me? Do I not look like a man to you? Who has been saying such a thing? Who? The boy? I will beat him, for saying such a thing. I tell you anybody tries to do such a thing to me, he is flat on the ground; he's on his back; he's dead."

It's worse than the accordion.

We keep pushing. The tears start again. "Why do you say such things to me? My wife, my daughter, is it not enough? Why are you tormenting me? When will it stop?"

Finally I say, "Let's finish."

Vesna just nods. I send her home. I said to her, I told her, I said, "We'll talk tomorrow, OK?"

We didn't need it in the end, the testimony. Skender was examined and they found damage completely consistent with the story, and that was good enough. The Paçakus got to Norway.

It's a miracle this café is still here. Wine's just as terrible. Tastes of blood. I was hoping to see Vesna.

I'm here on my VARI ... voluntary relief from isolation. You become so professional. I didn't know what it was at first, I just felt exhausted. They're sending me to the Rome office probably until I retire. I been lots of places.

My first was West Africa: Sierra Leone and Liberia. Then Zaire. That might be the worst. North Ossetia, then here. Pakistan, Zambia— lovely country, that was just persuading the Angolanos to go home. Now Chad, Darfur. It's all the same thing.

How can a pig love a duck?

Pol Pot's Beautiful Daughter

In Cambodia people are used to ghosts. Ghosts buy newspapers. They own property.

A few years ago, spirits owned a house in Phnom Penh, at the Tra Bek end of Monivong Boulevard. Khmer Rouge had murdered the whole family and there was no one left alive to inherit it. People cycled past the building, leaving it boarded up. Sounds of weeping came from inside.

Then a professional inheritor arrived from America. She'd done her research and could claim to be the last surviving relative of no fewer than three families. She immediately sold the house to a Chinese businessman, who turned the ground floor into a photocopying shop.

The copiers began to print pictures of the original owners.

At first, single black-and-white photos turned up in the copied dossiers of aid workers or government officials. The father of the murdered family had been a lawyer. He stared fiercely out of the photos as if demanding something. In other photocopies, his beautiful daughters forlornly hugged each other. The background was hazy like fog.

One night the owner heard a noise and trundled downstairs to find all five photocopiers printing one picture after another of faces: young college men, old women, parents with a string of babies, or government soldiers in uniform. He pushed the big green off buttons. Nothing happened.

He pulled out all the plugs, but the machines kept grinding out face after face. Women in beehive hairdos or clever children with glasses looked wistfully out of the photocopies. They seemed to be dreaming of home in the 1960s, when Phnom Penh was the most beautiful city in Southeast Asia.

News spread. People began to visit the shop to identify lost relatives. Women would cry, "That's my mother! I didn't have a photograph!" They would weep and press the flimsy A4 sheets to their breasts. The paper went limp from tears and humidity as if it too were crying.

Soon, a throng began to gather outside the shop every morning to view the latest batch of faces. In desperation, the owner announced that each morning's harvest would be delivered direct to *The Truth*, a magazine of remembrance.

Then one morning he tried to open the house-door to the shop and found it blocked. He went 'round to the front of the building and rolled open the metal shutters.

The shop was packed from floor to ceiling with photocopies. The ground floor had no windows—the room had been filled from the inside. The owner pulled out a sheet of paper and saw himself on the ground, his head beaten in by a hoe. The same image was on every single page.

He buried the photocopiers and sold the house at once. The new owner liked its haunted reputation; it kept people away. The FOR SALE sign was left hanging from the second floor.

In a sense, the house had been bought by another ghost.

This is a completely untrue story about someone who must exist.

Pol Pot's only child, a daughter, was born in 1986. Her name was Sith, and in 2004, she was eighteen years old.

Sith liked air-conditioning and luxury automobiles. Her hair was dressed in cornrows, and she had a spiky piercing above one eye. Her jeans were elaborately slashed and embroidered. Her pink T-shirts bore slogans in English: CARE KOOKY. PINK MOLL.

Sith lived like a woman on Thai television, doing as she pleased in lip-gloss and Sunsilked hair. Nine simple rules helped her avoid all unpleasantness.

1. Never think about the past or politics.
2. Ignore ghosts. They cannot hurt you.

3. Do not go to school. Hire tutors. Don't do homework. It is disturbing.
4. Always be driven everywhere in either the Mercedes or the BMW.
5. Avoid all well-dressed Cambodian boys. They are the sons of the estimated 250,000 new generals created by the regime. Their sons can behave with impunity.
6. Avoid all men with potbellies. They eat too well and therefore must be corrupt.
7. Avoid anyone who drives a Toyota Viva or Honda Dream motorcycle.
8. Don't answer letters or phone calls.
9. Never make any friends.

There was also a tenth rule, but that went without saying.

Rotten fruit rinds and black mud never stained Sith's designer sports shoes. Disabled beggars never asked her for alms. Her life began yesterday, which was effectively the same as today.

Every day, her driver took her to the new Soriya Market. It was almost the only place that Sith went. The color of silver, Soriya rose up in many floors to a round glass dome.

Sith preferred the 142nd Street entrance. Its green awning made everyone look as if they were made of jade. The doorway went directly into the ice-cold jewelry rotunda with its floor of polished black and white stone. The individual stalls were hung with glittering necklaces and earrings.

Sith liked tiny shiny things that had no memory. She hated politics. She refused to listen to the news. Pol Pot's beautiful daughter wished the current leadership would behave decently, like her dad always did. To her.

She remembered the sound of her father's gentle voice. She remembered sitting on his lap in a forest enclosure, being bitten by mosquitoes. Memories of malaria had sunk into her very bones. She now associated forests with nausea, fevers, and pain. A flicker of tree-shade on her skin made her want to throw up, and the odor of soil or fallen leaves made her gag. She had never been to Angkor Wat. She read nothing.

Sith shopped. Her driver was paid by the government and always carried an AK-47, but his wife, the housekeeper, had no idea who Sith was. The house was full of swept marble, polished teak furniture, iPods, Xboxes, and plasma screens.

Please remember that every word of this story is a lie. Pol Pot was no doubt a dedicated communist who made no money from ruling Cambodia. Nevertheless, a hefty allowance arrived for Sith every month from an account in Switzerland.

Nothing touched Sith, until she fell in love with the salesman at Hello Phones.

Cambodian readers may know that in 2004 there was no mobile phone shop in Soriya Market. However, there was a branch of Hello Phone Cards that had a round blue sales counter with orange trim. This shop looked like that.

Every day Sith bought or exchanged a mobile phone there. She would sit and flick her hair at the salesman.

His name was Dara, which means Star. Dara knew about deals on call prices, sim cards, and the new phones that showed videos. He could get her any call tone she liked.

Talking to Dara broke none of Sith's rules. He wasn't fat, nor was he well dressed, and far from being a teenager, he was a comfortably mature twenty-four years old.

One day, Dara chuckled and said, "As a friend I advise you, you don't need another mobile phone."

Sith wrinkled her nose. "I don't like this one any more. It's blue. I want something more feminine. But not frilly. And it should have better sound quality."

"Okay, but you could save your money and buy some more nice clothes."

Pol Pot's beautiful daughter lowered her chin, which she knew made her neck look long and graceful. "Do you like my clothes?"

"Why ask me?"

She shrugged. "I don't know. It's good to check out your look."

Dara nodded. "You look cool. What does your sister say?"

Sith let him know she had no family. "Ah," he said and quickly changed the subject. That was terrific. Secrecy and sympathy in one easy movement.

Sith came back the next day and said that she'd decided that the rose-colored phone was too feminine. Dara laughed aloud and his eyes sparkled. Sith had come late in the morning just so that he could ask this question. "Are you hungry? Do you want to meet for lunch?"

Would he think she was cheap if she said yes? Would he say she was snobby if she said no?

"Just so long as we eat in Soriya Market," she said.

She was torn between BBWorld Burgers and Lucky7. BBWorld was big, round, and just two floors down from the dome. Lucky7 Burgers was part of the Lucky Supermarket, such a good store that a tiny jar of Maxwell House cost US$2.40.

They decided on BBWorld. It was full of light, and they could see the town spread out through the wide clean windows. Sith sat in silence.

Pol Pot's daughter had nothing to say unless she was buying something. Or rather she had only one thing to say, but she must never say it.

Dara did all the talking. He talked about how the guys on the third floor could get him a deal on original copies of *Grand Theft Auto*. He hinted that he could get Sith discounts from Bsfashion, the spotlit modern shop one floor down.

Suddenly he stopped. "You don't need to be afraid of me, you know." He said it in a kindly, grownup voice. "I can see you're a properly brought-up girl. I like that. It's nice."

Sith still couldn't find anything to say. She could only nod. She wanted to run away.

"Would you like to go to K-Four?"

K-Four, the big electronics shop, stocked all the reliable brand names: Hitachi, Sony, Panasonic, Philips, or Denon. It was so expensive that almost nobody shopped there, which is why Sith liked it. A crowd of people stood outside and stared through the window at a huge home-entertainment center showing a DVD of *Ice Age*. On the screen, a little animal was being chased by a glacier. It was so beautiful!

Sith finally found something to say. "If I had one of those, I would never need to leave the house."

Dara looked at her sideways and decided to laugh.

The next day Sith told him that all the phones she had were too big. Did he have one that she could wear around her neck like jewelry?

This time they went to Lucky7 Burgers and sat across from the Revlon counter. They watched boys having their hair layered by Revlon's natural-beauty specialists.

Dara told her more about himself. His father had died in the wars. His family now lived in the country. Sith's Coca-Cola suddenly tasted of antimalarial drugs.

"But ... you don't want to *live* in the country," she said.

"No. I have to live in Phnom Penh to make money. But my folks are good country people. Modest." He smiled, embarrassed.

They'll have hens and a cousin who shimmies up coconut trees. There will be trees all around but no shops anywhere. The earth will smell.

Sith couldn't finish her drink. She sighed and smiled and said abruptly, "I'm sorry. It's been cool. But I have to go." She slunk sideways out of her seat as slowly as molasses.

Walking back into the jewelry rotunda with nothing to do, she realized that Dara would think she didn't like him.

And that made the lower part of her eyes sting.

She went back the next day and didn't even pretend to buy a mobile phone. She told Dara that she'd left so suddenly the day before because she'd remembered a hair appointment.

He said that he could see she took a lot of trouble with her hair. Then he asked her out for a movie that night.

Sith spent all day shopping in K-Four.

They met at six. Dara was so considerate that he didn't even suggest the horror movie. He said he wanted to see *Buffalo Girl Hiding*, a movie about a country girl who lives on a farm. Sith said with great feeling that she would prefer the horror movie.

The cinema on the top floor opened out directly onto the roof of Soriya. Graffiti had been scratched into the green railings. Why would people want to ruin something new and beautiful? Sith put her arm through Dara's and knew that they were now boyfriend and girlfriend.

"Finally," he said.

"Finally what?"

"You've done something."

They leaned on the railings and looked out over other people's apartments. West toward the river was a building with one huge roof terrace. Women met there to gossip. Children were playing toss-the-sandal. From this distance, Sith was enchanted.

"I just love watching the children."

The movie, from Thailand, was about a woman whose face turns blue and spotty and who eats men. The blue woman was yucky, but not as scary as all the badly dubbed voices. The characters sounded possessed. It was though Thai people had been taken over by the spirits of dead Cambodians.

Whenever Sith got scared, she chuckled.

So she sat chuckling with terror. Dara thought she was laughing at a dumb movie and found such intelligence charming. He started to chuckle too. Sith thought he was as frightened as she was. Together in the dark, they took each other's hands.

Outside afterward, the air hung hot even in the dark and 142nd Street smelled of drains. Sith stood on tiptoe to avoid the oily deposits and castoff fishbones.

Dara said, "I will drive you home."

"My driver can take us," said Sith, flipping open her Kermit-the-Frog mobile.

Her black Mercedes-Benz edged to a halt, crunching old plastic bottles in the gutter. The seats were upholstered with tan leather and the driver was armed.

Dara's jaw dropped. "Who . . . *who* is your father?"

"He's dead."

Dara shook his head. "Who was he?"

Normally Sith used her mother's family name, but that would not answer this question. Flustered, she tried to think of someone who could be her father. She knew of nobody the right age. She remembered something about a politician who had died. His name came to her and she said it in panic. "My father was Kol Vireakboth." Had she got the name right? "Please don't tell anyone."

Dara covered his eyes. "We—my family, my father—we fought for the KPLA."

Sith had to stop herself asking what the KPLA was.

Kol Vireakboth had led a faction in the civil wars. It fought against the Khmer Rouge, the Vietnamese, the King, and corruption. It wanted a new way for Cambodia. Kol Vireakboth was a Cambodian leader who had never told a lie and or accepted a bribe.

Remember that this is an untrue story.

Dara started to back away from the car. "I don't think we should be doing this. I'm just a villager, really."

"That doesn't matter."

His eyes closed. "I would expect nothing less from the daughter of Kol Vireakboth."

Oh for gosh sake, she just picked the man's name out of the air, she didn't need more problems. "Please!" she said.

Dara sighed. "Okay. I said I would see you home safely. I will." Inside the Mercedes, he stroked the tan leather.

When they arrived, he craned his neck to look up at the building. "Which floor are you on?"

"All of them."

Color drained from his face.

"My driver will take you back," she said to Dara. As the car pulled away, she stood outside the closed garage shutters, waving forlornly.

Then Sith panicked. Who was Kol Vireakboth? She went online and Googled. She had to read about the wars. Her skin started to creep. All those different factions swam in her head: ANS, NADK, KPR, and KPNLF. The very names seemed to come at her spoken by forgotten voices.

Soon she had all she could stand. She printed out Vireakboth's picture and decided to have it framed. In case Dara visited.

Kol Vireakboth had a round face and a fatherly smile. His eyes seemed to slant upward toward his nose, looking full of kindly insight. He'd been killed by a car bomb.

All that night, Sith heard whispering.

In the morning, there was another picture of someone else in the tray of her printer.

A long-faced, buck-toothed woman stared out at her in black and white. Sith noted the victim's fashion lapses. The woman's hair was a mess, all frizzy. She should have had it straightened and put in some nice highlights. The woman's eyes drilled into her.

"Can't touch me," said Sith. She left the photo in the tray. She went to see Dara, right away, no breakfast.

His eyes were circled with dark flesh, and his blue Hello trousers and shirt were not properly ironed.

"Buy the whole shop," Dara said, looking deranged. "The guys in K-Four just told me some girl in blue jeans walked in yesterday and bought two home theatres. One for the salon, she said, and one for the roof terrace. She paid for both of them in full and had them delivered to the far end of Monivong."

Sith sighed. "I'm sending one back." She hoped that sounded abstemious. "It looked too metallic against my curtains."

Pause.

"She also bought an Aido robot dog for fifteen hundred dollars."

Sith would have preferred that Dara did not know about the dog. It was just a silly toy; it hadn't occured to her that it might cost that much until she saw the bill. "They should not tell everyone about their customers' business or soon they will have no customers." Dara was looking at her as if thinking: *This is not just a nice sweet girl.*

"I had fun last night," Sith said in a voice as thin as high clouds.

"So did I."

"We don't have to tell anyone about my family. Do we?" Sith was seriously scared of losing him.

"No. But Sith, it's stupid. Your family, my family, we are not equals."

"It doesn't make any difference."

"You lied to me. Your family is not dead. You have famous uncles."

She did indeed—Uncle Ieng Sary, Uncle Khieu Samphan, Uncle Ta Mok. All the Pol Pot clique had been called her uncles.

"I didn't know them that well," she said. That was true, too.

What would she do if she couldn't shop in Soriya Market any more? What would she do without Dara?

She begged. "I am not a strong person. Sometimes I think I am not a person at all. I'm just a space."

Dara looked suddenly mean. "You're just a credit card." Then his face fell. "I'm sorry. That was an unkind thing to say. You are very young for your age, and I'm older than you and I should have treated you with more care."

Sith was desperate. "All my money would be very nice."

"I'm not for sale."

He worked in a shop and would be sending money home to a fatherless family; of course he was for sale!

Sith had a small heart, but a big head for thinking. She knew that she had to do this delicately, like picking a flower, or she would spoil the bloom. "Let's . . . let's just go see a movie?"

After all, she was beautiful and well brought up and she knew her eyes were big and round. Her tiny heart was aching.

This time they saw *Tum Teav*, a remake of an old movie from the 1960s. If movies were not nightmares about ghosts, then they tried to preserve the past. When, thought Sith, will they make a movie about Cambodia's future? *Tum Teav* was based on a classic tale of a young monk who falls in love with a properly brought-up girl, but her mother opposes the match. They commit suicide at the end, bringing a curse on their village. Sith sat through it stony-faced. I am not going to be a dead heroine in a romance.

Dara offered to drive her home again, and that's when Sith found out that he drove a Honda Dream. He proudly presented to her the gleaming motorcycle of fast young men. Sith felt backed into a corner. She'd already offered to buy him. Showing off her car again might humiliate him.

So she broke rule number seven.

Dara hid her bag in the back and they went soaring down Monivong Boulevard at night, past homeless people, prostitutes, and chefs staggering home after work. It was late in the year, but it started to rain.

Sith loved it, the cool air brushing against her face, the cooler rain clinging to her eyelashes.

She remembered being five years old in the forest and dancing in the monsoon. She encircled Dara's waist to stay on the bike and suddenly found her cheek was pressed up against his back. She giggled in fear, not of the rain, but of what she felt.

He dropped her off at home. Inside, everything was dark except for the flickering green light on her printer. In the tray were two new photographs. One was of a child, a little boy, holding up a school prize certificate. The other was a tough, wise-looking old man, with a string of muscle down either side of his ironic, bitter smile. They looked directly at her.

They know who I am.

As she climbed the stairs to her bedroom, she heard someone sobbing, far away, as if the sound came from next door. She touched the walls of the staircase. They shivered slightly, constricting in time to the cries.

In her bedroom she extracted one of her many iPods from the tangle of wires and listened to System of a Down, as loud as she could. It helped her sleep. The sound of nu-metal guitars seemed to come roaring out of her own heart.

She was woken up in the sun-drenched morning by the sound of her doorbell many floors down. She heard the housekeeper Jorani call and the door open. Sith hesitated over choice of jeans and top. By the time she got downstairs, she found the driver and the housemaid joking with Dara, giving him tea.

Like the sunshine, Dara seemed to disperse ghosts.

"Hi," he said. "It's my day off. I thought we could go on a motorcycle ride to the country."

But not to the country. Couldn't they just spend the day in Soriya? No, said Dara, there's lots of other places to see in Phnom Penh.

He drove her, twisting through back streets. How did the city get so poor? How did it get so dirty?

They went to a new and modern shop for CDs that was run by a record label. Dara knew all the cool new music, most of it influenced by Khmer-Americans returning from Long Beach and Compton: Sdey, Phnom Penh Bad Boys, Khmer Kid.

Sith bought twenty CDs.

They went to the National Museum and saw the beautiful Buddha-like head of King Jayavarman VII. Dara without thinking ducked and held up his hands in prayer. They had dinner in a French restaurant with candles and wine, and it was just like in a karaoke video, a boy, a girl, and her money all going out together. They saw the show at Sovanna Phum, and there was a wonderful dance piece with sampled 1940s music from an old French movie, with traditional Khmer choreography.

Sith went home, her heart singing, Dara, Dara, Dara.

In the bedroom, a mobile phone began to ring, over and over. *Call 1* said the screen, but gave no name or number, so the person was not on Sith's list of contacts.

She turned off the phone. It kept ringing. That's when she knew for certain.

She hid the phone in a pillow in the spare bedroom and put another pillow on top of it and then closed the door.

All forty-two of her mobile phones started to ring. They rang from inside closets, or from the bathroom where she had forgotten them. They rang from the roof terrace and even from inside a shoe under her bed.

"I am a very stubborn girl!" she shouted at the spirits. "You do not scare me."

She turned up her iPod and finally slept.

As soon as the sun was up, she roused her driver, slumped deep in his hammock.

"Come on, we're going to Soriya Market," she said. The driver looked up at her dazed, then remembered to smile and lower his head in respect.

His face fell when she showed up in the garage with all forty-two of her mobile phones in one black bag.

It was too early for Soriya Market to open. They drove in circles with sunrise blazing directly into their eyes. On the streets, men pushed carts like beasts of burden, or carried cascades of belts into the old

Central Market. The old market was domed, art deco, the color of vomit, French. Sith never shopped there.

"Maybe you should go visit your mom," said the driver. "You know, she loves you. Families are there for when you are in trouble."

Sith's mother lived in Thailand, and they never spoke. Her mother's family kept asking for favors: money, introductions, or help with getting a job. Sith didn't speak to them any longer.

"My family is only trouble."

The driver shut up and drove.

Finally Soriya opened. Sith went straight to Dara's shop and dumped all the phones on the blue countertop. "Can you take these back?"

"We only do exchanges. I can give a new phone for an old one." Dara looked thoughtful. "Don't worry. Leave them here with me. I'll go sell them to a guy in the old market and give you your money tomorrow." He smiled in approval. "This is very sensible."

He passed one phone back, the one with video and email. "This is the best one, keep this."

Dara was so competent. Sith wanted to sink down onto him like a pillow and stay there. She sat in the shop all day, watching him work. One of the guys from the games shop upstairs asked, "Who is this beautiful girl?"

Dara answered proudly, "My girlfriend."

Dara drove her back on the Dream and at the door to her house, he chuckled. "I don't want to go." She pressed a finger against his naughty lips, and smiled and spun back inside from happiness.

She was in the ground-floor garage. She heard something like a rat scuttle. In her bag, the telephone rang. Who were these people to importune her, even if they were dead? She wrenched the mobile phone out of her bag and pushed the green button and put the phone to her ear. She waited. There was a sound like wind.

A child spoke to her, his voice clogged as if he was crying. "They tied my thumbs together."

Sith demanded. "How did you get my number?"

"I'm all alone!"

"Then ring somebody else. Someone in your family."

"All my family are dead. I don't know where I am. My name is—"

Sith clicked the phone off. She opened the trunk of the car and tossed the phone inside it. Being telephoned by ghosts was so . . . unmodern. How could Cambodia become a number-one country if its cellphone network was haunted?

She stormed up into the salon. On top of a table, the $1500, no-mess dog stared at her from out of his packaging. Sith clumped up the stairs onto the roof terrace to sleep as far away as she could from everything in the house.

She woke up in the dark, to hear thumping from downstairs.

The sound was metallic and hollow, as if someone were locked in the car. Sith turned on her iPod. Something was making the sound of the music skip. She fought the tangle of wires, and wrenched out another player, a Xen, but it too skipped, burping the sound of speaking voices into the middle of the music.

Had she heard a ripping sound? She pulled out the earphones, and heard something climbing the stairs.

A sound of light, uneven lolloping. She thought of crippled children. Frost settled over her like a heavy blanket, and she could not move.

The robot dog came whirring up onto the terrace. It paused at the top of the stairs, its camera nose pointing at her to see, its useless eyes glowing cherry red.

The robot dog said in a warm, friendly voice, "My name is Phalla. I tried to buy my sister medicine and they killed me for it."

Sith tried to say "Go away," but her throat wouldn't open.

The dog tilted its head. "No one even knows I'm dead. What will you do for all the people who are not mourned?"

Laughter blurted out of her, and Sith saw it rise up as cold vapor into the air.

"We have no one to invite us to the feast," said the dog.

Sith giggled in terror. "Nothing. I can do nothing!" she said, shaking her head.

"You laugh?" The dog gathered itself and jumped up into the hammock with her. It turned and lifted up its clear plastic tail and laid a genuine turd alongside Sith. Short brown hair was wound up in it, a scalp actually, and a single flat white human tooth smiled out of it.

Sith squawked and overturned both herself and the dog out of the hammock and onto the floor. The dog pushed its nose up against hers and began to sing an old-fashioned children's song about birds.

Something heavy huffed its way up the stairwell toward her. Sith shivered with cold on the floor and could not move. The dog went on singing in a high, sweet voice. A large shadow loomed out over the top of the staircase, and Sith gargled, swallowing laughter, trying to speak.

"There was thumping in the car and no one in it," said the driver.

Sith sagged toward the floor with relief. "The ghosts," she said. "They're back." She thrust herself to her feet. "We're getting out now. Ring the Hilton. Find out if they have rooms."

She kicked the toy dog down the stairs ahead of her. "We're moving now!"

Together they all loaded the car, shaking. Once again, the house was left to ghosts. As they drove, the mobile phone rang over and over inside the trunk.

The new Hilton (which does not exist) rose up by the river across from the Department for Cults and Religious Affairs. Tall and marbled and pristine, it had crystal chandeliers and fountains, and wood and brass handles in the elevators.

In the middle of the night only the Bridal Suite was still available, but it had an extra parental chamber where the driver and his wife could sleep. High on the twenty-first floor, the night sparkled with lights and everything was hushed, as far away from Cambodia as it was possible to get.

Things were quiet after that, for a while.

Every day she and Dara went to movies, or went to a restaurant. They went shopping. She slipped him money and he bought himself a beautiful suit. He said, over a hamburger at Lucky7, "I've told my mother that I've met a girl."

Sith smiled and thought: and I bet you told her that I'm rich.

"I've decided to live in the Hilton," she told him.

Maybe we could live in the Hilton. A pretty smile could hint at that. The rainy season ended. The last of the monsoons rose up dark gray with a froth of white cloud on top, looking exactly like a giant wave about to break.

Dry cooler air arrived.

After work was over Dara convinced her to go for a walk along the river in front of the Royal Palace. He went to the men's room to change into a new luxury suit and Sith thought: he's beginning to imagine life with all that money.

As they walked along the river, exposed to all those people, Sith shook inside. There were teenage boys everywhere. Some of them were in rags, which was reassuring, but some of them were very well dressed indeed, the sons of Impunity who could do anything. Sith swerved suddenly to avoid even seeing them. But Dara in his new beige suit looked like one of them, and the generals' sons nodded to him with quizzical eyebrows, perhaps wondering who he was.

In front of the palace, a pavilion reached out over the water. Next to it a traditional orchestra bashed and wailed out something old fashioned. Hundreds of people crowded around a tiny wat. Dara shook Sith's wrist and they stood up to see.

People held up bundles of lotus flowers and incense in prayer. They threw the bundles into the wat. Monks immediately shoveled the joss sticks and flowers out of the back.

Behind the wat, children wearing T-shirts and shorts black with filth rooted through the dead flowers, the smoldering incense, and old coconut shells.

Sith asked, "Why do they do that?"

"You are so innocent!" chuckled Dara and shook his head. The evening was blue and gold. Sith had time to think that she did not want to go back to a hotel and that the only place she really felt happy was next to Dara. All around that thought was something dark and tangled.

Dara suggested with affection that they should get married.

It was as if Sith had her answer ready. "No, absolutely not," she said at once. "How can you ask that? There is not even anyone for you to ask!

Have you spoken to your family about me? Has your family made any checks about my background?"

Which was what she really wanted to know.

Dara shook his head. "I have explained that you are an orphan, but they are not concerned with that. We are modest people. They will be happy if I am happy."

"Of course they won't be! Of course they will need to do checks."

Sith scowled. She saw her way to sudden advantage. "At least they must consult fortune-tellers. They are not fools. I can help them. Ask them the names of the fortune-tellers they trust."

Dara smiled shyly. "We have no money."

"I will give them money and you can tell them that you pay."

Dara's eyes searched her face. "I don't want that."

"How will we know if it is a good marriage? And your poor mother, how can you ask her to make a decision like this without information? So. You ask your family for the names of good professionals they trust, and I will pay them, and I will go to Prime Minister Hun Sen's own personal fortune-teller, and we can compare results."

Thus she established again both her propriety and her status.

In an old romance, the parents would not approve of the match and the fortune-teller would say that the marriage was ill-omened. Sith left nothing to romance.

She offered the family's fortune-tellers whatever they wanted—a car, a farm—and in return demanded a written copy of their judgment. All of them agreed that the portents for the marriage were especially auspicious.

Then she secured an appointment with the Prime Minister's fortuneteller.

Hun Sen's Kru Taey was a lady in a black business suit. She had long fingernails like talons, but they were perfectly manicured and frosted white.

She was the kind of fortune-teller who is possessed by someone else's spirit. She sat at a desk and looked at Sith as unblinking as a fish, both her hands steepled together. After the most basic of hellos, she said, "Dollars only. Twenty-five thousand. I need to buy my son an apartment."

"That's a very high fee," said Sith.

"It's not a fee. It is a consideration for giving you the answer you want. My fee is another twenty-five thousand dollars."

They negotiated. Sith liked the Kru Taey's manner. It confirmed everything Sith believed about life.

The fee was reduced somewhat but not the consideration.

"Payment upfront now," the Kru Taey said. She wouldn't take a check. Like only the very best restaurants she accepted foreign credit cards. Sith's Swiss card worked immediately. It had unlimited credit in case she had to leave the country in a hurry.

The Kru Taey said, "I will tell the boy's family that the marriage will be particularly fortunate."

Sith realized that she had not yet said anything about a boy, his family, or a marriage.

The Kru Taey smiled. "I know you are not interested in your real fortune. But to be kind, I will tell you unpaid that this marriage really is particularly well favored. All the other fortune-tellers would have said the same thing without being bribed."

The Kru Taey's eyes glinted in the most unpleasant way. "So you needn't have bought them farms or paid me an extra twenty-five thousand dollars."

She looked down at her perfect fingernails. "You will be very happy indeed. But not before your entire life is overturned."

The back of Sith's arms prickled as if from cold. She should have been angry, but she could feel herself smiling. Why?

And why waste politeness on the old witch? Sith turned to go without saying good-bye.

"Oh, and about your other problem," said the woman.

Sith turned back and waited.

"Enemies," said the Kru Taey, "can turn out to be friends."

Sith sighed. "What are you talking about?"

The Kru Taey's smile was a wide as a tiger-trap. "The million people your father killed."

Sith went hard. "Not a million," she said. "Somewhere between two hundred and fifty or five hundred thousand."

"Enough," smiled the Kru Taey. "My father was one of them." She smiled for a moment longer. "I will be sure to tell the Prime Minister that you visited me."

Sith snorted as if in scorn. "I will tell him myself."

But she ran back to her car.

That night, Sith looked down on all the lights like diamonds. She settled onto the giant mattress and turned on her iPod.

Someone started to yell at her. She pulled out the earpieces and jumped to the window. It wouldn't open. She shook it and wrenched its frame until it reluctantly slid an inch and she threw the iPod out of the twenty-first-floor window.

She woke up late the next morning, to hear the sound of the TV. She opened up the double doors into the salon and saw Jorani, pressed against the wall.

"The TV . . . ," Jorani said, her eyes wide with terror.

The driver waited by his packed bags. He stood up, looking as mournful as a bloodhound.

On the widescreen TV there was what looked like a pop-music karaoke video. Except that the music was very old fashioned. Why would a pop video show a starving man eating raw maize in a field? He glanced over his shoulder in terror as he ate. The glowing singalong words were the song that the dog had sung at the top of the stairs. The starving man looked up at Sith and corn mash rolled out of his mouth.

"It's all like that," said the driver. "I unplugged the set, but it kept playing on every channel." He sompiahed but looked miserable. "My wife wants to leave."

Sith felt shame. It was miserable and dirty, being infested with ghosts. Of course they would want to go.

"It's okay. I can take taxis," she said.

The driver nodded, and went into the next room and whispered to his wife. With little scurrying sounds, they gathered up their things. They sompiahed, and apologized.

The door clicked almost silently behind them.

It will always be like this, thought Sith. Wherever I go. It would be like this with Dara.

The hotel telephone started to ring. Sith left it ringing. She covered the TV with a blanket, but the terrible, tinny old music kept wheedling and rattling its way out at her, and she sat on the edge of her bed, staring into space.

I'll have to leave Cambodia.

At the market, Dara looked even more cheerful than usual. The fortune-tellers had pronounced the marriage as very favorable. His mother had invited Sith home for the Pchum Ben festival.

"We can take the bus tomorrow," he said.

"Does it smell? All those people in one place?"

"It smells of air freshener. Then we take a taxi, and then you will have to walk up the track." Dara suddenly doubled up in laughter. "Oh, it will be good for you."

"Will there be dirt?"

"Everywhere! Oh, your dirty Nikes will earn you much merit!"

But at least, thought Sith, there will be no TV or phones.

Two days later, Sith was walking down a dirt track, ducking tree branches. Dust billowed all over her shoes. Dara walked behind her, chuckling, which meant she thought he was scared, too.

She heard a strange rattling sound. "What's that noise?"

"It's a goat," he said. "My mother bought it for me in April as a present."

A goat. How could they be any more rural? Sith had never seen a goat. She never even imagined that she would.

Dara explained. "I sell them to the Muslims. It is Agricultural Diversification."

There were trees everywhere, shadows crawling across the ground like snakes. Sith felt sick. One mosquito, she promised herself, just one and I will squeal and run away.

The house was tiny, on thin twisting stilts. She had pictured a big fine country house standing high over the ground on concrete pillars with a sunburst carving in the gable. The kitchen was a hut that sat directly on the ground, no stilts, and it was made of palm-leaf panels and there was no electricity. The strip light in the ceiling was attached to a car battery, and they kept a live fire on top of the concrete table to cook. Everything smelled of burnt fish.

Sith loved it.

Inside the hut, the smoke from the fires kept the mosquitoes away. Dara's mother, Mrs. Non Kunthea, greeted her with a smile. That triggered a respectful sompiah from Sith, the prayerlike gesture leaping out of her unbidden. On the platform table was a plastic sack full of dried prawns.

Without thinking, Sith sat on the table and began to pull the salty prawns out of their shells.

Why am I doing this?

Because it's what I did at home.

Sith suddenly remembered the enclosure in the forest, a circular fenced area. Daddy had slept in one house, and the women in another. Sith would talk to the cooks. For something to do, she would chop vegetables or shell prawns. Then Daddy would come to eat and he'd sit on the platform table and she, little Sith, would sit between his knees.

Dara's older brother, Yuth, came back for lunch. He was pot-bellied and drove a taxi for a living, and he moved in hard jabs like an angry old man. He reached too far for the rice, and Sith could smell his armpits.

"You see how we live," Yuth said to Sith. "This is what we get for having the wrong patron. Sihanouk thought we were anti-monarchist. To Hun Sen, we were the enemy. Remember the Work for Money program?"

No.

"They didn't give any of those jobs to us. We might as well have been the Khmer Rouge!"

The past, thought Sith, *why don't they just let it go? Why do they keep boasting about their old wars?*

Mrs. Non Kunthea chuckled with affection. "My eldest son was born angry," she said. "His slogan is 'Ten years is not too late for revenge.'"

Yuth started up again. "They treat that old monster Pol Pot better than they treat us. But then, he was an important person. If you go to his stupa in Anlong Veng, you will see that people leave offerings! They ask him for lottery numbers!"

He crumpled his green, soft, old-fashioned hat back onto his head and said, "Nice to meet you, Sith. Dara, she's too high class for the likes of you." But he grinned as he said it. He left, swirling disruption in his wake.

The dishes were gathered. Again without thinking, Sith swept up the plastic tub and carried it to the blackened branches. They rested over puddles where the washing-up water drained.

"You shouldn't work," said Dara's mother. "You are a guest."

"I grew up in a refugee camp," said Sith. After all, it was true.

Dara looked at her with a mix of love, pride, and gratitude for the good fortune of a rich wife who works.

And that was the best Sith could hope for. This family would be fine for her.

In the late afternoon, all four brothers came with their wives for the end of Pchum Ben, when the ghosts of the dead can wander the Earth. People scatter rice on the temple floors to feed their families. Some ghosts have small mouths so special rice is used.

Sith never took part in Pchum Ben. How could she go to the temple and scatter rice for Pol Pot?

The family settled in the kitchen chatting and joking, and it all passed in a blur for Sith. Everyone else had family they could honor. To Sith's surprise one of the uncles suggested that people should write names of the deceased and burn them, to transfer merit. It was nothing to do with Pchum Ben, but a lovely idea, so all the family wrote down names.

Sith sat with her hands jammed under her arms.

Dara's mother asked, "Isn't there a name you want to write, Sith?"

"No," said Sith in a tiny voice. How could she write the name Pol Pot? He was surely roaming the world let loose from hell. "There is no one."

Dara rubbed her hand. "Yes there is, Sith. A very special name."

"No, there's not."

Dara thought she didn't want them to know her father was Kol Vireakboth. He leant forward and whispered, "I promise. No one will see it."

Sith's breath shook. She took the paper and started to cry.

"Oh," said Dara's mother, stricken with sympathy. "Everyone in this country has a tragedy."

Sith wrote the name Kol Vireakboth.

Dara kept the paper folded and caught Sith's eyes. *You see?* he seemed to say. *I have kept your secret safe.* The paper burned.

Thunder slapped a clear sky about the face. It had been sunny, but now as suddenly as a curtain dropped down over a doorway, rain fell. A wind came from nowhere, tearing away a flap of palm-leaf wall, as if forcing entrance in a fury.

The family whooped and laughed and let the rain drench their shoulders as they stood up to push the wall back down, to keep out the rain.

But Sith knew. Her father's enemy was in the kitchen.

The rain passed; the sun came out. The family chuckled and sat back down around or on the table. They lowered dishes of food and ate, making parcels of rice and fish with their fingers. Sith sat rigidly erect, waiting for misfortune.

What would the spirit of Kol Vireakboth do to Pol Pot's daughter? Would he overturn the table, soiling her with food? Would he send mosquitoes to bite and make her sick? Would he suck away all her good fortune, leaving the marriage blighted, her new family estranged?

Or would a kindly spirit simply wish that the children of all Cambodians could escape, escape the past?

Suddenly, Sith felt at peace. The sunlight and shadows looked new to her and her senses started to work in magic ways.

She smelled a perfume of emotion, sweet and bracing at the same time. The music from a neighbor's cassette player touched her arm gently. Words took the form of sunlight on her skin.

No one is evil, the sunlight said. *But they can be false.*

False, how? Sith asked without speaking, genuinely baffled.

The sunlight smiled with an old man's stained teeth. *You know very well how.*

All the air swelled with the scent of the food, savoring it. The trees sighed with satisfaction.

Life is true. Sith saw steam from the rice curl up into the branches. *Death is false.*

The sunlight stood up to go. It whispered, *Tell him.*

The world faded back to its old self.

That night in a hammock in a room with the other women, Sith suddenly sat bolt upright. Clarity would not let her sleep. She saw that there was no way ahead. She couldn't marry Dara. How could she ask him to marry someone who was harassed by one million dead? How could she explain *I am haunted because I am Pol Pot's daughter and I have lied about everything?*

The dead would not let her marry; the dead would not let her have joy. So who could Pol Pot's daughter pray to? Where could she go for wisdom?

Loak kru Kol Vireakboth, she said under her breath. *Please show me a way ahead.*

The darkness was sterner than the sunlight.

To be as false as you are, it said, *you first have to lie to yourself.*

What lies had Sith told? She knew the facts. Her father had been the head of a government that tortured and killed hundreds of thousands of people and starved the nation through mismanagement. I know the truth.

I just never think about it.

I've never faced it.

Well, the truth is as dark as I am, and you live in me, the darkness.

She had read books—well, the first chapter of books—and then dropped them as if her fingers were scalded. There was no truth for her in books. The truth ahead of her would be loneliness, dreary adulthood, and penance.

Grow up.

The palm-leaf panels stirred like waiting ghosts.

All through the long bus ride back, she said nothing. Dara went silent, too, and hung his head.

In the huge and empty hotel suite, darkness awaited her. She'd had the phone and the TV removed; her footsteps sounded hollow. Jorani and the driver had been her only friends.

The next day she did not go to Soriya Market. She went instead to the torture museum of Tuol Sleng.

A cadre of young motoboys waited outside the hotel in baseball caps and bling. Instead, Sith hailed a sweet-faced older motoboy with a battered, rusty bike.

As they drove she asked him about his family. He lived alone and had no one except for his mother in Kompong Thom.

Outside the gates of Tuol Sleng he said, "This was my old school."

In one wing there were rows of rooms with one iron bed in each with handcuffs and stains on the floor. Photos on the wall showed twisted bodies chained to those same beds as they were found on the day of liberation. In one photograph, a chair was overturned as if in a hurry.

Sith stepped outside and looked instead at a beautiful house over the wall across the street. It was a high white house like her own, with pillars and a roof terrace and bougainvillaea, a modern daughter's house. What do they think when they look out from that roof terrace? How can they live here?

The grass was tended and full of hopping birds. People were painting the shutters of the prison a fresh blue-gray.

In the middle wing, the rooms were galleries of photographed faces. They stared out at her like the faces from her printer. Were some of them the same?

"Who are they?" she found herself asking a Cambodian visitor.

"Their own," the woman replied. "This is where they sent Khmer Rouge cadres who had fallen out of favor. They would not waste such torture on ordinary Cambodians."

Some of the faces were young and beautiful men. Some were children or dignified old women.

The Cambodian lady kept pace with her. Company? Did she guess who Sith was? "They couldn't simply beat party cadres to death. They sent them and their entire families here. The children too, the grandmothers. They had different days of the week for killing children and wives."

An innocent-looking man smiled as sweetly as her aged motoboy, directly into the camera of his torturers. He seemed to expect kindness from them, and decency. *Comrades*, he seemed to say.

The face in the photograph moved. It smiled more broadly and was about to speak.

Sith's eyes darted away. The next face sucked all her breath away.

It was not a stranger. It was Dara, her Dara, in black shirt and black cap. She gasped and looked back at the lady. Her pinched and solemn face nodded up and down. Was she a ghost, too?

Sith reeled outside and hid her face and didn't know if she could go on standing. Tears slid down her face and she wanted to be sick and she turned her back so no one could see.

Then she walked to the motoboy, sitting in a shelter. In complete silence, she got on his bike, feeling angry at the place, angry at the government for preserving it, angry at the foreigners who visited it like a tourist attraction, angry at everything.

That is not who we are! That is not what I am!

The motoboy slipped onto his bike, and Sith asked him: "What happened to your family?" It was a cruel question. He had to smile and look cheerful. His father had run a small shop; they went out into the country and never came back. He lived with his brother in a jeum-room, a refugee camp in Thailand. They came back to fight the Vietnamese and his brother was killed.

She was going to tell the motoboy, Drive me back to the Hilton, but she felt ashamed. Of what? Just how far was she going to run?

She asked him to take her to the old house on Monivong Boulevard.

As the motorcycle wove through backstreets, dodging red-earth ruts and pedestrians, she felt rage at her father. How dare he involve her in something like that! Sith had lived a small life and had no measure of things so she thought: It's as if someone tinted my hair and it all fell out.

It's as if someone pierced my ears and they got infected and my whole ear rotted away.

She remembered that she had never felt any compassion for her father. She had been twelve years old when he stood trial, old and sick and making such a show of leaning on his stick. Everything he did was a show. She remembered rolling her eyes in constant embarrassment. Oh, he was fine in front of rooms full of adoring students. He could play the *bong thom* with them. They thought he was enlightened. He sounded good, using his false, soft, and kindly little voice, as if he was dubbed. He had made Sith recite Verlaine, Rimbaud, and Rilke. He killed thousands for having foreign influences.

I don't know what I did in a previous life to deserve you for a father. But you were not my father in a previous life and you won't be my father in the next. I reject you utterly. You can wander hungry out of hell every year for all eternity. I will pray to keep you in hell.

I am not your daughter!

If you were false, I have to be true.

Her old house looked abandoned in the stark afternoon light, closed and innocent. At the doorstep she turned and thrust a fistful of dollars into the motoboy's hand. She couldn't think straight; she couldn't even see straight, her vision blurred.

Back inside, she calmly put down her teddy-bear rucksack and walked upstairs to her office. Aido the robot dog whirred his way toward her. She had broken his back leg kicking him downstairs. He limped, whimpering like a dog, and lowered his head to have it stroked.

To her relief, there was only one picture waiting for her in the tray of the printer.

Kol Vireakboth looked out at her, middle-aged, handsome, worn, wise. Pity and kindness glowed in his eyes.

The land line began to ring.

"*Youl prom,*" she told the ghosts. Agreed.

She picked up the receiver and waited.

A man spoke. "My name was Yin Bora." His voice bubbled up brokenly as if from underwater.

A light blinked in the printer. A photograph slid out quickly. A young student stared out at her looking happy at a family feast. He had a Beatle haircut and a striped shirt.

"That's me," said the voice on the phone. "I played football."

Sith coughed. "What do you want me to do?"

"Write my name," said the ghost.

"Please hold the line," said Sith, in a hypnotized voice. She fumbled for a pen, and then wrote on the photograph *Yin Bora, footballer.* He looked so sweet and happy. "You have no one to mourn you," she realized.

"None of us have anyone left alive to mourn us," said the ghost.

Then there was a terrible sound down the telephone, as if a thousand voices moaned at once.

Sith involuntarily dropped the receiver into place. She listened to her heart thump and thought about what was needed. She fed the printer with the last of her paper. Immediately it began to roll out more photos, and the land line rang again.

She went outside and found the motoboy, waiting patiently for her. She asked him to go and buy two reams of copying paper. At the last moment she added pens and writing paper and matches. He bowed and smiled and bowed again, pleased to have found a patron.

She went back inside, and with just a tremor in her hand picked up the phone.

For the next half hour, she talked to the dead, and found photographs and wrote down names. A woman mourned her children. Sith found photos of them all, and united them, father, mother, three children, uncles, aunts, cousins and grandparents, taping their pictures to her wall. The idea of uniting families appealed. She began to stick the other photos onto her wall.

Someone called from outside, and there on her doorstep was the motoboy, balancing paper and pens. "I bought you some soup." The broth came in neatly tied bags and was full of rice and prawns. She thanked him and paid him well and he beamed at her and bowed again and again.

All afternoon, the pictures kept coming. Darkness fell, the phone rang, the names were written, until Sith's hand, which was unused to writing anything, ached.

The doorbell rang, and on the doorstep, the motoboy sompiahed. "Excuse me, Lady, it is very late. I am worried for you. Can I get you dinner?"

Sith had to smile. He sounded motherly in his concern. They are so good at building a relationship with you, until you cannot do without them. In the old days she would have sent him away with a few rude words. Now she sent him away with an order.

And wrote.

And when he came back, the aged motoboy looked so happy. "I bought you fruit as well, Lady," he said, and added, shyly, "You do not need to pay me for that."

Something seemed to bump under Sith, as if she was on a motorcycle, and she heard herself say, "Come inside. Have some food, too."

The motoboy sompiahed in gratitude, and as soon as he entered, the phone stopped ringing.

They sat on the floor. He arched his neck and looked around at the walls.

"Are all these people your family?" he asked.

She whispered, "No. They're ghosts who no one mourns."

"Why do they come to you?" His mouth fell open in wonder.

"Because my father was Pol Pot," said Sith, without thinking.

The motoboy sompiahed. "Ah." He chewed and swallowed and arched his head back again. "That must be a terrible thing. Everybody hates you."

Sith had noticed that wherever she sat in the room, the eyes in the photographs were directly on her. "I haven't done anything," said Sith.

"You're doing something now," said the motoboy. He nodded and stood up, sighing with satisfaction. Life was good with a full stomach and a patron. "If you need me, Lady, I will be outside."

Photo after photo, name after name.

Youk Achariya: touring dancer
Proeung Chhay: school superintendent
Sar Kothida child, aged 7, died of "swelling disease"
Sar Makara, her mother, nurse

Nath Mittapheap, civil servant, from family of farmers
Chor Monirath: wife of award-winning engineer
Yin Sokunthea: Khmer Rouge commune leader
She looked at the faces and realized. Dara, I'm doing this for Dara.
The City around her went quiet, and she became aware that it was
now very late indeed. Perhaps she should just make sure the motoboy had
gone home.
He was still waiting outside.
"It's okay. You can go home. Where do you live?"
He waved cheerfully north. "Oh, on Monivong, like you." He
grinned at the absurdity of the comparison.
A new idea took sudden form. Sith said, "Tomorrow, can you come
early, with a big feast? Fish and rice and greens and pork: curries and
stirfries and kebabs." She paid him handsomely and finally asked him his
name. His name meant Golden.
"Good night, Sovann."
For the rest of the night she worked quickly, like an answering service. This is like a cleaning of the house before a festival, she thought. The
voices of the dead became ordinary, familiar. Why are people afraid of
the dead? The dead can't hurt you. The dead want what you want: justice.
The wall of faces became a staircase and a garage and a kitchen of
faces, all named. She had found Jorani's colored yarn, and linked family
members into trees.
She wrote until the electric lights looked discolored, like a headache. She asked the ghosts, "Please can I sleep now?" The phones fell
silent and Sith slumped with relief onto the polished marble floor.
She woke up dazed, still on the marble floor. Sunlight flooded
the room. The faces in the photographs no longer looked swollen and
bruised. Their faces were not accusing or mournful. They smiled down
on her. She was among friends.
With a whine, the printer started to print; the phone started to ring.
Her doorbell chimed, and there was Sovann, white cardboard boxes piled
up on the back of his motorcycle. He wore the same shirt as yesterday,
a cheap blue copy of a Lacoste. A seam had parted under the arm. He

only has one shirt, Sith realized. She imagined him washing it in a basin every night.

Sith and Sovann moved the big tables to the front windows. Sith took out her expensive tablecloths for the first time, and the bronze platters. The feast was laid out as if at New Year. Sovann had bought more paper and pens. He knew what they were for. "I can help, Lady."

He was old enough to have lived in a country with schools, and he could write in a beautiful, old-fashioned hand. Together he and Sith spelled out the names of the dead and burned them.

"I want to write the names of my family, too," he said. He burnt them weeping.

The delicious vapors rose. The air was full of the sound of breathing in. Loose papers stirred with the breeze. The ash filled the basins, but even after working all day, Sith and the motoboy had only honored half the names.

"Good night, Sovann," she told him.

"You have transferred a lot of merit," said Sovann, but only to be polite.

If I have any merit to transfer, thought Sith.

He left and the printers started, and the phone. She worked all night, and only stopped because the second ream of paper ran out.

The last picture printed was of Kol Vireakboth.

Dara, she promised herself. Dara next.

In the morning, she called him. "Can we meet at lunchtime for another walk by the river?"

Sith waited on top of the marble wall and watched an old man fish in the Tonlé Sap river and found that she loved her country. She loved its tough, smiling, uncomplaining people, who had never offered her harm, after all the harm her family had done them. Do you know you have the daughter of the monster sitting here among you?

Suddenly all Sith wanted was to be one of them. The monks in the pavilion, the white-shirted functionaries scurrying somewhere, the lazy bones dangling their legs, the young men who dress like American rappers and sold something dubious, drugs, or sex.

She saw Dara sauntering toward her. He wore his new shirt and smiled at her, but he didn't look relaxed. It had been two days since they'd met. He knew something was wrong, that she had something to tell him. He had bought them lunch in a little cardboard box. Maybe for the last time, thought Sith.

They exchanged greetings, almost like cousins. He sat next to her and smiled and Sith giggled in terror at what she was about to do.

Dara asked, "What's funny?"

She couldn't stop giggling. "Nothing is funny. Nothing." She sighed in order to stop, and terror tickled her and she spurted out laughter again. "I lied to you. Kol Vireakboth is not my father. Another politician was my father. Someone you've heard of...."

The whole thing was so terrifying and absurd that the laughter squeezed her like a fist and she couldn't talk. She laughed and wept at the same time. Dara stared.

"My father was Saloth Sar. That was his real name." She couldn't make herself say it. She could tell a motoboy, but not Dara? She forced herself onward. "My father was Pol Pot."

Nothing happened.

Sitting next to her, Dara went completely still. People strolled past; boats bobbed on their moorings.

After a time Dara said, "I know what you are doing."

That didn't make sense. "Doing? What do you mean?"

Dara looked sour and angry. "Yeah, yeah, yeah, yeah." He sat, looking away from her. Sith's laughter had finally shuddered to a halt. She sat peering at him, waiting. "I told you my family were modest," he said quietly.

"Your family are lovely!" Sith exclaimed.

His jaw thrust out. "They had questions about you, too, you know."

"I don't understand."

He rolled his eyes. He looked back 'round at her. "There are easier ways to break up with someone."

He jerked himself to his feet and strode away with swift determination, leaving her sitting on the wall.

Here on the riverfront, everyone was equal. The teenage boys lounged on the wall; poor mothers herded children; The foreigners walked briskly, trying to look as if they didn't carry moneybelts. Three fat teenage girls nearly swerved into a cripple in a pedal chair and collapsed against each other with raucous laughter.

Sith did not know what to do. She could not move. Despair humbled her, made her hang her head.

I've lost him.

The sunlight seemed to settle next to her, washing up from its reflection on the wake of some passing boat.

No, you haven't.

The river water smelled of kindly concern. The sounds of traffic throbbed with forbearance.

Not yet.

There is no forgiveness in Cambodia. But there are continual miracles of compassion and acceptance.

Sith appreciated for just a moment the miracles. The motoboy buying her soup. She decided to trust herself to the miracles.

Sith talked to the sunlight without making a sound. Grandfather Vireakboth. Thank you. You have told me all I need to know.

Sith stood up and from nowhere, the motoboy was there. He drove her to the Hello Phone shop.

Dara would not look at her. He bustled back and forth behind the counter, though there was nothing for him to do. Sith talked to him like a customer. "I want to buy a mobile phone," she said, but he would not answer. "There is someone I need to talk to."

Another customer came in. She was a beautiful daughter, too, and he served her, making a great show of being polite. He complimented her on her appearance. "Really, you look cool." The girl looked pleased. Dara's eyes darted in Sith's direction.

Sith waited in the chair. This was home for her now. Dara ignored her. She picked up her phone and dialed his number. He put it to his ear and said, "Go home."

"You are my home," she said.

His thumb jabbed the C button.

She waited. Shadows lengthened.

"We're closing," he said, standing by the door without looking at her.

Shamefaced, Sith ducked away from him, through the door.

Outside Soriya, the motoboy played dice with his fellows. He stood up. "They say I am very lucky to have Pol Pot's daughter as a client."

There was no discretion in Cambodia, either. Everyone will know now, Sith realized.

At home, the piles of printed paper still waited for her. Sith ate the old, cold food. It tasted flat, all its savor sucked away. The phones began to ring. She fell asleep with the receiver propped against her ear.

The next day, Sith went back to Soriya with a box of the printed papers.

She dropped the box onto the blue plastic counter of Hello Phones.

"Because I am Pol Pot's daughter," she told Dara, holding out a sheaf of pictures toward him, "all the unmourned victims of my father are printing their pictures on my printer. Here. Look. These are the pictures of people who lost so many loved ones there is no one to remember them."

She found her cheeks were shaking and that she could not hold the sheaf of paper. It tumbled from her hands, but she stood back, arms folded.

Dara, quiet and solemn, knelt and picked up the papers. He looked at some of the faces. Sith pushed a softly crumpled green card at him. Her family ID card.

He read it. Carefully, with the greatest respect, he put the photographs on the countertop along with the ID card.

"Go home, Sith," he said, but not unkindly.

"I said," she had begun to speak with vehemence but could not continue. "I told you. My home is where you are."

"I believe you," he said, looking at his feet.

"Then...." Sith had no words.

"It can never be, Sith," he said. He gathered up the sheaf of photocopying paper. "What will you do with these?"

Something made her say, "What will you do with them?"

His face was crossed with puzzlement.

"It's your country too. What will you do with them? Oh, I know, you're such a poor boy from a poor family, who could expect anything from you? Well, you have your whole family and many people have no one. And you can buy new shirts and some people only have one."

Dara held out both hands and laughed. "Sith?" *You, Sith are accusing me of being selfish?*

"You own them, too." Sith pointed to the papers, to the faces. "You think the dead don't try to talk to you, too?"

Their eyes latched. She told him what he could do. "I think you should make an exhibition. I think Hello Phones should sponsor it. You tell them that. You tell them Pol Pot's daughter wishes to make amends and has chosen them. Tell them the dead speak to me on their mobile phones."

She spun on her heel and walked out. She left the photographs with him.

That night she and the motoboy had another feast and burned the last of the unmourned names. There were many thousands.

The next day she went back to Hello Phones.

"I lied about something else," she told Dara. She took out all the reports from the fortunet-ellers. She told him what Hun Sen's fortune-teller had told her. "The marriage is particularly well favored."

"Is that true?" He looked wistful.

"You should not believe anything I say. Not until I have earned your trust. Go consult the fortune-tellers for yourself. This time you pay."

His face went still, and his eyes focused somewhere far beneath the floor. Then he looked up, directly into her eyes. "I will do that."

For the first time in her life Sith wanted to laugh for something other than fear. She wanted to laugh for joy.

"Can we go to lunch at Lucky7?" she asked.

"Sure," he said.

All the telephones in the shop, all of them, hundreds all at once began to sing.

A waterfall of trills and warbles and buzzes, snatches of old songs or latest chart hits. Dara stood dumbfounded. Finally he picked one up and held it to his ear.

"It's for you," he said and held out the phone for her.

There was no name or number on the screen.

Congratulations, dear daughter, said a warm kind voice.

"Who is this?" Sith asked. The options were severely limited.

Your new father, said Kol Vireakboth. The sound of wind. *I adopt you.*

A thousand thousand voices said at once, *We adopt you.*

In Cambodia, you share your house with ghosts in the way you share it with dust. You hear the dead shuffling alongside your own footsteps. You can sweep, but the sound does not go away.

On the Tra Bek end of Monivong there is a house whose owner has given it over to ghosts. You can try to close the front door. But the next day you will find it hanging open. Indeed you can try, as the neighbors did, to nail the door shut. It opens again.

By day, there is always a queue of five or six people wanting to go in, or hanging back, out of fear. Outside are offerings of lotus or coconuts with embedded joss sticks.

The walls and floors and ceilings are covered with photographs. The salon, the kitchen, the stairs, the office, the empty bedrooms, are covered with photographs of Chinese-Khmers at weddings, Khmer civil servants on picnics, Chams outside their mosques, Vietnamese holding up prize catches of fish, little boys going to school in shorts, cyclopousse drivers in front of their odd, old-fashioned pedaled vehicles, wives in stalls stirring soup. All of them are happy and joyful, and the background is Phnom Penh when it was the most beautiful city in Southeast Asia.

All the photographs have names written on them in old-fashioned handwriting.

On the table is a printout of thousands of names on slips of paper. Next to the table are matches and basins of ash and water. The implication is plain. Burn the names and transfer merit to the unmourned dead.

Next to that is a small printed sign that says in English HELLO.

Every Pchum Ben, those names are delivered to temples throughout the city. Gold foil is pressed onto each slip of paper, and attached to it is a parcel of sticky rice. At 8 a.m. food is delivered for the monks, steaming rice and fish, along with bolts of new cloth. At 10 a.m. more food is delivered, for the disabled and the poor.

And most mornings a beautiful daughter of Cambodia is seen walking beside the confluence of the Tonlé Sap and Mekong rivers. Like Cambodia, she plainly loves all things modern. She dresses in the latest fashion. Cambodian R&B whispers in her ear. She pauses in front of each new waterfront construction whether built by improvised scaffolding or erected with cranes. She buys noodles from the grumpy vendors with their tiny stoves. She carries a book or sits on the low marble wall to write letters and look at the boats, the monsoon clouds, and the dop-dops. She talks to the reflected sunlight on the river and calls it Father.

Blocked

I dreamed this in Sihanoukville, a town of new casinos, narrow beaches, hot bushes with flowers that look like daffodils, and even now after nine years of peace, stark ruined walls with gates that go nowhere.

In the dream, I get myself a wife. She's beautiful, blonde, careworn. She is not used to having a serious man with good intentions present himself to her on a beach. Her name is Agnete and she speaks with a Danish accent. She has four Asian children.

Their father had been studying permanently in Europe, married Agnete, and then "left," which in this world can mean several things. Agnete was an orphan herself and the only family she had was that of her Cambodian husband. So she came to Phnom Penh only to find that her in-laws did not want some strange woman they did not know and all those extra mouths to feed.

I meet the children. The youngest is Gerda, who cannot speak a word of Khmer. She's tiny, as small as an infant though three years old, in a splotched pink dress and too much toy jewelery. She just stares, while her brothers play. She's been picked up from everything she knows and thrown down into this hot, strange world in which people speak nonsense and the food burns your mouth.

I kneel down and try to say hello to her, first in German, and then in English. Hello, Gertie, hello, little girl. Hello. She blanks all language and sits like she's sedated.

I feel so sad, I pick her up and hold her, and suddenly she buries her head in my shoulder. She falls asleep on me as I swing in a hammock and quietly explain myself to her mother. I am not married, I tell Agnete. I run the local casino.

Real men are not hard, just unafraid. If you are a man you say what is true, and if someone acts like a monkey, then maybe you punish them. To be a crook, you have to be straight. I sold guns for my boss and bought policemen, so he trusted me, so I ran security for him for years. He was one of the first to Go, and he sold his shares in the casino to me. Now it's me who sits around the black lacquered table with the generals and Thai partners. I have a Lexus and a good income. I have ascended and become a man in every way but one. Now I need a family.

Across from Sihanoukville, all about the bay are tiny islands. On those islands, safe from thieves, glow the roofs where the Big Men live in Soriya-chic amid minarets, windmills, and solar panels. Between the islands hang white suspension footbridges. Distant people on bicycles move across them.

Somehow it's now after the wedding. The children are now mine. We loll shaded in palm-leaf panel huts. Two of the boys play on a heap of old rubber inner tubes. Tharum with his goofy smile and sticky-out ears is long legged enough to run among them, plonking his feet down into the donut holes. Not to be outdone, his brother Sampul clambers over the things. Rith, the oldest, looks cool in a hammock, away with his earphones, pretending not to know us.

Gerda tugs at my hand until I let her go. Freed from the world of language and adults, she climbs up and over the swollen black tubes, sliding down sideways. She looks intent and does not laugh.

Her mother in a straw hat and sunglasses makes a thin, watery sunset smile.

Gerda and I go wading. All those islands shelter the bay, so the waves roll on to the shore child-sized, as warm and gentle as caresses. Gerda holds onto my hand and looks down at them, scowling in silence.

Alongside the beach is a grounded airliner, its wings cut away and neatly laid beside it. I take the kids there, and the boys run around inside it, screaming. Outside, Gerda and I look at the aircraft's spirit house. Someone witty has given the shrine tiny white wings.

The surrounding hills still have their forests; cumulonimbus clouds towering over them like clenched fists.

In the evening, thunder comes.

I look out from our high window and see flashes of light in the darkness. We live in one whole floor of my casino hotel. Each of the boys has his own suite. The end rooms have balconies, three of them, that run all across the front of the building with room enough for sofas and dining tables. We hang tubes full of pink sugar water for hummingbirds. In the mornings, the potted plants buzz with bees, and balls of seed lure the sarika bird that comes to sing its sweetest song.

In these last days, the gambling action is frenetic: Chinese, Thai, Korean, and Malays, they play baccarat mostly, but some prefer the one-armed bandits.

At the tables of my casino, elegant young women, handsome young men, and a couple of other genders besides, sit upright ready to deal, looking as alert and frightened as rabbits, especially if their table is empty. They are paid a percentage of the take. Some of them sleep with customers, too, but they're good kids; they always send the money home. Do good, get good, we in Cambodia used to say. Now we say, *twee akrow meen lay*: Do bad, have money.

My casino is straight. My wheels turn true. *No guns*, says my sign. *No animals, no children.* Innocence must be protected. *No cigarettes or powders.* Those last two are marked by a skull and crossbones.

We have security but the powders don't show up on any scan, so some of my customers come here to die. Most weekends, we find one, a body slumped over the table.

I guess some of them think it's good to go out on a high. The Chinese are particularly susceptible. They love the theater of gambling, the tough-guy stance, the dance of the cigarette, the nudge of the eyebrow. You get dealt a good hand, you smile, you take one last sip of Courvoisier, then one sniff. You Go Down for good.

It's another way for the winner to take all. For me, they are just a mess to clear up, another reason to keep the kids away.

Upstairs, we've finished eating and we can hear the shushing of the sea.

"Daddy," Sampul asks me and the word thrums across my heart. "Why are we all leaving?"

"We're being invaded."

So far, this has been a strange and beautiful dream, full of Buddhist monks in orange robes lined up at the one-armed bandits. But now it goes like a stupid kids' TV show, except that in my dream, I'm living it, it's real. As I speak, I can feel my own sad, damp breath.

"Aliens are coming," I say and kiss him. "They are bringing many, many ships. We can see them now, at the edge of the solar system. They'll be here in less than two years."

He sighs and looks perturbed.

In this disrupted country two-thirds of everything is a delight, two-thirds of everything iron nastiness. The numbers don't add up, but it's true.

"How do we know they're bad?" he asks, his face puffy.

"Because the government says so and the government wouldn't lie."

His breath goes icy. "This government would."

"Not all governments, not all of them all together."

"So. Are we going to leave?" He means leave again. They left Denmark to come here, and they are all of them sick of leaving. "Yes, but we'll all Go together, okay?"

Rith glowers at me from the sofa. "It's all the fault of people like you."

"I made the aliens?" I think smiling at him will make him see he is being silly. He rolls his eyes.

"There's the comet?" he asks like I've forgotten something and shakes his head.

"Oh, the comet, yes, I forgot about the comet, there's a comet coming, too. And global warming and big new diseases."

He tuts. "The aliens sent the comet. If we'd had a space program we could meet them halfway and fight there. We could of had people living in Mars, to survive."

"Why wouldn't the aliens invade Mars, too?"

His voice goes smaller, he hunches even tighter over his game. "If we'd gone into space, we would of been immortal."

My father was a drunk who left us; my mother died; I took care of my sisters. The regime made us move out of our shacks by the river to the countryside where there was no water, so that the generals could build their big hotels. We survived. I never saw a movie about aliens, I never had this dream of getting away to outer space. My dream was to become a man.

I look out over the Cambodian night, and fire and light dance about the sky like dragons at play. There's a hissing sound. Wealth tumbles down in the form of rain.

Sampul is the youngest son and is a tough little guy. He thumps Rith, who's fifteen years old, and both of them gang up on gangly Tharum. But tough-guy Sampul suddenly curls up next to me on the sofa as if he's returning to the egg.

The thunder's grief looks like rage. I sit and listen to the rain. Rith plays on, his headphones churning with the sound of stereophonic war. Everything dies, even suns; even the universe dies and comes back.

We already are immortal. Without us, the country people will finally have Cambodia back. The walled gardens will turn to vines. The water buffalo will wallow; the rustics will still keep the fields green with rice, as steam engines chortle past, puffing out gasps of cloud. Sampul once asked me if the trains made rain.

And if there are aliens, maybe they will treasure it, the Earth.

I may want to stay, but Agnete is determined to Go. She has already lost one husband to this nonsense. She will not lose anything else, certainly not her children. Anyway, it was all part of the deal.

I slip into bed next to her. "You're very good with them," she says and kisses my shoulder. "I knew you would be. Your people are so kind to children."

"You don't tell me that you love me," I say.

"Give it time," she says, finally.

That night lightning strikes the spirit house that shelters our *neak ta*. The house's tiny golden spire is charred.

Gerda and I come down in the morning to give the spirit his bananas, and when she sees the ruin, her eyes boggle and she starts to scream and howl.

Agnete comes downstairs, and hugs and pets her, and says in English, "Oh, the pretty little house is broken."

Agnete cannot possibly understand how catastrophic this is, or how baffling. The *neak ta* is the spirit of the hotel who protects us or rejects us. What does it mean when the sky itself strikes it? Does it mean the *neak ta* is angry and has deserted us? Does it mean the gods want us gone and have destroyed our protector?

Gerda stares in terror, and I am sure then that though she is wordless, Gerda has a Khmer soul.

Agnete looks at me over Gerda's shoulder, and I'm wondering why she is being so disconnected when she says, "The papers have come through."

That means we will sail to Singapore within the week.

I've already sold the casino. There is no one I trust. I go downstairs and hand over the keys to all my guns to Sreang, who I know will stay on as security at least for a while.

That night after the children are asleep, Agnete and I have the most terrifying argument. She throws things; she hits me; she thinks I'm saying that I want to desert them; I cannot make her listen or understand.

"*Neak ta? Neak ta*, what are you saying?"

"I'm saying I think we should go by road."

"We don't have time! There's the date, there's the booking! What are you trying to do?" She is panicked, desperate; her mouth ringed with thin strings of muscle, her neck straining.

I have to go and find a monk. I give him a huge sum of money to earn merit, and I ask him to chant for us. I ask him to bless our luggage and at a distance bless the boat that we will sail in. I swallow fear like thin, sour spit. I order ahead, food for Pchum Ben, so that he can eat it, and act as mediary so that I can feed my dead. I look at him. He smiles. He is a man without guns, without modernity, without family to help him. For just a moment I envy him.

I await disaster, sure that the loss of our *neak ta* bodes great ill; I fear that the boat will be swamped at sea.

But I'm wrong.

Dolphins swim ahead of our prow, leaping out of the water. We trawl behind us for fish and haul up tuna, turbot, sea snakes and turtles. I can assure you that flying fish really do fly—they soar over our heads at night, right across the boat like giant mosquitoes.

No one gets seasick; there are no storms; we navigate directly. It is as though the sea has made peace with us. Let them be, we have lost them, they are going.

We are Cambodians. We are good at sleeping in hammocks and just talking. We trade jokes and insults and innuendo, sometimes in verse, and we play music, cards, and *bah angkunh*, a game of nuts. Gerda joins in the game, and I can see the other kids let her win. She squeals with delight and reaches down between the slats to find a nut that has fallen through.

All the passengers hug and help take care of the children. We cook on little stoves, frying in woks. Albatrosses rest on our rigging. Gerda still won't speak, so I cuddle her all night long, murmuring. *Kynom ch'mooah Channarith. Oun ch'mooah ay?*

I am your new father.

Once in the night, something huge in the water vents, just beside us. The stars themselves seem to have come back like the fish, so distant and high, cold and pure. No wonder we are greedy for them, just as we are greedy for diamonds. If we could, we would strip-mine the universe, but instead we strip-mine ourselves.

We land at Sentosa. Its resort beaches are now swallowed by the sea, but its slopes sprout temporary, cantilevered accommodation. The sides of the buildings spread downward like sheltering batwings behind the plastic quays that walk us directly to the hillside. Singapore's latest growth industry. The living dead about to be entombed, we march from the boats along the top of pontoons. Bobbing and smooth-surfaced, the quays are treacherous. We slip and catch each other before we fall. There are no old people among us, but we all walk as if aged, stiff-kneed and unbalanced.

But I am relieved; the island still burgeons with trees. We take a jungle path, through humid stillness, to the north shore, where we face the Lion City.

Singapore towers over the harbor. Its giant versions of Angkor Wat blaze with sunlight like daggers; its zigzag shoreline is ringed round with four hundred clippers amid a white forest of wind turbines. Up the sides of Mt. Fraser cluster the houses of rustics, made of wood and propped against the slope on stilts.

It had been raining during the day. I'd feared a storm, but now the sky is clear, gold and purple with even a touch of green. All along the line where trees give way to salt grasses, like stars going for a swim, fireflies shine.

Gerda's eyes widen. She smiles and holds out a hand. I whisper the Khmer words for firefly: *ampil ampayk*.

We're booked into one of the batwings. Only wild riches can buy a hotel room in Sentosa. A bottle of water is expensive enough.

Once inside, Agnete's spirits improve, even sitting on folding metal beds with a hanging blanket for a partition. Her eyes glisten. She sits Gerda and Sampul on the knees of her crossed legs. "They have beautiful shopping malls Down There," she says. "And Rith, *technik*, all the latest. Big screens. Billion billion pixels."

"They don't call them pixels anymore, Mom."

That night, Gerda starts to cry. Nothing can stop her. She wails and wails. Our friends from the boat turn over on their beds and groan. Two of the women sit with Agnete and offer sympathy. "Oh poor thing, she is ill."

No, I think, she is brokenhearted. She writhes and twists in Agnete's lap. Without words for it, I know why she is crying.

Agnete looks like she's been punched in the face; she didn't sleep well on the boat.

I say, "Darling, let me take her outside. You sleep."

I coax Gerda up into my arms, but she fights me like a cat. *Sssh sssh, Angel, sssh.* But she's not to be fooled. Somehow she senses what this is. I walk out of the refugee shelter and onto the dock that sighs underfoot. I'm standing there, holding her, looking up at the ghost of Singapore, listening to the whoop of the turbines overhead, hearing the slopping sound of water against the quay. I know that Gerda cannot be consoled.

Agnete thinks our people are kind because we smile. But we can also be cruel. It was cruel of Gerda's father to leave her, knowing what might happen after he was gone. It was cruel to want to be missed that badly.

On the north shore, I can still see the towers defined only by their bioluminescence, in leopard-spot growths of blue, or gold-green, otherwise lost in a mist of human manufacture, smoke, and steam.

The skyscrapers are deserted now, unusable, for who can climb seventy stories? How strange they look; what drove us to make them? Why all across the world did we reach up so high? As if to escape the Earth, distance ourselves from the ground, and make a shiny new artifice of the world.

And there are the stars. They have always shone; they shine now just like they would shine on the deck of a starship, no nearer. There is the warm sea that gave us birth. There are the trees that turn sunlight into sugar for all of us to feed on.

Then overhead, giant starfish in the sky. I am at loss, *choy mae!* What on Earth is that? They glow in layers, orange red green. Trailing after them in order come giant butterflies glowing blue and purple. Gerda coughs into silence and stares upward.

Cable cars. Cable cars strung from Mt. Fraser, to the shore and on to Sentosa, glowing with decorative bioluminescence.

Ampil ampayk, I say again, and for just moment, Gerda is still.

I don't want to go. I want to stay here. Then Gerda roars again, sounding like my heart. The sound threatens to shred her throat. The sound is inconsolable.

I rock her, shush her, kiss her, but nothing brings her peace. You too, Gerda, I think. You want to stay too, don't you? We are two of a kind. For a moment, I want to run away together, Gerda and me, get across the straits to Johor Bahu, hide in the untended wilds of old palm-oil plantations.

But now we have no money to buy food or water. I go still as the night whispers its suggestion. I will not be cruel like her father. I can go into that warm sea and spread myself among the fishes to swim forever. And I can take you with me, Gerda.

We can be still, and disappear into the Earth.

I hold her out as if offering her to the warm birthsea. And finally, Gerda sleeps, and I ask myself, will I do it? Can I take us back? Both of us? Agnete touches my arm. "Oh, you got her to sleep! Thank you so much." Her hand first on my shoulder, then around Gerda, taking her from me, and I can't stop myself tugging back, and there is something alarmed, confused around her eyes. Then she gives her head a quick little shake, dismissing it. I would rather be loved for my manliness than for my goodness. But I suppose it's better than nothing, and I know I will not escape. I know we will all Go Down.

The next day we march, numb and driven by something we do not understand.

For breakfast, we have Chinese porridge with roasted soya, nuts, spices, and egg. Our last day is brilliantly sunny. There are too many of us to all take the cable car. Economy class, we are given an intelligent trolley to guide us, carrying our luggage or our children. It whines along the bridge from Sentosa, giving us relentless tourist information about Raffles, independence in 1965, the Singapore miracle, the coolies who came as slaves but stayed to contribute so much to Singapore's success. The bridge takes us past an artificial island full of cargo, cranes, and wagons, and on the main shore by the quays is a squash of a market with noodle stalls, fish stalls, and stalls full of knives or dried lizards. Our route takes us up Mt. Fraser, through the trees. The monkeys pursue us, plucking bags of bananas from our hands, clambering up on our carts, trying to open our parcels. Rith throws rocks at them.

The dawn light falls in rays through the trees as if the Buddha himself was overhead, shedding radiance. Gerda toddles next me, her hand in mine. Suddenly she stoops over and holds something up. It is a scarab beetle, its shell a shimmering turquoise green, but ants are crawling out of it. I blow them away. "Oh, that is a treasure, Gerda. You hold on to it, okay?"

There will be nothing like it where we are going. Then, looking something like a railway station, there is the Singapore terminal dug into the rock of the outcropping. It yawns wide open, to funnel us inside. The concrete is softened by a screen of branches sweeping along its face— very tasteful and traditional, I think, until I touch them and find that they are made of moldform.

This is Singapore, so everything is perfectly done. PAMPER YOUR-SELF, a sign says in ten different languages. BREATHE IN AN AIR OF LUXURY.

Beautiful concierges in blue-gray uniforms greet us. One of them asks, "Is this the Sonn family?" Her face is so pretty, like Gerda's will be one day, a face of all nations, smiling and full of hope that something good can be done.

"I'm here to help you with check-in, and make sure you are comfortable and happy." She bends down and looks into Gerda's eyes but something in them makes her falter; the concierge's smile seems to trip and stumble.

Nightmarishly, her lip gloss suddenly smears up and across her face, like a wound. It feels as though Gerda has somehow cut her.

The concierge's eyes are sad now. She gives Gerda a package printed with a clown's face and colored balloons. Gerda holds the gift out from her upside-down and scowls at it.

The concierge has packages for all the children, to keep them quiet in line. The giftpacks match age and gender. Rith always says his gender is Geek, as a joke, but he does somehow get a Geek pack. They can analyze his clothes and brand names. I muse on how strange it is that Rith's dad gave him the same name as mine, so that he is Rith and I am Channarith. He never calls me father. Agnete calls me Channa, infrequently.

The beautiful concierge takes our papers and says that she will do all the needful. Our trolley says goodbye and whizzes after her, to check in our bags. I'm glad it's gone. I hate its hushed and cheerful voice. I hate its Bugs Bunny baby face.

We wait.

Other concierges move up and down the velvet-roped queues with little trolleys offering water, green tea, dragon fruit, or chardonnay. However much we paid, when all is said and done, we are fodder to be processed. I know in my sinking heart that getting here is why Agnete married me. She needed the fare.

No one lied to us, not even ourselves. This is bigger than a lie; this is like an animal migration, this is all of us caught up in something about ourselves we do not understand, never knew.

Suddenly my heart says, firmly, *There are no aliens.*

Aliens are just the excuse. This is something we want to do, like building those skyscrapers. This is all a new kind of dream, a new kind of grief turned inward, but it's not my dream, nor do I think that it's Gerda's. She is squeezing my hand too hard, and I know she knows this thing that is beyond words.

"Agnete," I say. "You and the boys go. I cannot. I don't want this." Her face is sudden fury. "I knew you'd do this. Men always do this."

"I didn't use to be a man."

"That makes no difference!" She snatches Gerda away from me, who starts to cry again. Gerda has been taken too many places, too suddenly, too firmly. "I knew there was something weird going on." She glares at me as if she doesn't know me, or is only seeing me for the first time. Gently she coaxes Gerda toward her, away from me. "The children are coming with me. All of the children. If you want to be blown up by aliens—"

"There are no aliens."

Maybe she doesn't hear me. "I have all the papers." She means the papers that identify us, let us in our own front door, give us access to our bank accounts. All she holds is the hologrammed, eye-printed ticket. She makes a jagged, flinty correction: "*They* have all the papers. Gerda is my daughter, and they will favor me." She's already thinking custody battle, and she's right, of course.

"There are no aliens." I say it a third time. "There is no reason to do this."

This time I get heard. There is a sound of breathing-out from all the people around me. A fat Tamil, sated maybe with blowing up other people, says, "What, you think all those governments lie? You're just getting cold feet."

Agnete focuses on me. "Go on. Get going if that's what you want." Her face has no love or tolerance in it.

"People need there to be aliens, and so they all believe there are. But I don't."

Gerda is weeping in complete silence, though her face looks calm. I have never seen so much water come out of someone's eyes; it pours out as thick as bird's nest soup. Agnete keeps her hands folded across Gerda's chest and kisses the top of her head. What, does she think I'm going to steal Gerda?

Suddenly our concierge is kneeling down, cooing. She has a pink metal teddy bear in one hand, and it hisses as she uses it to inject Gerda. "There! All happy now!" The concierge looks up at me with hatred. She gives Agnete our check-in notification, now perfumed and glowing.

But not our ID papers. Those they keep, to keep us there, safe. "Thank you," says Agnete. Her jaw thrusts out at me. The Tamil is smiling with rage. "You see that idiot? He got the little girl all afraid."

"Fool can't face the truth," says a Cluster of networked Malay, all in unison. I want to go back to the trees, like Tarzan, but that is a different drive, a different dream.

"Why are you stopping the rest of us trying to go, just because you don't want to?" says a multigen, with a wide glassy grin. How on Earth does s/he think I could stop them doing anything? I can see s/he is making up for a lifetime of being disrespected. This intervention, though late and cowardly and stupid, gets the murmur of approval for which s/he yearns.

It is like cutting my heart at the root, but I know I cannot leave Gerda. I cannot leave her alone Down There. She must not be deserted a second time. They have doped her, drugged her, the world swims around her, her eyes are dim and crossed, but I fancy she is looking for me. And at the level of the singing blood in our veins, we understand each other.

I hang my head.

"So you're staying," says Agnete, her face pulled in several opposing directions, satisfaction, disappointment, anger, triumph, scorn.

"For Gerda, yes."

Agnete's face resolves itself into stone. She wanted maybe a declaration of love, after that scene? Gerda is limp and heavy and dangling down onto the floor.

"Maybe she's lucky," I say. "Maybe that injection killed her."

The crowd has been listening for something to outrage them. "Did you hear what that man said?"

"What an idiot!"

"Jerk."

"Hey, lady, you want a nicer guy for a husband, try me."

"Did he say the little girl should be dead? Did you hear him say that?"

"Yeah, he said that the little baby should be dead!"

"Hey you, Pol Pot. Get out of line. We're doing this to escape genocide, not take it with us."

I feel distanced, calm. "I don't think we have any idea what we are doing."

Agnete grips the tickets and certificates of passage. She holds onto Gerda, and tries to hug the two younger boys. There is a bubble of spit coming out of Gerda's mouth. The lift doors swivel open, all along the wall. Agnete starts forward. She has to drag Gerda with her.

"Let me carry her at least," I say. Agnete ignores me. I trail after her. Someone pushes me sideways as I shuffle. I ignore him.

And so I Go Down.

They take your ID and keep it. It is a safety measure to hold as many of humankind safely below as possible. I realize I will never see the sun again. No sunset cumulonimbus, no shushing of the sea, no schools of sardines swimming like veils of silver in clear water, no unreliable songbirds that may fail to appear, no more brown grass, no more dusty wild flowers unregarded by the roadside. No thunder to strike the *neak ta*, no chants at midnight, no smells of fish frying, no rice on the floor of the temple.

I am a son of Kambu. Kampuchea. I slope into the elevator. "Hey, Boss," says a voice. The sound of it makes me unhappy before I recognize who it is. Ah yes, with his lucky mustache. It is someone who used to work in my hotel. My Embezzler. He looks delighted, pleased to see me. "Isn't this great? Wait 'til you see it!"

"Yeah, great," I murmur.

"Listen," says an intervener to my little thief. "Nothing you can say will make this guy happy."

"He's a nice guy," says the Embezzler. "I used to work for him. Didn't I, Boss?"

This is my legacy thug, inherited from my boss. He embezzled his fare from me and disappeared, oh, two years ago. These people may think he's a friend, but I bet he still has his stolen guns, in case there is trouble.

"Good to see you," I lie. I know when I am outnumbered.

For some reason that makes him chuckle, and I can see his silver-outlined teeth. I am ashamed that this unpunished thief is now my only friend.

Agnete knows the story, sniffs and looks away. "I should have married a genetic man," she murmurs.

Never, ever tread on someone else's dream.

The lift is mirrored, and there are holograms of light as if we stood inside an infinite diamond, glistering all the way up to a blinding heaven. And dancing in the fire, brand names.

Gucci. Armani. Sony. Yamomoto. Hugo Boss. And above us, clear to the end and the beginning, the stars. The lift goes down. Those stars have cost us dearly. All around me, the faces look up in unison. Whole nations were bankrupted trying to get there, to dwarf stars and planets of methane ice. Arizona disappeared in an annihilation as matter and anti matter finally met, trying to build an engine. Massive junk still orbits half-assembled, and will one day fall. The saps who are left behind on Ground Zero will probably think it's the comet.

But trying to build those self-contained starships taught us how to do this instead.

Earthside, you walk out of your door, you see birds fly. Just after the sun sets and the bushes bloom with bugs, you will see bats flitter, silhouetted as they neep. In hot afternoons the bees waver, heavy with pollen, and I swear even fishes fly. But nothing flies between the stars except energy. You wanna be converted into energy, like Arizona?

So we Go Down. Instead of up. "The first thing you will see is the main hall. That should cheer up you claustrophobics," says my Embezzler. "It is the biggest open space we have in the Singapore facility. And as you will see, that's damn big!" The travelers chuckle in appreciation. I wonder if they don't pipe in some of that cheerful sound.

And poor Gerda, she will wake up for second time in another new world. I fear it will be too much for her.

The lift walls turn like stiles, reflecting yet more light in shards, and we step out.

Ten stories of brand names go down in circles—polished marble floors, air-conditioning, little murmuring carts, robot pets that don't poop, kids in the latest balloon shoes.

"What do you think of that!" the Malay Network demands of me. All its heads turn, including the women wearing modest headscarves.

"I think it looks like Kuala Lumpur on a rainy afternoon."

The corridors of the emporia go off into infinity as well, as if you could shop all the way to Alpha Centauri. An illusion of course, like standing in a hall of mirrors.

It's darn good, this technology, it fools the eye for all of thirty seconds. To be fooled longer than that, you have to want to be fooled. At the end of the corridor, reaching out for somewhere beyond, distant and pure there is only light.

We have remade the world. Agnete looks worn. "I need a drink, where's a bar?" I need to be away too, away from these people who know that I have a wife for whom my only value has now been spent. Our little trolley finds us, calls our name enthusiastically, and advises us. In Ramlee Mall, level ten, Central Tower we have the choice of Bar Infinity, the Malacca Club (share the Maugham experience), British India, the Kuala Lumpur Tower View....

Agnete chooses the Seaside Pier; I cannot tell if out of kindness or irony.

I step inside the bar with its high ceiling and for just a moment my heart leaps with hope. There is the sea, the islands, the bridges, the sails, the gulls, and the sunlight dancing. Wafts of sugar vapor inside the bar imitate sea mist, and the breathable sugar makes you high. At the other end of the bar is what looks like a giant orange orb (half of one, the other half is just reflected). People lounge on the brand-name sand (guaranteed to brush away and evaporate.) Fifty meters overhead, there is a virtual mirror that doubles distance so you can look up and see yourself from what appears to be a hundred meters up, as if you are flying. A Network on its collective back is busy spelling the word HOME with their bodies.

We sip martinis. Gerda still sleeps, and I now fear she always will.

"So," says Agnete, her voice suddenly catching up with her butt, and plonking down to Earth and relative calm. "Sorry about that back there. It was a tense moment for both of us. I have doubts, too. About coming here, I mean."

She puts her hand on mine.

"I will always be so grateful to you," she says and really means it. I play with one of her fingers. I seem to have purchased loyalty.

"Thank you," I say, and I realize that she has lost mine.

She tries to bring love back by squeezing my hand. "I know you didn't want to come. I know you came because of us."

Even the boys know there is something radically wrong. Sampul and Tharum stare in silence, wide brown eyes. Did something similar happen with Dad number one?

Rith the eldest chortles with scorn. He needs to hate us so that he can fly the nest.

My heart is so sore I cannot speak.

"What will you do?" she asks. That sounds forlorn, so she then tries to sound perky. "Any ideas?"

"Open a casino," I say, feeling deadly.

"Oh! Channa! What a wonderful idea, it's just perfect!"

"Isn't it? All those people with nothing to do." Someplace they can bring their powder. I look out at the sea. Rith rolls his eyes. Where is there for Rith to go from here? I wonder.

I see that he, too, will have to destroy his inheritance. What will he do, drill the rock? Dive down into the lava? Or maybe out of pure rebellion ascend to Earth again?

The drug wears off and Gerda awakes, but her eyes are calm and she takes an interest in the table and the food. She walks outside onto the mall floor, and suddenly squeals with laughter and runs to the railing to look out. She points at the glowing yellow sign with black ears and says "Disney." She says all the brand names aloud, as if they are all old friends.

I was wrong. Gerda is at home here.

I can see myself wandering the whispering marble halls like a ghost, listening for something that is dead.

We go to our suite. It's just like the damn casino, but there are no boats outside to push slivers of wood into your hands, no sand too hot for your feet. Cambodia has ceased to exist, for us.

Agnete is beside herself with delight. "What window do you want?"

I ask for downtown Phnom Penh. A forest of gray, streaked skyscrapers to the horizon. "In the rain," I ask.

"Can't we have something a bit more cheerful?"

"Sure. How about Tuol Sleng prison?" I know she doesn't want me. I know how to hurt her. I go for a walk. Overhead in the dome is the Horsehead Nebula. Radiant, wonderful, deadly, thirty years to cross at the speed of light. I go to the pharmacy. The pharmacist looks like a phony doctor in an ad. I ask, "Is . . . is there some way out?"

"You can go Earthside with no ID. People do. They end up living in huts on Sentosa. But that's not what you mean, is it?" I just shake my head. It's like we've been edited to ensure that nothing disturbing actually gets said. He gives me a tiny white bag with blue lettering on it.

Instant, painless, like all my flopping guests at the casino.

"Not here," he warns me. "You take it and go somewhere else, like the public toilets."

Terrifyingly, the pack isn't sealed properly. I've picked it up, I could have the dust of it on my hands; I don't want to wipe them anywhere. What if one of the children licks it?

I know then I don't want to die. I just want to go home, and always will. I am a son of Kambu, Kampuchea.

"Ah," he says and looks pleased. "You know, the Buddha says that we must accept."

"So why didn't we accept the Earth?" I ask him.

The pharmacist in his white lab coat shrugs. "We always want something different."

We always must move on, and if we can't leave home, it drives us mad. Blocked and driven mad, we do something new.

There was one final phase to becoming a man. I remember my uncle.

The moment his children and his brother's children were all somewhat grown, he left us to become a monk. That was how a man was completed, in the old days.

I stand with a merit bowl in front of the wat. I wear orange robes with a few others. Curiously enough, Rith has joined me. He thinks he has rebelled. People from Sri Lanka, Laos, Burma, and my own land give us food for their dead. We bless it and chant in Pali.

All component things are indeed transient.

They are of the nature of arising and decaying.

Having come into being, they cease to be.

The cessation of this process is bliss.

Uninvited he has come hither

He has departed hence without approval

Even as he came, just so he went

What lamentation then could there be?

We got what we wanted. We always do, don't we, as a species? One way or another.

Acknowledgments

With gratitude to the people who published these stories. In no particularly order: David Pringle, Paul Brazier, Gordon Van Gelder, Ellen Datlow, Esther Salomon, Patrick Nielsen Hayden, Peter Crowther, Ra Page, Kelly Link and Gavin J. Grant, and Andy Cox.

Publication History

These stories were originally published as follows:

The Film-makers of Mars, Tor.com, December 2, 2008
The Last Ten Years in the Life of Hero Kai, *The Magazine of Fantasy & Science Fiction*, December 2005
Birth Days, *Interzone*, April 2003
VAO, PS Publishing, 2002
The Future of Science Fiction, *Nexus*, Spring 1992
Omnisexual, *Alien Sex*, ed. Ellen Datlow, 1990
Home, *Interzone*, March 1995
Warmth, *Interzone*, October 1995
Everywhere, *Interzone*, February 1999. The author was specially commissioned to write this story by Artists Agency as part of the Visions of Utopia project.
No Bad Thing, *The West Pier Gazette and Other Stories*, ed. Paul Brazier, 2007
Talk Is Cheap, *Interzone*, May/June 2008
Days of Wonder, *The Magazine of Fantasy & Science Fiction*, October/November 2008
You, *When It Changed*, Geoff Ryman, ed., 2010
K is for Kosovo (or, Massimo's Career) is published here for the first time.
Pol Pot's Beautiful Daughter, *The Magazine of Fantasy & Science Fiction*, October/November 2006
Blocked, *The Magazine of Fantasy & Science Fiction*, October/November 2009